Book Sense National Bestseller!

Amazon.com Editor's Choice!

"[A] beautiful story . . . brimming with touches of humor . . . well-developed characters . . . excellent writing and overall quality."

Publisher's Weekly

"[Musser] is an Atlanta native and keen observer . . . *The Swan House* is a sweet read for 'old Atlantans' and a vivid picture of a young girl living through the history of Atlanta in the 60's for newcomers . . ."

Atlanta Magazine

"A beautifully executed story . . . Highly recommended."

CBA Marketplace

"Musser has written an inspiring coming of age novel set in the segregated South of the early 1960's. Chock-full of suspense, the novel's heroine has an intelligent innocence that searches for truth in the most unyielding of places, the human heart."

Mary Rose Taylor, Executive Director
The Margaret Mitchell House, Atlanta

"The deep wounding of Atlanta by a plane crash in Paris in 1962 and the consequential insight of a questing motherless daughter—a fact and faith-based novel of assuring conciliation and comfort."

Doris Lockerman
Columnist

Books by Elizabeth Musser

FROM BETHANY HOUSE PUBLISHERS

The Swan House

The Dwelling Place

OTHER BOOKS

Two Crosses

Two Testaments

Two Destinies

THE
SWAN
HOUSE

a Novel

ELIZABETH
MUSSER

BETHANYHOUSE
MINNEAPOLIS, MINNESOTA

Published by Bethany House Publishers
11400 Hampshire Avenue South
Bloomington, Minnesota 55438

Bethany House Publishers is a division of
Baker Publishing Group, Grand Rapids, Michigan.

Printed in the United States of America

ISBN-13: 978-0-7642-2508-6
ISBN-10: 0-7642-2508-1

Library of Congress Cataloging-in-Publication Data

Musser, Elizabeth.
    The Swan House / by Elizabeth Musser.
        p.   cm.
    ISBN 0-7642-2508-1
    1. Children of the rich—Fiction. 2. Mothers—Death—Fiction. 3. Social
classes—Fiction. 4. Young women—Fiction. 5. Socialites—Fiction. 6. Poor—
Fiction. I. Title.
    PS3563.U839 S9   2001
    813'.54—dc21   2001002281

Dedication

This story is dedicated to my wonderful father, Jere Wickliffe Goldsmith IV, who loves Atlanta as much as anyone I know and who has spent his life supporting many of the organizations and endeavors that have made this city great.

Your generosity of heart and resources has been an example to me throughout my life. You have been not only a great, loving father, but also a confidant and friend; some of the most precious moments in my life are on our many walks together where we discuss life's joys and disappointments. We have walked in many different places around this globe, but my favorite by far is when I come back home and we walk around the block in that spot of Atlanta known as Buckhead.

I love you.

About the Author

ELIZABETH GOLDSMITH MUSSER, a native of Atlanta, Georgia, attended The Westminster Schools and then received her B.A. in English and French from Vanderbilt University, where she was a member of Phi Beta Kappa and graduated magna cum laude.

Though passionate about writing since childhood, Elizabeth's first book was not published until 1996. *Two Crosses* was the first of a trilogy set during both the Algerian War for independence from France (1957–1962) and the present day civil war in Algeria. Her work has since been translated into Dutch, French, and German.

Since 1989, Elizabeth and her husband, Paul, have lived in Montpellier, France, where Paul serves on the pastoral team of a small Protestant church. The Mussers have two sons, Andrew and Christopher.

Prologue

Abbie moved down to Grant Park today, and of course I helped her. Who would have imagined that my twenty-six-year-old daughter and her computer-whiz husband would be moving into the Grant Park district of Atlanta, Georgia?

Their little house is yellow with white trim, and there's an oval-cut etched glass in the front door. The yard is neat with green grass and a few pansies. Abbie and Bill have a hundred plans for what they want to do to the house. They've already spent a bundle having the outside repainted and the wood floors redone. And now they are moving in.

I smile and ooh and ahh as she shows me the rooms, but Abbie sees right through it. After all, she is my child, and she does know some of the stories, a few of them at least. I'm fifty-four now and learning to do everything by computer and glad for e-mail. Bill and Abbie gave me a scanner for Christmas to ring in the new millennium with pictures, and I haven't quite figured that out yet.

Abbie comes up and puts her arms around me. She's always been my most affectionate child. "Can you believe it, Mom? Our own home, and right here where it all began for you."

I breathe deeply, the way I learned in therapy, because I really do not want to cry today. But the deeper I breathe and the harder I blink to keep the tears back, the more I find it is useless. Abbie has not seen me cry in quite a while.

We are covered in sweat. My hair is pulled back in a bandana, and my jeans have a lot of yellow and white paint stains on them, besides the other colors that have been there for goodness knows how long. Abbie kisses me on the cheek. "Sit down, Mom, and I'll get you some tea." She knows I can't stand the coffee she makes or even the latte that comes from the new contraption that Bill gave her for her birthday.

So I sit there on the couch, which is covered in old sheets splattered with paint, and while she is out of the room, I start crying. And I don't want to do that because I'm afraid I may never stop. So I hop up and call to Abbie in the cheeriest voice possible, "Honey, I'm just going to take a quick walk down to the church, and I'll be right back."

"Sure, Mom," she calls from the kitchen.

So that's why I'm walking down Grant Street and admiring all the houses that have been recently redone and thinking how this is turning into a young, yuppie neighborhood. I am also thinking, with that crushing feeling in my chest, about how in 1962, Carl Matthews and I used to walk down this street, right past a house that is now a strange shade of purple, and how back then it was just white with peeling paint in what was a neighborhood of blacks and whites and Mexicans. And poor. So poor.

Then I get to the red-brick church with the sparse grass, and I smile, as always, when I see those stained-glass windows from the outside. The stained glass has gone through a whole lot. So I let myself think about Miss Abigail and Carl Matthews and Ella Mae and spaghetti meals for the poor and what I learned so very long ago.

I walk into the sanctuary because the church is unlocked on Saturday mornings, and there is a group of teenagers working downstairs. But I go into the sanctuary with the pretty stained glass, and I walk up to the altar. It isn't a big church; it only holds about 300 people when it's jam-packed. But today it's empty. I get on my knees before the altar, and I cry. I am swept back almost forty years when, as a teenager, I found myself in the same position in this sanctuary. Then I think of another moment in this church, and I can almost hear the voices singing and see the women wiping their eyes as they look at the painting.

Abbie has begged me a hundred times in the past six months to write down the story, or at least to tell it again so that she can record it. She's pregnant and suddenly becoming very family-oriented and wanting our history to be preserved. But, of course, I haven't written a thing down. I don't write anymore. But Abbie is right. The story bears telling and saving. For a hundred different reasons.

I guess I'm praying and crying together. A lot of times my prayers are like that. Of course, that's when I see the painting. It's been hanging there by the alcove of the church ever since the spring of 1963. Just seeing the painting there and thinking about the other one downstairs always makes everything come flooding back.

So I decide right there, in between wiping my eyes and staring at the stained glass and the oil painting, that I will go back and dictate the whole story to Abbie, even if it takes a month or two or even three. I'll stay with her in that house as she has begged me to do, while Bill is off at the convention next week, and we'll sip the hot tea and latte and she can hold the recorder and change the tapes and I'll talk and she can type it up later on the computer. . . .

So here I am, three days later, comfortably installed on Abbie's black leather couch, which has been mercifully spared from yellow and white paint. Bill is gone, and Abbie with her round belly is sitting across from me in this great old rocking chair that she and Bill found at a garage sale, and the tape player is on the floor.

"I'll try to tell it the way it felt, Abbie. As if I were sixteen again."

"Perfect, Mom." Things are always perfect with Abbie.

"I may cry a bit, but don't worry about it, okay?"

"Promise. No problem."

"I have to start with the Dare. It'll take me a while to get to Grant Park. I'll start with the Dare and then talk about the plane crash and Mama and then Ella Mae and the church. . . ."

Abbie rolls her eyes and smiles a half-patronizing, half-sympathetic smile. "Just start, Mom. Just tell it." Then I think she realizes that this is not a simple thing she has asked—for her mother to go back almost forty years to something very painful—so she gets up with difficulty and comes over to me and gives me a warm hug and kisses my cheek and whispers, "It really matters to me. After all, I wouldn't be here without your story. This is important."

I close my eyes and try to put myself back into a schoolgirl's body. So much is still the same and so much is completely different, but when I think about Rachel, I know I can start talking. And so, sipping my tea, I begin. . . .

Atlanta, Georgia
June 1, 1962

It wasn't that I went looking for trouble on a regular basis, but adventures seemed to follow me around like a frisky kitten, waiting to pounce whenever I stopped to contemplate my next steps. But my most famous mishap started out innocuously enough. I was in tenth grade at Wellington Preparatory School for Girls, sitting in Mrs. Wilson's Latin class, transfixed by the way this now-defunct language fit together like pieces of a puzzle. Several girls yawned; others fidgeted. It was our last day of classes. Exams started on Monday.

"Sum levis, et mecum levis est mea cura, Cupido," I answered enthusiastically to the teacher's challenge to recite a line from a poem by Ovid. No sooner had the words been spoken than a small piece of folded paper was slipped onto my desk. I hastily stashed it under my spiral notebook and tried to concentrate as Mrs. Wilson turned away from the blackboard and addressed another question to me. I stammered my reply, mortified at the thought that she might have seen the note being slipped to me. Perhaps she did, for she kept interrogating me for the last few minutes of class until I was sure that wad of paper was burning a hole in my notebook just as it was doing in my mind.

When the bell rang, the seventeen other girls sprang for the door, and I never had a chance to verify who had written that note. I read it as I walked down the hall to Honors English, and I'll swear I'm not making this part up. Scrawled in black pen across that small wadded paper were the three words that a sophomore girl at Wellington Prep School desired most to see in that year of 1962: *Quoth the Raven.*

When I saw those three words, the hairs on my arms stood straight up, even though it was as hot as the oil in a frying pan that June afternoon. I almost didn't go to Honors English because that note made me feel as if I might just wet my pants right there in the hall. But it wasn't like me to skip class, so I went into Mrs. Alexander's class and sat rigidly with my legs crossed twice (only girls with long skinny legs can do that), holding that note in my hands until it grew soggy like the cornflakes in the bottom of my cereal bowl.

It didn't help that for the past two weeks we'd been studying Edgar Allen Poe in class and that yesterday we'd watched a movie called *The Telltale Heart* based on Poe's short story by the same name. I could almost hear that heart beating under the floor of the classroom as it had beat under the floorboards of the house in the movie.

And now I had been chosen to be the Raven.

Looking back, I almost laugh to think that I was selected for this most elusive of honors at Wellington. The ritual of the Raven dated back to the school's inception in 1927 when a spunky junior had challenged the senior valedictorian to a battle of wits and won. That contest had something to do with Poe's poem, "The Raven," and since then, at the end of each school year, a "Raven" was chosen. She was always an end-of-the-year sophomore, someone considered "different and daring enough" to meet the new challenge thought up by the rising senior-class officers.

I was flat-chested with braces and straight brown hair, as plain as a girl can get, but the one good thing about me was that I had a big imagination. Sometimes before Mrs. Alexander came to English class, I'd start reciting the poem she'd had us memorize that week, only I'd change the words as I went along, to the great amusement of the other girls. The rhymes came to my mind as quickly and as simply as those chants we used to sing while jumping rope at recess in grade school, so that Mr. Tennyson and Mr. Keats and a whole bunch of other poets were probably turning over in their graves, their hearts beating as loudly and angrily as the one in Mr. Poe's story.

A few weeks earlier, I'd cast my spell on James Whitcomb Riley's "Little Orphant Annie" and twisted the words to be about dear Mrs. Alexander. So instead of reciting the first verse of the poem as it should be:

Little Orphant Annie's come to our house to stay
An' wash the cups an' saucers up, an' brush the crumbs away
An' shoo the chickens off the porch, an' dust the hearth, an' sweep
An' make the fire, an' bake the bread, an' earn her board-an'-
keep . . .

I simply said,

"Mrs. Alexander's come to English class to stay
And force the sophomores to throw up at all she has to say
And shoo the seniors off the porch and pick her nose and beep
And quiz the girls and pull their curls to earn her board and keep."

The class had dissolved into hysterical laughter when Mrs. Alexander entered the room, and I, gangly and giggling in spite of myself, was too terrified to move. I'm sure that story, among many others, had spread around school throughout the year, and that's how I got elected to be the Raven. Tradition held that the Raven's task would be revealed at midnight on the last official day of school, before exams began. The first challenge of being chosen to be the Raven was to find the paper that explained the Dare, hidden somewhere on the school grounds. I glanced at my watch. It was two in the afternoon. I had ten long hours to wait, but with an imagination like mine, there was plenty to keep me busy.

At precisely midnight on June first, my best friend, Rachel Abrams, and I shimmied over the large wrought-iron gate that separated Wellington from the rest of the world. As I sat perched atop the gate in my cotton shirt and pedal pushers, hands clammy, I whispered down to Rachel, who was already safely inside the campus, "How in the heck do I get down?"

Rachel laughed in her practical way and said, "You jump, stupid. Just jump!"

And so I did, all nine feet down. I landed with one foot twisted under me, and I was sure it was broken, but Rachel grabbed my hand and yanked me up. "Come on, you silly, scatterbrained girl! We've only got an hour before they come looking. You are so clumsy." That was part of the deal too. You had to get onto the school grounds at midnight, and you only had an hour to find the clue. At 1:00 A.M. the rising senior officers supposedly invaded the campus and took back an unretrieved clue.

I winced with pain and scowled at Rachel when she turned her back, but I obediently followed her. I limped along the paved road surrounded by flowering magnolia trees that led to the shadow of a large brick building way in front of us.

"Slow down, will you, Rach?" I whispered.

"Shh. Hurry up!" was her unsympathetic reply.

From somewhere behind the high shrubs near the security hut to the right of the main building, a dog barked. "Rachel should be the Raven," I muttered to myself. She was loving this. "How do you know where the clue is hidden?" I called after her.

"Idiot! Didn't you even study the map on the back of the paper?" Rachel held the wadded ball of paper that I'd received in Latin class in her hands. She stopped abruptly, pulled out a pocket flashlight, and held it to the paper. Sure enough, a map of the Wellington school grounds was sketched on the back.

"See. It's right here." She pointed to a spot on the map marked with an X. "They aren't very imaginative this year, Swannee. Using the old statue again. Same as five years ago."

"How in the world do you know that?"

"Julie Jacobs told me. Her sister helped find the Dare that year. It was stuffed in the mouth of Mr. Augustus Parks himself."

We were jogging now, I with great difficulty, and had reached the administration building of Wellington. It housed all the offices on the main floor, as well as the assembly hall, with the art classrooms and the drama rooms upstairs. Normally stately looking, with its red brick and thick white columns, the building struck me as spooky at midnight. Or maybe it was just a combination of Mr. Poe's influence and my overactive imagination that made the fluted columns look like strange, sturdy ghosts, ready for some ghoulish battle. Behind the administration building was a large open terrace, with immaculate gardens surrounding a bronze statue of the founder of the school, Mr. Augustus Parks Emerson Wellington. We called him APE for short.

"There's the ape-man," Rachel giggled. "You look in his mouth. I'll check his hands."

The APE had been sculpted by one of Atlanta's finest sculptors, and everyone who had known Mr. Wellington said it looked just like him—he was long since dead. The girls at Wellington found great merriment in the way his mouth was open and you could literally put your hand, well, at least three fingers, inside. Which is precisely what I did. But there was nothing there.

"No luck?" Rachel inquired, pulling herself off the ground where she'd been inspecting the pedestal with her flashlight.

"Nothing." I suppressed a giggle.

"What's so funny?"

"Your tights are black with dirt!"

Rachel stuck out her tongue and, unperturbed, began to search the rest of the monument.

"I don't see why they'd choose the statue again if it was the hiding place five years ago. Maybe it's a trick," I reasoned.

Rachel ignored me and continued her frantic search, groaning, "Swan, hurry, we've only got forty-one more minutes! Do you want to be the first nincompoop in twenty years who couldn't even locate the Dare?"

I certainly didn't, and I was grateful Rachel was with me, but I didn't have a clue what to do next. I sat down beside Old Ape-Face and tried to think. Rachel was chattering away. "Be quiet, will you, Rach? Give me a chance to concentrate. I'll come up with something."

I put my hands on my forehead, resting my elbows on my knees, and closed my eyes. I could still hear the dog barking off to my right and the sound of a car screeching somewhere in the distance outside the Wellington campus. Then I looked up. Straight in front of me were the woods, and dangling from one thin branch of a pine tree was something white.

"Hey, Rach, look!" I pointed to the tree.

Rachel jumped up from the ground, went to the branch, yanked the paper loose, and read:

"Just in case you need a hint
Behind the ape beneath the trees
A spot where many hours are spent.
No escape, get on your knees."

We reread the clue several times with the help of the flashlight. Suddenly I grabbed the paper and exclaimed, "I know where it is! It's at the Band Hut!"

"The Band Hut?" she said, incredulous. Then she whistled low. "Hey, Swannee, I bet you're right."

We took off through the woods on the path we knew so well. We trudged it nearly every day. Stopping before the white clapboard building, I tried the door. Locked, of course.

"Swannee, don't try the door—it says to get on your knees!"

I fell to my knees and stuck my arms under the Band Hut, which sat (rather precariously, it seemed to me at that moment) on piles of cinder blocks about a foot off the ground. I felt around, sticking my hand in spider webs and moist leaves and who knows what else. "Give me the light, Rachel."

And there it was. An old beat-up flute case, the one that usually sat opened on the front table as we entered the Band Hut. If anyone was late to orchestra practice, she had to place a penny in the case. I grabbed its handle from under a pile of leaves and backed out from under the hut. "Ta-da!" I said triumphantly, holding up the flute case for Rachel to inspect. "I bet it's in here."

Rachel frowned.

"Don't you get it, Rach? 'Just in case you need a hint.' *In case.* In the case. That's where the Dare is." To prove my point, I opened it.

A folded piece of paper with a big *R* printed on the outside sat neatly on the velvet blue lining of the flute case. My mouth went dry, and as I licked my lips, I slowly unfolded the paper and read the type-written words.

"You, Mary Swan Middleton, Raven of Wellington for the school year of 1962 and 63, have been chosen to locate three missing works of art before the end of the annual Mardi Gras Festival on Friday, February 8, 1963. These paintings were given to the Atlanta High Museum of Art by an anonymous donor and were due to be delivered on April 29 of the past year, 1961. But the paintings never arrived. There was rumor of theft, but the donor never complained to the authorities. In fact, there was never another word received from the donor, and no one knows who this mysterious person is. Locate the paintings and become one of the few successful Ravens in Wellington's history."

Below were written the names of the three paintings and their artists. It didn't surprise me a bit to see that one of the artists was Mama.

Spring Bouquet—Henry Becker, 1958
Child at Rest—Sheila Middleton, 1952
Joie de Vivre—Leslie Leschamps, 1956

My mind was spinning as Rachel grabbed the paper from my hand.

It was a commonly known story among Atlanta's art patrons, and especially our family, that three paintings which had been acquired for the summer of '61 collection had disappeared the night before they were to be displayed at the opening of a new exhibition at the museum. The riddle of the donor had never been solved. Mama and Daddy had tried to help the museum locate this mysterious person with no luck.

I immediately loved the challenge. The Raven had all summer and all fall and winter of her junior year to come up with an answer to the Dare. But, as every girl at Wellington knew, the Raven's identity had to remain a secret. If at any point during the course of the nine months she revealed herself, the Dare became moot and void. Fortunately, the Raven was allowed to choose two people to help her solve the mystery. I figured that I'd be just fine with Rachel. She had more brains than the rest of my class put together, at least in my humble opinion.

Of course, the Wellington girls spent nine months trying to figure out who had been named as the Raven. Sometimes someone guessed correctly, but since the Raven could not outright admit her identity, an aura of mystery surrounded the ritual right up to the time when the Raven was announced on the night of the Mardi Gras Festival, along with the fact of whether or not she had been successful in her quest. And, of course, the senior girls who had chosen the Raven had to keep their mouths shut.

It was the best of the school's rituals, and the motivation behind the Dare and the Mardi Gras Festival was not just class pride, but also philanthropy. Several of the major Atlanta companies pledged money to the charity of the junior class's choice if the Dare were met. Likewise, wealthy individuals also participated in the event. Daddy had offered a large amount of stock last year.

Wellington Prep School was a private Christian school for girls, starting with sixth grade and going through high school. It was considered one of the finest schools in the Southeast, and many wealthy Atlantans supported it. Graduating from Wellington almost always meant that the girl continued on to college, and if she was smart she had her pick of the top universities before her. Such was the reputation of Wellington.

Only once in the past ten years had a junior solved the Raven Dare. Rebecca Dewberry was the girl chosen to be the Raven in 1956.

She was one of those really brainy types with drab dresses and pointed glasses. But as the story goes, when she solved the mystery, she was transformed into the school heroine. Her wardrobe was completely refurbished to the latest style, and she did away with those atrocious red cat-eye glasses. She applied for the Morehouse Scholarship to UNC and got it, but turned it down to go to Radcliffe and became a lawyer in the time before women did things like that.

I couldn't remember what her task had been, but I had heard that her grandmother, who had been one of the founders of Wellington back in the 1920s, had helped Rebecca, along with the drama teacher. Apparently, Rebecca had wisely chosen her two faithful assistants and had brought glory to her class.

But I was no Rebecca Dewberry. My grades were Bs at best. I just didn't have the time to study. I much preferred sketching in the woods or making up silly poems or riding my horse. But at least I had Rachel Abrams for a friend. We'd been practically inseparable since our first year at Wellington as sixth graders. Rachel was what I called book smart. Her dad was some brilliant physicist at Georgia Institute of Technology. Where I lacked confidence, Rachel had enough for the whole school. And whereas I tended toward the melodramatic, Rachel was blunt. She liked to call a spade a spade, as my granddaddy would say. And for as plain as I was, Rachel was a real knockout. Long, thick blond hair and crystal clear blue-gray eyes. She'd started puberty by age eleven. I was sixteen, and for me puberty had just begun three months ago. But we were best friends.

Why she had picked me out to befriend, I'm not sure, except that we both played the flute in the school orchestra—she much better than I. We also both loved horses and had mares of our own, which we kept at the barn behind Rachel's house. So just about every afternoon we'd be together riding or practicing flute or cleaning out stalls or something.

And Rachel made me think. She was always coming up with bizarre questions about the meaning of life. But thank goodness, on this particular night, with the prize of the Raven Dare safe in my hands, she chose simply to chat happily as we headed back to the gate, me limping and she skipping.

"Good going, Swannee. Good job. This is going to be a piece of cake."

I wasn't so sure about that. My ankle was throbbing, and my hands were filthy with dirt and leaves. But I was excited. I had been chosen to be the Raven, and I had found the Dare!

If that task had been all I had to do in and of itself, then my story would not bear telling. But it seems to me now that the hand of God reached down in the midst of a harmless dare to alter my destiny and that of every other person I cared most about for so many years to come. It makes me shiver to consider it, but as I see it, the history of my family, and by and large of the city of Atlanta, is forever tied up in a schoolgirl's prank.

Chapter 1

In my mind, the nine months from the first of June 1962 until the end of February of the following year were what I afterward called "the year of death." I suppose it was the worst year of my life in many ways, certainly the most painful. And yet, as I have so often seen since, it was a year of discovery and change, and ultimately of hope. And there were wonderful parts too—the first time I fell in love, the first time I learned to really see someone else, the first time I dared to venture outside myself. And most importantly, it was the year that I discovered the truth, and truth always sets us free. So maybe I should call it not the year of death, but the year of freedom.

This is how it happened, as best I can piece those first days together from what I've been told and from what I lived.

John Jason Middleton, my forty-year-old father, lifted his arm and waved happily to his wife and my mother, Sheila, as she headed to the large aircraft. Then, on an impulse, he ran out of the glass doors and caught her in a tight embrace, kissed her on the lips, and pressed his hand against her fine silken hair. She laughed at him, her jade eyes twinkling and her wide, delicious mouth painted bright pink. "See you tomorrow, sweetheart."

He watched as his wife and many of their friends boarded the Boeing 707 bound from Paris to Atlanta. The three-week trip with over a hundred other Atlantans had been perfect in every way. A dozen different scenes flashed through his mind. Dancing with Sheila. Sheila on the Champs-Elysées. Sheila, arms piled high with packages from Galéries Lafayette. And of course Sheila weeping in front of a Rembrandt . . . a da Vinci . . . a Raphael.

Ah, Sheila! At thirty-eight, she was already called one of Atlanta's premier artists, and the contacts she'd made in Paris could almost assure a noteworthy exhibition there next spring. He squinted to get another look at his wife as she disappeared into the huge jet. The other members of the tour were tucked safely inside the plane as it taxied for takeoff.

But he and Mama had agreed two nights before to fly home on separate planes. Daddy, ever the cautious one, had preferred not to be on the same flight going home—for me and my brother Jimmy's sake. The others on the trip thought him silly, but I'm sure he must have had a premonition of what was to come. And several business options had presented themselves on Friday, so he had a good excuse to stay another day.

"Of course, Jason darling! It's a marvelous idea." Mama had sung the words in her slow, smooth Southern accent. Then she had pouted. "But what a bore to be on the plane all those hours without you!"

To which he had guffawed and playfully pinched her. "Yes, you'll be bored stiff, I'll bet. Nothing to do but chat with Rosalind Williams and Anne Berry and Elizabeth Bull."

"But you, dear Jason?" she said in mock sadness. "I'm thinking of you."

He laughed again hearing her words, both of them knowing how he relished the thought of a few hours alone to catch up on business before he got back to Atlanta.

The jet sped down the runway of Orly Airfield with the bright Paris sky at midday shining down on it, sending gleaming reflections from its sleek metal exterior. Daddy felt the familiar jump in his stomach as the plane accelerated, then an immediate sense of relief to see it poised, ready to pierce the sky, nose pointing confidently upward.

Then, as he was about to turn away, he saw the silver bird hurtle forward without leaving the ground, heavy streams of white smoke trailing behind it. The plane screeched to the left, wobbling horribly for what seemed an eternity as the white smoke turned black. Daddy watched, horrified, screaming out loud as the nose of the plane struck the runway with the force of an earthquake, splitting the pavement apart. There was the sound of an explosion and then the airplane burst into fierce, lapping orange and blue flames.

He ran toward the glass doors with a dozen other dumbstruck eyewitnesses, tripping over himself, and made it onto the field before a man in an Air France uniform stopped him, warning, "You can't go out there!"

"My wife's on that plane," Daddy cried hysterically.

"I'm sorry," the Air France official told him. "My brother's on it too."

Daddy stood there in shock, imagining the excruciating heat, hearing somewhere on a distant runway the scream of sirens. Hearing his own anguished voice, weeping and calling out, "Sheila, Sheila . . ."

Atlanta, Georgia
June 3, 1962

The way I always heard it afterward was that Ella Mae was sitting in church on the morning of June third, fanning herself the way she always did, her big straw hat covering the coarse black hair that was beginning to be laced with gray. She was a large woman, strong, sturdy, and jovial. When she would smile and show her white teeth amidst her ebony face, ah, to me, it was such a simple and profound picture of contrast. Dark and light that blended into one of the most beautiful faces that my young eyes had ever seen. Ella Mae was my family's maid in the year 1962. I lived on the northwest side of Atlanta in a big house. I had no idea where Ella Mae lived when she wasn't at my house. She was as much a part of my family as my mother and father and my thirteen-year-old brother, Jimmy. I loved Ella Mae, and even though the tides of racial change were sweeping through our country, and her skin was black and mine was white, I had never seen the difference between us in all of my sixteen years.

It was, in fact, the events of the next nine months that forced me out of my cocoon. But I am getting ahead of myself.

At nine in the morning on June third at the Mount Carmel Church in southeast Atlanta, the pews were filled, the singing loud and joyous. The black bodies were swaying to and fro, as Ella Mae loved to describe it, and a young soloist in the choir stepped forward to belt out the last verse of "Oh, Happy Day." It was a modest church of red brick and white woodwork that needed painting, and the pews had worn gray cushions. But it had ten breathtakingly beautiful stained-glass windows, and the piano was in tune, and the choir, my, could they sing! So caught up were they all in singing and praising the Lord that

21

no one seemed to notice that Pastor James was awfully late getting to his place. When he finally did step into the sanctuary and up to the pulpit, the singing stopped abruptly with one look at his stricken face.

"My brotha's and sista's in Je-, in Jesus," he said, stumbling over his words, something Ella Mae said he had never done before. His eyes were glistening as though he was trying to blink back tears. "Our hope is in the Lawd." The usual amens were suppressed. Every member of the congregation waited, hearts beating hard.

"I have jus' received the tragic news of a plane crash in Paris. A charter plane carryin' some of Atlanta's citizens crashed early this mornin' in Paris." There was a gasp throughout the congregation. "That plane carried on it many of Atlanta's most prominent citizens. The pain I feel for these people . . ."

But Ella Mae never heard the rest of Pastor James's eulogy or his sermon. She let out a loud wail of "Lawd Jesus!" and abruptly got to her feet. "I gotta git to Mary Swan and Jimmy," she cried out loud, but really talking to herself, and she left the church in a blur, barely noticing the others who reached out to her or asked, "Ella Mae. . . ?"

They figured it out later, and it made perfect sense that Ella Mae would be thinking about us, her chil'un, as she liked to say. Thinking about me asleep in that big house, oblivious to the fact that my whole life had just come to a screeching halt.

When I came downstairs that morning, the house was uncommonly quiet. My little brother, Jimmy, was still asleep, and I was still dreaming about the great Raven adventure and nursing my tender ankle. It was Sunday, and Grandmom and Granddad Middleton, Daddy's parents who were staying with us while Mama and Daddy were away, had already left for church. If Mama and Daddy had been home, we would've been at church too. But Grandmom had told us the night before that we could "slee-eep eyan," as she pronounced it in her dignified Southern way, and we had not argued. Later in the afternoon, Grandmom and Granddad would take Jimmy and me to the airport to pick up our parents. I could hardly wait. They'd been gone for three long weeks, and I was anxious to hear about their travels.

Ella Mae, the maid who had worked for us for as long as I'd been alive, was always there on weekdays. I could imagine the sound of her vacuum in one of the bedrooms and the smell of her fried chicken permeating the air and whetting my appetite. Sometimes, when I got home from school, I'd sneak into the kitchen and steal a chicken leg, devour it, and toss the bone into the trash can before Ella Mae could discover it. She knew, of course, and fried several extra pieces for my brother and me to enjoy after school.

But today there was no smell of chicken or soft, distant zooming of the vacuum. Today was Sunday, the third of June, and Mama and Daddy were already on the plane en route to Atlanta from Paris. I glanced at the grandfather clock in the entranceway as I came down the long, winding marble staircase. Nine thirty-two. Only six more hours.

My mother was a well-known painter in Atlanta and the South, often absent traveling to what I considered exotic places for art exhibitions. I'd grown up in the ample lap of Ella Mae, loving the smell of her soft black skin against mine as she read to me from *Uncle Remus* or sang songs about Jesus loving me, this I know. She was like a second mother to me.

Ella Mae's black hair was short at the time, but I remember when I was little I used to run my fingers through it and love the coarse feel and the way she let me twist it around my fingers and braid it. She never put on makeup that I could tell. Her eyes weren't that big, but she would lift her eyebrows and somehow show the whites of the eyes when she was mad. Her nose was straight and wide, which I thought was absolutely perfect because mine was so little and turned-uppish, and I always wanted to sketch her face. It was the most real face I had ever seen.

We called Ella Mae sturdy or round, but Mama, who loved to sneak up with a phrase from her French mother, would say, "She is not fat, just *un petit peu enveloppée*." I poorly translated that to mean she was well padded, but it sounded much more sophisticated in French.

I found Ella Mae that morning of June third in the den, listening through the static on the radio and rocking herself back and forth, back and forth, moaning, "Lawd Jesus, have mercy on us. Have mercy."

I don't think she heard me come into the room, because she let out a scream and then a "Lawd, chile, you done scared me ta daeth," and when she looked at me, that beautiful round face was shining with tears.

I'd never seen Ella Mae cry until that day. She was not supposed to cry. She was there to wipe my tears and listen to my stories and laugh at my pranks, but I felt a funny little quiver inside to see her face all wet with crying, and a cool shiver ran through my body.

"Ella Mae, what's the matter? Why are you here today? Why aren't you at your church?"

"My, my, chile. My, my," she said, shaking her head and pulling me toward her and holding me in her strong black arms, snuggling me in her big bosom the way she used to when I was a little girl.

"Ain't got no good news today, we ain't."

"What do you mean, Ella Mae?" It was then that I had my first premonition that whatever was making her cry would do the same to me when I found out. If it was bad news, I didn't mind hearing it from Ella Mae. I only wanted to get it over with before Mama and Daddy came home from the airport. Three weeks of touring museums around Europe with one hundred of the city's most generous art patrons had kept my parents away. I wanted everything to be perfect for their return.

"They's been a crash. A terribul crash, sugah. A plane in Paris, takin' off early this mornin.'"

The words froze me in place, and I narrowed my eyes, making them hard and angry, as if I were daring Ella Mae to tell me something too horrible to be true. "What plane crashed?" I mumbled after a moment.

The doorbell rang before she could answer, and we both jerked ourselves up. I left the den, ran through the entrance hall, and pulled the front door open, hearing my heart hammering in my chest. Our neighbor and Mama's best friend, Trixie Hamilton, was standing there looking stricken. Trixie was in her late thirties, petite and blond and loads of fun, but she had nothing happy on her face at that moment.

"Mary Swan," she whispered and pulled me close. "Oh, Mary Swan. I came right when I heard the news. I was on my way to church. I wanted to be here before you got up." Ella Mae's eyes met Trixie's, and she shook her head slowly. Trixie must have understood something, because she led me through the big hall to the kitchen, which was decorated in bright red, yellow, and blue—what we called Mama's artistic touch. Adjoining the kitchen was the breakfast room with a sturdy round oak table around which our family ate all our informal meals. We each took a chair, and Trixie held my hands.

"There's been a crash. A tragic accident. The plane . . ." She cleared her throat and started again. "The plane your parents were on that left Paris this morning has crashed. They don't think there are any survivors."

If I had been six, I would have melted into Trixie's arms or Ella Mae's bosom and sobbed for hours. But I was sixteen, at that awkward, proud age when even those closest to me seemed at times distant. I sat there rigid as a board and numb, and Trixie just sat there too, her arms wrapped loosely around me as though she was afraid to squeeze me because I might break.

It was Ella Mae who, crying quietly, fixed a glass of orange juice for me and one for Trixie, and then she took my hands as she had done so often in my life and began to hum very low and reverently, "Nobody knows the trouble I've seen. Nobody knows but Jesus."

It was when she was humming the part about nobody knowing but Jesus that I began to cry. And then I wept and I heaved, and the most excruciating pain I had ever known wracked my body. Not physical. A pain so deep down in my soul that it felt like a type of death itself. We sat there, me crying and Trixie biting her lip and Ella Mae humming, for a long time.

We went back into the den and listened to the radio, sitting there numblike, as the persuasive voice of some man selling sedatives ended, and the neutral voice of the newscaster came on the air, announcing the most awful tragedy in the most impersonal way. Then it would switch to singing commercials, and the hard-sell adman would come back on again, while we listened in agony, waiting. Waiting. Waiting to hear a list of names, waiting for a phone call to confirm our worst fears, waiting for time to start ticking again and assure us that there was a future out there. That morning, the morning without fried chicken or the sound of the vacuum cleaner, was a day when I, on the brink of womanhood, became again just a skinny flat-chested girl who wanted more than anything else to curl up in her maid's lap and be rocked to sleep.

It was Trixie who got up the courage to call the Air France office on Forsyth Street. The line was busy for so long that we gave up and just sat again, Trixie smoking one cigarette after another. The phone must have rung around ten-thirty, its shrill clanging bringing us out of our stupor. And not one of us wanted to answer it. But Ella Mae picked it up and said in a voice much changed from her usual robust greeting, "Middleton residence."

She listened intently for a moment, then screwed her face up in a perplexing expression and began to yell. "Hello. Hello! Who is this? Whatcha sayin'? Is you tryin' to trick us, Mista? Hurt us more than we already be hurtin'?"

Then she paused, leaned in even closer to the phone as if she were trying to peer through the lines to check out the caller. Finally she let out a "Lawd be praised, it *is* you, Mr. Middleton!" which caused me to jump up and grab the phone from her hand.

"Daddy! Daddy! Is it you? Is it really you? Ella Mae heard at church about a plane crash, and we thought it was yours. . . ."

But Daddy's voice was filled with anguish and punctuated by sobs as he said through a crackling phone line, "Mary Swan, sweetheart. Mama was on the plane. Mama . . . Mama died in the crash."

"No!" I screamed because the horror had been replaced by a moment of hope, and now the horror struck again. I let the phone drop and sank to the floor as Jimmy came into the room, his face holding a thousand questions. Trixie took the phone and Ella Mae held on to Jimmy, and somehow we got through the agony of that hour. I do not know how. All I remembered later was the delicious sound of Daddy's voice and then the sound of it breaking and then the realization that Mama was gone. Daddy was stuck thousands of miles away from us, alone in his grief, and we were in shock. I did not know anything except a shattering pain in my chest and a desire to run, run backward in time to when life was the way it had always been.

After Daddy's phone call, after so many tears, I fell back onto the couch in the study, completely exhausted. Grandmom and Granddad arrived soon afterward. They had been in church when they heard the news. As soon as they walked in the front door, I could tell they'd been crying, something I had never seen them do before. But Grandmom tried not to show it as she wrapped her tiny arms around me. She wasn't even as tall as Trixie, and her hair was a beautiful snow-white, and she wore a bright lavender suit that almost matched her eyes. I always thought of Grandmom as really classy and so full of life. But today she seemed frail, almost gaunt.

Granddad was a big man, a former football player at Georgia Tech.

He had a rather timid personality in social settings, but everybody said he was a genius at business where he dealt with the most intimidating men with a firm hand. That morning Granddad didn't look timid or tough. He looked broken.

The only thing I could think of saying was "Daddy's alive!" They stared at me pitifully.

"Poor child," Grandmom mumbled, pressing me into the lavender suit so that I could smell her perfume.

"It's true, Frank and Jennie," Trixie confirmed. "JJ just called." She bit her lip and blinked back tears. "He and Sheila decided to take different flights." She cleared her throat. "He saw the whole thing."

"Good Lord," Granddad whispered, and Grandmom gave a whimper that must have been a mixture of incredible relief and unimaginable sadness.

People started coming right away to the house to check on us, and Ella Mae and Trixie and Grandmom and Granddad faithfully stood guard, receiving them graciously and protecting us from all but a very few of those who came to offer their condolences. The conversations seeped up the stairs to Jimmy's bedroom where Jimmy and I were sitting crouched by his radio, and they always went the same. People in tears, Trixie explaining that Daddy had survived, the relief and then the pain when it was confirmed about Mama. All I wanted to know was when Daddy was coming home. But for that I would have to wait again.

Trixie came upstairs around noon with a tray of sandwiches. Her eyes were all puffy, and she sniffed and explained, "The street looks just like a parking lot, cars lined up for a mile in each direction, and I heard some women whisper that it's like that all over town, in front of every house who had someone on that plane."

When Jimmy and I peeked out the windows, we couldn't believe it. It did look like a parking lot with a bunch of people coming to a church service, walking all dressed up toward our front door. Only they weren't carrying Bibles but covered casseroles and tins of cookies. I pressed my face against the cool windowpane. I felt dizzy and weak and hot, like I had a fever.

Ella Mae came up at two and whispered, "Chil'un, it's yore preacher here with his wife. You'd best come on down."

"I can't," Jimmy sniffled. "I don't want to see anybody, Swan. Not a soul. You go down there. Please."

And so I did. We were Episcopalians, and Grandmom and Granddad and Daddy and Mama went to the Cathedral of St. Philip right up the street from us. The cathedral, which had recently been rebuilt, was a magnificent building constructed of what was called Tennessee quartzite—a pretty yellow-hued stone. It sat up on a hill on a small promontory that jutted out, not into water, but into Peachtree Road just as the road veered right, so that you couldn't help but notice the beautiful cathedral as you drove by. Jimmy and I usually went to church on Sunday mornings, although we'd slacked off the past few weeks with Mama and Daddy gone.

Walking slowly because my head felt so light and my ankle was still sore, I made it to the bottom of the staircase. Dean Hardman was there, extending his hand. "God bless you, Mary Swan. What an awful tragedy."

Mrs. Hardman gave me a warm hug. "We're so sorry about your mother," she whispered with a voice that had real compassion in it. Trixie had already told me that almost twenty people from our church had died in the crash. I wondered how many families Dean and Mrs. Hardman had already been to visit. I felt sorry for them.

But I had nothing to say at all except, "Thank you for coming." We sat in the fancy living room with the high ceiling and the sculpted cornices and the oil paintings and Oriental rugs, the Hardmans and Trixie and Grandmom and Granddad and me, with Ella Mae looking on, until Dean Hardman insisted she take a seat too. I stared down at my hands, which I kept twisting around in my lap, occasionally lifting one to wipe my nose. We must have sat there like that in absolute silence for fifteen minutes. And somehow that seemed the right thing to do.

Then Dean Hardman cleared his throat awkwardly and said, "There will be a memorial service at St. Philip's on Tuesday morning for all those who perished." He stood up, shook my hand again, and I swear I thought this middle-aged man was going to start bawling like a baby in front of me. His eyes were all misty, and Mrs. Hardman blotted her eyes with a white-laced handkerchief. I started crying again, and she hugged me tight and I let her.

When the people called from the newspaper to ask for information about Mama, I guess it was Grandmom who answered all the questions. I was back upstairs with Jimmy, who was lying listlessly on his bed. The next phone call was Daddy again.

Grandmom answered the phone and burst into tears when she heard his voice and kept repeating, "Oh, Johnny, thank the Lord. Johnny, I'm so sorry."

We were all crowded around the phone, and I heard him tell Grandmom, "I'll be home as soon as I can. Can you and Dad hold things together?"

"Of course, Johnny. We'll take care of the children."

But then Jimmy grabbed the phone. "Please come home, Daddy," he wailed. "It's the worst thing in the whole world. Please come home."

I don't know how many times Jimmy and I went up and down, up and down that winding staircase that afternoon, but we did it together, and somehow I felt a bitter-sweetness at putting my skinny arm around Jimmy's even skinnier shoulders and being a real big sister to him.

The telegram arrived at three-thirty. It came from the officials of Air France, and I guess everybody who was related to someone on the plane got one. I took it out of Ella Mae's hand and screwed my face up to read it. I'd never received a telegram before: *In this time of sorrow I convey to you on behalf of Air France our sincerest condolences. Please also know that I am at your disposition for any assistance we can render.* It was signed *Henri Lesieur, General Manager in North America for the airline.*

I gave the telegram back to Ella Mae and said, "There's not a thing they can do to help, and they know it." Jimmy just sniffed and nodded.

Late that afternoon Trixie went downtown to buy copies of an "extra" edition of the *Atlanta Journal*—the first "extra" published by the newspaper on a local story since Margaret Mitchell was fatally injured in a street accident thirteen years earlier. Trixie was gone for over three hours, so long that we were afraid there'd been another accident. When she finally got back to our house, she was crying again.

"All the streets going downtown near the *Atlanta Journal Constitution* building at Forsyth Street are jammed with traffic. You can't believe it. You just can't believe it. Nobody can. Not a soul can believe it." Her hands were trembling as she held out five copies of the special edition, and Grandmom and Granddad and Ella Mae and Jimmy and I each took one. I sank to the floor right there in the entrance hall, staring at the picture on the front page. In the foreground were a bunch of firemen with their hard hats on, and behind them was the tail of the plane all broken and sticking up toward the sky. The caption read, "Charred section of tail only recognizable part of plane."

"Oh my gosh," Jimmy mumbled.

On the right-hand side of the front page there was a long, long list of the Atlanta victims, typed in alphabetical order and bold print. I felt as if I might faint. The names were too numerous to fit on the front page but spilled over to another page, one after another, husbands and wives, a few children, and almost every one was a name that I recognized.

I saw Mama's name before the others did, and I let out a little sob. There it was, right after Mrs. William Merritt of Peachtree Battle Avenue and right before Mrs. Lawton Miller of Argonne Drive: Mrs. John Jason Middleton of Andrews Drive. Somehow, seeing her name in black-and-white made it final and sure. There was no way to fantasize that she had somehow escaped, especially when I examined the photo of the remains of the plane.

One of the main articles said that Mayor Ivan Allen was heading for Paris late that afternoon. "With this much of Atlanta there, I think we ought to be on the scene," he had said. And then the mayor had spoken on behalf of the whole city. "Atlanta has suffered her greatest tragedy and loss." And Mr. Carmichael, who was a close friend of Daddy's and the chairman of the board of the Atlanta Art Association, was quoted as saying, "It's like an atomic bomb has hit Atlanta. It's the most tragic thing for all of us. At the Art Association, it has simply wiped out our basic support. These were the hard workers, the people we depended on."

Mama and Daddy had always been very involved in the Art Association. I had grown up seeing my parents off at the door, me clinging to Mama's leg and then to Ella Mae as they left for some fundraising affair, both of them looking elegant. And now Mama would never dress up again, wearing the tight-fitting luxurious satin gowns for which she was known.

I couldn't bear to read anything else. I left the paper in the middle of the hall, ran up two flights of stairs and into my bathroom, and vomited. Then I fell on my bed. I was still lying there, in the same clothes and the same position, when I woke up late the next morning.

Chapter 2

T hose first two days were nothing but a constant flow of people, of radio and television announcements and newspaper articles, all talking about the crash. It was as if Atlanta was a walled-in city of medieval times, taken siege and oblivious to the rest of the world, so consumed were we all by what had happened. It was everywhere, and we were terribly drained. The hardest article to read was the one in the *Atlanta Constitution* that talked about my family. "Two young teens would have been orphaned by the Paris plane crash if their parents had not decided to take separate planes home from abroad. . . ." It sounded like Daddy was a hero in the article—the fact that he had decided not to fly with Mama for the sake of us kids. I really can't explain how strange I felt reading about myself and Jimmy in the paper and how we still had a daddy. It seemed to me like the reporters went too far, telling something so personal, something meant to make the readers cry, something sentimental to pull at their hearts. Well, everyone's heart was already breaking. It struck me all wrong. If Daddy was a hero, then there should have been some sort of celebration, but it was simply the blackest time in the world, the blackest time in my whole life.

For most of the day Monday, Jimmy and I just sat around the house waiting for Daddy to return and wearing our darkest clothes, since we were in mourning. Trixie and Ella Mae stayed at the house all day, helping Grandmom and Granddad. They spoke with all the callers who came, literally by the hundreds, bringing flowers and casseroles and custards and all kinds of delicious, mouth-watering goodies of the South. But none of us had any appetite. Somehow it seemed sacrilegious to enjoy something that tasted so good when Mama had just perished in that awful plane, burned to death in an explosion of heat.

And all during that day, we'd look out from the second-story window and see the cars parked down at the bottom of the hill, and Jimmy would lean out the window and tell me about every person who was walking up the driveway. Jimmy was at that awkward age of thirteen. I guess I had always loved my kid brother, but I was immensely grateful that we went to different schools so he didn't embarrass me in front of my friends. He had gotten Mama's blond hair and fine features and Daddy's dark brown eyes, which meant, all and all, he was a pretty good-looking kid. But, of course, since he drove me practically insane, I would never admit it. He had collections of rocks and baseball cards, and he liked to take the tops off of soda bottles and make weird art out of them, so that Mama had sometimes called him Jimmy Picasso.

But being there, just the two of us without Daddy, at the worst time in our lives, kind of drew us together. Daddy called twice a day just to hear our voices and explained that the French authorities needed him to help with the investigation. And I guess he was a big support to the mayor because they knew each other well.

Neither Jimmy nor I wanted to see all the people coming by. We'd hide upstairs and listen to the voices when the doorbell rang, looking down the staircase to see who was there, or we'd tiptoe down the back stairs and through the kitchen and peek through those doors. It became our twisted game, our way of simply surviving those first few days. When the doorbell rang, Jimmy would go tearing down the back stairs and through the kitchen, and I would peep around the corner of the upstairs. As soon as we discovered who the caller was, we'd race back to the bedroom. The first one there with the right answer won. And so the game continued for hours and hours as if we were preschoolers instead of teenagers. We clung to that game tenaciously, and I loved my brother all the more for the passion with which he played it.

It was after another lunch that Ella Mae fixed and no one ate that Papy and Mamie McKenzie, Mama's parents, arrived. They lived on a big cotton plantation in South Georgia and were in their late sixties. Papy looked as Scottish as his roots from the Borders, and he could imitate his father's brogue perfectly, even though he'd spent the last forty-five years in Georgia. He was a giant of a man with reddish hair that curled all over his head and piercing green eyes, and he loved to call me Lassie. At Christmas he would put on his family's McKenzie kilt and bring out his bagpipes and delight us with that haunting music and the jigs that he danced with Mamie.

Mamie was one hundred percent French and spoke English with an accent that I thought was beautiful and intriguing. Papy had met her while serving in France during the First World War and had fallen in love with her. I guess I could understand why, because, from what I could tell from the photographs, Mamie had been stunning. She'd had really dark hair, maybe black, and clear brown eyes with thick dark lashes, and she was skinny as a rail except for where it mattered most. But I think their love story had been a big scandal back in Scotland, because Mamie was from what they called "a different social class." But Papy had convinced her to marry him. Soon after, to the shock of his whole family, Papy bought a cotton plantation in South Georgia, and he and Mamie moved across the ocean. His family, Papy liked to say, had made their fortune in Scottish wool, and now he wanted to try his hand at spinning cotton. It had worked, I guess, because Papy certainly seemed to have loads of money.

I don't think Mamie ever really adjusted to life in the American South. She was always complaining about the lack of real cheese and the *faible vin*, and she insisted that Jimmy and I call her Mamie, which was the French equivalent of Grandmom. So my grandfather went along with her game, and that's why we called him Papy.

Mamie always scared me. If she got upset, *énervée* as she called it, she'd scream at us, and once she even slapped me in the face. When I went crying to Mama, she hushed me up and explained that was just how Mamie had been raised, the way things had been done in her family in France. She was a strange, high-strung woman, and I'd once overheard Daddy complaining to his parents that all she wanted from Papy was his money. She did like to travel back to France two or three times a year, and sometimes she spent months going to the most exotic places, without Papy. I always hoped she would invite me on one of her trips, but she never had. She did bring Jimmy and me back some great souvenirs.

But if Papy's marriage to Mamie had been kind of a scandal, I'd seen the old newspaper clippings about Mama and Daddy's marriage that touted their union as a great social success, bringing together the Middleton and McKenzie fortunes. And while all four of our grandparents smothered us with love in their own distinct ways, they barely tolerated each other. And Mamie distrusted Daddy.

So I watched carefully as Grandmom met Mamie at the door. Mamie's face was hard and creased, and the bright red lipstick she wore was smeared on so that it went above her top lip and left several specks on her front teeth. "Ian, Evelyne," Grandmom said. She kissed Papy gently on the cheek. "We are so sorry." Then she took Mamie by her frail shoulders and kissed her softly on each cheek, French style. That seemed to touch Mamie's heart, because the hard, pinched expression left her face, and it was replaced by genuine misery.

Papy grabbed Jimmy and me in his big bear hug and held us close and didn't say a word. But by the way his chest rose and fell and the horrible, deep sighs that accompanied the rising and falling, I knew he was crying too. Everyone in my life who had always seemed invincible was broken in two.

Trixie was so organized that she thought of everything, right down to the guest book that everyone signed after they'd expressed their condolences. I was leafing through the book on Monday afternoon when the bell rang once again. Before I could run to hide, in walked my best friend, Rachel, with a huge bouquet of flowers in her hands. "It's from everyone at school," she choked out. She handed the flowers to Trixie, and then she took me in her arms and just wept, and I wept, and she smoothed my long hair and said over and over, "Swan, I'm so sorry. So very sorry."

Rachel was made for crises. She took me upstairs and we sat in my room, and she talked on and on about everything and nothing and what the rest of our part of Atlanta looked like, how the cars really were lined up for miles in front of each home. She reported the facts without emotion, so it didn't make me want to cry anymore, and besides, I didn't have any tears left for the time being.

"It's just all over the news, you know, and your dad's picture with the mayor and all the photos of that plane just smashed into pieces." She glanced my way and continued. "And they say that they'll be raising lots of money for the art museum now—people are already giving huge sums in memory of those who . . . perished." Another glance at me. "You all right, Swan? You want me to stop talking?"

I shrugged. After a few moments of silence I said, "Rach, will you put on JP?"

"You sure?"

"Positive."

Soon the sounds of flute and harpsichord filled my room. Handel. Sonata in B Minor, Opus 1, number 9. Jean-Pierre Rampal, the brilliant French flutist who had gained international renown, played the Largo, his vibrato so strong and yet so soft and so smooth that it sent chills running up and down my spine. I closed my eyes and pictured mountain peaks and snow and a piercing sun breaking through the clouds. It felt at that moment like JP, as Rachel and I called him, was playing a funeral hymn for my mother, lovingly, slowly, with emotion. And as he played, I imagined a little girl delicately placing a bundle of handpicked wild flowers on a fresh grave in a field far below the snow-covered ridges.

"It's like he's mourning with me," I whispered, and Rachel nodded. We were transported by that music in an ethereal way that later we would try to explain and couldn't. But it was the first time I really felt what I had long understood: that something could be extremely beautiful and intensely painful at the same time.

"You're gonna be okay, Swan," Rachel stated in her practical way when we got up and headed downstairs. "If you can cry like that, it means that you're gonna be okay."

She was halfway out the door when Trixie caught up with us. "Swan, why don't you go to the barn with Rachel for a while? Get away from all the people."

I shrugged, already headed toward the kitchen and the *Atlanta Constitution*.

"Go on, sweetie," Trixie urged. "It'll do you good."

It was only a five-minute walk up the street from my house to Rachel's. I walked it almost every day, usually with a bounce to my step, because behind Rachel's house was a stable, and in the stable was my chestnut mare, Bonnie. The stable had five stalls and, behind it, a large riding ring and several acres of woods with trails. Most all of the houses in the part of Atlanta where I lived sat on spacious yards with plenty of land surrounding them. Some homes, like mine, had a pool behind them. Rachel's had a stable.

But I dragged my feet to the barn that day. Bonnie greeted me with a soft nicker, her head peering over the door of her stall, small ears pricked forward. I sat down across from her stall in the overflowing shavings that were stored there. The smells of horses and hay and shavings and manure and leather, the smells of this part of my life, permeated the air, but the excitement and fond memories they usually awakened in me were absent that afternoon.

"I think I better go home," I said to Rachel after I'd been there for only five minutes. "Sorry, Bonnie," I whispered, running my hand across my mare's soft muzzle. "I don't feel like riding today."

We walked back toward Rachel's house in silence. Her mother, Mrs. Abrams, met us in the backyard. She was a very attractive woman, a lot shorter than Rachel's five foot six, with blond shoulder-length hair and an oval face. She looked at the moment very prim and proper in her rose-colored suit, but I knew her to be as tough as nails. Mrs. Abrams loved horses as much as Rachel and I did, and most of the time she was at the barn with us, wearing worn jeans and a dirty sweatshirt and rubber boots, her hair covered by a bandana. The three of us shared the responsibility of feeding the five horses, cleaning out their stalls, and doing what Mrs. Abrams called the "general upkeep of the barn." That translated into a lot of hot, sweaty work, especially when the muggy summer hit.

"Mary Swan, my dear." She patted my shoulder. Mrs. Abrams was not usually an affectionate woman. "We are all terribly sorry." She had sent over a casserole that morning. Her eyes looked very red and swollen, and I guessed that she'd already made visits that afternoon to homes of several of her friends who had been on the Orly flight. Although our parents were well acquainted because of Rachel's and my friendship, they were not particularly close friends. They did see each other at the symphony, and Dr. Abrams, a well-respected professor, was one of Daddy's clients.

Mrs. Abrams came up close to me and looked me straight in the eyes, as was her habit. "Mary Swan," she said, "you know that you are always welcome here and at the barn. Always. But in view of what has happened—" She cleared her throat. "In view of what has happened, you certainly won't be expected to take part in the general upkeep of the place. Take your time. All the time you need." I believe that she blinked back tears.

"Thank you," I managed to mumble.

Rachel draped her arm around my shoulder and walked me down

her driveway. "They canceled all the exams at Welly. I guess you heard, huh?"

I nodded.

"Memorial service at school is Thursday. I'll come and pick you up for it, Swan, okay?"

I nodded again.

Then I forced one foot in front of the other as I walked back down that wide, winding street. Seeing the cars lined up again in front of my house, I found my way through the woods on the left, taking a well-worn path that led away from my house.

A few minutes later, I emerged from the woods and gazed longingly in front of me to where hundreds of yards of grass and trees and flowering plants led to the Swan House, an Italian-style villa that was well-known in Atlanta and had long ago captured my heart. It was called the Swan House because its owner, Mrs. Inman, used the swan motif throughout the residence. The first swan that greeted a visitor was above the porte cochere of the house. That swan, made of lead and surrounded by glass, was depicted amidst a spray of cattails, and the crescent shape that framed the swan emphasized the delicate beauty of the swan's curving neck.

Mama loved that house so much that it was part of the reason she named me Mary Swan. The other was the fact that Swan was the last name of some distant relatives of Daddy's. And since Mama and Daddy were friends of the Inmans, I'd been inside the house on several occasions. On my first visit as a young child, while the grown-ups played bridge and sipped brandy in the library, I spent several hours searching for all the swans in the house. At first Daddy and Mama had disapproved of my wandering in and out of every room, but Mrs. Inman just chuckled gaily and said, "Leave her alone. It's fine. Mary Swan is just looking for herself in my house." I had never forgotten those words.

Mama used to say that the Swan House was the place she escaped to when she got tired of painting portraits. I had many memories of playing around her legs as she stood in front of her easel at the bottom of the long yard and painted the house. What she never knew was that when I was older, I, too, often escaped through the woods all alone to contemplate this architectural masterpiece. Its beauty, its name, and its treasures inspired and encouraged me that someday maybe I would be graceful and poised and breathtaking. Someday I would find myself there.

And now, with my life unraveling around me, the simple sight of the elegant mansion, unchanged from my last visit, reassured me. If I had had pencil and paper with me, I would have sketched the house, as I had done so often before. But being empty-handed, I contented myself by sitting at the bottom of the long rolling yard and listening for sounds of birds and insects, hoping to hear echoes of Rampal's flute amidst the tranquil panorama. There, in one of my favorite settings, I could cry in peace.

I don't know how long I sat there. Later I plodded back through the woods to my house, which was like all the homes in our part of town, big and beautiful with immaculate green lawns that were carefully landscaped with the brightest flowers blooming at the appropriate season. Our house was white brick, three stories high, with a chimney on each side and a gable on the roof. It sat far back from the street on a gently sloping hill, and a little creek wiggled its way through the yard near the street, continuing on toward the Swan House. When we were younger, Jimmy and I built branch bridges over the creek and watched the frogs sunning themselves on the rocky little bank.

The trees that lined the front yard were hickory and oak and magnolia and dogwood and pine. The driveway wound its way up the left side of the property and opened into a wide turnaround behind the house. A guest quarters and two-car garage were located farther behind the main house, curving off to the right of the turnaround. Directly behind the turnaround on the left, there was a long expanse of grass that led to the swimming pool. A huge hickory tree rose rather magnificently up toward the sky, right in the middle of the lawn. And all the other trees, dogwood and oak and hickory and pine, made a tall green fence around the yard, so that you felt completely surrounded by nature and protected from the outside world.

The interior of our house had its share of antiques and art and real Oriental rugs and old elaborate chandeliers and stuff like that. But I preferred the poppy red, sun yellow, and berry blue kitchen, where Mama had framed some of Jimmy's and my childish art in big gilded frames and hung them on the wall that led into the breakfast room. And I liked the den because I could watch TV there, stretched out on a big comfortable couch, and I could set my glass of Coke on either of the end tables without Ella Mae chasing after me saying, "You gonna mess up Miz Sheila's fine table if ya aren't careful, Mary Swan."

It was the kind of house you could easily get lost in, and when we were young we loved to play hide 'n' seek in it with our friends. I liked to sneak down the front staircase and then run past the living and dining rooms and dash up the back stairs whenever anyone got close to finding me. And there were lots of doors in the hallways leading to closets that a small child could disappear into.

Mama and Daddy's bedroom was on the main floor, but upstairs were four more. One for Jimmy, with his own bath and an adjoining bedroom that had been transformed into a boy's playroom. Another bedroom for guests. And the last one with the best light and the big glass windows that opened onto the woods behind the house was Mama's studio, what she called her *atelier*.

The attic was my domain. When I turned twelve, Daddy had announced that it would be redone to become my private rooms, a whole floor all to myself, even though the house already had five bedrooms. Daddy wanted me to be far away from my younger brother and his friends, who loved action and fighting and never seemed to have time to curl up on a bed with a good book.

But that day, nothing about our house pleased me. As soon as I stepped inside the back door, I heard the voices of all those people who had come to express their condolences, and a horrible heaviness settled on me. I crept into the breakfast room, closed the door that led out into the hall, slumped into a chair, and picked up the newspaper from where it lay on the breakfast room table. I stared at the headlines of the *Atlanta Journal*'s final home edition. It read "Allen Arrives in Paris to Check Crash Victims."

I certainly wasn't in the mood to read more morbid details, and yet, there was this insatiable desire to know everything about the crash. So I read, "Paris, June 4—Atlanta Mayor Ivan Allen arrived Monday at the scene of the flaming jetliner crash that carried 130 persons to their death. One hundred and six of them were Atlantans, and many of those were Mayor Allen's personal friends." Mama was his friend. We had dined with the mayor on two different occasions in the past year. And now there was this awful picture splashed across the front page of Mayor Allen touching the burnt-up remains of the Air France jet.

"This was my generation . . . my friends," Mayor Allen had said, according to an article on page three of the Monday paper. "Our deepest sympathy is extended to the hundreds of families and thousands of friends of the victims. Atlanta mourns very deeply this group. There is no way to express adequately our sympathy to these families." And now the mayor was in Paris, personally representing Atlanta at the scene of the tragedy, and at this very moment I imagined he and Daddy were going from one morgue to the next, trying to identify bodies.

Another headline stated poetically: "City of Sorrow Too Hurt to Cry." Yes, that was true—the tears had stopped momentarily, and there was just the emptiest feeling in the air. It was suffocating grief, and I think we all just about went around numb for the first forty-eight hours. The flags were all flying at half-mast, and William B. Hartsfield, the former mayor of Atlanta who was very much respected among the people, called the crash "the greatest tragedy to strike Atlanta since the Civil War." President and Mrs. Kennedy sent their condolences to the Atlanta Art Association in a telegram that stated: "Mrs. Kennedy and I are terribly distressed to learn of the plane crash in France, which cost your community and the country so heavily. Please convey our deepest sympathy to the families who experienced this tragedy." Our Senators Talmadge and Russell wrote, too, as did, I guess, about every other important person in the country.

I forced myself to read all of that first article, and as I did so, I tried to imagine Daddy standing there waving as the plane hurtled down the runway and then watching it explode into flames. I could picture it in all its gruesome detail, and I could not shut it out even when I blinked my eyes. The printed page seared its words into my sensitive spirit as I read on:

> The crash took the lives of 121 passengers, all of them Americans, eight crewmen, and Air France's Atlanta agent. Many of the Atlantans were members of the Atlanta Art Association, en route home from a three-week tour of European art galleries and cultural sites. The big mystery is why the plane crashed. One of the two young stewardesses, the only people who survived the crash, said Monday that everything happened so quickly that she hardly had time to realize that she was involved in a disaster.
>
> Witnesses said that the captain, one of Air France's most experienced pilots, apparently tried to halt the airliner after the engine trou-

ble developed as it roared down the runway, but the plane was going too fast. The six-million-dollar, four-engine airliner rose only a few feet, if at all, then plunged to the ground and kept thundering ahead for 300 yards toward a cluster of homes in a village bordering the airfield. Spouting flames, the jet smashed through a fence at the end of the runway and raced wildly over a rolling wooded slope before coming to a halt at the doorsteps of homes in the hamlet of Villeneuve le Roi.

The takeoff just before 1:00 P.M. Paris time was in clear, bright weather—one of Paris's sunniest days this summer—and everything seemed normal as the plane warmed up for the Atlantic crossing. The recording of the pilot's last words with the control tower at Orly Field was requested by the district magistrate for use in the investigation of the crash. The magistrate said the pilot's exchange was routine—asking the tower for permission to take off and getting the go-ahead. . . . What the radioman described was one of aviation's greatest tragedies. The big Air France jet, chartered to take Georgians home from a "carefree and unforgettable vacation" in European art museums, as the brochure described the flight, careened across a bare field where one wing dug a trench in the soft earth and shattered a fence separating Orly Field from the adjacent village.

I stopped reading for a moment because everything was so blurry. There was a box of Kleenex sitting on the breakfast room table, and I guess I had used about half of it just to get through the first page of the evening paper. Another article at the bottom of the first page said, "Memorial for Paris Dead Considered at Meeting Here—A grief-stricken Atlanta turned its thoughts Monday to possible ways to memorialize the Atlantans who perished in the air crash in Paris. The subject was one of those taken up Monday afternoon at a specially called meeting of the executive committee of the Atlanta Art Association."

Jimmy had come into the kitchen and was eating a banana. "Look, Jimmy," I cried.

Startled, he said, "Gosh, Mary Swan! You don't hafta yell. I'm right here."

"Sorry," I replied sheepishly. "But did you see this? Did you see what it says? They're gonna do something at the art museum for the people, for the people in the . . . for Mama."

"I don't wanna hear it, Swan. I'm tired of that paper. I hate it all! I just hate it!"

He was definitely crying, but I pretended not to notice. I did get up and go over to him and give him a big hug and say, "It's gonna be all right, Jimmy. I swear it." But I didn't believe a word I said.

Jimmy tossed his banana peel into the trash can and left the room. I didn't even have the strength to say anything else to him. A minute later, I caught sight of him outside wrestling in the carport with his dog, a rust-colored Brittany spaniel named Muffin. Somehow it seemed perfectly appropriate that Jimmy could find consolation with his dog.

I stared at the article again. Daddy loved the High Museum almost as much as Mama did, and Jimmy and I knew it like the back of our hand. Whatever happened at the museum, the Middleton family would be there to help. Then I remembered—I was the Raven. A tragic twist of fate would make the Raven Dare all the more important. I *had* to help the museum, and one way would be by finding Mama's missing painting.

I turned the page and saw the next article, which brought the tears once again: "Thirteen Artists Among 130 Killed in Jet—Thirteen artists, at least three of whom were highly professional people with rising reputations, perished in the Paris air crash. . . ." It listed all the names, and Mama's was mentioned as being a very well-respected and sought-after artist, not only in Atlanta, but throughout the Southeast. The article ended with the quote, "They contributed in their enthusiasm and proved that art is worthwhile for life. They instilled their enthusiasm in their community and made life for themselves and others richer."

I found a very brief editorial on page twenty-two of the *Journal* that I thought pretty well summed up what we were all feeling. I read it over and over:

> There are some tragedies too great, some shocks too severe for the human spirit to understand and encompass at once. Such was the tragedy Sunday in Paris that took the lives of so many Atlantans and Georgians. Families were broken by it, and children were orphaned. The personal suffering and loss are so intense that years will pass before the sharp edge of grief is dulled.
>
> The loss will be felt, too, by those who were not bound by ties of

kinship and friendship to those who died. For these were the people who did things, who had the extra something that kept them in front. They were the ones who in times of crisis could be counted upon to come to the rescue of whatever worthy cause might be failing. They were the ones who could be depended upon to successfully sponsor whatever project might be important at the time. Their particular cares were the Art Association, the opera, the symphony, the Speech School, the agencies of the Community Chest, or whatever might bring greater richness and depth to life in Atlanta. The Journal *extends its deepest and most heartfelt sympathy to their families and friends.*

It was that same evening that I discovered the obituaries. I'd never read them before. In fact, I doubted I even knew such a page existed, but I learned a lot of new things in the summer of 1962. One of the most unimportant and yet most painful was the obituary page. Ever after, seeing it in a newspaper would bring back the terrible memories of that first discovery.

Somebody else had said it, and it was true. It felt as if I was being punched in the stomach with every name I read. Page after page, the obituaries listed the history of the crash victims, interspersed with their pictures, and I knew almost all of their names. Some of their daughters were attending or had graduated from Wellington Prep School. One of my classmates, Lanie Bradshaw, had suddenly become an orphan overnight. At least I still had Daddy.

Between the names and histories of the deceased were four ads of such extreme banality that I wondered at the insensitivity of the press. There was an ad for Supreme Coffee with musical notes floating around and the caption "Sparkling note for guests." Another ad claimed the benefits of using a special type of termite control. And then there was the ad for shoes to prove you appreciated your dad on Father's Day.

But the absolute worst was the ad for whiskey. "There's nothing to life but good living," the ad read. "Folks, here's my pride and joy. Friendships and whiskies improve with age." *There's nothing to life but good living.* Why did they print that on a page filled with death? How could they? It was right next to Mama's name. Mama wasn't living and nothing was good. Nothing.

On the second page of the *Journal* in bold letters was the headline:

"Negroes Rejected at Decatur High." I suppose if it had been any other day, I would have noticed that article, my being so staunchly, if naïvely, in support of civil rights. But I didn't see it until months later when I at last got up the courage to leaf back through the paper whose words proclaimed the news that had changed my life. When I did read that headline, long after all the heartache had happened, it occurred to me that the *Atlanta Journal*, in two brief pages, had summed up everything that would have meaning to me for the rest of my teenage years: a plane crash, a memorial museum, and a boy with dark skin who was not allowed to attend a white high school.

Chapter 3

I t was late on Tuesday afternoon when Ella Mae called out from
below. "Swannee! Jimmy! Yore daddy's here." I flew down the stairs
and into my daddy's arms, Jimmy close behind and impatiently waiting
his turn. Ever since Sunday, Jimmy and I had wavered between childhood and adolescence, wrestling with the emotions that bumped
around inside of us. But when we saw Daddy, we, or at least I, was
sure: I was just a little girl. His little girl.

Daddy's hug was fierce; he kept holding me and then Jimmy and
hugging us and saying things like "Thank God, you're both okay. Thank
God."

"Oh, Daddy," I sobbed. "It's the most terrible thing."

There he was without Mama. Without his Sheila. We walked, all
three of us interlaced arm in arm, back to Daddy's study.

I was stunned by the change in my father. In the space of the
month since I'd last seen him, he looked as though he had aged twenty
years. He was haggard and pale with dark circles under his brown
eyes, and it seemed as though he had indeed been carrying the grief
of a half million people on his shoulders.

I hugged him all the tighter and felt the prickle of his unshaven
face against mine. When I was a child, I had called his shadow beard
"pepper," and somehow it was comforting to feel that pepper again
while he was holding me. So we sat on the leather couch in his study,
me leaning on one of his shoulders and Jimmy on the other. I don't
know what Jimmy was thinking, but I was pretending in my big imagination that Mama was upstairs in her studio, painting a still life. At
any minute she would step into the study, paintbrush in hand, and dab
a bit of red on my nose, giggling and whispering in her soft Southern

drawl, "My, Swannee, don't you look marrrrvelous!" And then we'd all start laughing, as we had done so many times before.

"Your mama had the time of her life on the trip," Daddy was saying, and that brought me back to reality. "Of course she missed you both so much. There wasn't a day that went by when she didn't say, 'Now, JJ, don't you just wish Swannee could see this exhibit? She'd love it.' And 'Jimmy would spend hours in front of Napoleon's Tomb, can't you just see it?'" He chuckled a little with the memory, and that was okay. Then he sighed and said, "She was really happy during the whole trip."

Daddy looked at us hard, his eyes a little misty. But it wasn't the tears I saw, but that look of love in his eyes when he emphasized to us that she was really happy while in Europe.

As a painter, Mama was wild and sensitive and as fragile as a dry twig. I loved her fiercely for all her strange, deep ways. Daddy was kind of like her guardian angel, I think. But I don't think I ever realized how hard it was for Daddy to put up with the dark moods and the fits of crying that came along with what he called Mama's "gift." Jimmy and I knew about the black moods, too, although we didn't understand them or even try to. That was just how Mama was. There were days when she couldn't get out of bed and days when she'd lock herself in her studio and paint almost ferociously. Daddy was imperturbable, and Ella Mae was a rock, so it was okay that Mama was a leaf or a twig or a petal from a rose. That was how our family worked. And when Mama was in her happy moods, we were the luckiest kids in all of Atlanta.

Daddy was a stockbroker. He was born into what everyone called an "old Atlanta family." That meant they'd been in Atlanta for a long time and that they had money. Lots of money. Granddad was a great businessman, who had sensed the instability of the market back in 1929 and, fearing a crash, had put all of his money into what Daddy called "something safe." Thus the Middletons had not been hard hit when everyone else was. Daddy and his siblings, all five of them, grew up with his parents' wealth and heard Granddad's constant admonition, "Son, make wise investments and make lots of connections. Never hurts you to know a lot of people."

It certainly hadn't hurt Granddad. He'd been a friend of the Candlers, who owned Coca-Cola, and he was one of the early investors in

Coke stock. All along Daddy had seen what wise investments could do, and it got into his blood, I guess. As a stockbroker, Daddy successfully kept the money that he and Mama had inherited from their respective families and made a name for himself in the brokerage business. He was well respected in Buckhead, the part of northwest Atlanta where we lived. It was filled with these giant old homes with rambling yards, and I loved to ride around and admire the houses, especially in spring when all the dogwoods and azaleas were in bloom. And Buckhead was where most of the victims of the crash had lived.

"Did she get to do the sketches she wanted?" I asked, content to disappear into the past for a while.

"She did. She sketched so many things."

"But they were all destroyed, right, Daddy?" Jimmy interrupted.

And then this funny, sweet smile came over Daddy's face. "No, Jimmy, they weren't. I have all the sketches. Mama carried her art supplies in one of her suitcases, but the sketchpad was too big to fit in hers, so I kept it in the bottom of my case, where it was well protected."

"Oh, Daddy! Go get it!" we cried in unison.

And so he did. And there in his study, we drifted back in time, like in a sweet dream, as Daddy described his Sheila through the pages of her sketchbook.

"On our very first day in Paris, she insisted on sketching by the Seine. She said the light was perfect, and she could even see the Eiffel Tower way off in the distance. See how she did it? And of course she sketched Notre Dame right after that." He flipped the page, and the famous cathedral appeared.

"Oh, just look at the gargoyles leaning over with their wicked expressions," I said, peering intently at the page. Then I howled in glee. "Jimmy, look! She put your face on one of the gargoyles!" Mama was known for her touches of humor.

"Did not!" Jimmy insisted. Then upon closer inspection, he shrugged. "Who cares?" But I could tell he was thrilled. And then he snorted. "Look at you, Miss Goody-Two-Shoes. You're the Virgin Mary!" And he was right. "That's a good one! You the Virgin Mary!"

"I hadn't even noticed that," Daddy said, chuckling, but all too soon we were sniffling and brushing our sleeves across our eyes.

He flipped to the next page, and there was a little girl feeding a pigeon and in the background were lines of people waiting to get into the Louvre.

Daddy gave a nod, as if he'd just remembered something, and said, "It was the strangest thing, that little girl, oblivious to the crowds, intent on her pigeon. And your mama took off her shoes and sat in the grass in the Jardin des Tuileries and started sketching her, equally oblivious to those staring around her. Sheila was so much like a child sometimes. . . ."

Jimmy gave me this queer look, and I raised my eyebrows to warn him to be quiet and listen as Daddy reminisced. So Daddy took us to Rome and Florence and Madrid and Vienna and Amsterdam and London and Edinburgh, and every page was filled with the sketches from those great cities.

Then, quite suddenly, Daddy buried his face in his hands and gave this horrible, deep sigh. I quickly closed the pad. "I'm sorry, Daddy. We don't have to look at it anymore."

"You keep Mama's sketchpad, Swannee. She'd want it that way," he said, brushing my forehead with his bristly cheek.

I took it up to my room and set it beside my own sketchbook, the one I used almost daily, the one Mama had given me. Her sketchpad would be one of my most treasured possessions, and with the inspiration from her European trip tucked safely in its pages, I reaffirmed something that I'd felt from my earliest years: I was going to be a painter too.

But it turned out that for weeks I didn't sketch a thing. The June days were muggy and long, and I found myself slipping into a stupor that matched the sticky heat. I typically had a million ideas running around in my head, but now, as hard as I tried, there was nothing there at all. No energy, no interests, no appetite.

"You's gonna git too skinny, Mary Swan, if'n you don't eat nothin'," Ella Mae chided.

I shrugged.

Rachel Abrams's calls went unanswered. My mare was not ridden. My sketchpad lay closed. The lethargy seemed to swallow me up, and I sat for hours staring out the window of my bedroom into the backyard. I didn't know what was the matter with me. I just cried for days on end, and I couldn't eat, and my sleep was fitful.

And I couldn't get away from the articles and the reporters and the citywide grief.

Mrs. Alexander, my English teacher, stopped by my house one afternoon. At Wellington she was prim and proper and demanding, a straight-backed woman in her midforties. But standing there in the entrance hall, she took me in her arms and held me tight. "Mary Swan, I am so sorry."

Squashed against her bosom, I felt a stab of guilt. How many times had I made fun of her in class by sticking her name into some famous poem at just the right place?

"Would you like to sit down?" I offered. "And what about some lemonade?"

"No, no. I won't be long." She followed me into the living room, and we sat across from each other on the matching love seats. "Mary Swan, as you know I am the senior girls' advisor, and one of my roles is to supervise the Raven Dare. I know you were selected as this year's Raven—a wonderful choice. But I am also aware that, by a tragic twist of fate, this dare has become quite inappropriate for you. The senior-class officers and I would like to withdraw it."

"Withdraw the Dare?" I asked, startled, momentarily shaken out of my stupor.

"Yes. We have several options, though. If you would like to be the Raven, then the girls will simply come up with another dare. If, however, you feel that in light of the . . . the crash, you would rather forget the whole thing, then another Raven can be chosen. We want whatever would be best for you."

In truth, I had scarcely given the Dare a thought. "No, no. That won't be necessary, Mrs. Alexander. Don't change a thing." I hardly knew what I was saying, but with more feeling than I'd had in ten days, I said, "I want to be the Raven, and I want to solve the Dare." I nibbled a fingernail. "What I mean is that I *need* to solve the Dare. It's going to be important—for me and for Mama."

Mrs. Alexander leaned toward me, her expression intense. "Are you sure, Mary Swan? Do you really want that pressure on you, that constant reminder?"

"Yes. I don't know why, Mrs. Alexander, but somehow that dare is going to help me. I think it will. I hope it will."

She seemed flustered, unconvinced. "Well, then, please just know that if you ever change your mind, or if you ever just want to talk about it, I'll always be more than happy to meet with you."

"Thank you. Thanks a lot." I got tears in my eyes, and she hugged me again and said good-bye. As I watched her walk down the long driveway, I leaned against the opened door, thinking to myself, *That was your chance to get off the hook. Why didn't you just accept her offer?* And the only answer that came to me was what I'd told Mrs. Alexander. I *needed* to solve the Dare. Never mind that I had not one idea or ounce of energy to tackle it now. Later I would.

Our *LIFE* magazine showed up about two weeks after the crash. On the front cover was this great picture of Natalie Wood, who was kind of like my heroine. She was absolutely gorgeous on the cover, her black hair tousled and windblown, her dark eyes looking up, a wide smile on her face displaying her perfectly straight white teeth. Sometimes I'd fantasize that I might look a tiny bit like Natalie Wood, although there was not one iota of resemblance—she was so stunning and buxom, and I was so plain and flat-chested.

But then I saw the headline in the upper right-hand corner of the cover: "ATLANTA: A City's Time of Sorrow and the Enduring Art Legacy the Plane Victims Left Behind." I flipped through the pages until I found the article. There were pictures of the paintings that various victims had donated to the museum, and then a picture of a bunch of mourners kneeling outside the Cathedral of Christ the King for the memorial service held there. They were kneeling outside because there was no more room inside. Another picture showed a roomful of women, members of the Atlanta Junior League, standing with their heads bowed in the ballroom of the Piedmont Driving Club, grieving the loss of thirteen of their members. Mama was one of them.

There were shots of the artwork in some of the victims' bedrooms and an article about the different artists. There was a picture of a guard standing outside the museum, which was closed out of respect for the dead, with several wreaths of flowers in front of the door. And there was a picture of a self-portrait Mama had been painting, taken right in her studio. I remembered the day the reporters had come, invading our privacy for the benefit of the public.

I read every word about the crash written in *LIFE*, and when *Newsweek* came a few days later, I read it too. Maybe it was some kind of masochistic pleasure, but I don't think so. It was just me, Mary

Swan Middleton, trying to make sense of something that could never be explained.

> For days after the crash, the whole city of Atlanta seemed to be in mourning. She had lost over a hundred of her most prominent citizens, people whose lives had been spent investing in the culture of Atlanta. The churches were full that Sunday morning on the third of June when the news of the horrible tragedy was announced. The president of the Atlanta Arts Center was a victim along with his wife.
>
> "It is doubtful that any American city ever lost at a single stroke so much of its fineness," said editor Eugene Patterson of the Atlanta Constitution. Most of the victims were members of the tightly knit cadre of old families which makes up the motive force behind much of this Southern city's financial and cultural growth. They were the money raisers, the civic project backers, the city leaders who by letting it be known that they favored peaceful desegregation were responsible for Atlanta's orderly handling of that most difficult problem.
>
> Of the dead, six were board members of the Atlanta Art Association; thirty were members of the Piedmont Driving Club; twenty-one were members of the Capital City Club; thirteen were Junior Leaguers, of which two were former presidents. As editor Jack Spalding of the Atlanta Journal said, "They were all involved in some sort of civic work. . . ."
>
> "These people were of the type the city can ill afford to lose, the type who made Atlanta what it is," said ex-Mayor Hartsfield. "This is the greatest tragedy to strike Atlanta since the Civil War."
>
> As the week wore on, messages of sympathy arrived from President Kennedy, de Gaulle, the Pope, and many others. Homes in the Buckhead section were garbed in mourning wreaths, neighbors brought over food, and friends and relatives came to get the clothes and belongings of many of the thirty-one children orphaned by the disaster.
>
> At Orly Field, Mayor Allen grimly inspected the wreckage and the partly burned guidebooks, billfolds, travelers checks, souvenir ashtrays, menus, gold slippers, blackened opera glasses, charred cameras, and antique silverware. He picked up a charred vacation brochure ("Your trip will be carefree and unforgettable"), and it crumbled in his hand.
>
> After a trip to the morgue, the gray-haired mayor said wearily, "I had known most of these people since childhood, but I wasn't able to recognize any of them." The grim task of identification was left to experts, and Allen returned to Atlanta to comfort the bereaved.

On Friday, the Art Association executive committee decided to raise $1.5 million from donations for the purpose of building a new art school as a memorial to the victims. This, they believed, was much more meaningful than eulogies. Dr. Reginald Poland, director of the Art Association Museum, put it about as simply as one could, "Anything you say would be inadequate."

That was how the article in *Newsweek* ended, and that was how it should have. There was nothing else to say, no possible way to express the personal and communal grief that Atlanta was living. I was glad that the rest of America could know it, and yet I didn't want them to know too much, because, more than anything else, I thought that no one outside of those of us who were living this catastrophe could really understand it. And I didn't want it trivialized.

If I had been talented like Mama, I would have painted something to show how I felt. But every time I got my sketchbook out, all I could do was scribble horrible black lines all over the page. And day by day, I fell into a darker mood and a cycle of not eating and crying and sleeping and sitting on my bed just staring out the window.

When Daddy came home from Paris, he was greeted like the hero he'd been made into, since he was the one who had initially borne the grief for all of Atlanta. People said it again and again, whispered it with shining eyes, "Can you imagine what John Jason Middleton must be going through? Having watched the whole thing . . . seeing it explode with his wife inside."

But Daddy went around in a daze, and I think he spent a lot of time with other men who had lost wives in the crash. He would come into a room and hold me tight, his unshaven face tickling my cheek.

Daddy always shaved. Daddy was the most sophisticated businessman I knew. He was tall, on the thin side, with that kind of hair that turns gray around the temples and gives men a distinguished look. His hair was jet-black otherwise, and I thought his looks very intriguing. Not what some people would call knock-you-down handsome, but just so poised and honest. He was strong and sure of himself, but usually not overbearing. And he worked hard. Too hard, in my opinion, because I never felt I got to see enough of him. Even when he was at home, he seemed preoccupied with his job or with Mama. I longed for him to spend an afternoon alone with me. But that never happened.

Mama had been impromptu and sporadic. She'd be in the middle of painting when we'd come home from school. Suddenly she'd drop her paintbrush and grab Jimmy and me in a huge hug and say, "Y'all ready for a treat?" We loved Mama's treats because there was no way we could ever guess what they would be. One time she said she was going to take us out for a Coke, and it ended up we got a tour of the Coca-Cola Bottling Company in downtown Atlanta by Mr. Woodruff, the genius behind the soft-drink empire. Another time, we got ice cream as we sat on the back of a white Lipizzaner stallion that was in Atlanta for a very special circus. I don't know how Mama worked those things out. I never asked. I just enjoyed the times when Mama was really happy.

But now, with Mama dead and Daddy looking so awful and me feeling like there was no reason to keep on living, I started wondering if Daddy could take care of us alone. I decided that we needed Ella Mae more than four times a week.

"You can come live with us," I stated naïvely to her one day. "You could move in here. There's plenty of room."

"No, chile, I couldn't do that. I gotta take care o' Roy, and sometimes my daughter needs he'p with the gran'baby."

Amazingly, I had never thought of Ella Mae as having any family other than us. I knew she was married, because her husband, Roy, did yard work for Daddy occasionally. But I had never once heard her talk about her children, never seen a picture, and never thought that it might be odd that I did not know.

I guess Mama had known about Ella Mae's family. She often told the story of being nine months' pregnant with me and ready to deliver on the sidewalk. In that uncomfortable position she had decided that she must have a maid to help her after the baby came. And so she put an ad in the paper for help. When Ella Mae showed up at our house for an interview, Mama couldn't understand a word she said, not even her first name, which she repeated five times until finally Mama got it.

"Bring your family to live here, Ella Mae," I said stubbornly, determined that my world would not change.

"Chile, you think I could move my black family up heah and live with white folk—heah in the rich part of Atlanta? You don't know whatcha askin'."

Ella Mae's stubborn refusal to even consider my deepest request made me angry, and I left the room to sulk. I went up the two flights of stairs to the big open bedroom with the skylight that let in the afternoon sun. I didn't know what to do with myself. I had never been patient. When I had an idea, I wanted to get moving with it. And now I had an idea for the first time in weeks: Ella Mae would come live with us.

I stared out the dormer window, looking far below to where a massive hickory tree grew in the backyard, a rope swing attached to one of the lower branches. I could almost see Mama there, sitting in the yard with her easel and palette, painting me as I pumped my legs and forced the swing higher and higher, laughing in delighted four-year-old reverie, my light brown hair flying behind in a tangled swirl.

Mama was always happiest with a paintbrush in her hand. At other times she was sullen and pouty or sharp and critical, but a paintbrush almost always assured a smile and then a happy, if concentrated, intense look.

Why did you have to die, Mama, in a burst of flame? Angrily I rubbed the back of my hand across my face, wiping all the salty tears away. But it didn't do a bit of good. They came right back.

About an hour later I left my room, coming down the two flights of steps with slow deliberation. When my feet touched on the landing of the main floor, I caught sight of the portrait in the entrance hall. I loved it more than anything else that had ever belonged to me or ever would.

Mama painted many children's portraits. I remembered often coming home from school or waking from my nap to find Mama in her studio touching up a portrait of some finely clad child. The little girls were almost always dressed in pink taffeta, it seemed to me, with big pink ribbons in their long silky hair. Their expressions were serene and submissive, a flower or a kitten or a small book in their hands.

So when Mama decided that it was time to paint me at the age of four and a half, she went out and bought a beautiful taffeta dress, pink with smocking of little kittens and pansies across the front. And a wide pink ribbon for my hair. The dress lay across the twin bed in my room that I didn't use. Lay there for days. I tried it on for Mama and wriggled uncomfortably inside the scratchy new material. Mama laughed, with a little gleam in her eyes.

When the day came for her to do the sketch and take the photographs, I started up the stairs to my room, dreading the pink dress. Halfway up, Mama caught my arm and pulled me close. "Mary Swan," she whispered in the delightful way that meant she was really happy, "I don't much like the pink dress. Do you?"

Hesitantly I peered at her, wondering. Then I shook my head vehemently.

"Well, then, if you don't like it either, I think you should go up and pick out your very favorite clothes to wear while you pose for the portrait."

It was like the taste of your first strawberry in late March, so wild and sweet. Of course Mama knew what I would choose. I ran to my room, threw open the bottom drawer of my white wicker chest, the drawer reserved for my playclothes, and retrieved a pair of boy's denim overalls. Old, stained, twice my size, and terribly faded, with patches sewn all over, they had been cut off and rolled up above the knees. Underneath I pulled on a light blue T-shirt, equally faded and worn. No shoes. I turned and looked at the taffeta dress draped across my bed with the stiff pink bow lying beside it, and I laughed a luxurious little-girl laugh. Mama was painting my portrait in my favorite clothes!

She was a genius with expression. Even with the serene children whose hands were folded in their laps, Mama managed to convey their personality in the way the eyes shone or flashed and the turn of the lips. And for me, the child she knew best, she offered herself the luxury—*la gourmandise*, as she called it—of painting me just as I was. On the rope swing, bare feet stretching in the foreground of the painting, my mouth wide open in glee, and my tangled hair flying out behind me. The look in my eyes was of perfect, wild contentment, and even the big hickory from which the swing hung seemed to be smiling.

It was the kind of painting that made people smile when they looked at it, the kind that inspired you to hold out your arms and go running through the wind into a pile of freshly raked leaves, a picture that resonated with the vigor and spirit of childhood. Mama was proud of it.

Even Daddy could barely help stifle a hoot of laughter when he saw it. His brow wrinkled. He regarded me and then the portrait and then me again. "Well, darling, you seem to have captured our little Swan in all her exuberance!" Then he picked me up in his arms and swung me around, and we all shared in that delicious laughter.

It was the sweetest of my childhood memories. The sunny days swinging while Mama painted, humming happily to herself. Painting me was good therapy, she told me. It made her feel as though she had swallowed a butterfly that was flittering away inside her tummy, trying to get out. She couldn't wait to see what the painting would become.

And whenever I looked at it as a teenager, I felt that same warmth and truth. That rush of joy knowing that Mama had known me and understood the wild, free side of her daughter. Of course she had understood, for she had the same stubbornness, the same lust for adventure, the same determination to take in life in large gulps of fresh air.

One day in late June I was crying so hard that my face was all splotched and red and my eyes swollen. I wouldn't let Daddy into my room despite his pleading. I felt miserable, and I guess I was. Daddy must have thought I was on the brink of suicide, because after a while he stopped pleading, and all was silent. Then later I heard his footsteps on the staircase, accompanied by those of a high-heeled woman. I could tell immediately it was Trixie.

In whispered tones he said, "She won't come out. She's in there bawling her eyes out and heaven knows what else. Please, Trixie, do something."

Hearing the anguish in Daddy's voice made my sobs stop momentarily. Then it was Trixie's high-pitched Southern drawl that permeated the walls of my room.

"Sugar, Swannee, now I have a tall glass of lemonade out back by the pool, and you can just sit in the lounge chair and sip on it and dip your toes in the pool, and if you want, I'll give you a manicure and paint your nails. I don't know about you, but mine are simply atrocious. And I promised Lucy I'd do hers, so you might as well come on down. And I told your Daddy to go on and get to his meeting, that you'd be fine eating with us."

Hearing her talk like that, so natural, so trivial, about all the things we always did, somehow flooded me with relief. In spite of Mama's not being here, some things wouldn't change. Trixie was still my wonderful neighbor with the syrupy voice and the silliest ideas and a ten-year-old daughter named Lucy.

"I'll be waiting for you, Swannee. See ya in a minute," she called out.

I didn't see it, but I'd bet a million bucks that Trixie blew a puff of smoke from her cigarette and then nodded her head, winking at Daddy and shooing him out of the house. She'd done it a hundred times before. I heard her high heels clicking loudly on the steps and Daddy's heavy steps following, and then it was quiet.

I lay on the bed for five minutes without another tear flowing. I must have dozed a little, because I sat up with a start at the sound of Lucy's laughter and the splashing of water. I went to my window and peered outside, past the spacious yard. I couldn't see the pool, but I imagined Trixie sitting there, as she used to with Mama, bright pink straw hat on her blond curls, nicely tanned and toned legs stretched out on the chaise lounge, sipping something exotic. I hopped off the bed, scuttled to the bathroom, where I threw water on my face, wiped it quickly on a hand towel, and ran down the steps, taking them two at a time.

When I stepped out into the boiling, sticky heat of late June in Atlanta, the suffocating sensation made me thankful. It was the same. The smell of honeysuckle was the same, the tall hickory and oak trees without a breeze flickering their leaves were the same. And Trixie, wonderful Trixie, was the same as always. She smiled from under her straw hat and motioned for me to take the lounge chair beside her. Skinny Lucy with her long blondish brown hair splashed away in the pool. Maybe there was life after Mama's death after all.

Trixie was petite and blond and sweet. And I guess just her name made you think she was a bit superficial. And her high-pitched laugh. But she'd had her share of hard times too. Her husband had divorced her ten years ago when she was pregnant with Lucy. Anyway, Mama had loved her like a sister, and I loved her too. I had a hundred memories of Trixie rescuing me from eternal boredom while Mama painted. She'd arrive, always looking immaculate, every hair in place, wearing a wide straw hat and fashionable glasses, with a picnic basket draped over one arm. "Come on, Swannee, it's time you get yourself outside with us. Your mom needs a break."

It wasn't until after Mama's death that I realized the extent of

Trixie's love for Mama and for us. How she was in a sense Mama's personal savior when Daddy couldn't be there. She and Ella Mae and Daddy performed an intricate if unseen act of grace to keep my mother balanced and functioning. And I never once saw it. That was their gift to me as I grew up. Secrecy and love.

Chapter 4

There were several things that pulled me out of my depression at the end of June and during those early days of July: Trixie's attention and Rachel's constant phone calls insisting that we had to get a start on the Raven Dare were two. But it was especially Ella Mae who was determined to have her Mary Swan back.

"You is not much good to anyone, sugah, sittin' round as you are, feelin' sorry for yorese'f," she said one day when she found me flopped across my bed, staring at a magazine. "Ya know what would do ya good?"

"No idea," I mumbled unenthusiastically. "Give me a hint."

"You needs ta do somethin' fo' somebody else, Mary Swan. And I got jus' the thing."

I looked up from the magazine I was reading, the lack of interest evident in my eyes.

"You come downtown with me on Saturday mornin'. He'p out at Grant Park."

I'd never been to the part of Atlanta called Grant Park, but I knew where it was—in the slums, in the inner city. "What do you mean by 'help out,' Ella Mae?"

"I mean you goes to he'p people who are in a heap o' trouble and need a good hot meal and a listenin' ear. That's what I mean."

"Who'll be there?"

"Lotta blacks'll be there. And some white folk too, Swannee. It's not the kind of thing you can explain too well. Ya have to see it for yorese'f."

She didn't twist my arm or anything, but somehow, Ella Mae convinced me to go with her to Grant Park, a part of Atlanta's famous downtown that was now falling into disrepair. All the white families with money were moving out.

I was petrified to tell Daddy where we were going, but when I did, he just said, "If Ella Mae's taking care of you, that's just great." Anything that would get his Swannee out of the house seemed to be fine with him.

Ella Mae took the bus to our house and arrived around ten-thirty that Saturday morning. I was still asleep. She backed the old blue Cadillac out of our two-car garage. Daddy had taught her how to drive it years ago, and she used it to take Jimmy and me to different outings. She was one of the few maids who could drive at that time, and she was proud of it and even prouder of her "Caddylac," as she called it.

She honked once, and that got me out of bed. Five minutes later I rushed out of the house with a piece of toast hanging from my mouth. I hopped into the car, still munching, and gave Ella Mae a half smile. We rolled the windows all the way down, and I put my face to the wind and let the hot air blow over me.

Riding with Ella Mae at the wheel was always an adventure, the way she stomped on the brakes at stoplights and maneuvered the Cadillac along the streets. I decided I wasn't as scared of getting into trouble in Grant Park as I was of getting into a wreck before we ever arrived.

Eventually she pulled up in front of a red-brick church.

"You didn't tell me I was going to church," I complained.

"An' you didn' ask."

So I spent a good bit of Saturday morning and afternoon with Ella Mae in a big room in the basement of Mt. Carmel Church. Paint was peeling off the walls, except for where a mural had been painted near the side door, and a lot of long metal tables and folding metal chairs were arranged on the left side of the room.

"This is our fellowship hall, where we has our meals and such," Ella Mae explained. Then she led me into the adjoining kitchen to meet a white woman named Miss Abigail, whom Ella Mae called "an angel in the devil's boilin' pot." According to Ella Mae, Miss Abigail had moved to Atlanta in the midfifties from Detroit, where she'd worked in the slums for sixteen years.

Miss Abigail looked older than Daddy and younger than Ella Mae, which would have made her around fifty. Her hair was thick and mostly black with streaks of gray here and there, and she wore it long and pulled back in a ponytail, which struck me as odd for a woman of her age. But what I really noticed about her were her eyes. To this day I can never remember their color. I think they were just a very ordinary brown. But that day, as on most every other day I was with her, Miss Abigail's eyes sparkled. There's no other word for it. They sparkled as though she'd just been told she had won a million bucks.

She was of medium build and she wasn't very tall, several inches shorter than I, and I was five feet five. But according to Ella Mae, she was tough. She had spent her life on the streets, serving the poor and homeless, one of the first white women to do such a thing in Atlanta.

Miss Abigail was leaning over a big aluminum sink washing lettuce leaves. She turned around to greet me, wiping her roughened hands on her faded green apron. Then she extended her hand. "Thank you so much for coming down to help us today, Mary Swan." Miss Abigail's voice carried no hint of the Southern drawl we knew in Atlanta. I gave her a half smile and a shrug.

She didn't seem to notice. "There are over four hundred and fifty families living in Grant Park, and most of them are desperately poor. A large percentage of the kids have never known their fathers and are being raised by their grandmothers. About a year and a half ago, we started offering spaghetti lunch once a week to any who wanted it. Volunteers from both white and black churches take turns preparing and serving the food. Ella Mae is one of the most faithful." She stated the facts coolly. "You can help out with serving the sauce." She pointed out from the kitchen into the big room adjoining it. Steaming pots of spaghetti sauce and bowls of noodles were sitting on two long tables that separated the workers from the assortment of people milling around the room, waiting for lunch.

The spaghetti was overcooked and stuck together, the plates cracked, and the pots and pans dented and stained. Ella Mae said that all the silverware had been stolen the week before, so she and Miss Abigail had to go down the street begging the neighbors to loan them forks and knives at the last minute. I stood there, awkwardly holding a ladle in one hand, waiting for them to return. The people standing in line were mostly sad-looking men in thin shirts and greasy pants that hung on them, or heavyset women with thinning hair, or teenage girls with one or two little children in tow. There was a mixture of whites, blacks, and Mexicans.

I found myself serving spaghetti that Saturday beside a boy who was about eighteen or nineteen, strong looking and tall, over six feet, and black as the ace of spades, as Granddad would say.

"Hello. I'm Carl," he said, staring down at me with the ladle of spaghetti sauce in my left hand.

"Hi. My name's Mary Swan." My voice sounded a little strained, and I bet my face was crimson.

"Nice to see ya here, Mary Swan." His smile was wide and white.

"Nice to be here." I tried to smile, and then I cleared my throat. "Do you come here a lot, Carl?"

"Most weeks I come. Helping Miss Abigail."

"Why do you want to help her?"

He smiled again. " 'Cause she's the one who helped me get back in school. She helped me find an afternoon job so that I can make some money for my family and still go to school. She's one fine lady."

And that was how I formally met Carl Matthews.

I couldn't think of anything to say, which, as my friends often commented, was rarer than an uncooked piece of beef. It was just that it seemed more like I was in Africa or Haiti than in Atlanta. I'd lived here all my life, but I didn't know a thing about this side of the city.

"You have any brothers and sisters?" I ventured.

"Yep. Three of 'em. I live with my two younger brotha's, my little sista', and my aunt."

"What about your parents?"

"My mama's dead. She died when I was twelve."

That made my heart skip a beat. "Was she sick?"

"Got shot. Big fight between her and her boyfriend. You know what I mean?"

I didn't have the faintest idea, but it sounded absolutely gruesome. "What about your dad?"

Carl's smile was cynical. "I've never met my dad. Don't know him from Adam." He chuckled, but I wondered if there was bitterness behind those black eyes.

"My mom's dead too," I offered, feeling worse by the minute.

He shrugged, not a bit curious like I was. Maybe in his part of Atlanta it was the most common thing in the world to be an orphan.

To never know your father and to have your mama killed in an angry dispute, leaving four kids to fend for themselves.

Finally, after he'd slopped spaghetti sauce on several plates and murmured "The Lord bless you" to several men, he asked, "How'd she die?"

"In the plane crash in June. Did you hear about it?"

"Yeah, I know about that, Mary Swan." He looked almost offended. "I read the papers. I don't reckon there's a soul in Atlanta who didn't shed tears over that tragedy. Didn't know anybody on that plane, but it broke my heart. A whole lotta pain in Atlanta." Then he met my eyes, and I saw kindness and sorrow in his. "I sure am sorry for you, Mary Swan." And I knew, with a tingling down my spine, that he meant it.

But I didn't want to talk about the plane crash. After all, I was coming down to the inner city to get away from my problems and listen to someone else's. So I went back to asking about Carl's family. "So your aunt took care of you after your mom was killed?"

"No. My aunt was in no shape to care for us. It was Miss Abigail. Good thing she arrived in Atlanta 'bout that time. She took us in and fed us and got us to school and loved on us just as if she was as black as we were."

"But you're living with your aunt now?"

"That's right. Took us a while to get things back together, but we're coming along."

"And you go to school and then work in the afternoons?" I didn't know any teenager in Buckhead who had a job after school.

"Yep. I missed two years of school 'cause I had to be working. To help pay the bills, ya know what I mean? Like I said, Miss Abigail got me the job in the late afternoon so that I could go back to school. She says I'll be able to go to college one day if I want to. And I do."

I was glad that we ran out of spaghetti just then, so that when I went into the kitchen Carl thought it was just to get another pot of noodles. But really, I was crying, crying for this kind boy who told his tragic tale as if it were the most natural thing on earth. And it struck me then, that in his world, this world of the inner city of Atlanta, maybe it was.

The next Saturday morning I was up and dressed and waiting almost impatiently for Ella Mae to drive up. Daddy didn't say a word about it. He just watched me go with this mixture of pain and relief in his dark brown eyes. I think he considered anything that got me out of the house that sticky July a small miracle.

And Ella Mae was right. It did seem to help to leave Buckhead and its grief for a few hours and discover another type of pain in Grant Park. But mostly I think I agreed to go back because something deep and rebellious in me wanted to be friends with Carl Matthews. I'd never had a black friend my own age. Blacks weren't allowed at Wellington. Only one school district in Atlanta was desegregated, and it wasn't mine.

After the meal was served, Carl shooed Miss Abigail out of the kitchen. "You've got people to be talking to, now. Go on. I'll clean up." I noticed right away how protective he was of Miss Abigail. And I noticed something else. He knew how to clean up. The prospect of having his elbows in that sudsy water as he washed plates and silverware and pots and pans didn't seem to bother him a bit. "Wanna help?" he asked, smiling that same wide, white smile.

"Sure," I said with a shrug.

"You wanna wash or dry?" He was already rolling up his sleeves. "Don't make any difference to me."

I was petrified. I had no idea what to do; I'd never washed a dish in my life. But I was also proud. "I'll be glad to wash."

He had lined up all the pots and pans and plates and glasses and silverware on one side of the sink and put a stopper in the sink. The hot water bubbled into a foam when he squirted a little of the dishwashing liquid into it. I looked at the pile of dishes beside me and grabbed the biggest pan, caked with red sauce. Plunging it into the sudsy water, I stifled a little howl of pain. That water was hot! With a soggy sponge, I started scrubbing the pan with its stubborn sauce. The water was turning a dull shade of red, and I felt the sweat prickling my brow and upper lip. The pot would not come clean.

It took a moment for me to realize that Carl was staring at me with that same smile on his face. Then he scratched his head as if he were perplexed. "I've never seen anyone do dishes like that before. We always start with the glasses and silverware and save the pots and pans 'til last. Let 'em soak in the water. Ya know what I mean?"

My cheeks were burning, and I was inwardly cursing this boy who had the nerve to tell me how to wash dishes! My mind searched for a reply that would put him in his place. But before I could say a thing, he took up the rag and said, "Here, I'll show you, Mary Swan. I don't guess you've had the chance to do many dishes with Ella Mae there all the time."

He wasn't snooty or bitter or self-righteous. It was a statement. But it still bugged me to death, the way he smiled so politely and then changed the water and started all over. I felt like he had slapped my hands for committing a terrible sin. Humiliated, I grabbed a dish towel and started drying the glasses he placed in the dark green dish holder.

Somewhere between the silverware and the last pan, I got over my humiliation. When all the dishes were dried and stacked, we walked into the big room where Miss Abigail and Ella Mae were engrossed in a conversation with a sickly looking white-haired woman.

"Leave 'em be," Carl whispered to me. "They're always talkin' and prayin' with people. Wanna go outside? I'll take you to my house."

I shrugged, thinking I should at least tell Ella Mae what I was up to. When I did, she got a scowl on her face and said, "Fine little jaunt ova' ta yore house, Carl. Gonna take ya a while."

"We'll be careful, Ella Mae," Carl said solemnly.

Miss Abigail nodded at Ella Mae and smiled at Carl, so Ella Mae just shrugged and said, "Y'all be back fo' too long."

"Yes, ma'am," Carl said. And to me, "You can meet my brotha's and sista'."

It was hot and miserably muggy outside as we walked down the street. Carl pointed at a massive old Victorian house with trash in the yard and windows broken out. "Twelve different families live in there."

"In one house?"

"Yep. White families. That there's a tenement house. Lots of 'em round these parts."

Many of the houses were two-story and Victorian looking. Some, I could tell, had once been beautiful old homes. But now virtually all were in disrepair. "Whites and blacks live in this neighborhood?"

"Yep. Used ta be only rich white folks. Then they got scared and run lickity-split away from here, so that's when the poor whites moved in. Now ya got both blacks and whites, and Mexicans too, but they don't like mixin' together. 'Cept at the church when there's a free meal offered!" He chuckled a little. "Ova' where I live near Cabbagetown, it's all black families."

"Cabbagetown! That's really what it's called?"

He smiled. "Sure is. This here's Grant Park, and then there's Cabbagetown. And not far away there's Mechanicsville and Buttermilk Bottom and Summerhill and Reynoldstown. Those are all black neighborhoods."

"Funny names. But then again, I live in a place called Buckhead."

"I've heard of Buckhead. Lotsa ladies I know work in Buckhead."

"You know where the name came from?"

"Nope."

"Well, the story goes that back in the 1800s a man named Henry Irby shot a large buck near Paces Ferry Road and Peachtree." Peachtree was a wide road that ran smack through Atlanta from south to north. "He mounted the head on a post in front of his tavern, and people started calling the place 'Buck's Head.' "

Carl grinned. "Makes sense."

"And do you know where the name Peachtree comes from?"

"Now, Mary Swan, that ain't too hard. Comes from a peach tree, I reckon. Musta been a lotta them round these parts, the way they call everything in this city Peachtree somethin'."

"Well, it might be because of the peach trees, and it might be because of the pitch—you know, the resin, in pine trees."

"You mean it shoulda been called Pitchtree?" He narrowed his eyes in a teasing way.

"Yeah, maybe. Fact is, there weren't that many peach trees around back in Indian times. But one thing's for sure. Indians lived here, Muscogee and Cherokee, and there was a village known as Standing Peach Tree right where the Chattahoochee River meets Peachtree Creek."

Carl lifted his eyebrows. "They teach you stuff like that at your school?"

"No, I read it in a book."

"Well, that's just fine." He stopped then and said, "That's where I work in the afternoons." He indicated a gas station with a sign that read "Abe's Fill 'er Up."

"I don't know who named the place, but I figure it pretty well explains what it's here for." He was grinning from ear to ear.

I almost stuck my tongue out at him, but by now I knew his teasing was perfectly harmless.

"And over there's the Rite Price Laundromat where me and my friends hang out on the weekends."

We must have been walking for at least fifteen minutes, and I was beginning to wonder if I should have come with him. "Are we almost there?"

"Not far now, Mary Swan. Over there's the cemetery—they call it Oakland. Right famous place," he commented.

Oakland Cemetery! Way across the street, I could see a tall red-brick gateway rising in three arches with wrought-iron gates marking the entrance. Carved in the stone above the main arch was the word *Oakland*.

I nodded in the direction of the cemetery and said, "That's where my mom is going to be buried."

"Go on. Ya don't mean it?"

"Sure I do."

"She hasn't been buried yet?"

"No. Daddy and the rest of the people who lost family members in the crash are dealing with lots of red tape in getting the bodies back to the States. Most of the funerals are just now taking place. Mama's is scheduled for next Saturday." I suddenly felt a funny catch in my throat.

He walked with me to the entrance to Oakland, and I peeked through the gate. Tall oaks and magnolias lined a narrow red-brick cobbled road with stone monuments on each side. "Have you ever been inside, Carl?"

"Yep. Lotsa times. Big ole place, sprawlin' out all over. Kinda run-down now. But mighty lot of famous folks are buried in there." He got this distraught look on his face, just for a second, and then he turned away from the cemetery and kept sauntering down the street.

I watched him take his long, nonchalant strides. I wondered if he just liked to wander around in cemeteries, or if he went in there to attend funerals of people he knew. I was finding it hard to swallow. My head felt light, and I wanted to sit down on the curb, but Carl was already halfway down the street. I felt an awful aching inside for my dead mother, but even more so for this boy who was an orphan, who attended a run-down church and had a night job and had missed two years of school so he could help care for his siblings. I had to jog to catch up with him, and when I did, I was sweating and out of breath from the thick heat.

"It must be really hard to be a Negro," I said softly. Then I wished I hadn't.

He looked over at me, wrinkled his brow, and shrugged. "I'm used to it."

We walked a little farther without saying a word. The houses on this street were small, wood clapboard, different colors, mostly with peeling paint. Many had little porches on the front, and on some of those porches men and women sat rocking back and forth, fanning themselves and staring at me as if I were a Martian. And I guess I stared back, all the while thinking to myself, *This is what poverty looks like.*

It wasn't so much the unkempt homes or the sparse grass and trash along the route. It was the people. The children with a kind of dirtiness that meant they hadn't taken a bath for weeks. The men with toothless smiles and the wide women wearing clothes that looked like they'd picked them out of a rummage sale with their eyes closed. It was something I couldn't quite define—something that made me feel sad.

"Here's where I live," Carl said. He stopped in front of a white wooden house. Its yard was neat with potted flowers on the front porch. I couldn't help but notice the contrast with several of the surrounding homes, which had car carcasses in the front yards.

As soon as he opened the screen door, his siblings came to greet us.

"Carl's here," one of the boys called out. "He done brought a friend. A white girl!"

The two boys studied me solemnly at first. The little girl, who couldn't have been more than seven or eight, stood beside Carl and gave me a shy smile.

"Mary Swan, I'd like ya to meet my little brotha's, Mike and James, and my sista', Puddin'."

Mike, the oldest, stepped forward and held out his hand. "Pleased ta meetcha." He puffed out his chest and mashed my hand in his, so that I stepped back and said, "Ouch!"

"Mike, watch yorese'f, boy!" Carl remonstrated in a voice that was very different from the one he used when he talked to me. Then he said, "Excuse us, Mary Swan. He's mighty full of himself for a twelve-year-old, but he's all right."

"Nice to meet you, Mike," I said. "Good grip you've got there."

Immediately the other boy rushed over to shake my hand. "I'm James and I'm ten."

I regarded him warily with a sliver of a smile on my lips. "Good to meet you too. Be careful with my hand, please."

He opened his mouth in a smile, took my hand, and pumped it up and down several times. I pulled my hand away and shook it down by my side, pretending to be in pain. The boys stared at me silently. Then I winked at them, and they burst into laughter.

The little girl gazed at me timidly. "I'm Puddin', and I ain't never heard a name like Mary Swan before!"

I bent down to her level and shrugged. "I know. It's kinda weird. Family name."

Their eyes got wide at that comment, and James said, "You mean they's lotsa folks in yore family called Swan?"

I laughed. "No. That's not what I meant."

But Carl brushed it aside and said, "Why don't y'all take Mary Swan to the kitchen, and we'll fix her some iced tea?"

Puddin' took my hand in hers and said, "Come on in our front room." We left the porch and went through the "front room," which looked to me just like a bedroom. A table in the corner was piled with newspapers and old magazines, the floor had a dirty rug and a dirtier dog on it, and a skinny woman with droopy eyes that followed my every move sat on an unmade bed.

"Afternoon, ma'am," she said with a scowl on her face.

"Good afternoon," I replied and licked my dry lips.

"That's my Aunt Neta," Puddin' confided as she led me through the front room and into the kitchen. Mike opened the fridge, and James gave me a big grin and pointed to a chair. I sat down and tried my hardest not to stare at the flies that were swarming around several crusty plates beside the sink. I could hear Carl whispering something unintelligible to his aunt.

Mike placed a glass of iced tea on the table, and Puddin' whined, "I want some too, Michael. You betta' fix me some right now." Then she stood behind me and started twisting my hair around her fingers.

James gave her a hard look and said, "Stop it, Puddin'! Ain't polite."

"Oh no, it's fine," I said and winked at Puddin'. "Do you think you could braid it for me one day?"

Puddin' scrunched up her nose, looking unconvinced. Then she giggled. "I could try, I guess. Shore feels funny, yore hair, Mary Swan. All thin and straight." She giggled again.

For some reason, I pulled her into my lap and started tickling her the way I used to tickle Lucy, Trixie's daughter, when she was younger. Puddin' howled with delight, and Carl came into the kitchen to see what was going on. When he saw Puddin' squirming happily on my lap, he nodded at me in approval.

So I stayed at Carl's house for about an hour and listened to the kids babbling about their dog and their friends and their school, and I forgot all about Buckhead and Mama and Oakland Cemetery. And when Carl said we needed to be getting back to the church so that Ella Mae wouldn't worry, I didn't really want to leave. I felt all warm inside and nervous, sort of the way I'd felt when I'd been given the Raven Dare. Only this seemed so much better. I'd discovered a whole new world.

Chapter 5

I t was on July fourteenth that we buried Mama. Daddy chose that day because Mama, being half French, loved France, and that was France's Independence Day. The funeral services for the victims of the crash stretched over the whole summer, and I went to probably fifteen of them, along with Daddy and Trixie and about everyone else in Buckhead. Mama's service at St. Philip's was filled with the same sad people wearing their black suits and dresses, dabbing their eyes with handkerchiefs as they quietly cried.

Daddy's family had several plots in Oakland Cemetery. It was an historic place because it was the first cemetery in Atlanta, established in 1850. The first twenty-five of Atlanta's mayors were buried there, along with the great golfer Bobby Jones; the author of *Gone With the Wind*, Margaret Mitchell; a lot of Confederate soldiers; and a large portion of Atlanta's elite families, white, black, and Jewish. But as I'd seen with Carl, Oakland was located in the section of Atlanta that was fast becoming known as the bad part of town. As we drove to the cemetery, I thought of my peek through the bars the Saturday before. For a split second I forgot I was at Mama's funeral and remembered the afternoon with Carl and his family. It was a pleasure to lose myself for a moment, because I felt as though I was suffocating inside. We'd cried and grieved and hurt for over a month, and now we had to do it all over again. Would Atlanta never finish grieving for her dead?

A bunch of my friends were there and some of Jimmy's. After the graveside service, Jimmy wandered over to stand with his friend Andy Bartholomew. Andy's older brother, Robbie, was my age, and I'd met him several times before. Now he came up to me. He reminded me of a cross between a football jock and a Boy Scout—and actually, he was involved in both of those activities. He was as tall as Daddy, maybe six feet, with reddish brown hair that was cropped short and a tanned face and warm golden eyes. He had an athletic build, strong and svelte, but when he smiled, his face filled with dimples and he lost any suave look. He seemed, I don't know . . . he seemed nice, kind. Boy Scoutish.

"I just wanted you to know again how sorry I am, Mary Swan," he said, clearing his throat. He managed a half smile, and one dimple appeared. "You know my family's here if there's anything we can do."

"Thanks, Robbie." I felt suddenly awkward in my new black linen suit from J.P. Allen's. I nibbled on my lip. "You know, Andy's been great about inviting Jimmy over. It's no fun being alone with your thoughts in our big house."

"Andy's glad to have him over." He reached for my hand and held it briefly. "I am so sorry, Mary Swan." He started to leave, then added, "And if you need anything, if you ever want to get a burger or something, there's a bunch of us who meet at the Varsity on Sunday evenings." He smiled briefly again and met my eyes.

I could feel the heat running up my cheeks. "Thanks. Thanks, Robbie. I'll think about it. I will."

As soon as Robbie walked away, Rachel Abrams was by my side, poking me in the ribs. "Talking to Robbie Bartholomew, are you?" she teased.

"Rachel! Don't you have any respect for etiquette!" I scolded. "It's Mama's funeral."

Rachel gave me a quick hug and then took me by the shoulders. "I loved your mom, and I love you. And you know as well as I do that life has got to keep going. It can crawl by unnoticed while you suffocate at home, or it can be discovered." Then those magnificent blue-gray eyes of hers gleamed at me as she whispered mischievously, "And who are you to talk to me about etiquette anyway?"

I wiped the frown off my face and confided, "He offered, well, kind of offered, to ask me to the Varsity. I mean, he said I could come." I almost giggled.

Rachel glanced around and then pulled me away from the main crowd of people around the grave site. Her eyes were on fire. "Tell me more!"

I wiped my perspiring brow. "Not here, Rach. I have to see all these people. But come over tonight, and I'll tell you about it. And about something else."

"What else?"

"Someone I met," I answered ambiguously.

"Tell me now!"

"Tonight!"

She would have pulled it out of me if just then I hadn't seen Helen Goodman out of the corner of my eye. This flirtatious woman, who had quite a reputation, was deep in conversation with Daddy. Something inside me bristled, and I whispered, "I gotta go, Rachel. See you tonight."

It started to rain a little. Everyone stood there respectfully, talking in low tones, in spite of a steady drizzle and thunder in the background. It seemed fitting for Mama to be buried in the rain. She had died on a perfect summer day in Paris. But I didn't mind her being buried in the rain.

Late that afternoon after the funeral, I found Daddy in his study, his desk crowded with neat piles of papers, his head in his hands. I knocked softly on the opened door.

"Can I come in, Daddy?"

He looked up, gave me a weak smile, and nodded. "Sure, Swannee. What's up?"

"Are you okay, Daddy?"

"It was a hard day."

"Yep. Really hard."

He motioned for me to come to him and scooted his big leather chair with the brass studs on the sides back away from the desk so I could perch on one of the arms.

"What are you doing?"

"Looking over papers for the museum. And for my clients. Lots of legal problems with the crash, Swannee. Lots of money floating around."

"And you're in charge?"

He shrugged. "Yes, of quite a few of the estates. It's good for me to be busy."

"Are they gonna make that memorial arts school in honor of the victims? Has a lot of money come in?"

"Yes, quite a lot, but it's a bit complicated."

"You can tell me about it if you want."

"That's just what your mama would say. 'JJ, don't look so worried. Tell me about it.' But"—he smiled sadly, remembering something—"Mama couldn't handle business talk for too long. Pretty soon her eyes would glaze over, and I could tell she was far away thinking of a painting. Bless her soul."

"I'll listen, Daddy. I promise."

Daddy sat back in his chair and stretched his long legs out under the desk. "A lot of people think Atlanta is just a small Southern city with not much to offer, kind of backward. But many Atlantans, and plenty of them who died in the crash, felt differently. They wanted— we want—Atlanta to be a cultural center in the South. We have a long way to go. You know what Symphony Hall looks like."

I nodded. The Atlanta Symphony played in the Municipal Auditorium, a shabby building that was built in the early 1900s and was now only fit, as Mama used to say, to house cockfights and circuses.

"If we want our city to keep up with the likes of New York and Washington, we need a reputable arts center that fuses visual arts, performing arts, and art education into a single institution."

"You mean a place for the symphony and the theater?"

"Exactly. As well as an art museum and an art school." He chewed on a pencil. "So for a while we'd been trying to set up a big fundraiser to launch the project. Then came the crash, and gifts started pouring in to the Art Association. So we've got to decide what to do with that money, and the consensus is to use it to start a new arts school." He placed a hand lightly on my back. "You know what people are saying, Mary Swan?"

I shook my head.

"They're saying that arts in Atlanta will rise again, from the ashes of the plane crash, just like the city itself rose from the ashes of the Civil War."

"The phoenix, right?" I knew well that Atlanta's symbol was the beautiful mythological bird that was fabled to live 500 years in the Arabian wilderness, burn itself on a funeral pyre, and then rise from its own ashes into youth to live on in an unending cycle.

Daddy nodded. "The phoenix."

"Did lots of the crash victims leave money in their wills to help with the museum?"

"As a matter of fact, that's just what I'm working on. Look at this." He found a neat pile on his desk and pulled out a folder. *Weinstein* was marked across the top. "Remember Mr. and Mrs. Weinstein? They both died on the plane. Two days before the crash, Mr. Weinstein and I had been talking about the art museum's potential fundraiser while we sat in that famous café, Les Deux Magots, on the Left Bank in Paris. He said he had some money to give and that he'd show me what he was thinking when we got home. But he never got home. And I'm in charge of the estate and have to prove that the money is there for the museum."

"You can't get away from the crash, can you, Daddy?"

"No. No, sure can't. Not for a long time. A real long time." He turned toward the big picture window that looked out onto the carport. "They're setting up a memorial exhibition at the museum for the artists who perished in the crash. Two of Mama's paintings will be displayed."

"Really? When will it open?"

"Very soon, sweetie."

"Have you picked which paintings to show?"

"Yes, though it wasn't easy to decide. There are so many more to choose from than I would have thought."

"What do you mean, Daddy?" We both knew that Mama had never been considered a prolific painter. "Have you found more of her paintings?"

He had that far-off look in his eyes. "What? More paintings? No, no. Of course not, Mary Swan. Where would we find more paintings?" But the way he said it made me feel really funny inside.

"So which ones did you choose?"

"I figured we had to send one of the Swan House. Absolutely. And I wondered . . . I wondered if you'd mind if I lent the museum the painting of you on the tree swing?"

"Honest, Daddy? You want them to display that one?"

"Only if you don't mind." He started making excuses, misreading my thoughts. "Hard to part with it, even for a couple of months. Leave an awful kind of emptiness in the entrance hall, I guess. Maybe that's not such a good idea."

"Oh no, Daddy! I don't mind. It would be . . ." I got a lump in my throat. "It would be an honor for me."

"Good, then. We agree." He rested his hand on my back. "I've set up a special fund for donations that have come in specifically in memory of your mother. What do you think she'd want those donations to go toward?"

"Something about art, for sure," I said without hesitating.

"Exactly what I thought. I'm calling it the Sheila McKenzie Middleton Memorial Fund, and I've stipulated that it is to be a scholarship fund to help struggling artists get the training they need." The more Daddy spoke, the more his voice kind of quivered.

"It sounds good, Daddy. Really good."

"Yes, I thought it was the right thing to do."

I kissed him on his cheek, wishing it weren't so gaunt and prickly. Wishing that Daddy would sit up tall at his desk and talk loudly on the phone and then push back his big leather chair with the brass rivets and go to the closet and pull out his golf putter. That's what he always used to do. Play golf in his office. But he hadn't held that golf club since the crash, and from the look on his face, I didn't know if he ever would again.

Rachel rang our bell at seven that night. She had her driver's license, and her parents let her drive at night if she wasn't going too far. It didn't take her more than two or three minutes to drive from her Tudor-style house on the corner of Andrews and Cherokee to mine. She walked straight through the entrance hall and into the breakfast room, where she plopped down at the big round oak table.

"Tell all," she demanded. She was curled up in the chair, her thick blond hair falling on the table as she leaned on her hands.

"You want some ice cream?" I asked nonchalantly.

"Swan, quit stalling. Out with it!"

"Do you want some ice cream?" I repeated. "I'm dying for some. We just got some chocolate at the store." I opened the freezer and removed the carton.

She rolled her eyes at me. "Fine. Sure. So what's up?"

I took two bowls down from the bright yellow cupboards, the ones Mama had painted with different fruits on each door. This door was covered in cherries.

"I've met someone interesting," I stated as I piled the bowls high with scoops of chocolate ice cream.

"More interesting than Robbie Bartholomew?"

"Very different." I handed her a bowl and sat down.

"Okay, so? Where'd you meet him?"

"At church."

"Right. Come on, Swan. 'Fess up."

"It's true. I met him at church. He's nineteen and . . . and you may get to meet him sometime."

"Impossible. Remember, I'm Jewish. I don't go to church."

"No, not at church. You might meet him someday at Oakland Cemetery. He goes there a lot."

She rolled her eyes again and took a big bite of ice cream. "You're nuts."

"He lives right down the street from the cemetery."

I let that sink in.

Rachel set down her spoon, narrowed her eyes, and said, "You met him at church, and he lives near Oakland Cemetery. Hold on a minute. Do you mean that he's *black*?"

"Yep. Name's Carl."

Rachel had uncurled and leaned across the table, grabbing my hand. "This is not talk for the kitchen. Come on!" She pulled me up from my chair, leaving our bowls half filled with ice cream there on the table. We dashed through the hall and up the stairs until we reached the third floor and fell, laughing and panting, on my bed.

For a moment, every thought of Mama was gone. I reveled in my story. Rachel was as much of a rebel as I, and this ranked right up with the last poem I'd transformed in Mrs. Alexander's class. So I told her about Mt. Carmel Church and Miss Abigail and serving spaghetti with Carl and not knowing how to wash dishes. We giggled until our sides hurt. And then I told her about visiting Carl's house and his siblings and how his mother died and anything else I could remember, and I had the satisfaction of seeing her eyes grow bigger with each fact I related.

Finally she asked, "Do you like him, Swannee? Is that what you're telling me?"

"Yeah, I like him. We're gonna be friends. I guarantee it."

"What do you mean by 'friends'?"

"Oh, that you'll just have to wait and see."

We talked long into the evening, stretched out across my bed, the windows wide open and the faintest breeze ruffling the curtains. And I didn't consider once what I meant by the fact that Carl and I were going to be friends. But it wouldn't take me long to find out.

I could hardly wait for the next Saturday to roll around. The prospect of seeing Carl, and maybe Puddin' and Mike and James, and of visiting Mama's grave filled me with some sort of adrenaline. I thought about it the whole week, and how much I wanted Rachel to meet Carl, and then I had a crazy idea. I decided I would ask Carl to be my second assistant with the Raven Dare.

Way back in June I had made up my mind that I couldn't ask Daddy or Ella Mae to help me. Daddy would never have approved of me digging around in the past, and every time I mentioned anything about Mama, Ella Mae's eyes started shining with tears. Daddy and Ella Mae would have the surprise of their lives when they attended the Mardi Gras celebration and found out that I was the Raven and that I had solved the Dare. It was maybe a bit presumptuous of me to think like that, but it gave me the courage I needed to face each day. That became more important as the days slipped away and the new school year approached. It would be my secret, and I would solve that dare and bring Mama's lost painting back to the High Museum even if it killed me.

So that next Saturday at Mt. Carmel, standing beside Carl, I could not contain myself. He listened and at least acted interested as I explained the Raven tradition at Wellington, and how I'd been chosen and had found the clue at midnight with Rachel.

He made a face. "Sounds awful silly to me, Mary Swan."

"But it could be important for the school and the museum."

"If you say so, Mary Swan." He swatted at a fly that was hovering over the spaghetti sauce.

"Haven't you ever heard about the paintings that disappeared right before they were to be donated to the Atlanta Art Museum?"

"Nope. I've never been to no art museum. Never heard nothin' about it."

"You'd like the museum, Carl. I know you would. Two of Mama's paintings are going to be on display there. Another one should be, but it just disappeared. That's what the Dare is about."

"Two of yore mama's paintings are there, you say?"

"Yeah—they will be soon."

He whistled low and smiled. "They let black folks into that museum?"

"Of course!" I said indignantly, but really I had no idea. I couldn't recall ever having seen anyone black there except for Ella Mae when she went down with Mama and me.

"All right, then, Mary Swan Middleton. I'll go with you ta that museum, and I'll help you with that silly dare, if ya want." He poked out his lower lip, shook his head, slopped some sauce on a plate, and said, "My, my. If that don't beat all."

"But you've gotta swear you won't breathe a word about it to anyone, Carl."

"Gee, Mary Swan. Who in the world am I gonna tell about a big black bird?" His eyes twinkled.

"I don't know. But you can't tell Miss Abigail and certainly not Ella Mae. Or anyone. If you do, I'll be disqualified. Do you swear?"

"Ain't good ta swear, Mary Swan."

I started to protest, but he laughed and assured me, "I won't tell a soul. Not a soul."

I wiped my hands on my apron when the last plate had been served. Today I was ready to wash the dishes with Carl. I started with the glasses and felt rather proud when I'd washed the last pan and only changed the dishwater once. As I was taking off my apron, I caught sight of Ella Mae in the big room and called out to her, "I'm going down to Oakland Cemetery."

Ella Mae frowned, put her hands on her ample hips, and shook her head. "No, ma'am. You cain't be a goin' over there by yorese'f, Swannee. It ain't safe."

Miss Abigail came into the kitchen, wilted tendrils of hair sticking to her face. She ran her hand across her perspiring forehead and shook her head with a wry smile. "The Lord's provided again. Just the right amount, praise His name. We've only got a spoonful of sauce and half a pot of noodles left. And we just ran out of bread and brownies and iced tea. Everyone's been fed plenty." She held up the half-filled ladle of sauce as evidence.

She liked to remind us of "God's provisions," as she called them, how God always provided just enough, and the way she talked, you did kind of get caught up in her enthusiasm. She joined Ella Mae, and before long both women were sitting in those folding chairs talking to other women, the women Ella Mae had described as having a "heap o' troubles."

"I'll take ya to the cemetery, Mary Swan." Carl was drying his big hands on a wet dishrag and then wiping it across his shining face.

"You don't mind?"

" 'Course not. Go on."

So I ran over and told Ella Mae, who wrinkled her brow and admonished me to be careful. Carl left the dish towel on the back of a metal folding chair, and I followed him out the basement door of the church, squinting as the sun struck me hard in the face. The walk took us at least ten minutes, and we didn't say much, I don't think. But when we got to the opened gates, he said, "This cemetery is divided into different parts for the whites, the blacks, the Jewish folk, and the Confederate soldiers. And way over there"—he pointed with a long finger—"is what's called Potter's Field."

"What's Potter's Field?"

"It's where all the unmarked graves are."

"Oh."

I had just been to the cemetery a week ago, but my sense of direction wasn't too keen. I squinted in the distance, looking for a grave with lots of fresh flowers. The cemetery wound around in several interlocking circles, and it was easy to get turned around. The road inside the cemetery was cobbled with red brick, and over the years the ground had shifted so that the brick was broken and uneven, with little green weeds growing in it. I tripped once on the bricks as I searched for Mama's grave. Finally I found it.

I knelt down on the grass and let my knees touch the freshly turned soil. It was warm and moist from several days of rain. I reached into my jeans pocket and pulled out a little package of dirt and sprinkled it over the grave. Mama loved the feel of the red Georgia clay in her hands. Sometimes before she started to paint in the backyard, she'd stoop down and wipe her hands in the dirt, bring some to her nose and smell. She said it got her in the mood for painting.

"I know you're not here, Mama," I whispered. "But I just thought it would be kind of fitting for your grave to have some of the clay from home. So I brought it to you." The tears came.

Carl was standing off at a distance, as if he knew his place, and it wasn't by me. Then I saw him walk down the hill toward another part of the cemetery. I cried for a while, and then I knelt down again beside the fresh dirt and smelled the thick scent of the flowers. All of them had wilted in the heat. I picked a white daisy from one of the bouquets and placed it on an open patch of dirt. "I miss you, Mama," I whispered. Then I got up and brushed the dirt off my jeans.

I found Carl. "Thanks for bringing me," I said.

"It's okay."

We were just outside the entrance to the cemetery when three white boys walked up to us. They looked about seventeen or eighteen and were dressed as if they'd just gotten out from under some dilapidated car. One of them was staring at us with a sickly sort of grin on his face, which made my stomach twitter inside. He was skinny and even taller than Carl, and his blond hair was cropped in a crew cut.

"My, my, my. What do we have here?" he said sarcastically, his cheeks bright red. "Ain't this a sight to see? A white girl with a piece of black trash."

Carl touched my arm, and we started walking faster, away from the boys. But they followed us.

"Hey there, boy! Don't you ignore me when I'm talkin' to you! What are you doin' with this white girl? You aimin' to hurt her or somethin'?"

I wheeled around, heart pounding, furious, and said through clenched teeth, "It's none of your business. Leave us alone!"

I saw then, out of the corner of my eye, that Carl looked terrified. That was the only word for it.

"You're a feisty one, ain't you, missy!" This came from the boy with a reddish brown crew cut and a pudgy, smooth face. His T-shirt was soaked in sweat, and his jeans hung low on his full belly. "Not afraid to hang around with trash, eh? Maybe that's because you're just white trash yourself."

I stopped in my tracks, eyes flashing and hissed, "I'm not trash. You're the trash! Now leave us alone."

The sickly sweet smile on the first boy's face disappeared, and he grabbed my arm, squeezing it until it hurt. He was skinny as a rail, but his hand gripped my arm almost fiercely. I tried to pull loose. Then I saw that the others were circling Carl like two hungry wolves. Carl looked at me, and his wide eyes signaled me to be quiet.

"The colored boy knows when to be afraid," the skinny boy said. He motioned to the others, the pudgy one and his friend, who was shorter than the other two, wiry, with a head full of blond curls and greenish eyes and an evil sort of smile and a lot of muscles. They latched on to Carl savagely, just like wolves. I'm sure Carl could have beaten them both and gotten away if it hadn't been for me. But I knew he wouldn't leave me there.

They started hitting him in the face and the stomach while the skinny boy held me with my arms pinned behind my back. "Stop it!" I yelled. "Stop it!"

"Ain't no one around to hear you, girly," he whispered, obviously enjoying my mounting terror.

I bent my head down and bit his arm as hard as I could. He cursed and swung his hand hard on my face. I went reeling and fell to the ground, hitting my head on the pavement.

"Hey, watch out, Richie!" the short, wiry boy yelled in between punches. "You wanna get us in trouble for foolin' with a white girl?"

"She bit me! And anyway, I've got an idea. Knock the boy out. We'll have a little fun with the girl and then leave her here and tell the police we found that colored boy aggressin' her. They'll hang him for sure."

Carl groaned and I went numb, with my head throbbing and my cheek stinging. Richie dragged me behind a car, and I kicked and screamed and bit until he took his hand and slapped me hard again, cursing. I fell back against the pavement. I thought if I acted like I'd been knocked out, maybe they'd leave me alone. So that's what I did.

"You idiot," the wiry boy screamed. "We gotta git outta here. Quick. Tell the police it was him, but let's git!"

I lay perfectly still, forcing myself not to sob or heave or scream my guts out like I wanted to. Carl was about ten yards away, kind of crumpled up. I didn't know if he was unconscious or dead.

But when the three boys were gone, he pulled himself to his knees and crawled over to me, heaving as he did. "Come on, Mary Swan," he rasped. "We gotta get outta here quick. Real quick."

His face was all bloody and swollen, and he was holding his side, but he managed to help me up. We limped out of the cemetery, both of us trembling as we scrambled down the street toward Mt. Carmel.

"You liked to git us killed, Mary Swan," Carl panted. "Don't ya know not to argue with rednecks, girl?"

"They were going to hurt you, and I was scared." I looked up at him with one of my eyes shut. I could feel it beginning to swell.

He gave a weak chuckle. "If that's how you act when you're scared, I don't wanna git around you when you're feelin' real mean!"

"You know what they were planning to do?"

"Yep. And I bet you they're right now reporting somethin' to the police."

I don't know if I felt more angry or scared, but finally I said, "I'm sorry, Carl. It's all my fault for wanting to see Mama's grave. I didn't realize it was so awful here. Has that ever happened to you before?"

"Happens all the time round these parts."

"You mean you're used to it?"

He just nodded.

"But they could kill you!"

"Lotsa people git killed around here, Mary Swan. Either fighting over a girlfriend or trying to steal, or like with those boys—someone who just hates us because our skin is black. You learn to take a few punches, Mary Swan. If you fight back, those boys'll come back with knives and guns and a lotta friends."

By this time we'd reached the church and gone inside to the bathrooms. No one was around except for Ella Mae and Miss Abigail. With one look at us, they both came running.

"What in the world—"

"Some rednecks found us at the cemetery. Wanted to rough me up a bit, but Mary Swan wouldn't let 'em. She was determined to take all the brunt herself." He tried to smile.

"My, my, chil'un," Ella Mae kept repeating as she and Miss Abigail got the first-aid supplies and started cleaning our wounds. "I tol' ya not to go there, Mary Swan. Ain't safe." She grunted with disapproval. "Ain't safe."

I didn't say anything but kept looking at Carl and thinking about how he could have run off and gotten away. Left me with those white boys. But he didn't. And I wanted more than ever to be his friend.

As I went to sleep that night, it was one of the first times I could remember when I wasn't thinking about myself. I kept seeing that pudgy white face and Carl's terrified black one, and I was thinking how comfortable I was cuddled in my bed and of how glad I was that Daddy hadn't been around to see my bruised face when I got home. If I wanted, I could close my eyes and forget about all the events of the afternoon. If I wanted, I didn't ever have to go down to Mt. Carmel Church again.

But I was especially thinking that for Carl and Mike and James and poor little Puddin' and probably everyone else who lived on that side of town, the fighting was just a way of life. They got used to it somehow and survived amid the violence. It was really my first peek at another reality, at something dark that made me shudder. Cruelty. I'd never really seen cruelty the way I had seen it that afternoon. I decided it would be so much easier to never go back to that part of town, to never be confronted with that part of life.

But of course, I wasn't really the type to look for the easy way out. As I've said before, I seemed to have a knack for stumbling into adventure. So as I fell asleep thinking about Carl and Ella Mae and Miss Abigail and those three redneck boys, I imagined myself as the Raven. Not only of Wellington Prep School, but also as a big black bird that sat on a tombstone in Oakland Cemetery and warned the good people of the bad ones who were lurking somewhere just out of sight.

Chapter 6

The next morning after Carl and I had had the run-in with the redneck boys, I woke feeling the way you must feel after you've drunk a pint of bourbon. My head was throbbing, and when I looked in the mirror, I let out an involuntary scream. The right side of my face was puffed out as if I were hiding Jimmy's baseball in my cheek, and the skin was a grayish, purplish blue. My right eye was really swollen. I crawled back to bed. Fifteen minutes later, Daddy knocked on my door.

"Mary Swan. Time to get up for church."

I groaned. I'd forgotten it was Sunday.

"Mary Swan," he repeated, cracking the door.

With the covers pulled over my head, I mumbled, "Daddy, I feel awful, like I'm gonna throw up."

"What is it, Swannee?"

I could tell he was coming to the bed, so I said quickly, "Oh, it's nothing, Daddy. Just my time of the month, you know. I'll be all right."

Daddy was always embarrassed to talk about women's things, so he left the room quickly, saying, "Well, you just stay home today, Swannee. Jimmy and I'll go on to church. You'll be okay alone?"

"Fine!" I said a little too brightly, but he didn't seem to notice and left the room.

I waited in bed probably thirty minutes, until I heard the car go down the driveway. Then I got up, pulled on my overalls, and went downstairs. In the kitchen I gulped down a glass of orange juice and two aspirins. Ten minutes later, with sketchbook and charcoal pencils in hand, I headed through the woods to the left of the house.

There were several well-worn trails in the woods leading to the Swan House, trails that I had trampled with Mama when I was little and had made my own through the years. These were my woods, a long, luxurious hyphen between life at home and life in a dream. Sometimes I saw gray squirrels or brown rabbits scurrying along near me, and once I'd seen a little red fox, and another time a deer. The trees felt like my friends, so familiar were they to me. The thick-barked pines that shot straight to the sky and the majestic hardwoods, hickories and oaks and wide-leafed magnolias and sumac and dogwoods; all of them formed a protective canopy with their leaves far, far above me, a canopy that became a multicolored umbrella in the fall.

Today everything was green. I sat down on my favorite log, staring at the bright green moss at my feet. I listened intently to the caw of a blue jay and the delicate call of the whippoorwill, and I thought I could hear a woodpecker knocking his beak into the trunk of a tree. Not far away, water gurgled through a stream. *These woods are peaceful, dark and deep, but I have promises to keep and miles to go before I sleep.* I repeated the lines from one of my favorite poems by Robert Frost in my mind. Peaceful, yes. Only these woods, *my* woods, were infused with light today, light that filtered down through the leaves, light that I could almost reach out and touch as it sparkled on a sunray. A few minutes later, I stood up and followed the trail to where it burst forth onto the green lawn of the Swan House.

As I've already said, the Swan House was a beautiful old mansion. It had been built for the Inman family in 1928 by a very famous architect named Philip Trammel Shutze. Mama knew all about it. She told me that Mr. Shutze had spent several years in Italy studying architecture and had won some sort of fancy prize. When he came back to the States, his work was influenced by his time in Italy. Mama loved Italian architecture, so she was always explaining things about her favorite house to me. I could still hear her saying in her soft Southern accent, "The Swan House was modeled after a mix of graceful Italian villas and Palladian country houses. See how clean and symmetrical it is? It reflects a return to Classicism and away from the more ornate Victorian architecture." That had never interested me much, but now, with Mama gone, I wished I had listened to her better.

What I loved was the front of the house. When I stood on Andrews Drive and looked at the mansion, well, it almost took my breath away. First you saw two cloverleaf fountains near the bottom of the hill and a long ivy-covered retaining wall that cut across the property horizontally. Then a terraced lawn spread out long and wide in front of you on a gradual slope that led two hundred yards to the mansion. And then there was the mansion itself. Mama said it was built of cement blocks that had been stuccoed to look like the smooth, light gray stone of the eighteenth century. The house rose three stories high with six long windows on the first floor and eight on the second floor and one round one on the third. On either side of the round window were cornices, each with a statue on top, and behind the statues and over a little were the two chimneys.

But the best part were the cascading fountains that led to the horseshoe-shaped stairway at the front. Cascading fountains! There were five tiers of round stone basins holding water, starting with the smallest at the top and descending in ever-larger circles as the water cascaded from one basin to the next.

As a child I liked to sit in the woods, brushing away the gnats and contemplating the mysteries of the house. After all, I was in a way its namesake. Mary Swan. It was a fine name, rich in symbolism, Mama used to say, for which I took her to mean later that even I, the ugly duckling, might someday be transformed. But what she meant, she used to explain to me, was that my name embodied, like my portrait, all the fine subtleties of my personality, and that, like the swan, beauty and grace were part of me. "Mary Swan is just looking for herself in my house," Mrs. Inman had said. Maybe someday I would find myself there.

When I was twelve Mama bought me a sketchbook that looked a lot like hers. She also gave me some fancy drawing pencils and instructed me to "enjoy." After she died, I was sorry that I'd never let her know just how much I had enjoyed sketching. I could sit for hours sketching the fountains and the stately mansion. The Inmans never minded a bit, and one of the maids had commented years ago, "You's jus' like yore mama," which had made me feel proud.

I walked up the long yard to the boxwood garden on the right of the house. Mr. Shutze designed this garden to be a green garden, like one found in Rome, since Atlanta was on the same latitude as Rome. Two mimosa trees sat right outside a huge screened-in porch, their fuzzy pink flowers giving off a sweet fragrance that wafted up to guests in the summertime. Beside the mimosa trees grew the gardenia bushes, in full bloom before me, their waxy, creamy white flowers almost heavy with a luxurious odor. I stopped, closed my eyes, and breathed in the fragrances. In the middle of two islands of grass, surrounded by liriope, white wisteria grew with a perfume of its own. And there was crepe myrtle all along the retaining walls with their bright pink and purple blooms. And of course throughout the garden were neatly trimmed balls of boxwood.

I sat down on the stone bench at the end of the garden, staring back at the porch and the rest of the house. I felt wild and exotic because on either side of me rose these two columns, made to look like Greek temple ruins. A stone eagle, wings spread wide, was perched behind me, and slag hung from the columns to give the appearance and the feeling of something in a garden from Pompeii. Interspersed along the stone walls of the garden sat huge stone urns with the same slag dripping from their lips. In the spring and summer, buxom impatiens made a hedge under the crepe myrtle. And in the fall they were replaced by delicate, sweet-faced pansies. There were boxwoods surrounding the front of the house too, and on either side of the cascading fountains were big clay pots filled with oleander and other blooming plants.

I loved to try to recreate different spots in the garden on my sketchpad. Those sketches were never very good, but I left them in the pad nonetheless. I had grown up seeing Mama toss out sketches like the trash, impatient and childish in her mood. I didn't want to repeat that gesture, even if no one else would ever see my drawings. In my mind, they were something created out of my spirit, and I had a desperate hope that they were proof that I had inherited a smidgen of Mama's talent. Now, with her dead, I knew that I would save them forever.

So this morning, for the first time in several months, seated on that stone bench in the garden, I began to sketch. I didn't have a diary, which was popular at the time with girls my age. Somehow it was easier for me to draw what I felt. A tiny breeze occasionally ruffled the stagnant air, causing a corner of my paper to turn up. I welcomed the refreshment. I was sketching the screened porch on the side of the Swan House with the blooming mimosas and lavish gardenia bushes. I must have sketched for two hours without realizing it. While I sketched, I thought about Carl and those awful boys and how scared I'd been and how right now, sitting in this garden, that all seemed like a nightmare. I was warm and happy, and surely none of those things had really happened. I closed my eyes momentarily, choosing to forget the inner city and remember my adventures inside the Swan House.

I remembered standing as a young child in the great open hallway, called the rotunda, and bending down to touch the black and white squares on the smooth, cool floor. "That's Italian marble, Swannee," Mama had cooed. "And see the staircase with a bronze balustrade and walnut treads. It looks like it's floating!"

But of course, as a little girl, I had not been impressed. Instead, I had exclaimed gleefully, "There's a swan!" pointing to a shadow on the wall.

"Good for you, Swannee. You're right!" Mama had congratulated. "See, it's coming from the curving spires of the crystal chandelier. Mrs. Inman planned it that way, I think, so that at certain times of the day, when the sun hits the chandelier in just the right way, it casts a shadow on the wall that looks like a swan's neck."

I nodded happily, and off I went to find the swans. To the left of the rotunda was the library, but to get to it you passed under a thick archway with what Mama called a coffered ceiling, which meant all kinds of fancy stuff was carved into it. But as I strained my neck to look, I found no swans. On a desk in the library, a swan finial sat on a little wooden box. I picked it up and liked its smooth, metal feel. But Mama frowned and motioned with her eyes for me to put it back in its place.

So I left her there with the other adults and went into the room next door, what Mrs. Inman called the morning room. I never understood why. It seemed to me more like the living room in our house. I took a seat at the beautiful Steinway grand piano and plunked on several keys. Then my eye caught sight of the fireplace with its honey-colored marble from Siena, Italy. On either side of the fireplace was a swan, carved into the capitals of the fluted columns.

A few minutes later, I crept up that floating staircase and into Mrs. Inman's bedroom. It was in her bathroom that I found the most swans. They were painted on the ceiling by a famous Italian artist named Menaboni. Twelve of them! Twelve delicate swans! He had also painted lots of stars and the Olympic torch. And I found four bronze swans on the capital of the pilasters in between Mrs. Inman's mirrored closet doors.

Back downstairs in the dining room, behind a long table set for twelve, I discovered what Mama called two swan console tables. Mama thought they were perhaps the inspiration behind the swan motif in the house. I think they were very expensive. "Carved in the eighteenth century by a famous English woodcarver named Thomas Johnson," Mama whispered while I gawked at the large gilded tables, each with two delicate white swans staring at me from underneath the tables. I loved the wallpaper in the dining room—it was hand painted in England but made to look Chinese, with different groups of birds painted on each panel. And some of those birds were mating!

I shook myself back to the present and looked up from my pad. The sun was high and the right side of my face was throbbing, and I knew I'd better be getting home before Daddy and Jimmy returned from church. I planned to spend the afternoon back in bed, my face hidden from view.

So I hurried through the woods to my house. It wasn't until I got back to my room that I took the time to examine my sketch. I liked the way it looked as if you touched the petals of the flowers on the gardenia bush, they'd be smooth and soft, and how the mimosa seemed ecstatic and carefree with its small blooms. I especially liked the way that the morning at the Swan House had given me another glimpse of hope. My love for drawing had not vanished with Mama's death, as I had superstitiously and melodramatically imagined. I always got this tingling feeling in my head and running down my spine when I liked something I'd sketched. And today, the tingles came again.

I was in the middle of my thoughts about my sketch when I heard the car pull into the driveway. From my dormer window I could see Daddy's jade green Jaguar heading up the driveway. I hopped in bed and covered my face with a damp washcloth.

A few minutes later Daddy tapped on the door. "Swannee. You awake?"

"Barely, Dad," I mumbled.

"You want me to get you something to eat for lunch?"

"No, I really don't feel like eating."

"Do you need anything?"

"No, Daddy. Don't worry. I'll be fine."

And so I got away with it again. But when I went into the bathroom that adjoined my bedroom and looked in the mirror, I groaned. My face was still a terrible shade of purplish blue, and my left eye was definitely swollen. I wasn't sure I could keep up the hiding all day long.

About thirty minutes later I looked out my big window and saw Jimmy playing with Muffin in the backyard. Daddy wasn't in sight.

"Hey, Jimmy! Come up here quick!"

He must have caught sight of my face, because he came tearing into the house and up the stairs way too loudly. He flung open the door and stood gaping at me. Then his face went white. "Wow," he whispered. "I sure am glad I'm not a girl. Is that what happens to you every month?"

At first it didn't register. But then I let out a cackle. "You idiot! Of course not. I just made up that story 'cause I didn't want Daddy to see me."

Jimmy looked immensely relieved. I couldn't believe the naïveté of a thirteen-year-old boy.

"So what happened to you?"

"I fell down and whacked my head on the door last night," I lied.

"So? You could tell Dad that."

"No, I can't. He can't see it. So will you please go make me a sandwich and bring it up to me? I'm starving."

"I thought Daddy said you didn't feel like eating."

"Just shut up and get me something."

He glared at me, muttered something about his dumb big sister and why hadn't I gotten anything to eat while they were at church, and left the room. I ran after him and grabbed his arm. "Please don't say anything to Daddy. Promise."

He rolled his eyes. "Maybe I will and maybe I won't. What's it worth to you?"

By now I was wishing I hadn't called him. "Forget it, then. Just go away and keep quiet."

He shrugged, a smile playing on his lips, and started down the stairs.

"Oh, who cares. Say what you want!" I hissed after him.

I went back into my room and dialed Rachel's number, glancing all the while at my watch. Almost one. She'd be finished with lunch by now. She answered on the third ring.

"Come over quick!" I begged. "I'm in big trouble, and I need help!"

"You're always in trouble," she said, unimpressed.

"I know, but this is serious."

"Then I'll be right there." This was said with an obvious lack of enthusiasm.

"Use the back door."

I was waiting for her there. When Rachel saw me, she inspected my face and laughed. "Lovely, Swan. What'd ya do this time?"

"Shh." I put my finger to my lips as we tiptoed up the stairs. "It's not funny! Daddy can't know."

"Why not?"

"Because!" And I told her all about Carl and the cemetery and the three redneck boys.

"Mary Swan, you are really in a fix this time! That face will take days to heal! You have got to tell your dad something. Man, I'll bet they were Klanners, those guys."

"Klanners?"

"Oh, don't be so naïve. The Ku Klux Klan. You know."

"Carl said they were just rednecks."

"Well, I bet they were sons of some KKK men. They hate blacks and Jews like me. And they really hate anyone who associates with blacks and Jews."

"Great," I mumbled.

"What are you going to do?"

"How should I know? That's why I called you. You've gotta help me think of something!"

She got off my bed and began to pace around the room. She was wearing a teal green blouse that set off her eyes. Her thick, wheat-colored hair fell on the blouse in such a way that you wanted to stroke it. Man, was Rachel pretty.

"You've got to confess," she stated bluntly. "No way around it."

"But I can't! He'd forbid me to ever go anywhere with Ella Mae again!"

Then Rachel turned to me, took my hands, and gave me her slyest cat look. "You have to confess, Swan, but you don't have to tell the truth!"

"Huh?"

"Oh, come on, 'Miss Big Imagination.' Just make something up. Anything."

"I tried that. I told Jimmy I bumped into the door."

"Fine. You bumped into the door. Now write one of your poems and make your dad smile, and that will be that." She crossed her arms across her chest.

I hugged Rachel fiercely. "You're brilliant. Of course!"

So I wrote a poem, and with Rachel following me, I descended the stairs and went into Daddy's study, where he sat bent over his desk.

"Swannee!" Daddy was already out of his chair and coming to me. He stopped in the middle of his long stride, his expression changed from pleasure to concern, and he started to speak.

Immediately I held up my hand and began to recite:

"To dearest Dad,
Please don't feel bad,
The news I bring
Just must be had.
Don't scream, don't cry.
I'll tell you why.
I'm fine in spite of this bruised eye.
I hit the door—
The choice was poor.
It wondered what my face was for.
It made a knot
Right in this spot,
And at the time it hurt a lot.
But all is well,
I'm here to tell,
So don't scream or cry and please don't yell.
Forgive my fault of concealing
This bump which I am now revealing.
But, Dad, could you please quick call Trixie.
You know how she just loves to fixie
All your scrapes and mine as well.
She'll come right over
If you just tell.
I've learned my lesson.
(That's what mistakes are for.)

The next time I won't fight a door!"

I had read it with so much expression and drama that by the end of the rhyme, Dad's face, which had shown displeasure, anger, and guarded mirth, was full of laughter. He hugged me and clapped Rachel on the back.

"Fighting a door! Of all things! You could have told me."

"Sorry, Dad. I was too embarrassed. It was stupid of me, I know."

"Swannee! For goodness' sake." He examined the bruise. "You're right," he concluded. "Trixie should have a look. She'll know what to do."

When we got back from Trixie's thirty minutes later, Rachel and I hugged each other in triumph and decided a swim was just what we needed. Rachel always kept a spare swimsuit at the bathhouse, so we changed out there. I couldn't help but feel a bit jealous of the way she filled out her swimsuit so well. Especially when mine hung on me so pitifully.

"See, Swannee. Now, that wasn't hard, was it?"

"No, but it bugs me to lie to my dad."

"I know, but sometimes there's nothing else to be done!"

I could tell she was thrilled with the way things had worked out. She grabbed my hand, spun me around, and declared, "You are too skinny. Skinny, girl. You've got to eat!"

"I haven't been very hungry."

"Of course not."

I looked down at my flat chest and the way my swimsuit puckered out there. "There's no hope for me," I moaned.

We'd had this conversation a hundred times before, and Rachel assured me again, "Patience, dear Swannee! They'll grow!"

Then her face grew serious, and she changed the subject. "Swannee. Do you think you should be hanging around with Carl? I mean, I like action, but that's plain dangerous."

"I know, Rach. But he saved me." Then I got melodramatic again. "He could have run away! And anyway, I like him."

Rachel did a dive off the side of the pool, plunging deep into the water. When she came up, long lashes glistening wet, she didn't say anything else about Carl. "Now, look, Swannee. We have to get going on the Raven Dare. It's the end of July, and we haven't done one thing."

I liked the way she always said "we."

Then she hunched her back and, moving toward me like a cat about to pounce, started quoting Poe's poem.

"Once upon a midnight dreary, while I pondered weak and
  weary,
Over many a quaint and curious volume of forgotten lore,
While I nodded, nearly napping, suddenly there came a tapping,
As of someone gently rapping, rapping at my chamber door.
'Tis some visitor,' I muttered, 'tapping at my chamber door—
Only this and nothing more.' "

I smiled at her and she continued.

"Ah, distinctly I remember it was in the bleak December,
And each separate dying ember—"

"Oh, Rach!" I exclaimed suddenly, interrupting her recitation. "I completely forgot to show this to you! Hold on! I *have* done something about the Dare." I ran into the house and up to my room and retrieved a spiral notebook from under my bed.

"Listen!" I ordered, out of breath, when I was back at the pool. I, too, fell under the Raven spell and began quoting,

"Once upon a midday dreary while I pondered weak and weary
Over many a trite and teary volume of such rotten bore
While I nodded nearly napping, suddenly there came a tapping
Of Mrs. Alexander harshly rapping, rapping my fingers 'til
  they're sore.
'Tis a cruel trick,' I sputtered, 'rapping on my fingers four!'
Only this and nothing more.
Ah, distinctly I remember it was not in bleak December
But in June that some sole member of the senior ladies' lore
Put a message in these fingers, words from writers or from sing-
  ers.
How that memory still lingers of the feel in fingers' sore
Of the note unknown to nudge me into Wellington's wild war
Between two classes evermore."

I was beaming as I finished, but Rachel stuck out her tongue and then began chasing me around the pool, calling out, "You silly girl! I should write a book called *Poems corrupted by Mary Swan!* Corrupted! Do you hear me?"

I squealed as she caught up to me. Then I tossed the spiral notebook onto a lounge chair and dived into the pool. When I came to the surface, there she stood hunched over the water, waiting. I pulled myself halfway out of the water, resting my elbows on the warm cement and watching. Now Rachel lifted her arms, high and folded like birds' wings on each side, sucked in her cheeks, wrinkled her brow, and began chanting quickly, madly, the whole long poem by Poe. She swooped and turned and almost flew around the pool, eyes glaring in frenzy and delight until she came to the last verse, and standing bent and mocking before me, whispered softly,

"And the raven, never flitting, still is sitting, still is sitting
On the pallid bust of Pallas just above my chamber door;
And his eyes have all the seeming of a demon's that is dreaming,
And the lamplight o'er him streaming throws his shadow on the
    floor,
And my soul from out that shadow that lies floating on the floor
Shall be lifted—nevermore!"

I burst into applause, calling "Bravo!" and "Encore!" while Rachel, making her eyes into condescending, dignified slits, bowed before me.

And with that, we were back to talk about the Dare and silly poems and boys. But I didn't show Rachel my sketch from that morning, and I didn't tell her that Carl knew about the Raven Dare, and I certainly didn't say that he had agreed to go with me to the High Museum sometime soon.

Chapter 7

A nd so the summer just went right along into muggy, sticky August. Marilyn Monroe died. She took an overdose of sleeping pills and killed herself. I wasn't a big fan of Marilyn Monroe—not the way I was with Natalie Wood—but still, everyone knew about her, and the fact that she'd killed herself did nothing to help my depression.

Robbie Bartholomew never called about the Varsity, and Daddy stayed in his office and politely received casseroles from a lot of single ladies who seemed to have their eye on him.

About twice a week Rachel came to spend the night. Sometimes she and I stayed up late into the night brainstorming about the Raven Dare, Rachel curled under the sheets of the twin bed in my room. We didn't seem to be making much progress, except that I did finally tell her about Carl being my other assistant, and I did ask her to go with Carl and me to the High Museum and gather all the information available about the disappearance of the three paintings. But we couldn't set a date because I hadn't seen Carl since that day we met up with the rednecks.

Ella Mae dusted and mopped and vacuumed and fried chicken and watched me out of the corner of her eye. But mostly, she refused to take me back to Mt. Carmel.

"Ain't safe," she said a hundred times, scowling at me in a disapproving way. She'd been mad at me ever since my dad remarked that I'd had a mighty big problem with a door. "I don't approve of ya lyin' to Mista Middleton, Mary Swan. Ain't right."

And when she was really irritated, she'd say, "I've a good mind to tell him myself. My, my, young'un. Yore gonna git me in a heap o' troubles, Mary Swan. A heap o' troubles."

But I knew she'd never say anything to Daddy. It wasn't her place. And off she went mumbling and perspiring in that gray-and-white maid's uniform that was at least two sizes too small for her.

One day I trotted after her, saying, "I'm sorry, Ella Mae. Pleeese take me back this Saturday. I promise to stay at the church. I promise! My face is all healed, and I won't step outside if you don't want. I promise."

"Hmmph!" was her reply. She must have thought about it all day, waddling from room to room and humming some of those Negro spirituals that I knew so well. Right before she left that afternoon, she took me aside and said, "All right, Mary Swan. Ya can come on Saturday. Stay all day long and follow Miss Abigail around. Ya stick with her—ya hear me?"

"Oh, Ella Mae! Thanks!" I wrapped my skinny, white, freckled arms around her thick waist and hugged her so tight that she said, "Mary Swan! My, my! Ya like to squeeze me ta death!" She wrinkled her black brow as though she was cross, but I could see a smile playing on her lips.

Three long weeks had passed since my last visit to Mt. Carmel, since three white boys taught me about hatred and cruelty, and since I had seen Carl Matthews. My heart was hammering in my chest when Ella Mae and I entered the big room in the basement. Immediately the smells of spaghetti sauce and garlic bread overtook me and I felt— how did I feel? Good, happy to be there, like a part of me had just walked in the front door of a house I'd never known was home.

When I saw Carl, I didn't know what to say. I felt like hugging him and thanking him again for saving me from the rednecks and apologizing for being away for so long.

"Nice to see ya, Mary Swan." Those white teeth! He looked intently at my face, then smiled again. "You look good as new."

I swallowed hard and nodded. But all the things I had planned to say to him just went straight out of my mind. We served up spaghetti in silence.

When we were washing up the dishes, Miss Abigail came over. "I guess I'm following you around today," I said. She nodded. "Is there something you want me to do now?"

"You'll see, Mary Swan," she answered in her no-nonsense way and hurried off to greet a young black girl with a baby.

Carl and I washed every dish and put them away and swept the kitchen and the main room while he told me all about what Mike and James and Puddin' had been up to lately. I finally got up the courage to ask him a question. "Would you be willing to come with me to the museum next week? After we finish up here, I mean?"

He cocked his head and shrugged. "Shore, Mary Swan. Why not? I want ta see your mother's paintings." Then he winked. "And it's about time we get our hands on that big black raven, ain't it?"

I felt my cheeks burning. I nodded and then peeked out into the main room to see if Miss Abigail was ready for my help. She was engrossed in conversation with a young black teen who had the skinniest arms I'd ever seen. And she was holding a baby. A really small baby.

After a while, the baby started screaming so loudly that I guess the two could hardly hear themselves think. I was waiting, a little impatiently, and wondering if Miss Abigail had forgotten that I was staying with her today. But she hadn't.

"Mary Swan," she called out to me. I was poised holding the broom, staring at the pitiful girl and her baby.

"Could you please take little Jessie so that Cassandra and I can talk?" When Miss Abigail wanted something, she stated it nicely but firmly. I didn't dare say no.

But inwardly I was horrified. I didn't know what to do with a screaming baby. I wasn't the kind of girl who oohed and ahhed over babies. They made me nervous. In fact, I don't think I'd ever held a baby in my life.

I bent down, and Miss Abigail must have seen how petrified I looked, because she took the baby out of Cassandra's arms and carefully placed her in mine. "Just snuggle her tight on your shoulder, Mary Swan. Be careful of her head. You need to support it."

I smiled faintly, feeling my pulse pounding in my head. Little Jessie was furious.

"If'n ya keep walkin' her, she'll git quiet," Cassandra said, looking relieved to not be holding the baby. Cassandra couldn't have been more than fourteen or fifteen.

So there I was, holding this tiny black baby girl, my head throbbing, wondering what in the world I was supposed to do with her. I remembered I'd seen Ella Mae patting an infant's back, so I tried that, to no avail. Jessie screamed all the harder.

I walked outside, because Miss Abigail and Cassandra were back into their conversation, and I could tell that I was supposed to leave. Right beside the church was a patch of land all grown up with brown grass and weeds. I walked her there. I wasn't about to walk her down the street and have all the neighbors staring at me, wondering why some white girl was holding a black baby and why she couldn't get her to calm down.

And then Carl appeared. I thought he'd already gone home. He was smiling that smile again, and I thought if he said one word about how to hold a baby, I'd explode.

"My, my, Jessie!" he said, drawing his face up to the little one's. He was talking in a soft, sweet way. "Ain't you mad today, young'un."

I was holding her awkwardly with both arms in front of me, and Carl just reached down and took her from my hands and cradled her in his arms as if he'd been doing it all his life. And he looked that baby right in the eyes and cooed at her and bounced her really gently until she stopped screaming and stared at him.

That was the first time I really looked at Jessie. She had round black eyes and perfectly smooth black skin and tiny black curls on her head. And when she smiled, her whole little body seemed to be smiling.

"How did you get her to do that?"

"Do what?"

"Stop yelling and smile?"

Carl laughed lightly, shrugged, and said, "Mary Swan, I've been takin' care of babies ever since my mama died. Ya know what I mean? I helped raise Mike and James and Puddin' and my aunt's children and just about every other kid around here. Miss Abigail's always bringing babies over who need a bit of lovin.' "

I swallowed hard, feeling that fierce pride rise within me and that shame, too, for not having any idea of how to handle a baby. But Carl didn't seem to notice. He went on talking to Jessie and patting her bottom and walking around in the dying grass.

Finally Miss Abigail came outside with Cassandra, and they were both smiling in a funny way. Their faces looked happy but wet, like they'd been crying.

"Thank you, Mary Swan. Carl." Miss Abigail took Cassandra's

hand. "Let me introduce you to our new sister."

Carl broke into his wide, white grin and said, "Well, ya don't say. That's mighty fine, Cassandra. Mighty fine."

I furrowed my brow and looked from Carl to Miss Abigail to Cassandra. I had no idea why Miss Abigail was calling Cassandra their new sister. Had she adopted her? But Carl seemed to understand perfectly and to be more than pleased.

Miss Abigail took little Jessie in her arms and snuggled her close. "Your mama's made a very important decision," she whispered. "The most important one in her whole life. You are a blessed baby."

Then she gave Jessie to Cassandra, hugged them both, and said, "You go on home now, dear. I'll be along later with some diapers and food and that refrigerator."

"Thank ya, Miss Abigail. Thank ya for everything. And thank ya, Mary Swan and Carl," Cassandra said in a trembling voice. As she left, I wondered how this girl, probably younger than I, could possibly take care of that little baby, and the inner city once again felt like some foreign country.

"I best be goin'," Carl said to Miss Abigail. "Got a lot of work to do for Monday." He nodded to me, and I felt a funny little quiver in my stomach, as if I didn't want him to leave.

So I cleared my throat and said, "See ya next week." And off he went while I tried, to no avail, to keep my face from turning two shades of pink.

Miss Abigail didn't seem to notice but said, "Bye, Carl," with the sweetest look on her face. Then she turned to me. "Would you like to stop by my house for a glass of iced tea, Mary Swan?"

"Go to your house? Why not?" I said. "Thanks." At that moment iced tea sounded as refreshing as a dip in the pool.

Miss Abigail's old Ford station wagon was parked across the street from the church, its backseat crammed with bags full of clothes. When she opened the door, the air inside was so thick I thought I might be able to scoop it up in my hand. The cracked vinyl on the seats was broiling hot. I rolled down the window and stuck my head out. We drove past row after row of houses, their miniscule yards at times littered with spare car parts or children's toys or beer cans. The men and women sitting on the front porches would lift a hand and wave as Miss Abigail drove by.

She told me about her past, how her dad had made a lot of money in the automobile industry and how she lived in a "very comfortable neighborhood," as she put it, in Detroit. But she'd left all that years ago, first to work in the slums of Detroit and now here in Atlanta. I wished she could live in a big white antebellum structure with a wraparound porch and sparkling hardwood floors and a big mimosa tree hanging over the porch. I wanted the inside of her home to be filled with her family china and silver and old photographs of family members, and I wanted her to have a long, curving wooden staircase leading to the second floor. Miss Abigail deserved a place like that, a retreat after her long days in the inner city.

But, of course, I knew all that was just another romantic dream from my big imagination. Still, I wasn't prepared for where she really lived. She pulled into the driveway of a pale blue house with peeling paint and a front porch cluttered with boxes and brown bags. It looked a lot like the other houses in Grant Park, badly in need of repair. She parked the Ford by the sidewalk, turned off the motor, and said, "Welcome to my house."

Nothing fancy or new or different. No safe retreat. Just a roughshod house about a mile from Mt. Carmel Church. At first, I felt sorry for Miss Abigail, then I felt inspired by her, proud of her sacrifice. Those were fleeting emotions. I finally settled on the one that fit her. Everything I had observed about Miss Abigail in the past six weeks testified to one fact: This woman would naturally live among the people she worked with and loved.

On one side of the porch sat three old vinyl chairs with cracking upholstery and what looked like about ten brown bags filled with toys and puzzles and clothes. On the other side of the porch there was a wooden swing where a big brown-and-white cat was sleeping. An old refrigerator was lying on its side behind the swing.

Miss Abigail pushed open the screen door. I noticed that the screen had come loose in one corner and was rusted, and the door made a grinding squeal when she opened it. "Carl said he'd fix this door next week," she stated unapologetically.

The front room had a sagging couch covered in a floral material that had long since faded, two old armchairs, and a coffee table. Plus there was a big desk along one wall that was stacked high with different piles of papers. Miss Abigail must have noticed me staring at her desk, because she gave a dry laugh and said, "What I need is a secretary to help me keep up with all the paper work."

We walked to the back of the house. "Here we are," she said happily, indicating a large, airy kitchen. "Have a seat, Mary Swan." The table was rectangular and bigger than the oak table in our breakfast room. "A table is my most important piece of furniture. As long as I have a table, I can feed the children. The Lord knew I'd need a big kitchen and a big table for my work. And He gave me just that!"

She brought out two tall glasses and placed them on the table, and there was real pleasure in her gesture. Then she took a tray of ice from the freezer and dropped ice cubes into the glasses, filling them from a pitcher she took from the refrigerator.

"Thank you," I murmured.

The refrigerator door had rust spots showing through, but mostly it was covered with pictures that had been taped all over it. Pictures of smiling children and young girls and a few elderly couples. And a picture of Carl with his siblings.

The iced tea tasted like a mixture of lemon and raspberry, and I closed my eyes, relishing the cold drink and the ice as it touched my lips.

"My, that's good, isn't it?" Miss Abigail sang out.

Maybe it was my head throbbing so hard, or the tension from dealing with baby Jessie, or the shock of seeing Miss Abigail's house. Probably all of it combined. But I asked, "How can you live here, Miss Abigail? How can you live in this part of town?"

She didn't flinch. "This is my home, Mary Swan."

"But why? Why would you do this when you had such a nice home?"

"This is where God called me. He called me to live among those with whom I work."

"Oh."

She broke into a prayer. "Lord Jesus, how we thank you for this new life. For Cassandra's decision for you. Protect that child. Give her courage to do what she must. Let her trust you. Amen."

I had not closed my eyes right away because I didn't realize she was saying a prayer. After all, I'd never met anyone who would just start praying over a glass of iced tea. But her hands were clasped together and her eyes closed. When she said, "Amen," I opened one eye to see what I should do next. She had unclasped her hands and was smiling at me.

"Do you understand what happened to Cassandra today?"

"No idea."

"She made the decision to become a follower of Christ."

"Oh. You mean a Christian?"

"Exactly."

"Wasn't she already a Christian? Didn't she go to church?"

"Going to church doesn't make you a Christian, Mary Swan."

I didn't argue, but I didn't agree.

"When you let God enter your life, things change. His Holy Spirit inhabits you, and He starts working in ways you could never do on your own."

I wasn't following Miss Abigail and was feeling extremely uncomfortable, so I changed the subject to my previous topic.

"So why do you live here?"

"I told you. God called me here."

"For what?"

"To help out. To love these people."

I smiled. "I knew you'd say that."

"It's the truth, Mary Swan."

"Does anything ever get better, Miss Abigail? Do their lives ever get any easier? It must be so discouraging to live here and see how miserable they are."

"I don't work here because it is easy or fun or comfortable, Mary Swan. I work here because it is good. Maybe the outside doesn't change. And sure, there are a thousand heartbreaks. But the inside is changing in some of them. They have hope. Carl has hope." When she said his name, her face softened just as if she were his real mother.

"When I was about nine years old, I felt God calling me to be a missionary. I wanted more than anything in the world to go overseas and tell people about their need for Christ, about their need for His forgiveness and love. But when I got old enough to apply to be a missionary, I was refused. Bad eyes, bad heart. I was devastated. I knew God had called me."

"How did you know?" I interrupted. "What do you mean He called you? Out loud?"

"No." She smiled. "But I knew it was God nonetheless. There was a longing in my heart that He confirmed as His call when I'd read the Bible. It's hard to understand if you've never read the Bible, but sometimes a verse you're reading will just jump out and snatch your heart. And you'll say, 'That's it! That's me!'

"One of those verses for me was in the book of James in the New Testament, at the end of the first chapter. It says, 'Pure religion and undefiled before God and the Father is this, to visit the fatherless and widows in their affliction and to keep himself unspotted from the world.' That verse and many others that speak of God's love for the poor made an impression on me early in my life. As I got older, I prayed a lot about the desire of my heart, and I talked to people I trusted. People who were sensitive to God's Spirit. Again and again over the years, He kept showing me that I was to be a missionary."

This startled and intrigued me. How could she be so sure it was God calling her? But I didn't say a word.

"Then this letter arrived saying that although my health wouldn't permit me to go overseas, I could be a home missionary. I was thrilled. And then I got my assignment: the inner city of Detroit. Mary Swan, if you think this is depressing, you should see that place. Devil's den, for sure. I couldn't believe they'd send me there. After all, I was from Detroit. There was nothing exotic or exciting about working among the poor there. You see, Mary Swan, God was trying my heart. Asking me if I really wanted to follow Him, or if it was more that I wanted to go on a romantic adventure."

My ears perked up at that.

"So I had to confess to the Lord my sin—"

"Your sin!" I was horrified. "Since when is it a sin to want to be a missionary!"

She chuckled. "Not a sin to be a missionary. My sin was wanting my way and pretending it was God's."

"Oh," I said, nodding as if I understood; but I didn't have a clue what she meant.

"Well, I ended up accepting the job in Detroit. And that's when I started seeing the humor of God. He placed me smack in the middle of twelve different nationalities. I was a foreign missionary after all!"

My head was throbbing again, and I didn't really understand, but I couldn't quit asking questions. "But why do you do this, and how?"

"Mary Swan, every morning when I wake up, I ask Jesus, 'What do you want me to do today?' *Why* isn't the right question. Lots of things I can't explain. But I ask *what* and He always shows me what and then how."

I looked at her skeptically. I was beginning to think that maybe Miss Abigail had a screw loose somewhere.

"For instance, take that refrigerator on the porch. Somebody brought it over yesterday. Looks like a mess, but it works. And today I find out that Cassandra's family needs a fridge. So on the same day as she sees that Jesus is her Savior, she's learning that He provides for all her needs too. Some people don't ever learn that because they never need to. They are too busy providing for themselves." She stopped, saw how intently I was staring at her, and patted my hand.

"Jesus shows me what and how every day, and I leave all the whys to Him. I certainly don't have all the answers."

"I could never do what you do."

"On your own, no. Neither could I."

"I don't mean that. I mean I would never in my life *want* to do what you do. Come down and help, sure. But live here? If you start 'following God,' as you call it, is that what He asks?"

"He doesn't ask the same thing of all of us, Mary Swan." She stopped talking, brushed several wisps of gray hair out of her face, and started again. "Well, yes, He does ask the same of us: love and obedience and total devotion. But how that plays out in each individual life is never the same. Why do you come along on Saturday mornings?"

I thought for a moment. "Because it makes me feel good to know I'm helping out. And then I can go back to my home and be comfortable."

She laughed hard, a deep, delicious laughter that made you hope that whatever could make her laugh like that was contagious. "Mary Swan, you have just admitted to something that most adults won't touch with a ten-foot pole."

"What?" I asked suspiciously.

"We help out so we'll feel better about ourselves, but we always like the knowledge that we can go back to our side of the tracks and be comfortable. Deep down, that's what we all do."

"What's the matter with that?"

"Nothing, I suppose. But that's not what Jesus calls service."

I liked talking to Miss Abigail. She seemed like someone I could trust with my hardest questions. But I couldn't trust her with my thoughts about Carl. Not yet anyway. After all, she was practically his mother. I couldn't admit to her that a lot of the reason I came to the church was to see Carl.

She glanced at her watch and said, "We'd best be on our way. We have a lot to do before I take you home this evening."

We spent two hours driving around inner-city Atlanta. I saw winos sprawled out on park benches, prostitutes sitting in corner houses, abandoned shacks, garbage strewn around the parks, little children playing unsupervised. Every time Miss Abigail stopped the car and let down the back, men, women, and children crowded around it. She usually went inside a house to deal with some crisis, so I was left to hand out the clothes and food. It only took me a few minutes to figure out which bags held kids' clothes and which were for the women and the men. Sometimes a lady would come up and ask for something specific like a stroller or some diapers or, in a whisper, some sanitary pads. All I could do was mumble, "I'll tell Miss Abigail about it, and she'll see what she can do."

I breathed a sigh of relief when the back of the Ford was finally empty. "Time to get you home, Mary Swan," Miss Abigail said. "On the way back, I'll take you through the worst part of town."

I wasn't ready for what she showed me.

"Here's the worst." She stopped in front of a nondescript building on Peachtree Street, smack in the middle of downtown Atlanta, the part of downtown where the whites congregated. The building was twelve stories high. "The Cotton Corporation takes up the first three floors. Other businesses occupy the top floors. But in the middle are the offices of the Ku Klux Klan. That's where the ideas of white supremacy and hatred for blacks and Jews are bred and nourished. There and in a hundred other places like it across the city. You've gotten a glimpse of that, unfortunately."

We had not talked about the run-in with the rednecks since the Saturday it happened. "Would they kill, Miss Abigail? Would those boys kill Carl?"

"Many have been killed because of hatred, Mary Swan. And many more because of indifference." She paused. "Which is worse, Mary Swan? Hatred or indifference?"

I didn't answer her, but I had a feeling she was asking one of those rhetorical questions we talked about in English class.

"It's not pretty to realize what life is like for others. It's messy and heartbreaking. But it's real. The blacks of the inner city are real."

So I said what I had been wondering for weeks. "And the people in Buckhead are fake?"

"No, nothing is all black or white."

We laughed when she realized her pun, and I couldn't resist saying, "Nothing except for Buckhead is all white and the inner city is all black!"

She winked at me.

"So there are a bunch of religious hypocrites in my church, is that what you're saying? That's what my friend Rachel always says."

"Not at all! It's not up to us to judge. Only God can see the heart."

"You think it's better to go to church at Mt. Carmel than in Buckhead? Is that what you mean?"

"Absolutely not. That's not what I'm trying to say. We're not talking about *better*. God doesn't call us to *better*. He calls us to truth and obedience to Him, not to comparisons with others. That's man's religion. Comparing churches and good works and budgets. God is so much bigger and broader than we can possibly imagine. He calls us to serve Him wherever He has put us, be that Buckhead or Grant Park, Detroit or Africa. He knows what He's doing. He's got people all over this planet who love and serve Him. Rich folks and poor folks, middle class and clergy. If a person is liberated in his soul, he will have hope for a different future.

"Mary Swan, you just concentrate on what God's trying to do in your heart. That's all you need to do right now."

By the time we got into the Buckhead section of town, it was late afternoon. I was almost embarrassed for her to see where I lived, but she drove up our long driveway as if it was right next door to her little house.

"Thank you for joining me today, Mary Swan." She patted my hand. Then she asked, "Do you have a Bible at home?"

"Sure, somewhere."

She looked at me with those sparkling eyes and said, "Examine everything by the truth, Mary Swan." She was patting the Bible that sat beside her on the seat. "Don't just automatically believe everything you're taught. Examine it by the truth. You know what Jesus said, don't you?"

I shook my head, wishing I did know.

"He said, 'And ye shall know the truth and the truth shall make you free.' Gospel of John, chapter eight, verse thirty-two. You'll notice He didn't say the philosophies in Buckhead or Grant Park or at Georgia Tech will make you free. He said the truth. Jesus is truth. His word, this good book, is truth. Find out what it says, and you'll know what to do. The truth will set you free."

But when I got inside, I didn't read that verse. I walked over to the bookshelf in my room and touched the spine of the white leather Bible I'd gotten for my confirmation. It sat in an appropriate place beside the leather-bound copies of *Oliver Twist* and *A Tale of Two Cities*.

I'd never once taken it down to read. And I wasn't about to do it now. Not yet. I didn't want the words from this book making me feel bad. I didn't want to think about God or Miss Abigail's work or anything else. All I wanted to do was to change into my swimsuit and dive into the fresh clean water of the pool behind my house.

Chapter 8

So the next Saturday, after we'd finished helping out at Mt. Carmel, and after we'd spent ten minutes convincing Ella Mae that we would be careful and arranging for Miss Abigail to pick us up later in the afternoon, Carl accompanied me to the High Museum of Art. Rachel was supposed to meet us there, but she had called early that morning and said she was as sick as a dog and couldn't come. Since Rachel wasn't the type to weasel her way out of an adventure, I believed her. But I felt a bit let down. I had so hoped that Rachel and Carl would meet.

It took twenty minutes for us to ride the bus from Capitol Avenue down to Peachtree and 16th Street, where the museum was. Of course when Carl and I sat next to each other, we got a few stares. Mostly blacks were on the bus, and a few white teenage boys, which made my stomach churn and my heart start doing a tap dance in my chest. They weren't the same boys, but their faces wore the same pompous sneer, and they talked among themselves and stared quite rudely at us. When we got off the bus, so did they. Carl kind of pushed me along, away from the boys. Unfortunately, they followed right behind us, making comments like "Now, ain't that cute—black and white together, just like an Oreo cookie!" But I had learned my lesson and didn't say a word or turn around.

I just whispered to Carl, "What's up with those guys?"

"Nothin'."

"Something's bothering you about them."

"Ain't nothin', Mary Swan. Don't pay any attention to them." His voice was firm.

They left us near the entrance to the High Museum. As soon as the rednecks were out of sight, I exploded, albeit in a whisper, "I hate guys like that. I hate them! Why do they have to act that way?"

But Carl didn't say a thing.

"Don't you hate them? Don't you think they're awful?" I asked, when I had calmed down a bit.

Carl cocked his head to the side, as if he wasn't sure whether to confide in me. Finally he said, "It's just the way things are, Mary Swan. It's like just because of the color of your skin, you're cursed forever. And there's nothing you can do about it, no matter what the people say. I respect Reverend King. I have a friend who went on the Freedom Rides, and I was involved in all the sit-ins in the cafeterias downtown last year, and I intend to be a part of every freedom rally I can. But I can feel it, Mary Swan. It'll be a long time comin' before we aren't judged by our skin color, before we ever get to say a word.

"We made some progress. At least we can sit where we want on the bus." He gave me a wry grin. "We can even sit beside a white girl. But we aren't equal. Far, far from it."

For the first time, I saw a look of discouragement on Carl's face.

"It ain't no fun being a Negro, Mary Swan. It ain't no fun." Then he asked, "Are we almost to that museum?"

In answer, I stopped in front of a red-brick building at 1032 Peachtree Street. "The High Museum," I announced dramatically. We walked up the steps leading to the entrance, which was all glass with four white columns out front.

Carl held the door open for me, and we went into the lobby with its marble floors. I must admit Carl looked out of place as I presented my dad's patron's card to the woman who was taking tickets at the reception desk. I knew Mrs. MacIlvain well, so I said, "This is my friend Carl. He's with me." To which, with more than a quizzical look, the woman let us in.

"So this is what you call a museum?" Carl said right out loud.

"Shh!" I reprimanded him. "Whisper in a museum. Whisper." I pointed out the window. "The museum started out in that old Tudor house next door. It was sold to the Art Association in the 1920s by this lady named Hattie High." I knew the history of the museum by heart.

"Hattie High—now, don't that beat all."

"What do you mean?"

"I thought it was called the High Museum 'cause it was tall or somethin'."

I smiled. "Everybody thinks that. No, it's named after Mrs. High. She was a wealthy widow who was very involved in civic affairs. The Art Association had been looking for a place to build a museum for years, and then, out of the blue, Hattie High sold them her house for ten dollars."

"Ten dollars!" Carl screwed up his face. "You're pullin' my leg, girl."

"No, it's absolutely true." And to prove it, I led him to the portrait of Hattie High that was prominently displayed in the lobby. Mama had always liked the painting. Hattie High sat comfortably but aristocratically in a chair, her graying hair pulled back from her face, a long strand of pearls falling over her shimmering silk dress, and a delicate silk scarf around her shoulders.

"She looks like royalty or somethin'."

"She's about as close to royalty as we come in Atlanta. Mama said she was a member of nine different ancestral societies. Traces her family back to European nobility."

"Ya don't say." Carl was standing smack in front of the portrait, so close that his wide nose almost grazed Hattie High's sequined dress.

"You're not supposed to stand so close. Makes the security guards nervous. They'll think you're going to touch the painting."

He rolled his eyes at me, so I added, "It's really bad for a painting to be touched."

Carl smiled. "I may know more about washing dishes and calming screaming babies, but you got me beat when it comes to museums."

I don't think he really cared, though. "When Mrs. High was alive, the museum mostly displayed works by American artists, like the man who painted her portrait the year the museum opened."

"Sidney Edward Dickinson. Mighty fine name." Carl read the plaque on the wall.

"Come on upstairs. There's lots more to see," I said as we climbed the stairs to the second floor. "This is where the museum's two most important collections are housed. One is the Kress Collection. This new museum was built in 1955 to house it. The man who owns the dime stores called Kresgee's, Mr. Kress, divvied up his private art collection to thirteen cities. It was said to be worth 75 million dollars.

Atlanta was one of the cities, but we had to agree to provide an appropriate facility for the collection—they're all Italian Renaissance—so the Art Association had this new museum built."

"Italian Renaissance?" Carl screwed up his face. "What in the world does that mean?"

"It's the period of history when these works of art were painted. And they're all by Italian artists."

He shrugged, saying, "Makes sense." He stopped in front of a painting of the Madonna and Child. "Pa-ol-o dee Gee-o-van-i Fay," he read. "Sure is hard to pronounce that artist's name. But I like the figures of Mary and Jesus—the way they're so much bigger than the angels and the other folk." And slowly he walked around in the first gallery, admiring the works of art in the Kress Collection.

After a few minutes I interrupted him and said, "I'll show you something you'll really like."

I led him into an adjoining gallery. "This room holds the Haverty Collection. Mr. J. J. Haverty was one of Atlanta's foremost art collectors." We stopped in front of a landscape painting. "This one was painted by a colored man."

"Ya don't say. Got pictures by Negroes in this museum?" He looked at the plaque. "Henry Ossawa Tanner. *Destruction of Sodom and Gomorrah*."

"Mr. Tanner was the son of a preacher, and he was very religious himself. Lots of his paintings are about things in the Bible. He even traveled to the Holy Land several times at the end of the century."

Carl backed up and studied the painting intently. Then he exclaimed, all excited, "Why, that does just look like the story in the Old Testament. Mighty fine. Look at that sky! Just look at it! God's showin' His power right through nature. Looky there! Look at those colors—the layers of green and blue paint. You can barely see Lot and his daughters in that painting, but you shore can feel God's power!"

For at least ten minutes Carl examined the painting. He'd stand back across the room, peer at it with a wrinkled brow, then walk so quickly toward it that I was sure he'd touch it. He squinted his eyes and laughed and talked to himself, saying things like, "Those wicked, awful men, trying to entice Mr. Lot to give 'em the angels!" and "Now, if only he'd painted Lot's wife turning into a pillar of salt. . . ." And he chuckled.

I think Carl had forgotten I was beside him. I got a tingly feeling in my arms and head, the same as I got when I was pleased with one of my sketches.

Finally he nodded in approval. "That there is a mighty nice painting, Mary Swan."

"You seem to know a lot about it."

" 'Bout the story, sure. I know that story by heart." He cocked his head and asked, "Haven't you ever read that story in the Bible?"

"Never." I was a little embarrassed that I'd never once thought of reading about the stories that Henry Tanner's paintings represented.

"You don't know anything about Sodom and Gomorrah, Mary Swan?" He was incredulous.

"Well, I know they were cities God destroyed because of their wickedness."

"That's right. Ole Abraham tried to talk God out of it, seein' as how his nephew Lot lived there." He chuckled again. "Good ole Abraham had a mighty int'restin' conversation with the Almighty. But in the end, there weren't any righteous folks in that town. Only a whole lot of wicked ones. And so the Lord jus' up and annihilated them all. And Lot and his family ran for their lives. But Lot's wife—" He stopped in midsentence. "Surely you've heard about Lot's wife, Mary Swan?"

"Well, you just said it, Carl. She turned into a pillar of salt."

"Exactly. She disobeyed the Lord. He'd told them not to look back at the destruction. And poof, she became a pillar of salt."

"Kind of a wild story. You don't believe it, do you?"

He was genuinely shocked, " 'Course I do, Mary Swan. It's in the Bible."

I was naïve, but even I knew that lots of stuff written in the Bible sounded like a fairy tale. But I didn't dwell on that. What I was thinking was that I liked watching Carl discover art. Because that's just what it was. A discovery. Nothing sophisticated. He reacted to it in the most natural way. It made me shiver again. Observing his enthusiasm, I decided I wanted to create art that anyone, black or white or rich or poor, could enjoy. Someday I wanted Carl to stand before one of my paintings with his eyes shining and say, "That's mighty fine, Mary Swan. Mighty fine."

When we came to the gallery set up in memory of the artists who perished in the plane crash, I suddenly felt sickish inside, and I broke out in a cold sweat. "I need to go to the bathroom," I mumbled, heading downstairs to the lobby with Carl following.

"I'll wait for you here," he assured me, standing near Mrs. MacIlvain's desk.

"If you need to use the rest room," she said, clearly embarrassed, "the rest room for Negroes is downstairs."

"I'm fine," he answered, declining her offer as I hurried down the hall. I hadn't even considered the possibility of separate bathrooms for blacks and whites. I was feeling worse by the second.

But I had regained my composure by the time I joined Carl at Mrs. MacIlvain's desk. Lillian MacIlvain had been a dear friend of Mama's. She smiled at us politely, but her cheeks turned light pink under her perfectly placed makeup.

"How can I help you, Mary Swan?" Her voice was syrupy sweet and tinged with a dose of pity.

"Well, can you keep a secret?" I asked. She nodded, leaning closer toward us. "A big secret?" Another nod and a bit of interest in her eyes. "I'd like to do some research on the three missing paintings. You know, the ones that disappeared last year before the exhibition."

Mrs. MacIlvain's face fell, and she said softly, "Isn't that a bit morbid?"

"No, I need to find out, for me and for Mama. Please."

"Do you really think it's wise, Mary Swan, especially right now, so soon . . ."

After the crash, I bet she thought, but she didn't say it. She'd already been to our house five times during the summer, bringing food and helping Daddy sort through Mama's things. Fortunately, contrary to several other women who came a little too often to our house, she never posed a threat to Daddy. She was married with four kids, one of whom was in my class at Wellington.

"Oh yes, I need to. But you can't breathe a word, Mrs. MacIlvain. Not to Daddy or anyone else."

She eyed Carl suspiciously, but I didn't feel like trying to explain why he was with me, helping in something I called secret. Lillian MacIlvain and Carl and I stood there awkwardly until at last I said, "Mrs. MacIlvain, I was wondering if you have any records about the paintings. The newspaper articles about the exhibition that was planned. Anything that might help me do a bit of research."

She cleared her throat. "Yes, of course, we could get you that information, Mary Swan, if you're sure."

"I'm sure, Mrs. MacIlvain. I need to do this."

"I understand," she said sweetly, and I think she really did. "Have you seen the exhibition upstairs in memory of the artists on the plane?"

"Not yet," I said too quickly. "I was just going to take Carl up there."

While Mrs. MacIlvain went searching through the files, Carl and I ventured back upstairs through the Kress Galleries. I hesitated before entering the gallery reserved for paintings painted by the crash victims. Then, taking a deep breath, I walked into the room with Carl close behind.

"There's Mama's painting," I said proudly.

And he rewarded me with a real live, "Ya don't say!" He practically stuck his nose on the plaque and read, "Sheila McKenzie Middleton, *The Swan House*."

It was one of Mama's numerous paintings of the famous mansion. "Beautiful, isn't it?"

Carl stared at the painting and then at me and then back at the painting. "Is it something symbolic, Mary Swan? Like those snakes in *Huckleberry Finn* or the turtle in *The Grapes of Wrath*?" Both of us had studied those books in school last year, and we'd talked about them just that morning.

"Sure, there's always symbolism in Mama's paintings."

"No, I mean is that about you, Mary Swan? The Swan House—is that you?"

The way he asked the question, I could tell he really wanted to know. I liked the way Carl thought about things.

"No, it's not about me," I said quickly, not wanting to confide that secret to him. "The Swan House really exists. In fact, it's right next door to where I live."

"Ya don't say! You live next door to a mansion with fancy, tumblin' fountains in the front yard."

I nodded. "Someday I'll take you to see it, if you'd like."

His eyes grew wide, and he smiled and looked embarrassed. "We'll see about that, Mary Swan."

"Come here quick," I said. And then, "This *is* a painting of me." I got tears in my eyes just seeing my beloved portrait hanging there in one of the museum's galleries.

"Ya don't say. That's you as a little girl!" He backed up, crossed his arms over his chest, and just stared at the painting. Finally, he said, "I like it. I like it a whole lot. I think your mama got it right. I think that must be just how you were as a little girl. All wild and free and pushing your feet out like you're trying to touch somethin' in another world. I do believe that's you."

Something in my chest hurt, that tingling feeling combined with a squeezing pain. I wanted to understand this young man who had never been to a museum and who understood a painting without anyone having to explain it to him.

Miss Abigail had promised to pick us up at five in front of the museum. We went out ten minutes early. I was carrying a folder filled with copies of newspaper articles and information that Mrs. MacIlvain had loaned me. But as soon as we stepped out into the sunlight, Carl looked around and cursed. Then he grabbed my arm and pulled me back inside the museum.

"What in the world—"

"Those rednecks are still hanging around. Just waitin'. I thought they'd have left by now, but they haven't." He was holding on to my arm kind of tightly, and his voice trembled for a fraction of a second. "Can you get a ride home with that Mrs. MacIlvain?"

"What do you mean?"

"It isn't good for them to see us together, Mary Swan. I'll ride back with Miss Abigail. You go ask now." His voice sounded worried, serious, so I went over to the desk where Mrs. MacIlvain was sitting. She gave me a funny look, but said that she was happy to drive me home when she closed the museum in half an hour.

I followed Carl to the exit. He touched my arm, more softly this time. Tingles again. "Mary Swan, you stay inside, you hear?"

"But what about you?"

"I'll be fine." He took hold of both of my shoulders and smiled down at me. "You be careful now, Mary Swan. Be careful."

But when he left, I sneaked a peek out of the door and saw the boys from the bus sitting on a step. One of them yelled to Carl, "Hey, boy! What'd you do with your white girly?"

Carl ignored them completely, walking by without a sideways glance. They stood up and started after him, but Miss Abigail was already waiting by the curb. Carl hopped in and slammed the door to the old Ford, and then he looked past the three boys to the front of the museum. He couldn't see me from where I was standing inside the door, but I saw those black eyes with their worried look, and I kept thinking about the way he had touched my arm.

When I got home, I found Daddy in his study and went over and kissed him on the cheek.

"Have a good day, Swannee?"

Daddy still had a grayish tint to his skin and a preoccupied look in his eyes, and I don't think he was sleeping much at night. After the plane crash I was afraid that maybe he would become overprotective of Jimmy and me. But he didn't. Maybe deep down inside, I wanted him to worry about where I spent my days. I wanted him to spend time with me. But today I was glad he didn't ask any questions. He smiled faintly when I said that the day with Ella Mae at church had gone well. I don't even think he had noticed that it was almost six, or that I'd been gone a lot longer than usual.

And something inside of me felt sad, like the time a couple of years ago when he was supposed to pick me up at school because Mama was gone for an exhibition, and he completely forgot. I finally called Trixie to get me, and when I got home, Daddy had his head buried in the paper, and he never realized that I was late or that he was supposed to pick me up.

The main word for Daddy was preoccupied. I'm not sure if it was because of the corporations he was advising, or the stocks and bonds jumping around, or Mama's temperament, but all I saw as a child growing up was that he didn't seem to have a lot of free time. That hadn't changed. Maybe it had only gotten worse.

I guess Daddy had a lot to keep inside. But in public he had a life-of-the-party personality, at least he had before the plane crash. He lit up around a crowd. When he went to a party or invited guests to our house, he was the center of attention, cracking jokes and making deals as he sipped on his Scotch and soda. He seemed to know everyone in Atlanta, and he predicted that our small Southern city had a big future ahead of her.

His heart was in Atlanta making a name for herself, and he, along with so many of those who had been in the Orly crash, had invested hundreds and thousands of hours and dollars to accomplish just that. I never could guess how much money Daddy gave away in a year, but I did know that a lot of it went to the Art Association and the church and the symphony and charities like the Lung Association.

He believed that a good education was absolutely the best and most secure thing he could give to his children, along with a good family name. So I grew up thinking that being born in Buckhead somehow meant I deserved to be born there, that I had been doubly blessed, and that I had a duty to give back to the community my time and talent. Sometimes as we were growing up, Daddy would quiz Jimmy and me about trivial details of history, and one wrong answer brought on a half-teasing, half-serious response. "What has happened to your fine education?"

Preoccupied and a perfectionist, that was my dad.

Jimmy came down the stairs, interrupting my thoughts, his Oxford cloth shirt rumpled and untucked from his khaki pants. I could tell he'd been eating potato chips, because a few crumbs lingered around his mouth and on his shirt.

"Some guy called you a while ago, Swan," Jimmy announced absentmindedly.

"Who?"

"Andy's big brother."

"Robbie? Robbie Bartholomew called me?" My voice slipped up an octave.

"Yeah."

"Well?"

"Well, what?" Totally uninterested.

"Well, what did he say, you idiot?"

Jimmy grinned. "Nothing much. We talked about the convertible he got for his seventeenth birthday. Cool car, sounds like."

"And what did he want?"

"Beats me. He said he'd call back later." With that, Jimmy went into the kitchen and started making a peanut butter and jelly sandwich. Thirteen years old and still eating peanut butter and jelly sandwiches. He drove me crazy!

Daddy seemed pleased with the news of the phone call. "Nice boy, Robbie Bartholomew. Fine family." We traipsed into the kitchen, and

Daddy grabbed two slices of bread and slopped peanut butter and jelly on them. Weekends without Ella Mae's cooking were disastrous. But if Daddy was eating a peanut butter and jelly sandwich, at least that meant no eligible ladies had come by today with a casserole.

I felt a weird kind of twittering in my stomach, and I knew I was definitely not hungry for peanut butter and jelly. Robbie Bartholomew had called! I gnawed on a fingernail, a bad habit I had when I felt nervous. Finally I asked, "How long ago did he call?"

Jimmy shrugged. "Beats me. An hour or so."

So I sat there, watching them eat their sandwiches and drink their glasses of milk and then take out the ice-cream carton from the freezer and eat straight out of it. I fumbled through the papers that Mrs. MacIlvain had given me, heart racing, trying desperately to think of anything but Robbie. I failed miserably.

When the phone rang, I leapt up and said, "I'll get it!" much too loudly. Daddy and Jimmy just smiled.

"Hello?"

"Hello. Mary Swan?" A boy's voice.

"Yes, this is she." *Wham, wham, wham* went my heart against my ribs.

"Mary Swan, this is Robbie Bartholomew."

"Oh, hi, Robbie." I tried to sound casual and a little surprised. If only Rachel was here, she'd tell me what to say. Boys didn't usually call me.

"I was just wondering how you're doing."

"Oh, fine. Okay. We're getting along okay." I could feel Jimmy and Daddy's eyes on my back.

"Well, I'm glad to hear it." Silence. He cleared his throat. "Um, well, um, I was calling because I wondered if you might like to go to the Back-to-School Ball with me. It's on Friday night, September tenth."

I leaned into the phone. Had I heard right? The Back-to-School Ball! It was the biggest social event of the fall for the rising juniors and seniors—a party open to all those attending the private schools in Buckhead. It was almost more important than the junior-senior prom at the end of the year. All girls talked about in August was if they'd been invited to the Back-to-School Ball.

"Sure! Sure. Yes, that would be fun."

"Oh. Well, good. Great."

Then without thinking, I said, "Um, well, let me just check with my dad first." I winced as soon as the words were out of my mouth, but it was too late. So I covered the phone with one hand and whispered to Dad, "Robbie Bartholomew just invited me to the Back-to-School Ball! Can I go?"

"Of course, sweetie," Daddy said, and Jimmy slopped up his melting ice cream and regarded me gleefully.

"Dad says it's fine," I stammered to Robbie.

"Oh, good. Well, I'll plan to pick you up around seven, then."

"Okay."

Then he added, "And I was wondering if you'd like to go to the Varsity with a bunch of us tonight. We were gonna head down there in about half an hour. I could come by and pick you up."

"Well, sure." I hoped he didn't hear the way my voice kept cracking. "Just let me check."

I whispered to Daddy, who just nodded with a smile.

"It's fine!"

"Good, see you in a few minutes."

I hung up the phone with a shaking hand, and Jimmy laughed loudly. "Swan, your face is as red as this strawberry jelly!"

I stuck out my tongue and left the kitchen in a hurry. Sometimes I was convinced that Jimmy didn't have a heart.

Safe in my room, I locked the door and dialed Rachel's number automatically. "You'll never believe it! Robbie Bartholomew just invited me to the Back-to-School Ball, and then he asked if I'd like to go to the Varsity with him in thirty minutes."

We both squealed into the phone at the same time. "But, Rachel, what will I wear?" I'd never been on a date in my life, which had been the topic of many a late-night discussion with Rachel. She, on the other hand, had boys asking her out all the time. And not just guys our age. Older guys.

"Don't worry, Swannee. The Varsity is the perfect place for a first date. Now, just go put on your pale yellow blouse—the one with the scalloped collar—and those light blue pedal pushers. You look great in those."

"And my hair? What about my hair?"

"Just pull it back in that nice barrette you got at Davidson's last week. And put a little rouge on and some lipstick."

"I don't have any lipstick, Rachel."

"Look in your mom's vanity drawer. I'm sure she had some."

I hesitated, and Rachel added, "Swannee, she'd be thrilled for you to borrow her lipstick for your first date."

"Okay, thanks a ton. I've gotta go."

"Call me when you get back!"

"Of course!"

Daddy and Jimmy were still in the kitchen, so I sneaked into Mama's private dressing room and sat down at her vanity. I opened one drawer. All kinds of lotion. Another held eyebrow pencils and mascara. The third had rouge and lipstick. How had Rachel known? I picked a bright pink tube and smeared it across my lips, then parted them in a smile. Bright pink lipstick and braces were completely incongruous. I wiped it off with the back of my hand.

"Oh, Mama, I'm no good at this. Why can't you be here for my first date?" I felt a sting in my eyes, so I dug through the drawer and tried another tube—a paler pink. Not too bad, I thought. Rachel would say it was a gentle hint, nothing too brash. I rushed back upstairs to my room and had just tucked my pale yellow blouse into those light blue pedal pushers when the doorbell rang.

The Varsity was touted as the biggest drive-in restaurant in the Southeast. Maybe in all the world. It was right across the street from the Georgia Institute of Technology, my daddy's alma mater. The story goes—and it's true—that in the early 1930s a guy named Frank Gordy had been kicked out of Georgia Tech for not making the grade. When he'd asked one of his professors what he should do, the man answered, "Why don't you go across the street and start a hot dog stand?" And that's exactly what he did. Now the Varsity was famous, and I guess that Frank Gordy was probably a lot richer than most of the bankers and stockbrokers and architects who had graduated from Georgia Tech.

In the thirties and forties, the parking lot of the Varsity touched the Georgia Tech campus and spread out all around it. Then in the fifties an expressway had come to Atlanta, knocking out a part of the Varsity's immense parking lot and separating it from the campus. But that didn't daunt its customers. Everyone ate at the Varsity. Rich, poor, black, white, student, businessman.

This evening I sat in the front seat of Robbie Bartholomew's 1962 bright red convertible and watched Robbie. As I've already said, he kind of reminded me of a cross between a football jock and a Boy Scout. His auburn hair matched his eyes. Everything about him matched, which was what bugged me about him. I wanted to take a fountain pen and flick it all over his pressed shirt and his loafers. Or ruffle his hair.

"Robbie, you are just too perfect," I told him that night, which made him blush and grin a little foolishly.

Virginia Lawson and Herbert Thomas sat glued together in the backseat. Virginia was a senior at Wellington, but I didn't know her very well. Herbert attended Mendon's Private School for Boys, which was also where Robbie and Andy and Jimmy went to school.

In the convertible next to us were two other couples, friends of Robbie's whom I knew slightly. As soon as we drove into the parking lot, a black curbside waiter jumped onto the back of Robbie's convertible, yelling, "What d'ya have?" I recognized him as a man called Flossie Mae.

Rumor had it that the waiters—they were called carhops—made so much in tips that they actually paid to work there, but I don't think that was true. The most fascinating and famous waiter was Flossie Mae. Years ago, he had put the menu to music and sang it for his customers. He never wrote a thing down when taking an order, but he could repeat the entire order back to you, never making a mistake. To add to the folklore, in addition to the white jacket and red pants that all the waiters had to wear, Flossie Mae wore outlandish hats. That night, he had on a vegetable colander turned over his head with pre-scription pill bottles, spice containers, plastic forks, and heart-shaped lollipops sticking out of it.

Sometimes guys went inside to order, but women couldn't go in-side. That night Robbie ordered from the curb, telling Flossie Mae, "We'll have a naked dog, a regular C dog, one naked steak, one glo-rified steak, two orders of strings, an order of rings, two frosted or-anges, and two PCs." That was Varsity lingo, which translated meant, a plain hot dog; a chili dog; a plain hamburger; a hamburger with mayonnaise, lettuce, and tomato; two milkshakes made out of frozen orange juice and vanilla ice cream; and two cups of plain chocolate milk, served over ice.

"Pick up in Snellville," belted a voice over a loudspeaker, and a waiter ran over to the part of the parking lot by that name. There were different names for each section, names like Techwood and Morningside and Buttermilk Bottom, places that really existed around Atlanta.

Robbie smiled that Boy Scout smile, and Virginia Lawson and Herbert Thomas held hands in the backseat.

"Flossie Mae's the smartest colored guy I ever knew. He ain't bad at all for a Negro," Herbert laughed.

I bristled and shot him a look that said *You jerk!* But I didn't say a thing.

When Flossie Mae came back with the order, I smiled at him and said thank you, but I don't think he noticed. He ran off yelling, "What d'ya have?" to another car.

It had never before made one bit of difference to me that all the waiters were black, or that we mocked the way they talked and made crude jokes behind their backs. But tonight it suddenly mattered.

"Since when are you so kind to colored boys, Mary Swan?" Herbert asked with a sneer.

I was boiling inside while Robbie distributed the food.

"Let's drop it, Herb," Robbie said a little nervously.

Soon Virginia and Herbert and Robbie were all laughing about some silly joke, but Robbie kept watching me out of the corner of his eye. I hardly said a word. I just nibbled at my hamburger and slurped the frosted orange.

It wasn't until after Robbie had let off Herbert and Virginia that I spit out what was bothering me. "Do you hate Negroes?"

"No, should I?"

"Of course not! What I mean is, do you treat them bad and call them names?"

"You pick a fine subject for a first conversation, Mary Swan."

Suddenly I felt extremely unconfident and foolish. "Sorry. Never mind."

"No, doesn't bother me. Fact is, I've never thought too much about it. Lou Ann has worked for us for almost as long as I've been alive, and so has Danny. They're practically like family." He made a face and squirmed. "Tell you the truth, I probably am nice to the ones I know and not so nice to the others. But I'd never act like Herbert. He's just like that. Don't let it bother you."

I almost said, "But it *does* bother me," then decided against it. We didn't talk much while he drove me home. But I was thinking hard. I wanted Robbie Bartholomew to like blacks if he was going to be my date to the Back-to-School Ball.

When he dropped me off at the house, I jumped out of the car and waved back, saying "Thanks" before he ever had a chance to open his door.

He smiled his Boy Scout smile, shrugged, and waved back. "See you soon, Mary Swan."

Daddy had left the porch light on. If it had been Mama, she would've been waiting at the window, watching. As it was, Daddy was holed up in his study. I peeked in the door and said, "I'm home."

Daddy was bent over a stack of papers. He looked up, letting a smile erase the worn look, and asked, "How'd it go?"

"Fine."

"Fine. That's all?"

"Yep. That's all for tonight." I kissed him on his bristly cheek and ran all the way up the stairs to my room, flopped on the bed, and grabbed the phone. Rachel and I talked for an hour about Robbie and Carl and the rednecks who followed us to the museum and how I hoped Robbie really did like blacks. And then for some reason, after I hung up the phone, I buried my head in my pillow and cried.

Chapter 9

On Monday afternoon, Rachel and I sat cross-legged on the floor of my room with the papers I'd gotten from the museum strewn all over the floor. "Are you sure you feel good enough to do this?" I inquired. She'd slept all morning after being awake half the night with the trots.

"I feel absolutely awful, but you've got a bathroom close by, and I might as well do something instead of sitting in bed all day. Two days of that is enough to drive a person crazy."

Rachel had a mind for organization. Whereas I had randomly spread all the newspapers and files on the floor, she immediately set about putting an order to it. As we worked, she threw out a quote from Shakespeare, which launched us into a little game we often played, recalling poetry and plays we'd been forced to memorize over the years at Wellington.

" 'This above all, to thine own self be true, And it must follow as the night the day, Thou canst not then be false to any man.' "

"Oh please, Rach," I lamented. "I'm not an idiot. Something a little more challenging next. Everyone knows that's from *Hamlet*, Polonius speaking. Now my turn. 'Though this be madness, yet there is method in't.' " I winked at her, indicating the papers on the floor.

"Clever, Swan! But also cinchy. Polonius again. My turn. 'Out, out, brief candle! Life's but a walking shadow. A poor player that struts and frets his hour upon the stage and then is heard no more. It is a tale told by an idiot, full of sound and fury, signifying nothing.' "

"Oh, that is just awful. So sad!"

"Quit stalling, Swan."

"I'm not stalling. Who could forget Macbeth's great soliloquy? But I hope it's not true, Rachel."

"What?"

"That life is just an hour on the stage that amounts to nothing in the end. I want my life to count."

"Well, look who's getting deep on me."

So I left Shakespeare for the moment, stood up, and quoted in a lyrical voice that sped up and slowed down according to the words of the poem,

"Out of the hills of Habersham,
Down the valleys of Hall,
I hurry amain to reach the plain,
Run the rapid and leap the fall,
Split at the rock and together again,
Accept my bed, or narrow or wide,
And flee from folly on every side
With a lover's pain to attain the plain
Far from the hills of Habersham,
Far from the valleys of Hall."

With the first line, Rachel was standing too, and quoting along with me one of our favorite poems. The Chattahoochee River ran through Atlanta, and six girls in our class lived on Habersham Road, named after the hills of Habersham in North Georgia. " 'Song of the Chattahoochee!' " Rachel cried. "By Sidney Lanier!"

Rachel was really getting into our game, momentarily healed of her stomach virus. She started galloping around my spacious room like a frenzied stallion, chanting,

" 'Forward, the Light Brigade!'
Was there a man dismayed?
Not though the soldier knew
Someone had blundered."

She screeched to a halt, became a soldier who dismounted from her steed, saluted me with a make-believe sword, and continued,

"Theirs not to make reply,
Theirs not to reason why,
Theirs but to do and die,

Into the valley of death,
Rode the six hundred."

"Bravo, Rachel!" She bowed to my applause. "Excellent performance, but you kind of gave it away! Tennyson, 'Charge of the Light
Brigade.' "

And not to be outdone, I stood up and, in my most dramatic stage
voice, said,

" 'Why, what an ass am I! This is most brave,
That I, the son of a dear father murdered,
Prompted to my revenge by heaven and hell,
Must like a whore unpack my heart with words and fall a-cursing
like a very drab, a stallion!' "

I had picked up one of the newspapers halfway through the soliloquy and now fairly shook it in my hand.

Rachel's eyes grew wide. "Wow, Swan. You make a great Hamlet.
It's really spooky, when you think about the lines."

I let go of the paper and gave a wry smile. "Yeah. I'm no prince
of Denmark, but my dear mother has been killed, and I swear I'll have
my revenge, and it will be by solving this dare. I swear it." My heartfelt
outburst turned our silly game into something a bit too serious, and
we fell into silence.

Then Rachel whispered sadly as she flopped across my bed,

" 'No! I am not Prince Hamlet, nor was meant to be;
Am an attendant lord, one that will do
To swell a progress, start a scene or two, advise the prince; no
      doubt an easy tool,
Deferential, glad to be of use,
Politic, cautious, and meticulous;
Full of high sentence, but a bit obtuse;
At times, indeed, almost ridiculous—
Almost, at times, the Fool.' "

"Oh, Rachel, how in the world did you remember that!" I was
frankly more than impressed. "It's what's-his-face. Don't say it. We just
studied him." I closed my eyes and nibbled a fingernail. "Prufrock!
That's it! 'The Love Song of J. Alfred Prufrock' by T. S. Eliot." Rachel
could tell I was proud of myself for having recalled the poet and the

poem. "But we never had to memorize that."

Rachel shrugged. "I know. But I liked it. I liked the whole thing."

"Please don't tell me you memorized the whole stinking poem. Just for fun?"

She didn't answer but turned over on her back and stared up at the ceiling. "We are wasting a bunch of time, Swan."

"I know it."

"Last one. Your turn. Then we've got to get busy. Give me something challenging, my dear."

I groaned. Nothing was challenging to Rachel. I think she had a photographic memory. Then I got an idea and quoted, " 'Ye shall know the truth and the truth shall make you free.' "

Rachel narrowed her eyes, made her lips into two thin lines, and thought for a moment. "Sounds like Martin Luther King, Jr."

I made a loud, obnoxious buzzing sound. "Aannnh! Wrong! Try again."

"Did we have this in class?"

"Maybe we did and maybe we didn't."

"Come on, Swannee. Cheater." She thought for a while longer, then shrugged. "I give up."

I smiled triumphantly and exclaimed, "The Bible!"

Rachel didn't let that pass. "Hey, you can't just say 'The Bible.' You have to give the author and the name of the work."

"Okay, the Bible; author, God. How's that?"

"No good. As I recall from our class at dear Wellington, the Bible was written by a bunch of different men and has a whole lot of books. Sixty something in all. So spit it out, Miss Know-It-All. Who said it and where?"

"Drat, Rachel." It was something Miss Abigail had said ten days ago, but she was always quoting stuff from the Bible and then telling me to look it up at home, which I never did.

"I'm sure it's somewhere in the New Testament," I replied lamely. "Jesus probably said it."

"Well, if you don't know for sure, it doesn't count," Rachel announced matter-of-factly as she neatly folded a copy of the *Atlanta Journal* to the page that spoke about the art exhibition. That marked the end of our little game and the beginning of some serious work.

For an hour we nibbled Saltines and sipped Coke and read everything Lillian MacIlvain had given me about the mysterious disappearance of the paintings. Rachel had divided the papers by date. She took all the articles that were written before the disappearance and gave me the ones dated after April twenty-ninth.

"Listen, Swannee," she commented after we'd silently perused the papers. "This is from the *Journal*, dated April 23, 1961.

"A new exhibition has been planned at the High Museum to honor Southern painters. Three previously unshown paintings by Georgia artists Henry Becker, Leslie Leschamps, and Sheila Middleton will be featured. An anonymous donor has graciously agreed to give these three paintings to the museum. The exhibition opens on April 29 for art patrons, where a seated dinner will be followed by a viewing of the newly acquired paintings as well as the rest of the exhibition. Sheila Middleton, whose portrait and landscape work is already known to many Atlantans, will deliver a brief talk about her newest painting. When asked if the other two Southern artists would be present, Mr. Shaw, the museum's curator, said no. He did verify that art specialists had examined all three paintings and that they were impressed by the 'very high quality of painting.' "

"Did you know your mom was supposed to speak at that dinner?"
"Nope."
"Well, then, you need to ask your dad about that. Find out if she really did speak, and if so, what she said." Rachel pulled out a pen from behind her ear and noted the questions in a small spiral notebook.
"I can't ask Daddy! I'll be disqualified if he finds out."
"You can ask about the exhibition. You have to. He doesn't have to know that you're the Raven. You can ask as a daughter wanting to find out as much as she can about her mom."
"Well, that might work."
"Of course it will. Now, listen to this. It's from the *Northside News*." That was the weekly society paper in Buckhead.

"For art enthusiasts, this Saturday marks the opening of a new exhibition at the High Museum. Three paintings have been donated to the museum. One of the artists, Buckhead resident Sheila Middleton of 3083 Andrews Drive, will speak briefly at a fundraising dinner to be held the night before the opening of the exhibition. Mrs. Middleton is the wife of Atlanta broker John Jason Middleton and daughter of Ian and Evelyne McKenzie, the well-known cotton magnate and his wife whose plantation is located in Griffin, Georgia."

"Nothing new there."
"Wait, let me finish, Swannee.

"Mrs. Middleton said that she was 'surprised and pleased that one of her paintings was being donated to the museum.' She was flattered that the donor regarded her work so highly. When asked to identity this person, she smiled and said she had been instructed not to reveal the name.

"You, see, Swan! Your mom knew who the donor was. If your mom knew, then your dad probably did too. And if you can find out who donated the paintings, I'll bet you a million bucks you'll find the paintings too."

I watched her scribble down, *Ask Mr. Middleton about donor.*

"Okay, what have you got, Swan?"

"Let's see. On April thirtieth, the headline in the *Atlanta Journal* was:

"Three Paintings Mysteriously Disappear the Night Before Major Exhibition Is to Open at High—While the High Museum's best patrons were savoring a dinner of filet mignon, scalloped potatoes, and a strawberry trifle, the museum's curator, Harold Shaw, waited in vain for the delivery of the three paintings to be viewed later in the evening. No complaint of theft by the anonymous donor was made. Police have combed the area of the museum to no avail. The donor has not contacted the museum's curator. 'It is a most disappointing and puzzling situation,' Mr. Shaw said Saturday afternoon. The exhibition, featuring fifteen Southern painters, opened yesterday, despite the absence of the three paintings that were to be donated to the museum.

"And this one, dated May first, says,

"Sheila Middleton, whose painting was to be shown at the exhibition, declined to comment on the disappearance. Her husband, stockbroker John Jason Middleton, called it a terrible loss and expressed his wife's chagrin."

"Aha! There you have it! Your dad was protecting your mom! She knew something!" More scribbling. "This is gonna be easy, Swan. Your dad will have all the answers. He just didn't want to reveal them to the press." She stuck the pen behind her ear, smiled, then suddenly got a sick look on her face. She groaned, "Be right back," and took off for my bathroom.

The afternoon turned out to be a great success, but even with all the progress we made, my thoughts often strayed from the Raven Dare to Grant Park. I could not stop thinking of Carl and how he had never been in a museum before and how he had loved the paintings. There was a part of me that was dying to sweep him out of inner-city life and a part of me whose heart broke in two just thinking about the people who were trapped, as literally as if prison bars held them there, in poverty. Smart, kind, decent kids who, even if they could quote Shakespeare and Eliot, would never have a chance to escape that inner-city prison. I felt suddenly embarrassed about my obsession with the Raven Dare. I wished all the money I would raise for solving the Dare could help liberate the desperate people who came to Mt. Carmel for spaghetti meals. I wished I could hand Carl a check for $100,000 and tell him to go anywhere his heart desired.

What had Miss Abigail said? *"If a person is liberated in his soul, he will have hope for a different future."* And then she'd said that verse about knowing the truth and the truth making you free.

"Swan, you're off in space again," Rachel chided.

"Sorry," I said, not about to admit to Rachel that I was daydreaming about Carl yet again.

"Okay, now on to the other artists, Leslie Leschamps and Henry Becker. Question number one for your dad or for the donor is, did your mom know these people? If we could interview them, that would be the best. As well as an interview with the donor. Let's see, it says in the *Northside News* that they aren't local artists. So we have to find out who they are and where they live and go talk to them."

"Even if they live in California?"

Rachel stuck out her tongue. "Don't be impertinent. They're from somewhere in Georgia. This lovely state isn't that big!"

"And what if they've moved away from Georgia?"

"Well," she said, straightening up all the papers into one pile, "then we'll just have to find out where they live now. And call them. But first on your list is to talk with your dad. And you've got to be convincing. He can't have a clue it has to do with the Raven."

"Should I make up another poem?" I asked sarcastically, rolling my eyes. "Ella Mae didn't speak to me for days after that!"

"No. Poetry is definitely out." She removed the pen and nibbled on it. "You're the grieving daughter who wants to honor her mother by finding out as much about her past as possible. That's it!"

"You know, Rach, that really is it."

And so Rachel helped me plan my speech to be presented to Daddy. But if either of us had had any idea of everything I was going to find out about Mama, I think we would have both stuffed that big black bird as far back in our minds as possible and left it there to die.

It took me five days to get up the courage to talk to Daddy. I wanted to make sure he was in a good mood. Late Friday afternoon, when he came home from the office, I flopped into a chair at the breakfast room table, where he sat reading the sports page of the *Atlanta Journal*, and sighed dramatically.

"Daddy, I need your help." Rachel and I had practiced that ridiculous line for three days, until she was satisfied with my intonation.

He looked up from the paper and asked, "What is it, Swan?"

"It's something serious, Dad. Is it okay to talk to you now, or should I wait?"

He set the paper on the table and gave a half smile. *Why does your face have to look so gray all the time?* I thought. But aloud I said, "I went to the High Museum last Saturday." I let that sink in. "I asked Mrs. MacIlvain for all the information about the three paintings that disappeared before that exhibition a year and a half ago."

He pushed his chair back and looked worried. "Why, Mary Swan? What made you want to go digging up the past like that?"

Those were the exact words I'd predicted he'd use, and I was ready with my reply. Rachel had forced me to memorize it too.

"Just missing Mama. And looking for a way to, I don't know, to honor her. I thought maybe I could talk to the donor. Find out what he did with the paintings." Then I showed him the newspaper articles I'd gotten from Mrs. MacIlvain.

He skimmed them, commenting, "Yes, Mary Swan. I've seen them all. Strange thing, that whole incident." He fiddled with his tie, which hung loosely around his neck. "Imagine you digging up this stuff."

But he wasn't really talking to me. He had that vacant look in his eyes, as if he had just arrived in another city and didn't have the faintest clue which road to take. "You just let that whole thing rest, Swannee," he sighed. "There's nothing you can learn about your mother from that scandal."

"Why do you call it a scandal, Daddy?"

"Because that's all it was. Some nut trying to get attention, offering paintings to the museum."

"But, Daddy, it says here, see——" I sifted through the papers until I found the right article—"that the curator met the donor and that art experts examined the paintings. It wasn't just a hoax. Those paintings existed. Surely you saw Mama's painting. She knew who the donor was. Look what it says:

"Mrs. Middleton said that she was surprised and pleased that one of her paintings was being donated to the museum. She was flattered that the donor regarded her work so highly. When asked the identity of this person, she smiled and said she had been instructed not to reveal the name.

"So, Daddy, you must have known too. Just tell me who the donor is, and I'll do the rest."

That got his attention, and he jerked up straight in his chair. "I'm sorry, Swan. The whole thing is a bad memory, and I was happy to let it go. Maybe your mother did know who this donor was, but I swear she never told me. She wasn't really very excited about the whole thing. She was a nervous wreck having to speak at the opening."

"Did she speak? I mean, even though her painting wasn't there?"

He grimaced. "The whole evening was a bit of a flop, Mary Swan." He took the newspapers from me and shuffled them around absentmindedly. It looked to me as though he was just wasting time.

"You really don't want to talk about it, do you, Daddy?"

"No, Swan. I don't. But you have to believe me, sweetie. If I knew anything that could help you, I'd tell you. I swear I would." He got up and said, "Come with me."

I followed him into his study. I was barefoot, and I liked the feel of the smooth carpet on my toes. Daddy went to his filing cabinet, opened the third drawer down, and pulled out a thick manila file. He laid it on his desk. "Your mother didn't want to have a thing to do with the disappearance. She refused to speak to the authorities. She didn't know the other artists. I'd certainly never heard of them. Anyway, you're welcome to look through the file. Most of it is the same as what Mrs. MacIlvain already gave you." He slid it across his desk to me. "But, Swan, please. There's nothing there. Remember your mother just as you do now."

The way he said it, I felt as though he was begging me to read between the lines of a letter he had never written me. Begging me to keep the memory of Mama the artist neatly arranged like a new box of oil paints.

"Could I go through her things, Dad? Could I look in Mama's studio? Please?"

"I don't think it would be wise."

"Daddy, if you don't want to think about Mama, that's okay. But thinking about her and doing something for her is the best way I'm going to make it through all this. So please. Please let me."

He got up and came to the other side of his desk and ruffled my hair, the way he used to do when I was young. "Her studio's not locked. You can go in there anytime you want, Swan." His voice had dropped about an octave, and I was pretty sure he was holding back tears. But I didn't look into his eyes, because he caught me in a hug, a tight, emotional hug. "Oh, Swan. I just want whatever is best for you and Jimmy."

To say that Rachel was disappointed with the lack of information I gleaned from Daddy was like saying Shakespeare was a half-decent playwright. To lift her spirits, I invited her to come with Ella Mae and me to Grant Park the next day. She sounded fairly interested until she remembered that her older brother, Jamie, had his baseball playoffs that afternoon, and the whole family was expected to go.

As I was finishing up serving lunch I spotted Cassandra, who was trying to eat her spaghetti while Jessie howled in her arms. I don't really know what made me do it, but I went over to her and said,

"May I hold Jessie for you? Give you a chance to eat?"

Her face lit up. "You mean it, Mary Swan? Thanks! My mama's usually here to he'p, but her cousin's doin' right poorly, and she's stayin' with him today."

With a confidence that surprised me, I took the cloth diaper, tossed it over my shoulder, and then gently held Jessie in my arms, cooing at her as I'd seen Carl do. Jessie delighted me with a real smile, and I noticed that in the course of just two weeks she seemed to have grown and changed.

When Carl saw me with Jessie on my shoulder, he gave me an approving nod and a wide grin. "Puddin's hopin' to see you today, you know. Can you come over to the house for a little while, soon as we finish up here?"

I nodded happily.

So that Saturday, after serving spaghetti and holding Jessie, I found myself sitting in Carl's "front room" with the dirty rug and the dirtier dog, and as I sat there, I thought to myself, *How could anyone hate these people?* How? How could you hate a little baby who already had a head full of curls? Or a little girl like Puddin' who was sitting in my lap braiding my hair, her bright eyes dancing with satisfaction as she inspected her work and then let the braids undo themselves when she let go? It would take someone truly evil to hate this child.

Then I thought about Carl, who was settled in the big old easy chair across from us, his almost black eyes looking with so much love at his little sister and his big feet with those worn imitation-leather loafers propped up on the rickety table. Tall and strong, the kind of strong that comes from just a lot of hard, honest work. Why would anyone hate him? A boy who had become a man too early, who raised his siblings and worked a job and went to school. Nothing about the stereotypes of lazy blacks or unintelligent blacks or anything else I'd heard fit Carl.

When Puddin' got up to go outside and play, he asked, "Did you find anything in those papers to help you with that Raven Dare?"

"Yeah, some stuff." I filled him in on my conversation with Daddy the night before.

Then he asked, "Do ya wanna see my saxophone?"

"Yes, of course!"

And so he brought it out. We didn't have a saxophonist in our

orchestra, but I knew the instrument well from all the theory classes
I'd taken. His wasn't new. It even looked a little banged up.

"Do you play in a band?" I asked.

"Yep. At school. Marchin' band, Mary Swan. Best marchin' band
in Atlanta."

That was true, now that I thought about it. Everyone had heard
about Fair Oaks taking the prize last year.

"Do you practice a lot?"

"Practice a whole lot during football season, Mary Swan. A whole
lot. Lots of us in the band. Two hundred."

I ran my hands over the saxophone. "Nice horn."

"Mighty fine, she is. She isn't mine, though. Lease her from the
school. Someday I'll buy her." He talked about the horn as if it was a
good friend.

"Well, play it for me."

He sat back on the bed and started running his long fingers up and
down the keys as he played a bunch of scales. Then he adjusted his
reed, placed the strap over his neck, stood up, and leaned back the
way I'd seen guys do in the movies. He closed his eyes and blew into
the horn.

I played the flute the way I did math problems—adequately, with
a lot of difficulty and practice. But Carl played the saxophone with his
heart and soul. Listening to him made chills run up and down my
spine, even though it was hot as Hades that afternoon.

"Someday you'll have to meet Rachel. She plays her flute like
that—eyes closed and fingers just running all over the keys."

"You and your friend Rachel should bring your flutes down here
sometime. You could play with my band."

"You have a band? All your own?"

"Shore, Mary Swan. A jazz band."

"I don't know much about jazz. And I can't improvise like you."

"Aw, Mary Swan, you might have it in you if you tried." Then he
grinned mischievously. " 'Course it's a known fact that we blacks have
got jazz in the blood. Just runs in our veins. Know what I mean?"

"I wish I knew. I don't think you can teach someone to improvise."

"Sure you can, girl! Anyway, you're already a master at improvi-
sation. You told me yourself about making up those poems. That's
what got you the Raven Dare, isn't it?"

"But that's different. I mean making up poems is easy for me. It's . . ."

"It's in your blood, flowing through your veins." The way he looked at me when he said that made my face get all red. Mainly it was because our eyes met and locked, and it was as if he was daring me not to let him see inside my mind. I don't think Carl ever meant to flirt with me. But I'm pretty sure that at that moment something passed between us, something that Rachel would call "chemistry."

"I'll bring my flute the next time if you want," I said quickly.

He didn't answer but went back to playing the saxophone, swaying his body to the left and to the right and leaning his head back and making his instrument sing the way it was supposed to. When he stopped, his skin was glistening with sweat. He held out his saxophone and asked, "Wanna try it?"

And before I could answer, he'd put the strap around my neck, stood behind me, and started placing my fingers on the keys. Then he chuckled and said, "Blow, Mary Swan!"

I knew that reed instruments took a different kind of embouchure than woodwinds, so I wasn't a bit surprised that the first sounds that came out of the horn were horrible squeaks, which set Carl to chuckling even harder. But eventually I got out an A and then a B and then a C.

"Good goin', girl!" He patted me on the back.

That suddenly made me feel even hotter and a bit dizzy. I told myself it was from blowing so hard, but I knew it was from something else. I handed the sax back to Carl and said, "I'd better be going. What time is it anyway?"

Carl just smiled at me and said, "I'll walk you back to the church. Ella Mae'll have my hide if I let you walk these streets alone."

We stepped back out in the sun, and I blinked my eyes several times to adjust to the fierce light. Puddin' was jumping rope with a friend, and for a moment I stood and listened to them chanting as they jumped.

"Einy, meeny, miny moe, catch a rabbit by his toe, if he hollers let him go, einy, meeny, miny moe."

I went over to her, and when she stopped, I ran my fingers along her braids and kissed her cheek and said, "See you soon, Puddin'." She dropped her jump rope and gave me a quick hug.

Carl fell into stride beside me. I didn't say a word.

"Somethin' the matter?"

"No. Not at all. Just thinking about how well you play the sax. You've got a lot of talent for music. Just like Rachel." He smiled at that. "I'll see if I can get her to come next week, and we'll bring our flutes."

But what I was really thinking was that I liked Carl; I liked him a lot. And I kept repeating in my mind, as if I were talking to Daddy, *But we're the same. We like music and kids and books. We're the same.*

But, of course, we weren't the same at all. And when I waved good-bye to him that afternoon, I swallowed hard and had to force myself to find something to talk to Ella Mae about while she drove me home, so I wouldn't be remembering the way Carl had looked at me with his head tilted back and his eyebrows slightly raised and a puckered smile on his lips.

Chapter 10

School started on Tuesday, September fourth, the day after Labor Day. I hadn't been on the campus of Wellington since the night Rachel and I climbed the wall and searched for the riddle. When Ella Mae drove me through the gates that morning, I felt an odd mixture of excitement and heaviness. My life had been so simple and uninterrupted on June first. Today the administration building's columns did not look ghostly at all as I hopped out of the car, book satchel in hand, and waved good-bye to Ella Mae. I fingered one of the fluted columns and walked into the garden area where the ape-man statue stood. I stuck three fingers in his mouth, then leaned on the statue and cried. Everything had changed!

Dear, dear Rachel appeared beside me, resting a hand on mine, draping an arm over my bent shoulders, and led me into the assembly hall. That's how we filed into the big auditorium where morning assembly was held—all of us in our cotton blouses and gray jumpers with our heads turned down, as though the weight of our dead parents was pressing down on our shoulders.

So the morning of the first day of school at Wellington in the fall of 1962 was very subdued. That's the only word for it. All of us had seen each other at the funerals, but it did something awful to the spirit of the school when we got together and realized that thirteen of us had lost loved ones in the crash. The usual silliness and gossip and chatter were replaced by a common grief.

The morning assembly was a memorial service, and each of us who had been robbed because of Orly went forward and received yellow roses. Lanie Bradshaw, the girl in my class who had lost both of her parents, walked down the aisle in front of me. Lanie had always been considered a tomboy and was a real athlete, with short-cropped jet-black hair and a thick, compact build. But walking behind her that morning, I thought she looked misshapen, her shoulders slumped and her jumper hanging loosely. I wanted to reach out and give her a hug and ask her how she was doing, *really*. But I didn't because I was concentrating hard on not sobbing out loud. Not that it would have mattered, because everyone else was crying too.

Dr. Stadlander, the principal, a stout woman of German descent with an impossible accent that we loved to imitate, began to speak. "Girls. This tragedy will be used to make us stronger. We will pull together and embrace those who are grieving. Wellington . . ." I shut my eyes, wishing she would stop reminding me of what I'd tried all summer to forget. But of course, I would never, we would never, forget.

By nine-fifteen all the tears were dried, and we left the auditorium in little clusters. Just ahead of Rachel and me, Patty Masters launched into a story about one of her infamous capers. "Y'all aren't gonna believe what happened to me the other day."

When she talked, her big brown eyes grew wide, and her blond eyebrows lifted high on her forehead, and her softly curled blond hair, which fell practically to her waist, swished from side to side.

"I was at the A&P with my mom and had the grocery cart loaded full, sweating up a storm. All of a sudden my bra snapped and got all tangled somehow in my shirt. . . ." Patty, all five feet eleven of her, was well developed, to say the least. But much greater than her physical size was her incredible sense of humor and timing, and at that moment, we needed her genius as never before. The tension evaporated in the stuffy auditorium, and ten of us around Patty began to laugh hysterically, the kind of laughter that makes everyone else stare and then laugh too, so that pretty soon everyone was laughing. Most of the girls had no idea what they were even laughing at, but we were all thankful for the excuse to turn our thoughts from morbid memories.

Wellington was an elite private day school. The boarding program had ended two years earlier when Lilly Bawden was caught smoking in the bathroom for the fourth time. She wasn't smoking cigarettes. The Honor Council decided that boarders brought nothing but trouble and extra expense, so the boarding program, which had never housed more than fifteen girls from any one class, was done away with. Now fifty-nine socialites-in-training made up the junior class, with about the same number for each of the classes from sixth grade through senior year. Four hundred thirteen girls in all. Four hundred thirteen girls in gray jumpers and white cotton button-down blouses and white bobby socks and saddle oxfords.

But although we were all dressed alike, we did not in any way all look the same. I was just average in every way, but some of those girls were what we called "cream of the crop." I did have long fingers, which were good for playing the flute, I guess, but I bit my fingernails whenever I was nervous. The beautiful girls, some of them at least, wore makeup and paid twenty dollars to get their hair cut at that fancy new salon at Rich's. Rachel said I was paranoid about my looks, but she didn't know what it was like to be so terribly plain and skinny in a school filled with remarkable brains and beauty. She couldn't possibly understand.

But I think she understood another type of paranoia, even though she wouldn't admit it: paranoia over religion. Wellington had a reputation to uphold, so getting in was rather difficult—unless, of course, your family had a lot of money, which many of the families did. But Wellington being a Protestant Christian preparatory school, first choice was given to what we called the WASPs—white Anglo-Saxon Protestants. So no matter how rich a Jewish girl's family was, what mattered most were her grades. At least that's what Rachel always said, and knowing all the Jewish girls in my class, I had to agree with her. They were smart.

The school was considered one of the top in the Southeast, so good Jewish families, concerned for their daughters' education, chose Wellington. There was no rule against it. They simply had to agree to comply with the school etiquette. Chapel every morning. Prayers in homeroom. Mandatory Bible classes—Old *and* New Testaments. I guessed the parents figured their girls could hear a little about Jesus for the sake of their education. But it wasn't exactly easy to be Jewish at Wellington.

There was this unspoken thing, this difference that I could never really understand. Being a WASP placed you on a higher social level at Wellington than being a Catholic or a Jew. Well, no one ever said that, but we understood it, as if it were as much a part of the dress code as our gray jumpers and black-and-white saddle oxfords.

And if Catholics and Jews had a hard time getting into Wellington, blacks were not even considered. In the spring of 1963 a hot story in the news would be the fact that Reverend Martin Luther King's five-year-old son's application had been turned down at another private school. In the end, the school relented because its church-based funding required it. The church adopted a definite policy saying that segregation on the sole basis of race was inconsistent with the Christian religion. But that was still months away, and to my knowledge, no black family had ever tried to enroll their daughter at Wellington.

We were all friends with each other at Wellington, but each girl knew her social position. Sometimes it seemed that the Catholic girls felt like second-class citizens, and the Jewish girls felt almost like outcasts. Except for Rachel Abrams. She never cared one iota for stupid traditions, and she refused to be bullied by some unwritten rule. And anyway, as she told me frequently, her family were not practicing Jews. They were staunch atheists.

By the end of that first day, our love for gossip returned, and the buzz was all about the Back-to-School Ball and who had invited whom and what we'd be wearing on Friday night. Will Weston had asked Rachel, and I was hoping we could double-date, because I really had no desire to be stuck in a car with Herbert and Virginia again. Although the prospect of attending the ball with Robbie Bartholomew made me blush with pleasure, I think my greater excitement was for the fact that Rachel had agreed to go to Grant Park with me on Saturday. With my thoughts bouncing back and forth in my brain like a tennis ball between Robbie and Carl, I didn't know how I'd make it through the rest of the week.

The day before the ball, I laid four different outfits out on my bed and tried to figure out which one to wear. Rachel had already given me her opinion, and when Ella Mae came into my room, dragging the vacuum cleaner behind her, I thought I'd get her advice too.

"Which of these dresses will make me look beautiful, Ella Mae? I mean, as beautiful as someone who looks like me can be?"

Ella Mae glanced at the dresses and frowned. "Don't ya be worryin' none about bein' beautiful, Mary Swan. Uh-un. No, ma'am."

Mama always said that if and when Ella Mae said more than two sentences at a time I should pay attention. "I don't always understand what she means," Mama confided with a laugh, "but I know this. It's important, and she's usually right." Mama said Ella Mae wasn't what I called book smart—I don't even think she could read—but she had been through a lot, and according to Mama, "That grows you up fast and gives you character."

Ella Mae's husband, Roy, was small and skinny and had the reddest eyes. He drank a lot and couldn't hold down a job, so Daddy sometimes had him come out and do yard work, but it always ended up with Ella Mae chasing after him and saying, "Git yorese'f ta work, Roy!" And twice Daddy had caught him nipping at his bottles of gin, and once he was asleep by the pool with a girlie magazine.

Anyway, when Ella Mae started harping on me about what was beautiful, I guessed I should at least give it some thought.

"Ain't no blessing to be born beautiful, Mary Swan, I tell you it ain't. That kind of thing don't have nothin' to do with who you are really, deep down inside. Ain't nothin' you's done to deserve beauty. It jus' happens." Ella Mae spoke with such conviction that it seemed almost like a speech she had given somewhere before. "But we's a twisted world, chile. Jus' 'cause someone's got a perty head, we's ready to fall down and worship 'im, without him ever provin' he has anything worth worshippin'. And often it's the opposite. We make them beautiful people into some kinda celebrity without payin' one bit o' attention as to how they lives their lives."

That made me think about the way everyone at school kind of worshipped Elvis Presley and Marilyn Monroe. And Natalie Wood.

"Uh-uh, my chile. Don't you be worryin' none about beauty. You'll turn out jus' fine. Be sure of what you want, of what you pray for. If I was you, I'd want to have a good head on my shoulders and a heart that loves God. He's the one in charge, ya know. My, my, chile." She plugged in the cord to the vacuum cleaner and took another look at the dresses. Then with a smile on her lips, she pointed to the pale yellow off-the-shoulder dress. "Dat one will be mighty fine on you, Mary Swan. Mighty fine."

While Ella Mae vacuumed, I looked at my face in the mirror and wondered if it really was okay to be how I was. I had braces on my teeth, the color of my hair was a rather plain mousy brown. I was skinny, that was the only word for it. Skinny when all the other girls were becoming nicely rounded in all the right places. But I did like my eyes. They were a bright blue-green with black lashes, thick and long, surrounding them. Once Mary Alice Underwood, one of the popular girls in my class, but not particularly known for her tact, had remarked, "Too bad, Mary Swan, that the rest of you doesn't match up with your eyes."

They were Mama's eyes, striking. Of course all of Mama's appearance had been striking. A natural blonde with a little red in her hair (and a little help now and then), she had perfect jade green eyes and black lashes and a pouty, full mouth. She always looked like she should be on the cover of a magazine. She called herself *coquette*, which in French meant that she loved stylish clothes and fancy affairs, but at home she looked terrific in Dad's paint-splattered old blue Oxford shirt and those tight Audrey Hepburn black stretch pants with ballerina slippers.

I thought about Ella Mae's words and agreed with her. Mama's beauty had been an asset in some ways, but I think it had driven her crazy too. She wanted to be recognized as a fine painter without the addition of the "very lovely Sheila Middleton" tagged on, as if the fact that she was physically attractive made her a better painter.

Ella Mae was right. Beauty was nothing you earned. It didn't deserve the recognition we gave it. It was a curse for those who had it and those who admired it. I agreed with all of that in my head.

But in my heart, for the night of my first dance, I longed with everything within me to be beautiful.

When Robbie picked me up the next night, I had on that off-the-shoulder dress and a little of Mama's blush and lipstick and perfume, and Rachel had shown me how to curl my hair on the ends. Robbie wore a plaid sport coat and khaki pants and white bucks. He had slicked down his auburn hair and parted it to the side, which made him look a little older. That night I noticed how his eyes really were topaz, almost like the gem I had on a ring Mama had given me. He towered over me, which made me feel safe.

I liked the way he looked that night, even if everything about him did match. Plus he said the words I had longed to hear.

"You look great, Mary Swan. Really pretty."

I beamed. "Thanks." And after an awkward moment of Robbie

shaking Daddy's hand, while Jimmy raced down the steps to say hello, we went outside and got into his fancy new convertible. I noticed with a mixture of excitement and relief that no one else occupied the backseat.

It took us forty-five minutes to drive to the party, so with the top down on the convertible, my hair was pretty much ruined before we even arrived. But that didn't matter. Robbie and I laughed and talked about all kinds of stuff, and to my great delight, I found it wasn't hard at all to make conversation. He even thought that my jokes were funny.

For the third year in a row, the Back-to-School Ball was held on George Dixon's sprawling horse farm in Carollton, Georgia. Mr. Dixon had two sons at Mendon's Private School for Boys and a daughter at Wellington and enough money to treat half of Atlanta to a party. Under one striped tent were four long tables, the kind you can rent, laden with rare roast beef and horseradish, spicy meatballs, stuffed mushrooms, cheese balls, fresh fruit, raw vegetables and dips, smoked salmon, and various potato and vegetable salads. Robbie and I sampled every bit of food on each table, and then, when we were stuffed beyond belief, we laughed foolishly and arm in arm made our way to the other big tent, the one with the live band.

"You want to dance?" Robbie asked, a little shyly.

"I'd love to, but I'm not that great at it."

"Me either. Let's give it a try."

So we danced to almost all of the songs the band played, and when Robbie held my hands as we jitterbugged, I felt those familiar prickles. My hair fell limply on my bare shoulders and perspiration dotted my cheeks, but I didn't care. I felt like Mama's portrait of me as a little girl, happy, happy, happy! I thought that maybe this was the best night of my life, and I hoped it would go on forever.

We were both burning up after the latest jitterbug. "Need something to drink?" Robbie asked, wiping perspiration from his forehead.

"Yes, some punch!"

So with punch glasses in hand, we stood outside the tent and listened to the laughter and the music, and I looked up at the sky, which had turned suddenly very dark and was flecked with stars. "A million of them, don't you bet, Robbie?"

"At least."

I closed my eyes and breathed so deeply. "Absolutely perfect."

"What is?"

"This evening."

"Then make up a poem about it, Mary Swan." His eyes were twinkling, and a shy smile played on his lips. "Everybody says that you're a genius with poems."

"They do?" I blushed.

He nodded eagerly.

"Okay, but you have to understand that it's not really poetry. Just silly rhymes."

"That's fine by me." And the way Robbie was looking at me, I felt like I might be able to reach up and grab one of those million stars.

I ran my fingers through my damp hair, crinkled up my nose, and made my eyes into little slits that captured a half moon and a few hundred twinkling specks. "I'd rather see stars than ride in cars or eat cookies out of jars or go to bars. I'd rather see stars. I'd rather see lakes than have tummy aches from chocolate cakes or double-takes. I'd rather see lakes. . . ."

"I'd rather dance."

I shrugged. "Okay. I'd rather dance than wear your pants or water your plants or advance in a trance."

"That's a good one!"

"I'd rather stay up late than contemplate or radiate or initiate. I like to stay up late."

"Me too."

"I'd rather read a book than ever cook or take a look at a—"

"Fish on a hook!"

"Exactly. A fish on a hook. I'd rather read a book. I'd rather laugh out loud than be in a crowd or learn to be proud or live on a cloud. I'd rather laugh out loud." Which we both did, and which made the moment seem suddenly almost magical.

"Where'd you learn to do that anyway?" he asked with admiration.

"Oh, I didn't ever learn it. I was just born with silly rhymes in my head. I guess the way some people are good with numbers. Not that it's worth anything."

"Someday it might be. Can't say playing football is worth that much either."

"Are you crazy? Everyone knows you'll get offered a bunch of scholarships to college."

He shrugged. "Yeah, I guess." I liked the way he didn't seem very impressed with himself. "Do you want to write later on? I mean, as a job?"

I didn't hesitate. "No, I don't want to write. I want to paint. Like Mama."

He fumbled with a button on his shirt and took a sip of punch. "Is it hard, thinking about her. . . ?"

"Since she's dead," I helped him out. "Actually, I think that knowing about Mama's talent gives me a lot of motivation. . . ." *To solve the riddle,* I almost said, and stopped myself just in time. "Gives me motivation to pursue art. Someday. In her honor, you know? Mama sketched in almost every famous European city. Someday I'll go back and visit." I rattled on as we walked back to the food tent. "And someday her paintings are going to be hanging in the most famous museums."

"Really?"

"Well, I hope so. Two of her paintings are at the High right now, as part of a special exhibition for—well, you know, for the painters who were victims."

"Yeah, I remember Mom saying something about it."

A group of three other couples stood beside us, half listening to our conversation. All three of the girls were in my class at Wellington, Millie Garrett and Julie Jacobs and Gail Anderson, and their dates were from Mendon.

"I've seen your mom's paintings there," Millie Garrett commented. "Julie and I went with our moms right before school started." She lowered her voice respectfully. "I love that painting of the Swan House. It makes you want to *live* in that mansion. And that painting of you as a little girl—well, I laughed and I cried when I saw that!"

I felt like hugging Millie at that moment, the way she was raving about Mama.

"I didn't realize that your mom was such a good painter, Mary Swan!" Julie Jacobs added enthusiastically. "I mean, I knew she was an artist, but imagine maybe one day having her paintings in really famous museums!"

Somehow, talking about Mama as an artist didn't hurt. I felt proud. "She painted the most beautiful things."

Herbert Thomas and Virginia Lawson joined the group at that moment. I hardly paid any attention until Herbert stumbled over to me and I caught a whiff of alcohol on his breath. For those students who craved beer, the Dixons' land offered a number of woodsy areas where kegs could be concealed. I don't think the adults worried much about beer, anyway. The hard stuff was what bothered them.

By this time in the evening Herbert had found plenty of hard stuff, and his swagger and slightly drooping eyes betrayed him before he even opened his mouth. When he did speak, the words were slurred and almost incomprehensible.

Robbie rolled his eyes and whispered, "Let's go back outside."

But I ignored him. "As I was saying, she painted great portraits and still li—"

"Your mama was crazy, Mary Swan. A raving lunatic, that Sheila Middleton," Herbert butted in. He started to laugh this awful, drunken cackle. Everyone stopped talking and stared. He had fairly shouted it.

At first I didn't react. Robbie's face turned a dark-stained red, and he started to say something to Herbert, but before he could, I blurted out, "What are you talking about? She was an artist!"

"A lunatic," he repeated.

An extremely uncomfortable silence ensued. Everyone in the group was staring at me, and I got a sick, quivery feeling inside.

"My mother was not a lunatic."

Eyes sagging, Herbert shrugged, "No one ever wanted you to know the truth about your mom. That's all."

Virginia's face was bright red. "Herbert, please," she said with a nervous little giggle. Then she whispered, "You're talking about the dead. It isn't right."

He fiddled with his glass and muttered, "Sorry," with a silly smile.

"You should be sorry, Herbert!" Robbie said angrily, coming right up to his face.

"You're the lunatic!" Millie Garrett seethed at Herbert. "You make me sick."

And the others in the group were nodding their heads and saying things like "Don't pay any attention to him, Mary Swan. He's just a good-for-nothing louse."

Robbie took hold of my arm. "He has no idea what he's saying, Mary Swan. He's drunk out of his mind."

I shook off his arm when we were outside and whispered way too loud, "But he said Mama was crazy!" I was shaking.

"Forget it, Mary Swan. He doesn't know anything."

"But he does! He knows something I don't. A secret about my mother!"

"Mary Swan." Robbie was both alarmed and annoyed by my reaction. "For heaven's sake, the guy's drunk. Don't you think you're being a little bit oversensitive?" Then he saw the blaze in my eyes and added, "It's understandable, of course. With all you've been through. Come on, let's go get a Coke." He took my arm again gently, but I flung it away.

"I need to be alone for a minute," I said, half angrily, half apologetically, walking away from him. Something was throbbing in the back of my head, some memory trying to escape. Then it came to me.

I was about five years old, and I was sitting in Ella Mae's lap as I often did at the end of the day, waiting for Mama to get home from the doctor's. Except that this day she didn't go to the doctor's office. This day, for some reason, she was still at home, upstairs in her studio. And suddenly I wasn't in Ella Mae's lap anymore, but standing wide-eyed in the entrance hall watching Ella Mae carry Mama's limp body into Daddy's study and lay her on the couch.

Ella Mae turned and saw me and did something she'd never done before. She yelled, "Git up to yore room, Mary Swan!"

Me climbing the steps to my room and seeing blood on the carpet in the hall.

Trixie appearing from nowhere. Jimmy crying. The sound of a siren screaming outside.

Trixie explaining, "Your mama fell and hurt herself. But it'll be okay. It'll be okay."

Me looking at Trixie's tear-stained face that was all smudged with mascara.

And later, Daddy and Jimmy and I going to visit Mama at a fancy kind of hospital. Mama had been sick, was all they told me.

I put my head in my hands, sank to the ground, and cried.

Poor Robbie found me there. "Mary Swan! What's the matter?"

But I shook my head and motioned with my hand for him to stay away. He must have gone to find Rachel, because a moment later she came running over to me.

"Swan—what in the world. . . ?"

"I want to get drunk," I whispered.

Rachel narrowed her eyes. "What is the matter with you?"

I took her hand and pulled her after me, leaving poor Robbie standing in the field. "Show me where the hard liquor is hidden," I demanded.

"Swan, for heaven's sake . . ."

So I left Rachel too, and I found Billy Martin, who was known to be practically an alcoholic, and begged him to fix me a drink. He led me to a yellow ice cooler, lifted the top, and I grabbed a bottle without bothering to read the label.

Robbie caught up with me. "Look, Mary Swan, I won't take you home drunk."

"Then let someone else do it, Boy Scout!" I grabbed the glass from Billy and stomped off in a fury, feeling panicky inside. I gulped down the wretched liquid, coughing and sputtering as my eyes filled with tears. And I kept saying to myself, *Why are you reacting like this, idiot? What in the world is the matter with you?*

"Swan, come back here!" Rachel pleaded.

"Leave me alone! Both of you leave me alone!" I cried angrily. And then in a whimper, "Alone, please."

I flopped down in the woods, out of sight of the festivities and moaned, low and doleful. *"Your mama was a lunatic. Raving crazy. No one wanted you to know."*

Herbert's slurred words had triggered something painful in my memory. I knew Mama had had her dark moods, but I had never let myself think about what those dark moods meant. It had never mattered before. Daddy had called it her artistic "gift." But Herbert had given it a different name. *"Lunatic."* And suddenly, I wasn't at all sure that Herbert was wrong.

After I'd cried alone for a while, I went back to the yellow cooler and drank and drank that stinking stuff until my throat was burned red and I was ready to puke. I kept drinking with Robbie watching helplessly, begging me to let him take me home, and Rachel cursing at me and tugging on my arm.

So instead of being the best day of my life, my first dance ended up being the worst. The absolute worst. Even worse than when I learned about the plane crash. When Mama had perished in Paris, my memory of her had been sweet. Now her name had been slandered, and instead of shaking my head and calling Herbert a fool, something inside of me was exploding in pain. *"Crazy. A lunatic."*

Robbie did drive me home around midnight. I laughed horribly and cried and yelled, "My mama isn't crazy!" and "Why didn't you tell me she was crazy?"

The light to the front porch was on, and I stumbled out of the car and up the flagstone steps with Robbie holding my arm.

"I'm so sorry, Mary Swan," he said miserably.

I hiccuped and said, "Don't worry about it, Boy Scout," then fell in his arms, giggling and then crying.

"Are you gonna be all right?"

"Great. Just great, Robert H. Bartholomew. A greeeaaat time to-night. A real good time." I fumbled for the doorknob, turned it, and left him standing there with his mouth hanging wide open.

Chapter 11

The next morning when I woke up I remembered the long night of vomiting, and my throbbing head told me immediately that a hangover felt a lot different than getting slapped in the eye by rednecks. Neither were very good memories. This one left me listless. But I had to talk to Trixie. Not Daddy or Ella Mae or Rachel, but Trixie. She'd tell me the truth.

So I dragged myself to the bathroom and threw a bunch of cold water on my face. I didn't bother to brush my hair, which was one tangled mass. I pulled on a pair of Bermuda shorts and a T-shirt and wobbled down the two flights of stairs and out the door, barefoot. I walked straight through the yard and crossed the street. The pavement was already hot. I banged on Trixie's door.

She answered it, her blond curls made blonder by the sun and her face tanned and her lips painted with bright pink lipstick.

"Swannee!" she sang out in several slow syllables. Then, "Swannee, you look aw-ful!"

I marched into the spick-and-span house, through the hall with its high ceiling and hardwood floors, and plopped on the Louis XIV sofa, as Mama had called it, that was covered in green chintz.

"Was Mama really crazy, Trixie? I have to know." No hello, how are you. No hug. She got nothing from me except an exasperated groan and red eyes and those two sentences.

Trixie had followed me into her living room, her high heels clicking on the hardwood floor. She sat down beside me all ladylike and furrowed her brow. "What are you talking about, honey?"

I sniffled, ran my finger under my nose, and asked, "Do you have any orange juice, Trixie?" Every other adult I knew, I addressed as Mr.

or Mrs. or Dr. or whatever. But not Trixie and not Ella Mae.

"Shore do, honey," she sang out sympathetically.

So sipping on some orange juice, I told her the whole horrible story of the Back-to-School Ball and Herbert's drunken announcement and my reaction.

"It was the most awful thing. Poor Robbie. I was terrible to him. And I just kept drinking and drinking. Why did I act like that? If I'd just ignored Herbert's comment, everything would have been all right. But I couldn't, Trixie. I couldn't. Somehow I just knew he was saying something that his mother had sworn him to secrecy about years ago." I leaned forward and pronounced the next words carefully. "It's true, then, isn't it, Trixie? Mama was crazy."

When Trixie got nervous, she mashed her lips together several times, the way you do when you're putting on lipstick. Her tanned face, perfectly made up, showed a hint of perspiration. Her blue eyes, usually carefree, clouded. And those perfect lips that met in the center with two perfect peaks quivered slightly. "Mary Swan, people say all kinds of things. You can't pay any attention to it. You said he was drunk."

"But it feels true." That came out in a sob.

I could smell the delicate aroma of her perfume. She took my hand, the way she liked to do. I noticed the perfectly manicured nails, her pale yellow silk suit, everything about her in place, except her sad eyes and quivering lips. "Your mother was a wonderful woman whom I loved dearly." Her voice caught. "Whom so many loved. Don't listen to careless words at a party, Mary Swan. People say all kinds of cruel things." She reached for a pack of cigarettes, pulled one out, and lit it.

I felt a little shiver go through me, and I remembered the scandal from years and years ago. Trixie's scandal. Remembered her crying on Mama's floral couch and Mama shooing me upstairs when she caught me peeking around the corner. People had certainly said a lot of cruel things about Trixie when her husband had left her years ago for a nineteen-year-old brunette. Apparently Tony Hamilton had been having an affair with a co-ed for over a year when Trixie finally figured it out. Not that anyone was really surprised. Tony Hamilton had a reputation as long as his arm.

I was only six or seven at the time, but I clearly remembered how Trixie, pregnant with Lucy, would spend hours crying at our house.

Of course, it wasn't until much later that I understood why she had been crying, and why Daddy and Mama had seemed so angry, and why Ella Mae kept saying "My, my. That poor woman."

Divorced and well-off, Trixie had gotten to keep the house, stayed there, raised her daughter, and I guess she'd probably heard all the gossip that I had heard about her. That's how I knew that behind her appearance of a perfectly beautiful Southern belle, she really had a lot more substance to her. And that's what I thought of that morning as I cuddled on her couch with my glass of orange juice.

All those thoughts had taken no more than a couple of seconds, and now Trixie was saying something else. "You knew your mama, and you remember the way she was. Please don't let careless words tarnish that memory. Please don't, Swannee." I noticed for the first time how crinkled the lines were beside Trixie's eyes.

"But I told you, Trixie. It feels true. You've got to tell me about Mama. I'm not stupid, you know. I remember how she locked herself in her room. I remember the time Ella Mae carried her downstairs and the blood on the carpet and how she went away for a 'rest' and how Daddy took Jimmy and me to visit her in that big old house. I remember all the bottles of pills by her bed. If I try hard, I'll piece it all together, Trixie. But don't make me guess. Tell me the truth."

"Swannee, there's really not much to say."

"Please, Trixie. Daddy won't ever tell me. You know it. And Ella Mae will be loyal to death to whatever Daddy and Mama have sworn her to. It has to be you."

She licked her lips and took a deep breath. "Yes, your mama struggled with depression. Sometimes severe depression. Usually at a certain time of the year. I think maybe it was the genius in her that made her so delicate and yet so strong. She had to be strong to deal with all those battles in her head. She saw doctors and she took pills, but she said the pills killed her inside so that she couldn't paint.

"It's a sickness, Swannee. I'm sure it is. But most people just take it for pure craziness. Your daddy was so careful with Sheila. We all did what we could to help. That day that you remember, well, it was then your father knew she needed more help than she was getting. The psychiatrist admitted her to a clinic. Poor Sheila. She had a heart for people who suffer. She understood. . . ."

By now Trixie's eyes were moist, and I felt as though her heart and mine might just break in two again. I knew right then that I didn't want to hear any more. Not yet. I grabbed her in a fierce hug and whispered through the tightness in my throat, "You don't have to say any more. Thank you for telling me."

I left her house a little before eleven and walked back across the street, more resolved than ever to solve the Raven Dare. In the course of twenty-four hours the whole thing had become a lot more personal. Now the black bird spread his powerful wings out wide and cast his shadow like an omen, not just on an art museum or a plane crash or even an artist, but on a family. *My* family. I wasn't sure I wanted to find out things that Daddy and Ella Mae and Trixie had obviously tried to hide from me all of my life.

"You knew your mama, and you remember the way she was. Please don't let careless words tarnish that memory. . . . He was drunk, Mary Swan. He had no idea what he was saying. . . . You just let that whole thing rest, Swannee. There's nothing you can learn about your mom from that scandal."

Why did my imagination push me along, past all reason? Why did I have to ignore the warnings of those I loved and who loved me? Was it the curse of the Raven? Or was it just fate? Fate that caused me to run headlong into the truth? Miss Abigail had said that the truth would make me free. It was even in the Bible. And so I determined I would know the truth, no matter what.

When I got back home that Saturday morning, Jimmy met me at the door. "Where've you been, Swan? Daddy just left to play golf and was all worried, and Ella Mae's been waiting on you for fifteen minutes, and Rachel has called twice, and Robbie just phoned too."

"I was just at Trixie's."

"Well, you look horrible. Anyway, call Rachel back." Even though his words were insolent, I could tell that Jimmy had been scared for me too. In fact, as he left the room, I think he wiped his eyes.

I picked up the phone and dialed Rachel's number. When she answered, I simply said, "How awful was I last night?"

"Awful. Very awful. You need to apologize to Robbie."

"I can't. I'm mortified. I'm sure he hates me anyway."

"You're mean, Swan. Just plain ole mean."

"It's not mean; it's despair. I've been sitting in Trixie's den hearing her tell me about my mother, and if you think that's fun, well, think again. I can't help it if that drunken Herbert said something that triggered a lot of memories."

"Fine, then. Just explain that to Robbie. He deserves an explanation. He'll understand."

"He's already called, but I wasn't here."

"Well, call him back."

"Impossible. I can't just call a boy on the phone!"

"Imbecile. Well, then don't count on me going with you to Grant Park today." She hung up on me, really mad.

Ella Mae waddled into the kitchen and said, "Lawdy, chile, if you don't look like somebody done hit you over the head with a fryin' pan!"

Jimmy, who kept finding reasons to come back into the kitchen, added, "Yeah! You do, Mary Swan. You really do."

"Oh, shut up!" I spat at Jimmy. "Ella Mae, can you get me some aspirin?" She showed me the whites of her eyes and a very crinkled forehead before she left the kitchen in search of aspirin. When she came back, Jimmy was gone.

"You done got yorese'f a hangover, Mary Swan? Did you git into the likker at that there party?"

"It's not what you think, Ella Mae," I said as I swallowed the aspirin with the aid of a glass of water. "I'll be okay."

"Well, you ain't gonna go downtown lookin' like that. No sir, you ain't."

"Oh, come on, Ella Mae," I said lamely, but in truth, the absolute last thing I felt like doing was serving up pots of spaghetti. Even with Carl. And my head started throbbing twice as hard at the thought of trying to play my flute or listen to Carl making his saxophone moan in its loud, jazzy way.

"Okay, I guess you're right. You go on, Ella Mae. I'll be here with Jimmy. Tell Miss Abigail I'll see her next week, and—" I almost said, *Tell Carl hi,* but stopped myself. It didn't matter. Ella Mae knew.

She smiled in her cross way and said, "I ain't gonna be leavin' you here like that, with yore daddy gone and you in one foul temper. Heaven knows what you'd do ta Jimmy. Un-unn." And so it was decided.

I dragged myself up the stairs to my room and flung myself across my bed. After a while my headache subsided, and I drifted off to sleep.

When I woke, it was after three. I groggily got off my bed and made my way down to the kitchen, where I poured myself a tall glass of lemonade. Daddy was still playing golf, which I thought was a good sign that maybe he was feeling better, and Jimmy had left a note on the kitchen table saying he'd gone to play at Andy Bartholomew's. I groaned to myself, remembering Robbie. Poor Robbie. Then I called Rachel, but she had gone horseback riding, so I left a message with her brother, Jamie, for her to come over when she got back.

I found Ella Mae in the den, ironing in front of the TV with her back turned to me. I tiptoed away, and that's when I decided to go to Mama's studio. I climbed the stairs to the second floor and walked down the hall of the west wing with my heart racing. It was somber, almost dark, because all the doors leading to the rooms were shut and there was no window at the end of the hall. I hardly ever went into Mama's studio, and I had no idea what I expected to find.

The door to the studio was shut but not locked. When I pushed it open, it creaked. Then a burst of sunlight rushed upon me. The studio had one wall that was nothing but big wide windows. That made me smile unexpectedly. The room was big and airy and smelled of oil paints, especially after having the door closed for four months.

Several paintings were stashed on shelves; others, unfinished, leaned against chairs and a table. The unfinished self-portrait that had appeared in *LIFE* magazine was still sitting on an easel. I looked away quickly. Another easel held the bare beginnings of an outdoor scene of dogwoods, about to sprout blossoms of pink and white. Except that Mama had never gotten to finish it.

I walked to the window that looked out on the backyard and pressed my nose to the pane, trying to remember something important about this room. I closed my eyes and saw myself pumping my legs, the swing on the hickory tree carrying me higher and higher as I squealed with delight. And Mama was there with her paints and easel and palette. That made me smile again. I had always been happy when Mama was painting.

Then I remembered another day when I was about four or five. Ella Mae must have been sick or tending to a family matter, because she wasn't there. I was home with Mama. She had just put Jimmy down for a nap and she said, "Would you like to come into my *atelier* and watch me work?" She always called her studio her *atelier* and pronounced the word with a delicious French accent.

My eyes got really big and excited, and I just nodded. Mama's *atelier* was off limits to everyone else. We never dared to intrude on her privacy there. Consequently, I had rarely ventured inside. On this day, Mama took my hand and led me in, as if it were a big castle. I was immediately entranced by the smell of the paints and the vivid colors that were splashed on her canvases and all the many different sizes and textures of paintbrushes.

"It smells good in here, Mama. A different kind of good."

"Mmm, yes, Swannee. Isn't it heavenly? Paints and life and nature. That's what it smells like."

Daddy and Mama had moved into the house in 1949, right before Jimmy was born. Right away Mama, eight months pregnant, had wanted to set up a place to paint. She had picked her room—in the back right-hand corner of the house with the windows that opened out onto the backyard, giving a view of the flowers and the hickory tree and the green, green grass. And she had Daddy put in enormous glass windows so that light came in from every direction. Her easel was always facing these windows, and usually two or three dirty coffee cups lay around on the floor.

"All you can see is the woods and the yard, everywhere you look!" I had exclaimed in childish wonder.

"There's your swing and the hickory tree. I can sit in here and imagine you swinging every single day."

"And sometimes I am swinging with Ella Mae and Jimmy, Mama. Sometimes I can look up and see you painting!"

"Look, Swannee, I've set up your own little easel here. You can paint while I paint."

"Oh, Mama! Thank you!"

Looking back, I can see Mama's idealistic, spontaneous nature taking over and her imagining that I would sit calmly in my little corner and paint. But of course I didn't. I spilled my cup of water and I cried over my first painting and I asked Mama a hundred questions. And I didn't see how nervous she was getting.

"Stop your whining, Swannee! Stop it right now!" she yelled at me finally, just as her mother Mamie often did when she was mad. "If you can't sit still and be quiet and paint, then you'll have to find something else to do and leave me alone. Mama has to work. Do you understand?"

I nodded and bit my lip, unsure of what to do.

"Well, don't stand there like that, Swannee. Go to your room!"

I ran out of the *atelier* and flopped on the bed in my room, which was at the time just down the hall from her studio. I waited for Mama to come and console me, but she never did. A few minutes later, I heard Jimmy starting to wail from the nursery. I tiptoed back to Mama's *atelier*. She was humming happily to herself and painting, oblivious to anything else.

Heart pounding, I approached her easel and squeaked out, "Mama?"

"Swannee! What are you doing out of your room? I told you not to bother me!"

I sniffed. "But, Mama, Jimmy's crying. He's crying really loud."

"Well, go tell Ella Mae to take care of him!"

"But, Mama, Ella Mae isn't here."

That seemed to register vaguely, but then she got this nasty, angry look on her face. "Oh, that child! Impossible child!" She pushed her chair back impatiently, and it scraped against the floor and knocked over a half-full cup of coffee. She ran down the hall in those tight pants and ballerina slippers with me following behind.

When she got to the nursery, Jimmy, red-faced and hysterical, stood in his bed whimpering, "Ma, ma, ma . . ." with his little chest heaving up and down. Mama scooped him up, all anger erased momentarily from her face.

"Oh, the poor little boy. Jim, Jim. Now, don't cry. Mama's here with you. Right here." She rocked him a minute and changed his diaper, but Jimmy was inconsolable. She took him on her hip downstairs into the kitchen, sat him in his high chair, and tried to fix him a bottle or something, but Mama was getting tenser by the minute. And Jimmy kept crying so loud. Wide-eyed, I watched from the door of the kitchen. That's when I realized that Mama didn't know how to fix the bottle. She didn't know what Jimmy had after his nap! But I did.

I ran to the cupboard and grabbed a chair and climbed up, the way I always did with Ella Mae, and got the baby food jars and picked out one for carrots, because Jimmy loved carrots, and a chicken one.

"Here, Mama," I said proudly, handing them to her. "This is what Ella Mae gives Jimmy after his nap."

She bent down and touched my hair, and there were tears all over her face and she looked kind of scared and wild in her eyes. "Oh, Swannee, sweetheart. I scared you. I'm sorry. I'm so sorry." She hugged me tight, which made me feel not quite so scared.

Jimmy was still crying. I got his bib, and Mama opened the jars and started feeding him from a way-too-big spoon without even warming the food. So Jimmy spat it all out, and Mama started saying awful things and crying. And I thought she might even hit Jimmy.

So I turned and ran out of the kitchen and out the front door and down the long, long driveway and across the street and ended up breathless in front of Trixie's door. I banged on it, in tears myself, until Trixie's maid Tottie opened the door.

"Mary Swan, dahlin'! What in heaven's sake is the matter?"

"Is Trixie here?"

"She's busy right now, honey chile."

My bottom lip quivered and I blurted, "But I have to see her! Ella Mae's gone and Jimmy's mad and Mama's crying!"

A moment later, Trixie appeared in her nightshirt with rollers in her hair. "Swannee, what in the world. . . ?"

"Mama's crying and Jimmy's screaming and Ella Mae isn't home." I was sobbing by then.

In less than a minute Trixie was dressed, with a bandana wrapped around her curlers, and we both ran across the street. When we got to the kitchen, Mama was sitting on the floor bawling right along with Jimmy, and they both had baby food all over them.

Trixie tried to act as if she was laughing, but I could tell she was nervous. "Sheila, for goodness' sake, get up and give me that child." She turned to me and said, "Swannee, you go on over and play with Lucy and Tottie. You be careful crossing that street, you hear?"

She scooped Jimmy out of the high chair and followed me to the front door, leaving Mama, I guess, crying on the floor. She watched me go back down the driveway and across our wide, calm street, and I felt so thankful that she cared.

That was what I remembered, staring out at the hickory tree, letting my tears well up in my eyes and my heart hurt. That memory was another confirmation that Herbert's accusation and Trixie's confession about Mama were true. But I couldn't bear that squeezing kind of pain, so I turned and left the studio, closing the door behind me.

Rachel rang the doorbell at four-thirty. "You've been crying again," she stated in her matter-of-fact way.

"I'm sorry I was such a pill last night, Rach. I was so awful." I started crying again, and Rachel put her arm around my shoulders.

"Quit thinking about it, Swannee. It won't do any good."

I sniffed and nodded and laid my head on the kitchen table. That's when I saw the note again, the one from Jimmy.

Rachel snatched it up and demanded, "Jimmy's at Andy Bartholomew's? Hmm. Well, it doesn't matter. You've got to call Robbie right now."

"I can't. I'll die if you make me talk to him. It was the most awful, embarrassing evening of my life. Anyway, look at me. I'm a wreck."

In response, Rachel got the address book that sat by the phone in the kitchen and started leafing through the pages. "Aha! It's here. Bartholomew." She picked up the phone and dialed the number and then held out the phone to me. I could hear it ringing.

Mortified, I shot her a hateful look, breathed in deeply, and took the phone out of her hand.

Amazingly, thankfully, it was Robbie who answered. "Hello?"

"Robbie?" My tongue was pasted to the roof of my mouth.

"Yes?"

"Robbie, this is Mary Swan."

"Mary Swan! Did Jimmy tell you I called? How are you?" He sounded genuinely concerned.

"Okay. Better. Lots better." This was torture. Rachel glared at me all the while. "Look, um, Robbie. I'm sorry about last night. I . . . I was, well, wretched."

"Don't worry about it, Mary Swan. It wasn't your fault."

I chuckled nervously. "Oh yes, it was. No one made me drink all that stuff. Anyway, I'm sorry, and, and I really did have a good time with you, honest . . . until all that stuff about Mama."

"I'm glad you feel better," he said, and then there was an awkward pause.

"Well, thanks."

"Well, bye."

"Bye." And I hung up the phone.

"Good, Swannee. I'm proud of you," Rachel said with a smug smile on her face.

"He hates me. I could hear it in his voice. He thinks I'm out of my mind, just like Mama." That brought tears again.

But Rachel refused to let me dwell on my misery. "Ridiculous. You can be as mean as you want to Robbie Bartholomew. He's smitten."

I gave her an incredulous look. "Smitten. Are you crazy?"

"No. I'm smart. And even the biggest dummy there last night could see how he looked at you. Smitten. Too bad you had to pull that drinking spree."

I started to protest, but she added, "At least you apologized."

That Robbie Bartholomew could possibly like me, let alone be "smitten," was beyond my comprehension. Then I thought about the dancing and the silly poem and the way I'd felt when he held my hand. Maybe I was smitten too. Maybe. But mostly I was just completely confused.

Rachel insisted that I get away from my house for a while, so we walked over to hers. I liked Rachel's house. It had that Tudor look, the red and white brick and the dark brown wood interspersed. I think there were five chimneys popping out of the roof and, in the wintertime, it seemed like every room had a fire burning in its own private fireplace. Somehow, even though the rooms were big and the ceilings high, her house had a cozy feeling.

We hopped over the low flagstone wall that sat near the street, instead of taking the driveway on the left, and walked straight up the gentle incline that was her front yard. It was every bit as long and wide as mine, and we loved to sled down it on those rare occasions when Atlanta got half an inch of snow. Today, nothing but the September sun beat down on the grass that was showing signs of thirst in certain dry patches.

"Hello, Mary Swan," Mrs. Abrams greeted me when we came in the kitchen. She'd obviously just returned from a golf game, because she had on plaid shorts and a polo shirt and golf cleats, and she wore a sun visor over her blond hair. "I heard you all had such fun at the Back-to-School Ball last night."

I shot Rachel a look that said, *What am I supposed to say?*

She filled in the blanks for me. "Yeah, I told Mom about the yummy food and how good the band was. And how you and Robbie danced the night away."

I smiled sweetly as Rachel handed me a glass of iced tea and pulled me out the kitchen door into her backyard. "Sorry," she whispered once we were out of her mom's hearing. "I didn't think she'd be back from the golf course yet."

As I've mentioned before, Rachel didn't have a pool in her back-yard, but she had something much better: a stable with five horses and, beyond the stable, a riding ring. I hadn't been riding all summer, despite Rachel's numerous pleas. True to their word, the Abramses had graciously cared for Bonnie all summer long without a word of complaint. But Rachel knew that if she could just get me to the stable, the smell of the horses, the hay and grain, and even the manure would transport me into another world, far away from my personal pity party.

I set down my glass of tea in the tack room where the bridles and saddles hung on wooden racks nailed to the walls, and I breathed in deeply. Then I picked up a currycomb from a bucket filled with brushes and opened the door to my mare's stall.

"Hello there, Bonnie," I said in a voice I used exclusively for her. She was a big chestnut, over sixteen hands tall, with an off-center star on her forehead and a white ring around her left front fetlock. At that moment, her fiery mane and tail were filled with new shavings. She nickered as I rubbed my hand on her smooth muzzle. "Sorry I've been away so long."

I brushed her for at least fifteen minutes without saying a word to Rachel. Then I went back into the tack room and grabbed a bridle and a hard hat and said, "Let's go."

So even though Rachel had just spent the afternoon riding, she happily joined me as we slipped the bridles on our mares and led them out of the stable and up a hill to the riding ring. Then we climbed onto the fence, coaxed the mares to come alongside us, and hopped onto their bare backs. And as soon as my bottom touched Bonnie's warm sleek coat and I wrapped my legs around her smooth, rounded barrel, I forgot about Mama and Herbert and the Back-to-School Ball. It was the best therapy in the world, riding around the ring with a cloudless blue sky above and the faintest hint of autumn in the air.

Chapter 12

"Mary Swan, time for church!" Daddy's voice carried up the stairs. Then he added, "We'll be eating lunch at the club with Grandmom and Granddad."

I groaned. The last two places I wanted to be that Sunday were at church and at the club. Plenty of kids who were at the Back-to-School Ball would be both places. And Rachel wouldn't be at either. Her parents belonged to the Jewish club in town.

Eating lunch at the club with Grandmom and Granddad after church on Sundays was as much of a tradition in our family as going to church itself. But we hadn't been to eat at the club since Mama and Daddy had left on the European tour.

During the church service I ignored Virginia Lawson as she peered over the top of numerous ladies' hats to stare at me from three pews up and over on the right side. Jane Springfield was sitting by her, and as soon as she caught my eye, Virginia whispered something to Jane and they laughed into their white gloves. Millie Garrett looked away quickly when I caught sight of her coming down the aisle with her family. At least Herbert didn't attend St. Philip's.

I considered crawling under the pews to hide from any other possible sources of embarrassment, but settled instead on simply sinking to my knees on the kneeler. Then the congregation stood and began singing a hymn as the verger, the crucifer, and the acolytes paraded solemnly down the aisle. I was hiding my face in a hymnal when, to my horror, Robbie passed right beside me, carrying the tall gold candle holder. Of course Robbie the Boy Scout was also Robbie the acolyte.

Without missing a step, he mouthed the words, "Are you okay?" and I nodded so quickly that my straw hat with the blue satin ribbon and the fake daisies floated off my head and onto Jimmy's lap. Robbie was long past and Jimmy still guffawing by the time I got the hat back on my head. And Daddy gave me a stern look that meant, *Really, Mary Swan! We're in church.*

Usually after church a group of teenagers stood outside in the gardens to talk. Today I hid in the bathroom and waited for fifteen minutes to pass so that I could safely head to the car without seeing any of them.

Unfortunately, Patty Masters stepped into the powder room just as I was stepping out. "Mary Swan," she said sympathetically. "How are you?"

"Fine," I said dryly.

"Real convincing, Swan," she teased. "I saw you nipping in the bourbon the other night." She took me by the shoulders in a playful way, but since she was almost six feet tall, it still seemed a bit intimidating. "That's not like you. Don't you let a scum ball like Herbert drive you to drink. There are better things in life." Then she stuck her tongue in her lower lip and made one of the ridiculous faces she was known for, and I giggled in spite of my foul mood.

"Half fine, then," I confessed.

"Good ole Herbert. Leave it to the idiot of Mendon to spoil a perfectly delightful evening."

I shrugged.

"If it makes you feel any better, I heard that Virginia broke up with him that night after he insulted your mom. He's heartbroken." She made a mock-sad face, stuck her tongue in her lower lip again, and crossed her eyes.

This time I laughed out loud.

"Anyway, don't let it get to you. Not someone like him. Now quit powdering your nose and go on out to the parking lot. Robbie's looking all over for you." Right before she closed the door to the bathroom stall, she added, "Swell guy, that Robbie Bartholomew."

But I didn't want to see Robbie. Apologizing on the phone was one thing; dealing with it face-to-face was another. In the end, Robbie found me walking swiftly to my dad's Jaguar. He jogged to catch up with me, and his cheeks were all red when he got there.

He grabbed my hand and before I could pull it away, said, "Thanks for calling yesterday. I was so worried about you. I didn't sleep a wink Friday night. Are you okay now?"

"Yeah. I'm fine, except that everyone is looking at me like I have two heads. I really have to go, Robbie."

"Wait, Swan. Please." The topaz eyes met mine. "Could we maybe go somewhere tonight?"

"Don't even mention the Varsity. Out of the question."

He smiled, but with a pained look on his face. "I was thinking somewhere alone, just you and me."

I felt a twinge in my stomach. "I don't know, Robbie. Why would you possibly want to go anywhere with me after the way I acted Friday night?"

He grinned, "To give you another chance? Naw, I'm just kidding. I thought a movie would be fun. Light. Popcorn and Coke. Definitely no bourbon."

I found myself smiling and blushing. Robbie Bartholomew had a sense of humor!

"Well, I don't know. I've gotta go. Daddy's taking us all to the club for lunch."

"See you at seven, then," he said, touching my arm and giving me a wink. He left before I could say anything else.

"Wooweee, Swannee and Robbie," Jimmy sang triumphantly when I got to the car.

"Oh, hush up," I hissed.

"Seems like such a nice boy," Grandmom Middleton commented as she got into her big Cadillac, which was parked close to Daddy's car.

"Fine family," Granddad mumbled. "And I believe he's quite the football player. Tall and smart. Halfback."

They puttered out of the parking lot with Jimmy in the backseat making faces at me while Daddy and I followed in the Jaguar.

"Nice boy, that Robbie Bartholomew," Daddy said. "From a real fine family."

I rolled my eyes. Sometimes it was scary how much he and Granddad thought alike. He turned on the radio and listened to the news and then adjusted the dial to the sports station. So with the radio blaring and the windows down, I settled into my seat and thought about how Robbie Bartholomew had cracked a joke and winked at me and was taking me to the movies in just six hours. And I forgot to be worried about whom I might see at the club.

As it turned out, it wasn't who I saw at the club that was the problem. It was all about who wanted to see Daddy.

The Capital City Country Club sprawled over many acres way out Peachtree Street. The main building was built of beautiful sand-colored stone. A black valet always met us at the entrance, opened the car doors, let us out, and then parked the car. Club members could choose between the snack bar by the pool or the fancy restaurant upstairs. The club had a golf course and a swimming pool and tennis courts and a great lake for fishing.

When I was little, Granddad used to take Jimmy and me fishing. But I hated to see the half-dead fish floating on their sides in the bucket of water, and one time, when we were halfway back to his house, I had made Granddad turn around and let me throw the fish back into the lake. That was my last fishing expedition with Granddad.

Heading to our table in the formal dining room, I noticed with relief that Daddy stopped to joke with a few men on the way. "Did ya see what the Dow Jones did Friday, Bill? Looks like Coca-Cola might be on the move again."

"Listen, John Jason, you better get ready for the biggest surprise of the year when there's a merger in the automobile industry. And that Disney stock is gonna be worth something someday. I swear it!"

Daddy slapped Bill Henderson on the back and walked over to Jerry Webster, one of his fraternity brothers from Georgia Tech. "Got any tips on the Yellow Jackets for the fall, Jerry? Didn't look half bad yesterday against the Blue Devils."

And so the friendly banter went. I felt in a wonderful, hopeful mood for a number of reasons. I had a date later that night, and my reputation apparently wasn't tarnished beyond repair. Daddy had played golf at the club yesterday and was swapping stock stories with his buddies today. And he was all shaven and looking handsome. Jimmy was his same ole bratty self. And we were with Grandmom and Granddad, just like old times. So maybe that meant we were all on the road to recovery.

The waiters put us at a new table, not the one we used to sit at when Mama was alive. This table was in front of the big window that looked out onto the swimming pool. It was a round table with just enough room for the five of us, so it didn't seem like someone was missing, even though we were all probably feeling awkward that Mama wasn't there asking for her Bloody Mary.

"Sure do love those buttered crackers," Grandmom said to break the silence, reaching for the small silver tray that held the club's specialty. "And I've just got to try the vichyssoise today!"

"That's what you have every time, Jennie," Granddad said, raising his eyebrows and winking at me.

A waiter came over and silently placed himself by Granddad. When Granddad finished speaking, the waiter said, "Good to see you here today, Mr. Middleton. You doin' all right?"

"Just fine, Tony. Just fine. And how are you today? Lotta business, it looks like."

"Business goin' well, Mr. Middleton. Are y'all ready to order?"

"I believe we are," Granddad said jovially. So Tony turned to Grandmom first, and one after another we ordered.

All the waiters knew every club member by name, and most of the members knew the waiters by name too. I noticed in a different way from before that all the waiters were black. They wore black tuxes with starched white shirts and black bow ties, and the waitresses wore black dresses with bright white, frilly aprons tied around their waists. I wondered if a white person could be hired to work as a waiter at the club.

The meal went along just fine with me telling Grandmom all about the dress I wore to the Back-to-School Ball and how the Dixons had decorated the farm and the big tents and the food and the band and the dancing. I made it sound like the whole evening had been a dream come true. Daddy and Granddad droned on about the stock market, and Jimmy watched the swimmers and would occasionally comment, "Nice dive!"

But then, near the end of the meal, several women stopped by the table, one at a time, to say hello to Daddy. Very charming and very unattached women. I'd heard it said that there was nothing like a rich widower to attract the best and worst of the city's women, and I found out it was true. That day at the club, I recognized these three as women who had periodically shown up at our house throughout the summer with all kinds of steaming casseroles: Helen Goodman and Amanda Hunnicutt and Jennifer Peabody. They'd never stayed long, and I'd not given it a second thought.

But on this day, each one at separate intervals stopped by to chat with us as we were eating. And for some reason, that made me feel queasy inside. I lost my appetite and couldn't finish my absolutely favorite meal of prime rib and scalloped potatoes. Amanda Hunnicutt even found a way to lean over close to Daddy so that her more-than-ample cleavage showed. Then, at Daddy's invitation, she joined us for coffee.

"Oh, JJ. How sweet of you. Well, I can only stay for a sec. Just a sec," she said in her syrupy voice, and then she let out this piercing giggle that sent shivers down my spine.

Daddy motioned to a waiter and asked him to bring a chair over for Miss Hunnicutt, and I had to scoot over closer to Grandmom so that Miss Hunnicutt could fit in beside Daddy. Jimmy just sat and stared at her with his mouth hanging half open. I think he was more fascinated with her low-cut dress than her high-pitched laugh. I finally stomped on his foot under the table, and he snapped his mouth shut.

I didn't say a word but silently appraised the situation. Didn't these women know anything about proper etiquette? I was sure it was written in Emily Post somewhere that widowers got a year of peace to grieve before they were preyed upon by society's most eligible ladies.

If there was one thing I had learned at my girls' school, it was etiquette. In our sophomore year, we were required to take a class called Fashion and Poise, which met once a week to instruct us young ladies in all the essentials of womanly grace. We had been unapologetic in our ridicule of the class and of the teacher until I had gotten one of my great ideas. I had announced to my classmates one day before the teacher arrived that the course had been given a new name. Hereafter, instead of learning about Fashion and Poise, we were gleaning helpful hints about Passion and Boys. My classmates loved the name, so it stuck. And every sophomore soon was whispering gleefully about their class on Passion and Boys. Somehow that made learning about how to use an emery board and paint your fingernails and apply deodorant and what to wear to a funeral much more bearable.

But in the fall of 1962 it was Passion and Women, and Daddy was the target. And I made up my mind, sitting there at the round table at the club with Grandmom and Granddad and Jimmy and Daddy and Amanda Hunnicutt, that not a one of these high-society ladies would get her hands on Daddy and his fortune.

Robbie picked me up at seven o'clock sharp, and we drove with the top down on the convertible to the drive-in where the latest Elvis Presley movie was showing. Since his fancy little red convertible had the gearshift in the middle, I couldn't exactly sit next to him, and he couldn't really get his arm around my shoulder, so we watched the movie passing the box of popcorn between us. The credits were rolling at the end of the film when we first heard the skirmish behind us. A black boy with a ridiculous-looking paper hat on his head advertising a soft drink was serving a car several rows back.

"Nice hat you got there, darkie. Let me try it on." That came from a white teenager with an overabundance of muscles.

"That'll be fifty-five cents," the waiter said, ignoring the insult.

"Did you hear me?" the white boy demanded, getting out of his car. Then he said the "n-word."

"Gotta keep my hat, mister."

The white teenager laughed out loud and grabbed the waiter by the collar. "You do what I say, ya hear?" He shoved him hard, causing the frightened boy to fall down, spilling his tray of Cokes. Several other white boys hopped out of their cars and surrounded the hapless waiter, laughing and calling the black boy all kinds of derisive names.

I was already out of the convertible, with Robbie on my heels. "Leave him alone!" I shouted.

The group of boys snickered at my outburst, and one jeered in an effeminate-sounding voice, "Y'all leave him alone! Listen to what the girl's saying!"

I suddenly remembered my episode with Carl at Oakland and felt goose bumps on my arms. The boy who had started the whole thing turned from me and went over to the black waiter, pulled him back up, and started shaking him hard. The waiter's hat now lay in the middle of the parking lot, wet with Coke.

"Put your hat back on now," the white boy demanded.

As the waiter reached down to get the hat, the white boy punched him hard in the chin. The black boy went reeling, hit the hood of a car, and caught himself. It looked as though he was going to fight back, but he held himself off. The other boys crowded in closer, eyes flashing with excitement.

"Come on, darkie. Stand up for yourself. You 'fraid or something?" one of them taunted.

"Robbie!" I squealed. "Do something!"

And to my great surprise, he did. He walked through the circle of smirking teens and over to the black boy, who was cowering in the middle, eyes turned down, rubbing his chin. Blood was trickling out of his mouth. Robbie picked up the withered hat and handed it to him. Then he gathered up the cups of spilled Coke and handed them to the white teen and said, "That's enough, Ed." Disgust was on Robbie's face, just as it had been when Herbert had spewed out his information on Friday night. "Pay him for the drinks, Ed, and leave him alone."

Ed's face got all constricted and red. "You stay out of this, Bartholomew. And I'm not paying for my drinks. They're spilled all over the parking lot. I don't call that very good service." Ed spat on the ground, turned around, and got into his car. "Let's git outta here," he said to the others, and they sped off.

Robbie fished in his pocket for a dollar bill and handed it to the humiliated waiter.

"Thank ya, sir," the boy mumbled, his head turned down. "I'll get you your change."

"Don't worry about it," Robbie said. "Get back to work before you get into trouble."

The waiter nodded and scurried off.

That was the first time I saw Robbie's courage and his generous heart, and I would never forget it. We walked back to his car, his hand on my arm in a protective way.

I was shaking.

"Why are people so awful, Robbie? Why do they want to be cruel? Cruel. For absolutely no reason."

"I think the reason is hate, Mary Swan. Whites hating blacks because it's been bred into them to hate."

We were in the car now, and try as hard as I could, I could not stop my legs from shaking.

"Mary Swan, are you all right?"

"Let's just say this hasn't been that great of a weekend." Then I began to cry. It was awkward because Robbie wanted to hug me, I guess, but with the gearshift between us, he just leaned over so that we were touching heads, of all things, and he was holding my shoulders.

"I'm sorry, Mary Swan. I really am sorry," he kept saying, and occasionally he wiped away a tear that was running down my face with the handkerchief that he'd withdrawn from his pocket. We sat there so long that the same film started playing again. But Robbie didn't pay any attention.

Finally, I dried my tears, and we left the drive-in theater.

"Everywhere I look now, whites are mean to blacks," I stated in between little sniffs.

"I think it's just that you're seeing it now, Mary Swan. It's always been this way." He had that pained looked on his face again, as if he was trying to think of something reassuring to say.

"And all these women are after my dad!" I suddenly burst out.

"What?" Robbie looked startled.

So on the way home I told him about lunch at the club, and then we suddenly started giggling about Amanda Hunnicutt's low-cut dress and Jimmy's wide eyes. When we got to my house, he drove to the back carport, parked the car, and turned off the engine. He got out, came around to my side of the car, and opened my door. I think he was determined to walk me to the door this time. "We don't have much luck with our dates, do we? I'm sorry about the skirmish tonight," he apologized.

I suddenly felt this rush of tenderness and excitement as I watched him by the back porch light. His hair was kind of sticking to his face, all sweaty, and I brushed it back with my hand. "Thanks for doing what you did. It was really brave of you. And really kind."

"Just what every Boy Scout would do," he said with a twinkle in his eye.

That made me laugh. "No, I mean it, Robbie. You were great. It's me that ends up being a rotten date every time. First I pick on your friends, then I get drunk out of my mind, and now I practically get into a fight with a bunch of rednecks."

"You're a swell date, Swan. It's just that a lot of rotten things have happened lately."

I stood there, not wanting to rush off like the other times. Not wanting to go inside. Not wanting him to leave.

"Well, thanks for a nice evening," I said stupidly, because while it had been exciting and scary and romantic, it certainly hadn't been "nice."

And then he leaned forward, holding my right arm gently with his left hand, and he pressed his lips on mine. Just for a second or two. Not nearly long enough. Just barely long enough for my heart to start thumping. And long enough for me to long for more.

"Good night, Mary Swan," he said softly. I watched him go to the convertible and turn it around and drive down the driveway, waving as he went. I leaned against the column of the back door and sighed.

My first kiss. I walked out into the backyard and leaned against the hickory tree and stood there for a long time. My first kiss. It was something so sacred I didn't even want to share it with Rachel. Not yet, at least.

So going back to school on Monday wasn't nearly as bad as I had expected. Rachel and I had Latin and French and Honors English and PE together. When I told her about the kiss after English class, she dragged me into the bathroom and wanted all the details.

"I told you he was smitten, Swan!" she stated triumphantly.

And that was all that was on my mind for the whole day. The other girls whispered and giggled about the Back-to-School Ball, but it didn't bother me in the least. No one breathed a word about what Herbert had said or my response. And Rachel confirmed the gossip Patty had given me at church: Virginia had indeed broken up with Herbert. I gloated over that fact all day.

When I got back home that afternoon I didn't tell Ella Mae about Robbie, but I did tell her all about the women who had been flirting with Daddy. "You've got to help me protect him from them," I pleaded in my most dramatic voice.

"Yore daddy don't need no he'p from me, Mary Swan. Un-unn."

"But, Ella Mae, if you'd been there, you'd have seen how they were trying to seduce him. Daddy's a sitting duck. He's lonely. He's grieving." I leaned in close. "He's hungry for affection."

"Mary Swan! You leave all that alone. He's a grown man, he is."

"I don't care. He's extremely vulnerable right now. If you won't help me, I'll get Jimmy to." I thought that threat would do it, but Ella Mae just ambled out of the room, admonishing me with "Don't you git me involved in none of your silliness, Mary Swan. I won't have it. I tell you, I won't."

So I went outside to the backyard where Jimmy was throwing a ball with Muffin.

"What did you think about those women around Daddy yesterday?"

"Disgusting. Especially Amanda Top-Heavy Hunnicutt."

I squeaked out a laugh. "Shh. Don't let Ella Mae hear you!" I picked up a stick and tossed it as hard as I could toward the woods. Muffin went racing after it. "I've got an idea about how to keep Daddy safe from those women."

"You do? What is it?"

And that's how Jimmy and I started our campaign called Save JJ from the RASCALS, our acronym for Rich Available Sexy Cunning Admiring Ladies of Society. We planned our strategy, and I made Jimmy rehearse it with me, despite his protests. I knew we had no time to waste. Those women had one thing on their minds: JJ's money. I expected them to appear at the front door at any minute.

True to my instinct, the doorbell rang around six-fifteen. Ella Mae had taken the bus home at five-thirty, and thankfully, Daddy had not gotten home from work.

"It's Helen Goodman!" I wailed to Jimmy, who was making a robot out of bottle tops in his room. I raced down the steps from my room, taking them two at a time.

Helen Goodman looked to me like a model for *Vogue*. She had tanned skin all year long—I don't know how she did it—and big brown eyes so heavy with mascara that it looked like she was perpetually surprised and glad to be. She walked with a deliberate swing to her hips. That day, her hips were nicely concealed in a tightly fitting linen skirt.

"Looks like she's got something yummy on that cake plate," called Jimmy, who must have gone to the window. "Don't chase her off before she leaves the cake!"

I opened the door. "Oh, hello there, Miss Goodman. So nice to see you."

"Well, I just had to come by. Seeing JJ—seeing Mr. Middleton yesterday at the club, I felt so relieved that he seems to be doing better. And you children. Such sweet children. So perfectly behaved." She said it as if we were three and six instead of thirteen and sixteen. "I thought you might like my chocolate marble cake." Helen Goodman lowered her voice. "I wondered if your father might be here?"

"No, ma'am. He's not home from work yet. Working late today, I think."

That was Jimmy's cue. He ran down the steps, making a great commotion. "Hello, Miss Goodman. Oh, gosh, that cake looks delicious!" Then he turned to me, and with his eyes wide and innocent, said, "Mary Swan, don't you remember?" He turned toward Miss Goodman with her plastic smile and eyes stuck open. "Daddy's not at work. He left early because Jennifer Peabody invited him to that tour of homes, and then he's going with her to look at flowers."

Helen Goodman's surprised eyes now became astonished and flustered, so Jimmy added, "Women are coming around all the time. Especially Miss Peabody."

Miss Goodman's tanned face turned two shades deeper as she stammered, "Well, well, my goodness," handed me the cake plate, and turned and left without so much as a good-bye.

The next afternoon Jimmy burst into my room where I was practicing my flute and confided to me, "Guess who's eating dinner with us at the club tonight?"

I put down my flute and demanded, "Who?"

He smiled again.

"Not Helen Goodman, I hope."

"Worse."

"Well, who?"

"Amanda Top-Heavy Hunnicutt!"

"No!"

"Come see for yourself."

We sneaked down the two floors of stairs and peered from the entrance hall into the living room. I could barely see Daddy's polished black shoes. But we heard the laugh. It was Miss Hunnicutt's all right.

"JJ, you don't me-ean it!" she squealed, adding one or two extra syllables to every word.

Daddy was laughing nervously, and I could imagine the well-endowed Miss Hunnicutt scooting closer to him on the sofa.

"Daddy told me just before she got here that she was coming by for drinks and then we were all eating together at the club," Jimmy whispered way too loudly.

"Oh no!" I groaned. I yanked him into the kitchen. "We can't let her come." My melodramatic pitch came naturally. "We've got to do something quick!"

So Jimmy went upstairs and got his pre-algebra book and rather rudely walked into the living room. Without so much as a hello, he whined, "Daddy, can you please help me with these math problems?"

Listening in the hall, I could hear the irritation in Daddy's voice. "For goodness' sake, Jimmy, ask Swan."

When Jimmy left the room, we waited precisely five minutes before I traipsed in. "Hello, Miss Hunnicutt," I said, polite as could be. "Dad, I'm starving. Can I have a piece of that heavenly chocolate cake that Helen Goodman brought over yesterday?"

Daddy furrowed his brow. "Well, really, Swan. What do you mean. . . ?"

"Well, I just thought I should check, in case you were saving the last four pieces for us to eat when she comes by again."

Miss Hunnicutt gave me an annoyed look and then daintily lifted her glass of Scotch and soda to her lips.

Daddy examined his wristwatch. "Swan, you don't need a piece of cake now. We'll be leaving for the club in fifteen minutes. Our reservations are for seven."

"Oh, JJ, for goodness' sakes, she's practically grown. Let her have a piece of cake."

I'd barely left the room when Jimmy dashed in again, freckled face red and tears in his eyes. "Dad, come quick! Muffin's gotten out. Went chasing a dog down the road."

Daddy swore under his breath. "Excuse me for a second, Amanda." He set down his glass, muttering unkind words about Muffin, and strode out the front door. Jimmy ran after him, winking at me as he went.

When Daddy came back ten minutes later, he was puffing and sweating in his business suit. "Amanda, I am sorry. The dog's gone."

"Well, I'm sure he'll come home, JJ, for heaven's sake. There's no worry."

Jimmy's sour face sprouted tears. "No! He's never run away before. Somebody might try to steal him! We have to keep looking."

Daddy, mad and flustered, shrugged, and I guess Amanda caught on because she left in a big huff, saying something about kids and dogs. And so the rest of the evening was spent searching for Muffin, whom

Jimmy had actually hidden in the bathhouse. Two hours later, Jimmy just happened to find Muffin somewhere in the woods, and as far we could tell, Daddy never suspected a thing. We all ate peanut butter and jelly sandwiches for dinner.

But the next evening when he got home from work, Daddy called me into his study. "Listen, Mary Swan. I know exactly what you and your brother are trying to do. And it won't work. Do you understand?" His face had this strained look on it. Then he relaxed. "Swannee, there's nothing I wouldn't do for you and Jimmy. But honestly. Please don't embarrass me in front of visitors."

"But they're just after your money, Daddy!"

He smiled at that. "Mary Swan Middleton. I do believe I am old enough and, I do hope, wise enough to take care of myself and my money." Then he added, "And my dates."

"It's too early for you to be dating, Daddy! You're a grieving widower!"

"Swannee, for goodness' sake, the last thing I need is for my teenage daughter to give me dating tips. Anyway, I'd rather talk about your dates. You've been out with Robbie three times now." He got a faraway look in his eyes. "Do you like Robbie Bartholomew?"

So Daddy had been counting. At least he seemed to want to know. "Yeah, I like him. He's nice."

"He's from a good Atlanta family. I've known his dad for years."

I could tell he was slipping away into his thoughts, but I desperately wanted him to talk to me. "What does his dad do?" I asked, even though I knew perfectly well.

"He's in finance at the Trust Company. President of the Board at the Capital City Club." He listed a string of accomplishments that did not impress me. Robbie would probably grow up to be just like his father, successful, a pillar of society, boring. In my head I could hear the strident moaning of a saxophone.

Daddy cleared his throat and rubbed his chin. "If your mama were here, I guess she'd tell you all kinds of things about dating. . . ." He let the phrase hang. "But, um, well, I trust you to be good, Mary Swan."

I went over to Daddy and kissed him on the cheek. "You don't have to worry about me, Daddy. I'll be good." I thought about Robbie's kiss. That had not been boring! Maybe there was hope for Robert H. Bartholomew, Jr.

Daddy seemed relieved and turned back to his papers, and I left the room without a sound. But I couldn't help but wish for a few more minutes of Daddy's undivided attention.

Chapter 13

On Saturday Rachel promised to meet me at Mt. Carmel after lunch, so I laid my flute case on the seat in between Ella Mae and me as I slid into the Cadillac that morning. Ella Mae eyed me rather suspiciously. "You gonna be playin' for us over lunch, Mary Swan? A solo or somethin'?" she teased. She knew how much I detested playing my flute in front of others.

"No," I said casually. "Just with Carl later on. Rachel is coming down, too, after lunch."

"Mmm-hmm. I see." She was sitting up straight, hands gripping the steering wheel. I don't think Ella Mae ever felt perfectly comfortable driving. She never took her eyes off the road. "Gettin' along perty well with Carl, ain't ya?"

"Yeah. He's really nice."

"You and him, you stay outta trouble, Mary Swan. Won't do for no white girl to be hangin' round too much with a black boy." She sneaked a glance my way and frowned slightly. "Yore daddy trusts me with you down here, Mary Swan. You understand?"

I swallowed. "Of course I do, Ella Mae. You know good and well that I just go to his house and play with Puddin' and talk with Mike and James. And Carl. That's all."

"Well, you keep it like that. 'Specially with Rachel coming down. You two together is always into mischief. Mmm-hmm. You is."

So I considered myself as having been warned. But that didn't make the butterflies go away when we got to the church and Carl greeted me out in the yard, and it didn't keep me from glancing at my watch at least three times, wishing the line of folks waiting to be served would end. Usually I grabbed a plate of spaghetti once everyone had been fed and ate it in the kitchen with the other volunteers. But today, since I wasn't on clean-up duty, I went out into the big open room and sat down at a table across from Cassandra.

"Where's Jessie?"

"She's over there with her grandmama." Cassandra pointed to the back of the room where several women were huddled around the baby.

"Which one is your mother?"

"Well, the one holdin' Jessie, of course."

I squinted to get a good look at the woman. She didn't look more than thirty.

Ever since I'd been coming down to Grant Park, I'd been trying to figure out the way things worked in poor, inner-city Atlanta. I dared to ask Cassandra about it. "Do you think you'll get married to Jessie's father?"

"Married to him?" she giggled. "Ain't no way I'll be marryin' a rascal like her father. Un-unn."

"You mean you don't even like him?"

"I like him okay. And with Jessie, I'm keeping a piece of him. Ya know what I mean?"

That startled me a bit, but I didn't let it show. "What did your parents say when they found out you were pregnant?" I prodded.

"Well, ain't seen my daddy since I was knee-high to a grasshopper. But, Mama! Well, she said jus' what Pastor James said. 'Ain't right to be foolin' around, Cassandra. You goin' be bringin' a whole lotta trouble on yorese'f.' But I didn't pay her no neva' mind, 'cause she done got pregnant with me when she was fifteen."

I tried to hide my surprise. No wonder her mother looked so young. She was.

"And it didn't bother you that you weren't married when you got pregnant?"

"Happens all the time round these parts." She squinted at me and got this mischievous smile on her face. "Ya don't gotta be married, Mary Swan, to do what it takes to git pregnant, ya know."

My face probably turned five shades of red. I changed the subject. "And your mom's taking care of Jessie so you can go back to school?"

"Well . . ." Cassandra shrugged. "If I wanna go back to school."

"You don't like school, don't like to learn?"

"Nope. Boring as a Sunday sermon." She clapped her hand over her mouth and whispered gleefully, "Can't let Miss Abigail hear me say that!"

"But you need to go to school."

"Why? I already knows all I need to know about takin' care of a baby. Know how ta cook and change a diaper and stuff like that. Ain't gonna learn nothin' ta he'p me at that there school."

I considered her statement. Wellington's unspoken motto was that we were the cream of the crop, being groomed for the best colleges. Radcliffe, Vassar, and Smith. I certainly wouldn't learn how to cook or change a diaper at Wellington.

"You got a boyfriend, Mary Swan?" Cassandra interrupted my thoughts.

I shrugged. "No. Not really."

"Got your eye on somebody, though?"

I laughed self-consciously. "Maybe."

"Well, I do too!" She leaned across the table and motioned with her eyes toward the kitchen. Then she whispered, "I got my eye on Carl. I sure do."

My mouth went dry. "On Carl? Really?"

"Sure 'nuff, I do. So do a lotta other girls, though. Mighty fine boy, Carl. Smart, educated, goin' to college in a year, he is." She grimaced. " 'Course Miss Abigail watches him like a hawk. I guess if I'm gonna git me Carl, I'll jus' have ta go back to school. That'd sit right well with Miss Abigail. And I'd git Carl to be my man! Ain't ya seen how he looks at little Jessie? He's crazy 'bout my baby." Then she leaned even farther over the table. "An' I'm perty shore he's takin' a likin' ta me too."

I felt dizzy.

" 'Course, Miss Abigail says that now that I'm a Christian, I need to stop foolin' around. Ya know what I mean?" she giggled.

I had a good idea what she meant, even though I'd just had my first kiss. I remembered how a senior a few years ago had quietly disappeared from Wellington. Later we learned she was pregnant. "So are you going to stop?"

She grinned again. "I'm gonna try. For right now, I'll try."

Well, at least she's honest, I thought. I really did not want to talk about Carl or about "fooling around," so I asked her about something else that had been bothering me for a while. "Do you feel any different since you and Miss Abigail . . . since y'all talked together last month?"

"You mean after we prayed, and I asked Jesus in my heart?"

"Yeah, that's what I mean."

"Well, shore I do. Heap o' difference. Got me my sins forgiven, got me a place reserved up in heaven. Not gonna let that ole devil be botherin' me no more. Yeah. I feel clean, Mary Swan. Clean in here." She pointed to her heart. "And I know I gots Somebody lookin' after me and Jessie now. For real. The Lawd Jesus be lookin' out for us. I want Him to be in charge from now on." She had such a strange, radiant smile on her face that I felt uneasy. I certainly didn't understand what she meant.

"But weren't you already a Christian? Didn't you go to church?"

"Shore did. Every Sunday. Even sang in the choir. But that didn't make me a Christian. I had to invite Jesus to come in. And I'm gettin' baptized next Sunday!"

"In my church we get baptized as a baby."

"Ya do? Well, I ain't been baptized yet, but Miss Abigail says it's mighty important for me to do it. She says that the Bible says baptism is a symbol of what you's done in yore heart. Shows everybody in the church that you has asked Jesus in yore heart, that you want Him to be in control. So I'm gonna do it."

Just then Carl came over and sat down next to me, and I saw right away how Cassandra's face brightened. I watched her schoolgirl flirting and the way he responded, and I wondered what I had stumbled into. Carl was the heartthrob of Grant Park. What in the world did I think was going to happen between him and me? He came from a place where young girls became mothers at fifteen and grandmothers at thirty, where you didn't marry but had a man's baby to keep a piece of him with you. Where there was no dream of anything beyond this squalid existence.

"What do you say, Mary Swan?"

"Huh?" I hadn't heard Carl's question.

"I asked if you brought your flute and if your friend was coming?" He was smiling at me that same smile, but I felt a bunch of rocks in the pit of my stomach.

"Yeah, Rachel will be here at two. I told her we'd meet her here at the church." Then I slid away and left Carl and Cassandra to talk and laugh and flirt, and I found Miss Abigail in the kitchen.

"Can I talk to you when you have a second?"

She was wiping her hands on a dish towel. "I've got time now, if you want, Mary Swan."

"It's a little private."

So Miss Abigail took me up the stairs and across the hall into what she called the sanctuary. It was the first time I'd been in there. Compared to St. Philip's, where the sanctuary seated 1,200, Mt. Carmel was small. Kind of quaint. The pews were wooden with worn gray cushions, and there was a slot on the back of each pew for the hymnals and Bibles. The walls were painted white, and on each wall were big stained-glass windows divided into three sections, rising into an arch. The ceiling had wooden rafters across it. A piano stood at the front of the church to the left of a plain wooden pulpit. And behind the pulpit there was an alcove whose ceiling rose in a point. It was filled with pews for the choir and behind them, the biggest of the stained-glass windows.

We sat down on the front pew, and Miss Abigail closed her eyes and seemed to be meditating. Then she took hold of my hands and said, "What can I do for you, Mary Swan?"

"I want to know, I need to know, how this culture works. I don't mean the black culture, but this part of it. The poverty. The way they have families. Does anyone get married? Do grandmothers raise all the kids? What was Carl's family like? I want to know."

Miss Abigail smoothed a few tendrils of hair away from her face and then ran her hands behind her, tightening the rubber band that held her hair in that long ponytail. "Poverty is a terrible thing, Mary Swan. So often it seems hopeless. You can't really imagine how some of these people live. Or maybe I should say survive, because it doesn't always seem like a life. An existence. A condemnation." There was something in her voice that made me feel uncomfortable, something like a righteous indignation.

"The poor inner-city culture doesn't see morality the way you and I do, Mary Swan. The girls don't dream of a husband and a home and a good education for their kids. Their dreams are for survival. Sure Pastor James preaches abstinence, and I teach on sexual purity. And the mothers in the church talk about it with their children. But it's hard for a mother to tell her daughter to stop fooling around when she herself got pregnant at fourteen. Sex isn't the first thing I deal with down here. It comes later."

"Cassandra said you told her that now that she's a Christian, she needs to stop fooling around."

"I did. But that wasn't the first thing I told her. First I told her about Jesus and how much He loves her, just as she is. How much grace He's got for her, how He can turn bad into good. If you look at Jesus in the Bible, He didn't start with a list of do's and don'ts when He talked to the adulteress or the Samaritan woman. He asked them questions, good questions. And He listened and understood their need. Then He told about himself, of love and forgiveness and eternal life. It was only after He'd given the good news that He said, 'Go and sin no more.' "

Something in the way Miss Abigail described Jesus' interaction with these women suddenly made me want to read the Bible. She was preaching me a sermon I'd never heard before. Or maybe it was simply that I'd never wanted to hear it.

"I'll tell you how I found Carl, Mary Swan." Her voice suddenly sounded raspy and pained. "A policeman came to the church early one morning explaining that there had been a shooting down the street the night before. He asked me to come and see.

"I'd been in Atlanta barely three months at the time. I walked into a slum hovel—that's the only way to describe it. There was blood on the floor where the body had fallen. And squatting and crying in the three filthy rooms of that place were a bunch of children. Eight in all. Five belonged to Carl's mom, and three of them to his aunt. The aunt and her brother were trying to manage with all those children. They were in shock—all of them.

"Carl was the oldest sibling. At twelve he was trying to calm down all the little ones—skinny, dirty kids with runny noses and lice. His aunt's oldest daughter was thirteen and pregnant and had epilepsy. She died giving birth to her baby three months later. Two others of those eight children had TB and eventually died. One of them was Carl's other sister. She died at the age of eight." Her eyes got a little misty. "It was nothing but a pure miracle that little Puddin' survived. Just a little scrawny, sickly baby.

"I'd seen places like that in the Detroit slums too. The dirty toilet on the back porch was their only link to anything modern. No hot water, no window screens, no lavatory, tub, or shower. And nothing in the refrigerator but an opened can of tuna. Flies all over the kitchen counter, along with a lot of other things I won't mention."

Her story repulsed me. Surely Carl hadn't lived that way! "What did you do?" I asked.

"I gathered up those children and took them home with me. What else could I do? Got them clean and in school. But you know, Mary Swan, I never could have done it without all those lovely volunteers. Those ladies from your church and other churches in Buckhead who came down here and helped me wash the children and feed them and just hold the babies. The wealthy white ladies from Buckhead who loved Jesus bridged a gap in the inner city, Mary Swan. They became Jesus' hands and feet right here in this place."

"Rich white ladies helped you care for Carl and his brothers and sisters?" I asked incredulously.

"Mary Swan," she said, a peaceful expression on her face. "I love Buckhead. I love those precious women who volunteer their time down here. Did you think it was all me? The Lord knows how many a day He has kept me going because some sweet lady from Buckhead or another part of Atlanta was willing to help out."

"They didn't mind the poverty or the smell or how dirty everything is?"

She got this twinkle in her eye and said, "Mary Swan, those ladies may live in fine homes in the northwest part of Atlanta, but their hearts are given to Jesus. And He shows them what to do. Every day."

This was a revelation to me. "So you don't think it's bad to have money, lots of money?"

"No, I praise God for those kind women and their husbands. Many give generously, more than generously, to all kinds of charities, including the work going on here in Grant Park. Money is not the problem, Mary Swan. Do you know the verse that says, 'Where your treasure is, there will your heart be also'?"

I shrugged and shook my head.

"Look it up sometime. It's in the seventh chapter of the gospel of Matthew. And in the epistle to Timothy, the apostle Paul says it's the *love* of money that causes all the problems. Anything we worship above the Lord gets us into trouble. It could be our big fancy house in Buckhead or a bottle of beer here in Grant Park. It could be a car or our education or a man. . . ."

She looked away as though she was remembering something. "Carl and his siblings are going to make it, and they are going to make a difference because of all the help those ladies gave us. And those children know it. They know that God reached down to them in the middle of their suffering and picked them up. They've seen God do some mighty things in their lives. Miracles, Mary Swan.

"Lotta temptations out there for them, but I pray every day they remember how many people came, how many still come, week after week, just like you, to help out. I pray they remember what the hands and feet of Jesus look like. They may be white or black or any other color, but they are hands and feet that put Jesus first."

When Miss Abigail felt really passionate about something, her voice rose and her eyes got misty. I felt as though I had a golf ball in my throat. I couldn't speak.

She kept right on talking. "That's what God does with suffering, Mary Swan. Where it could breed violence and hatred and cruelty, God's love changes it into a sacrifice of love for Him. He changes it." Quite suddenly, she dropped to her knees and began to cry.

I think I was sitting up really stifflike, my back straight against the pew. I wanted to be on my knees, weeping beside Miss Abigail. Her story absolutely broke my heart. But I could not bear to let it get inside me. Not all that stuff about God and sacrifice and Him changing all the awful circumstances into good. Somehow I knew that if I really concentrated on her words, the God she spoke about so freely, so intimately, might come into my heart too. And I wasn't ready.

"Bless the children, mighty, holy Lord," she was praying with her eyes closed, tears trickling down her face. "You keep these children safe, all of them. I can't and their parents can't. But you can."

By now I had pushed my emotions so far back in my mind that my whole body felt hard and embarrassed by the open tears of Miss Abigail. The crushing, vulnerable feeling inside my chest was gone. When I spoke, I was surprised to hear the aloofness in my voice. "Do you always have children living with you?"

She got off her knees rather slowly, stood up, and walked over to one of the stained-glass windows. "Often, but not always."

"And you've never had any kids of your own?"

"No."

"Did you ever want to be married?"

"I was married once, Mary Swan." She turned around to face me, and suddenly her voice caught. "Married a boy I knew from school, a boy from a fine family in Detroit. Smart and funny and a head full of black curls, and eyes that could sweep you away with a look." Her smile was sad.

"I was really young, barely eighteen. He was three years older, had been off to school, and knew a lot of things. And he'd been with a lot of women. Of course, I didn't know that then. I don't know why he married me—yes, I guess it was love." But she said it as though she was trying to convince herself that it was true.

I wanted to tell her to stop, stop talking because she had already broken my heart with Carl's story, and I could tell that this one was going to be awful and sad too, and I didn't have any right to hear it.

But she kept on. "He married me, and right away, I was scared of him. He'd drink and stay out late with friends—fine young boys too, mind you—and do heaven knows what. He hardly ever even touched me, and then when he did, he'd slap me in the face. I used to have to use a whole pot of makeup to cover up the bruises before going to Sunday dinner at his mother's or mine. Mama and Daddy must have known something was going on, but they couldn't bear to admit it. Then one time he really hurt me, and I left. I left, and I never went back. And oh, Mary Swan, it was like a knife sticking through me, because I loved that man. I did."

I swallowed hard and started to say something, but Miss Abigail didn't even notice. "I was always thankful we never had kids, and then I was heartbroken at the same time, because I wanted a child. But you see, God has given me many, many babies to care for after all that."

The whole time she'd been talking, I was thinking to myself, *Why is she telling me this? Why?* I blurted out, "What kind of a good God would give you such a rotten husband and make you go through all that and then ask you to leave your nice comfortable home and live in the inner city and work with these poor, pitiful people who never change? I don't want a God like that!"

But Miss Abigail just said, "Mary Swan, do you think Carl is pitiful? And what about Puddin'? Or Cassandra and Jessie?"

"Oh gosh," I mumbled, so ashamed of myself that a wave of nausea swept over me. "I'm sorry."

Her voice was full of sympathy. "What God called me to do has nothing to do with what He's asking of you. Don't look at me and compare and be afraid. If you look at Scripture, you'll see it. God always provides just what is needed for what He asks, only it takes His supernatural strength to do it. But He still keeps in mind our person-alities and our hearts' desires. And if you let Him, Mary Swan, He'll change those desires until they become exactly what He has planned for you. It says in the Psalms, 'Delight thyself also in the Lord and He shall give thee the desires of thine heart.' Your desires become His desires, because you love Him so much and want to please Him. And He'll give you the biggest peace and joy you ever knew. He's done that for me, right here in the middle of the inner city." Her face got all radiant again.

"It's always easier to hold out your arm and say, 'Don't get near me, Jesus,' and then just criticize all the bad things around us. It is scary, Mary Swan, to get to know Jesus the way you know your best friend. But if you want to change, that's what has got to happen. There's no other religion that has a personal God, Mary Swan. No other religion where their god came down to earth and sacrificed him-self out of love. If you want to be a Christian, you've got to realize that it's all about knowing God, knowing Jesus. Not a religion. Not just going to church."

After a minute, when I didn't say a word, she added, "Anyway, Mary Swan, it seems to me you're putting the cart before the horse, as they say. Right now you should be more concerned with getting to know Jesus than with what He wants you to do with your life. 'Cause He can't be directing you until you're His."

I started feeling really uncomfortable then, especially when she kept saying *Jesus*. I don't know why, but it was almost like she'd said some horrible word. I didn't want her to pronounce that name again. My palms got all sweaty, and I glanced down at my watch and said too quickly, "I need to get back downstairs. A friend of mine is meeting me here."

Miss Abigail didn't budge. I got up and left her standing by the stained-glass window as I ran out of the sanctuary and down the stairs to the basement.

Rachel showed up about ten minutes later. I met her out on the street where her brother, Jamie, let her off. She waved to him and whispered, "Mom and Dad would absolutely die if they knew I was here."

"Are you ready to go inside?" I asked, a bit dramatically.

"Of course," she retorted, as though I'd insulted her.

I'd told her to dress casually, but casual to Rachel was chic to Grant Park. Right away heads began to turn. Carl was still talking to Cassandra. When he saw me come back into the basement with Rachel, he stood up, with Cassandra at his heels, and came over to us.

Rachel had that self-confidence that never wavered; she stuck out her hand and smiled and said, "Nice to meet you, Carl. Mary Swan's told me a lot about you."

"Same here, Rachel. Glad to meet you."

Cassandra looked a bit bewildered, so I quickly introduced her. "And this is Cassandra. Cassandra, my best friend, Rachel."

"Hi, Cassandra," Rachel said.

"Hi there," Cassandra responded, grinning. "Y'all gonna make some music for us?" she asked, nodding at the case that Rachel had stuck under her arm.

"No. Just practicing a little. For fun."

"You gonna play too, Carl?"

" 'Course. I invited them. If you wanna come round, Cassandra, you're mighty welcome."

She beamed at Carl and giggled. "I've gotta git Jessie home for her nap. Nice to meet ya. Bye." And she hurried over to where her mother was still talking with the other women and patting little Jessie on the back.

On the way to Carl's house, he commented to Rachel, "Mary Swan's told me all about you being a much better flutist than she is." He winked at me.

"Don't believe a word she says!" was Rachel's comeback.

"That's what I told Mary Swan. I don't have to believe it. I'll hear it soon enough. Then I'll know."

His aunt didn't look one bit pleased to see Rachel and me arriving at her house. She was sitting on the front porch talking to a man who was leaning over the railing. Carl shook the man's hand. "Nice to see you, Mr. Jones."

The man spit a wad of tobacco in the yard and just nodded at Carl.

We walked inside the house. "This is Puddin'," Carl said, hugging his little sister to him.

Rachel leaned down and said, "Good to meet you, Puddin'."

Puddin' let go of her brother and grabbed hold of my hand, and then whispered in my ear, "She's perty! Really perty!"

"I know," I whispered back.

"Y'all 'scuse me for a minute," Carl said. "You can start practicing if you want." He motioned for us to stay in the front room. "I just want to listen to the news on the radio for a minute." He went into the kitchen and fiddled with the radio dials while Rachel and I waited.

"He's hopin' to hear about James Mer'dith," Puddin' said, as if she was confiding a great secret. "Today's the day we'll know if Mr. Mer'dith gits into that white college in Miss, Missa, Mississippi."

I gave Rachel a perplexed look and she leaned over and whispered, "Haven't you heard about James Meredith applying to get into Ole Miss?"

I shrugged. I wasn't much for news.

She rolled her eyes as if to say, *You're hopeless.* "Today's the day they're supposed to let him in. The first time a Negro has been allowed to attend a white university."

Carl had his ear practically pinned to the radio, so I suggested, "Turn it up louder. We want to hear too."

A commentator was explaining how the Mississippi governor, upon learning that a Supreme Court justice was ordering him to admit Meredith at once, had cried, "Never! We will not surrender to the evil and illegal forces of tyranny!"

Carl turned off the radio and shrugged. "Not gonna happen today, that's for sure. But next week, they say he'll be enrolled." He smiled confidently and said, "Shore ain't fair to turn him away on the basis of race alone."

Carl had never really talked to me much about civil rights, but he and Rachel launched into a discussion about the Freedom Riders from last year. Carl seemed pleased and fascinated that Rachel would be so interested. "My cousin was part of those rides last year," he said proudly. "I went to most of those peaceful demonstrations in downtown Atlanta, ya know, letting the blacks eat at the same restaurants as whites. And have ya heard about all the stuff going on down in Albany? Even locked up Reverend King for a couple of weeks over the summer. My cousin's involved in all the demonstrations in Albany. I told him I'd go help out sometime. Someday, I even hope to meet Reverend King."

He got an angry look in his eyes. "Don't know what'll happen with Meredith. I know what it feels like to be turned down for school. Miss Abigail tried to get me into a white high school for this year, but they wouldn't have it. Wouldn't dare hear talk of it."

"Well, you know that since the Supreme Court's desegregation decision in 1954, only one school district in Georgia has desegregated, and that was here in Atlanta," Rachel commented. "Last fall a school in our part of town took in black students. Caused quite an uproar."

While listening to their conversation, I got my flute out and put it together. I had never really wanted to play the flute. Mama and Daddy thought every kid should have a musical background, and so, in the third grade, I'd chosen the instrument that looked the lightest and prettiest to me. Never mind that it took me two months of private lessons to even get a sound out of it. For three years I had struggled along with the flute.

Then, in sixth grade, I had met Rachel. If Rachel was book smart, she was also gifted with music. I'd never heard anyone else my age play the flute like she did. At the end-of-the-year banquet at Wellington, Rachel had stood up and played "The Carnival of Venice" from memory. Daddy had been so impressed that he'd signed me up with her flute teacher in seventh grade. Every Friday afternoon, Rachel and I rode together to Mrs. Hancock's house for flute lessons. We giggled and complained and acted like we hated those lessons.

Actually, I did hate them. I hated hearing Rachel play her scales perfectly, and I was jealous of the way she had already months ago finished the theory book I was struggling through. My legs shook and my stomach twitched as I listened to Rachel's skill. Then it would be my turn, and boy, was my teacher in for a letdown. That was what I thought. But to her credit, she never really compared me to Rachel. She did compare me to an off-key toad, though, and said my flute squeaked like a mouse.

When Rachel and Carl had finished talking about the civil rights movement, they immediately took out their instruments. Right away they started improvising. I sat back on the bed, my flute on my lap, enjoying listening to them and relieved to escape Carl's scrutiny. But he said, "Hey, Miss Lazy. What do you think you're doing? We're having a practice."

Rachel and I were tuning our flutes when his aunt banged her way into the room and, with a disapproving look announced, "Carl, you'll have to go somewhere else to play. Those flutes are giving me a headache."

"Yes, ma'am," he replied politely. Then, after she'd left the room, he whispered, "She's in one of her grouchy moods today. Don't let it worry you." He flashed his smile. "Anyway, I've got an idea. Come on, ladies."

We left his house and followed him down the street past Oakland Cemetery to his high school, Fair Oaks. It didn't have any fancy entranceway or grounds like Wellington's. There was just a parking lot in front of a bunch of nondescript brick buildings. I noticed the trash that lay in front of the main door. But behind the buildings lay a football field that seemed to be in much better shape than the school buildings.

Carl motioned for us to sit in the bleachers. Then he stepped out on the field and started playing his saxophone, head tilted back and happy as a lark, marching—prancing, I'd call it—and twisting. Rachel and I were doubled over in hysterics.

"See how easy it is, girls," he yelled up to the bleachers. "Nothin' to it."

I'd never seen this side of Carl—the performer.

"He's adorable," Rachel whispered admiringly.

We urged him to keep on marching, and he did, as if the whole two-hundred-piece band were out there with him performing for a halftime show. We were mesmerized. I think at different times, both Rachel and I had wanted to play in a marching band. At Wellington we had only an orchestra. A very well-known and respected orchestra, the only completely feminine one in the state. But seeing Carl having so much fun on the field brought back, at least to me, memories of attending football games with friends and applauding the marching band.

Finally a perspiring Carl came and joined us on the bleachers. He started making the sax moan again, the way he'd done for me. "Let's do some jazz, girls," he said, lifting his eyebrows.

Seeing my baffled expression, he set down his saxophone, and he came and sat behind me in the bleachers and reached forward, holding his hands over my eyes and whispering in my ear, "Hear the music, Mary Swan. Hear it. Just let your fingers play a scale." I could barely concentrate on anything except his smooth voice and the warmth of his hands over my eyes, but I tried to relax. "There you go," he said as, trembling with a mixture of fear and anticipation, I let my fingers play around with the keys on my flute. "Now make it a minor key. That's right, Mary Swan. Mm-hmm. That's right."

And by the time he let me go, I almost fell right back into his arms. Every cell in my body was screaming for more—more of his touch, of his time, of his music.

Ella Mae was waiting for us with a scowl on her face and her hands on her hips when we got back to church. "Sorry we're late," I squeaked out, trying not to grin foolishly while inside I felt like flying.

So Rachel and I didn't say a word on the way home, but when we were tucked safely in my room with the door shut, Rachel grabbed me by the shoulders and said, imitating Ella Mae, "You're in a heap o' trouble, Swan." Then she announced delightedly, "Carl is smitten too."

"I told you he was nice. And cute."

"And charming." We simultaneously burst into a high-pitched scream.

"He's never kissed you, has he?"

"Are you insane? Of course not. Never. Never even thought about it, I'm sure."

"I wouldn't be so sure."

"He's not like that."

"Like what? He's a man, isn't he? Same hormones as any other man. Believe me, Swan, he's thought about it."

"What do I do?"

"What do you mean, 'What do I do?' "

"I mean, is it okay to like two boys and for two boys to like me?"

"Of course it is!" Rachel stuck out her tongue and then laughed really hard. "What you do, Mary Swan, is enjoy it! You simply enjoy it!"

So I figured for the time being I'd follow her advice, because if there was anybody who knew about enjoying getting attention from boys, it was Rachel Abrams.

Chapter 14

Robbie had called twice that week, each time right after football practice. But his game on Friday night had been one of the few played out of town, so I had not gone. And Saturday night he lamented that his whole family had to attend his great-uncle's eightieth birthday party. "But I'll see you at church," he promised and sounded happy about it.

So instead of hiding in the bathroom as I had last Sunday, I met him at the back of the church after the service, and we walked out into the gardens.

"Congrats on the game," I stammered, all of a sudden flushed with excitement. "How'd the birthday party go?"

"Boring." He grinned, showing his dimples, and I saw that his cheeks were flushed too. "Poor Uncle Oscar has a hard time hearing, and he really isn't all there, so he never could get straight who had given him which gift. I think he received seven ties and four silk handkerchiefs." We laughed together. "What'd you do yesterday?"

"Oh, me?" I knew I couldn't tell him about Grant Park. "Not much. Rachel and I went riding in the late afternoon. Took a trail down by the Chattahoochee. And then last night"—I made a face—"Jennifer Peabody joined us for drinks at the Magnolia Room, and Jimmy was absolutely awful. Rude. I, on the other hand, acted like a perfect lady. Daddy was pretty furious with me last week after we chased off Amanda Hunnicutt. So I just sat there and acted interested in Miss Peabody's endless chatter about the Junior League raising money for something."

Then Robbie took my hand in his and looked straight at me with his topaz eyes wide and sincere. I thought he was going to ask me out again to the movies, but he didn't. He just said, "It's great to see you, Mary Swan. Do you think we could go out after the football game Friday night? I have to be there real early, but if your dad could drop you off, I'll take you home later."

If I had been Rachel, I would have known whether to act aloof, seductive, or enthusiastic. But as Mary Swan Middleton, I just got a goofy grin on my face and said "Gee, that sounds great." And I waved after him like a little kid saying good-bye to her grandma.

Late Sunday afternoon, after church and a meal at the club with Daddy and Jimmy and Grandmom and Granddad, and Amanda Hunnicutt unfortunately joining us for dessert, I needed time alone to think about what my mind was processing. I had to get to the Swan House.

I grabbed up my sketchpad and pencils and left the house. Back in the woods, with the flowering gardens in sight, I sat down. And although I wanted to think about Robbie and Carl, all I could hear in my mind was Miss Abigail talking about Someone who could make good out of bad and about white ladies from Buckhead loving those inner-city children. My pencil flew across the page, scratching and sketching something from inside my head.

The faintest tinge of fall kept the gnats away that afternoon in mid-September. From where I was sitting the mansion was almost out of view, but I could see the tumbling fountains, and if I listened carefully, I could hear the water splashing from one fountain to the next. Peaceful. That's what it felt like. Peaceful, when my mind was crowded with too many things: Miss Abigail's sad stories, kind white ladies, black hands covering my eyes, a kiss, Mama's struggles, a dare, a swan. Without realizing it, I started chanting verses from "Song of the Chattahoochee" while I sketched. "Out of the hills of Habersham down the valleys of Hall, I hurry amain to reach the plain, run the rapids and leap the fall. . . ."

I finally got up and tucked my sketchpad against my chest with the pencils clutched tightly in my hand. I retraced my steps on the well-worn path through the woods to my house. When I was safe in my room I fell onto my bed, opened the pad to the afternoon's sketch, and stared at it. The foreground held the cascading fountains, sketched fairly realistically. I sensed the flow of the water. Squatting on the steps to the right of the fountains was the figure of a black man. He was smiling and dipping his hand in one of the pools where a miniature swan swam. Embarrassed by the sketch, I slapped the sketchbook closed and went down to the second floor, slipping into Mama's studio. It was quite obvious to me that I needed inspiration from her *atelier*.

The wall with the built-in shelves beckoned to me. I counted the shelves. Six wide and four high, reaching all the way from floor to ceiling. These were big shelves, boxlike, the kind Mama could lean several yard-high paintings in. I had inherited my creativity and lack of organizational sense from Mama. I could almost hear her laughing with Trixie as she described her studio in perfect French. *"C'est la pagaille!"* A disaster area! Well, she'd been right.

A bottom shelf held her paints and palettes, all of which looked as if she had randomly tossed them inside, as someone might toss empty Coke bottles into a big trash can. Half of the tubes of paint lacked tops, so that the paint was caked on, hard and useless. The palettes, covered in rainbow colors, had apparently been stacked with wet paint on them, because several were stuck together. Another shelf held unused canvases, but most of them had smudges of paint from other projects on them.

One shelf was filled with sketchpads, lying one on top of the other as if Mama had thrown them inside in a hurry. I pulled two from the bottom of the stack and then plopped onto the floor. I flipped through the pages one by one. Mama had the habit of writing the date of when she started a sketchpad on the inside cover. The first one said 1955, and inside were several sketches of Jimmy when he was about six. The rest I recognized as other children whom Mama had eventually painted.

The other sketchpad was the one she'd used to sketch me as a little girl on the tree swing. Sweet Mama. *You said it was good therapy to sketch me.* I had not understood how much that one sentence meant at the time, but now I was beginning to see it. Mama the artist and Mama the tormented soul. I studied the way she had drawn my face. I liked the way my cheeks had been round and ruddy then, healthy and full. I liked the way I could feel myself moving back and forth on the swing. And I especially liked realizing how much time Mama had put into the sketches before she ever put paintbrush to canvas. No matter what had been running through her head in those months, she had taken the time lovingly and painstakingly to sketch me in a dozen different positions on that tree swing. Finally she had created the one that embodied her Swannee, the one with my toes fairly puncturing the paper, so far were they flung out in front of me as I leaned back, clutching the rope swing and giggling.

But as I set down the sketchpad, a completely different, gnawing question pierced through me. *Mama, if you were alive, what advice would you give me about boys and blacks and church?* It was more than an adolescent's question. It was me trying to figure out how much of what I had lived and believed in these sixteen years was a lie.

Then slowly, almost apprehensively, as if I thought Mama might be watching, I searched through the rest of those shelves, first stacking all thirteen of the sketchpads into a neat pile and then pulling out each unfinished painting and lining them up against the wall. In all, there were five unfinished paintings, including Mama's self-portrait, the one that photographer from *LIFE* had shown to the world. I wondered if it was normal for an artist to leave so many of her paintings unfinished. Maybe Mama had had too many ideas rushing around in her head, just like me. Maybe she hadn't had time to finish one before another scene thrust itself into her mind, begging to be painted.

In two of the bottom shelves on the far left of the wall, she'd had wooden boards nailed across the center and stacked the resulting four shelves with big heavy books on art history and painting. I took one off the shelf and leafed through it, then replaced it and absentmindedly withdrew another. That's when I noticed that those nailed-in, makeshift shelves were made of narrow planks of wood that left a space of about six inches behind them between the books and the back wall. I also noticed that the weight of those books on the narrow planks of wood had caused them to sag. So I took all the books from the top shelf and laid them on the floor. Then I did the same for the next shelf. And when I went back to repeat the action yet again, what I saw left me feeling momentarily like Nancy Drew. Something had been placed behind the now empty shelves in that space between the planks and the wall.

I reached behind, and my hands felt the coil of a wire. I pulled out a sketchpad. Thrilled with the discovery, I stuck my hand back behind the shelf again and found that Mama had stacked a bunch of old sketchbooks back there. I don't know if she had deliberately meant to hide them, but the heavy art books had certainly hidden them from view. There were seven of them, all the twenty-by-thirty-inch kind. Big, heavy, and spiral. Out they came, scattered on the floor on top of the art books. I chose one and opened it. On the inside cover, Mama had written in her flowery cursive: *Resthaven, 1951.*

Now I was really intrigued, especially when I saw no portraits or still lifes, nothing of the Swan House or other well-known homes in Buckhead. Only page after page of an old elegant mansion with white columns in front. Some sketches showed the front of the building, some focused on a woman sitting on a bench in a flowering garden with the brick building visible in the background. In one sketch, a black man with callused skin and a great crooked-toothed smile was leaning on a rake, and again that building loomed in the distance. He looked so real that I almost thought I could hear the laughter that was behind his eyes.

Mama had written at the bottom of the page *Henry B., 1951.* I was about to flip to the next page when I stopped, my heart pounding. I told myself it was just my overactive imagination starting up again. After all, how many Henry Bs were there in the world? But somehow, with tingles starting in my scalp and running down my spine, I just knew that Henry B. was Henry Becker, one of the artists of the Raven Dare. A breakthrough! This was definitely what Rachel would call a breakthrough.

It didn't look to me like Henry B. could possibly own the big red-brick mansion, especially since he had that rake in his hand and seemed perfectly comfortable and content with it. Maybe Henry B. worked at the house called Resthaven, for the obviously rich people who inhabited it. I couldn't wait to tell Rachel!

I quickly flipped through the other sketchbooks, and the thing that struck me right away was that Mama had written the same thing on the inside cover of each pad: *Resthaven* and then the year. *1951, 1953, 1954, 1957, 1958, 1960.* The final one was from 1961. Resthaven. All from Resthaven. All filled with sketches, and most held at least one sketch of the stately brick mansion.

I spent the rest of the evening sitting cross-legged on the floor with the seven newly discovered spiral sketchpads and the art books and all the contents of the file Daddy had given me several weeks ago scattered on the floor. I only left the studio once, to make a ham and cheese sandwich and get a glass of milk and bring that upstairs and set it on the floor too. Of course, with all that mess around me, I wasted several hours, completely at a loss of what to do next.

I knew I should have just waited for Rachel's help. She couldn't come over because she was in the middle of reading *Wuthering Heights*, which had to be finished for Honors English by the next Tuesday. I was only on page fifty-eight. Sometimes Rachel was just too practical! Forget Heathcliff and Cathy! I needed her here with me now!

Several things became painfully clear that evening. First, Daddy had been right about his file. I'd seen all of the articles before in the stuff Mrs. MacIlvain had given me. I'd hoped to find a bill of sale with the name of the person who'd bought Mama's painting, or at least some reference to it, but the file contained nothing new.

Second, I *had* to find out what and where Resthaven was. This place had obviously been very important to Mama, so much so that she went there fairly frequently to sketch. I wracked my brains to try to think of any friends Mama and Daddy had who called their home Resthaven. Lots of people in Buckhead named their homes and their property, but I didn't recall any place named Resthaven.

And third, the thing that worried and excited me the most was that it looked as if Mama didn't want anyone else to know anything about the sketchbooks from Resthaven. Surely that was important! Especially since no one else ever ventured into her studio. Not Daddy or Ella Mae or Jimmy or me or anyone. That photographer from *LIFE* was probably the first person to step foot inside the *atelier* in many, many months. The *atelier* was Mama's private refuge. So why would she hide these sketchpads when there was virtually no chance of their being discovered anyway?

About eight-thirty or nine I was suddenly tired of it all and then suddenly petrified that Ella Mae or Daddy might out of the blue walk in there the next day and find this mess. So I placed the Seven Secret Sketchpads, as I dubbed them, back into their hiding place, crammed the shelves with the art books, and stuffed the newspaper articles back into Daddy's manila file before I left the room.

Late that night Jimmy was watching *The Twilight Zone* in the den with the sound up so loud that its creepy music blared down the hall and into Daddy's study. I was curled up on Daddy's couch while he scribbled notes on his big yellow-lined ledger and wrote checks.

In my most casual voice, I asked, "Daddy, have you ever heard of a beautiful mansion called Resthaven?"

Daddy let his fountain pen drop and looked up at me with suspicion and surprise on his face. Then he regained his composure and said, "Resthaven. Hmm. Yes, I've heard of it."

"Well, where is it?"

"Why do you want to know?"

"I was going through some of Mama's things and found a sketchbook she had titled 'Resthaven.' It was full of sketches of this neat old mansion."

Daddy looked suddenly uncomfortable and squirmed in his chair. That's the only word for it. "Yes, I know of Resthaven." He cleared his throat.

"Well, where is it?"

"In the North Georgia mountains."

"On the way to Highlands?"

"Yes, in that general direction. Closer to Lake Burton, really."

"Did you and Mama know the people who lived there?"

"Well, yes, we did, Mary Swan. We knew them well. I guess your mother enjoyed sketching the mansion. A beautiful old historic home. You know how Mama loved historic homes."

It seemed to me that Daddy was being deliberately evasive. So I decided to risk being discovered as the Raven. I traipsed upstairs and brought a sketchpad back down to Daddy.

"Look, Daddy. Look at this sketch. This man. Mama calls him Henry B."

Daddy was not paying any attention to me as he thumbed through the sketchpad.

"Where did you find this?" he asked, almost accusingly.

"In Mama's studio. You said I could look in there."

He sighed deeply and closed the pad. "You're right, Swannee, I did. I'm sorry. It's simply that I've never seen this book. It's still quite painful to see your mother's work."

Gingerly I asked again, "Do you think the man Mama calls Henry B. could be the artist Henry Becker? The one whose painting was to be dedicated along with Mama's?"

Daddy peered at the sketch for a moment. "No. Impossible. The Henry in this picture looks like a yardman."

"Well, was he the yardman, Daddy? Did you ever see this man when you and Mama went to visit these friends?"

Daddy's brow furrowed as he thought. "Goodness, Swannee. I don't remember. We haven't been there in years. . . ."

Something about the way he said it didn't quite ring true, and I wanted to scream, "But Mama has seven sketchbooks from Resthaven, and the last one is dated 1961!" But I left him alone. Rachel and Carl and I could surely find the Henry B. who lived somewhere in North Georgia and smiled when he held a rake in front of a home called Resthaven. And if all else failed, I could always ask Trixie.

So I went up to bed and started reading *Wuthering Heights*, which turned out to be the best book and the worst I could be reading. Its haunting story fit in perfectly with my new discovery and my thoughts about the Raven Dare. But reading about Heathcliff, tormented Heathcliff, sent chills up my spine. What had Mrs. Alexander said in class yesterday? *"The literary figure of Heathcliff remains one of the most passionate and pitiful pictures of mental illness in modern literature."*

Mental illness. Resthaven. Mama. A lunatic.

And then I knew. I remembered. Me in tears running to Trixie's house, begging her to help Mama, who was crying on the floor with baby Jimmy. Me in Ella Mae's lap, and then me watching her carry Mama. Me and Daddy and little Jimmy visiting Mama in the big red mansion. Mama gone for such a long time. Me crying to Ella Mae every day that I missed Mama. And what did Ella Mae always answer? What was it?

"Yore mama be right tired out, Mary Swan. Right tired. But she'll be back soon 'nuff, honey chile. Don't you worry none."

And she had come back. She had! And I was absolutely certain that I'd never gone to visit Mama at Resthaven again. I counted backward in my mind. I would have been five in 1951. Resthaven! 1951!

Well, with that revelation, it was completely impossible for me to return to Heathcliff or to fall asleep, so I did what I'd been dying to do all evening. I called Rachel. Never mind that it was past eleven. She had a private line. I prayed that she'd answer and not Jamie.

Two rings later, Rachel's irritated voice said, "Hello?"

"Sorry, Rach, to call you so late."

"Swan, you idiot. You scared me to death. I hope Mom didn't hear the phone from her room."

"Listen, I've had the most unbelievable breakthrough in the Raven Dare and I wanted to call you earlier, but I didn't because I knew you were reading *Wuthering Heights* and I didn't want to bother you and I wouldn't have except that then I started thinking about Heathcliff and how he was so tormented and I remembered what Mrs. Alexander said about mental illness yesterday and then I thought about what Herbert had said about Mama being a lunatic and then I remembered, Rach, I remembered going to visit her at this big house when I was five, right after I'd been so scared, and I put it all together and it turns out that where she was and where I visited is the same place in the Seven Secret Sketchpads. It's Resthaven." I finished, out of breath.

Rachel took a long pause to recover from my babble. "What in the world are you talking about, Swan? Slow down a sec. You lost me way back there with Heathcliff!"

And so I told her, and we must have talked until well past midnight. And the last thing Rachel said before she hung up was "Wow, Swan. You really are on to something. See ya in the morning."

The first chance that Rachel and I had to talk on Monday was on the way to orchestra practice. Every time we trudged that path to the Band Hut, I couldn't help but think of our mad midnight pursuit of the clue and me sticking my hands under the building and pulling out the old flute case. So it seemed to me perfectly appropriate that I'd be explaining my incredible breakthrough to Rachel on the very same path where the adventure had begun.

Rachel didn't seem to care for the symbolism, but her blue-gray eyes flashed with energy and she said excitedly, "Look, Swannee. You said your dad admitted that Resthaven existed and that it was somewhere in the North Georgia mountains, near North Carolina, right? So a little snooping around and a few carefully asked questions to Trixie should get us the information we need. Then all we have to figure out is how to get to Resthaven."

"Good point." Silence. Then I had an idea. "Could Jamie drive us?"

Rachel made a face. "He already threatened to tell Mom and Dad about driving me to Grant Park. And just because I stayed on the phone with you too long the other day. No. Not Jamie."

"And not Ella Mae. Definitely not. She'd be scared out of her wits to drive outside of Atlanta. But I bet you a million bucks she knows all about Resthaven."

"Yeah. Too bad you can't pull it out of her."

"No way. She gave me a piece of her mind on Saturday about you and me going over to Carl's. It won't do to have her suspicious about anything else. Anyway, she might mention it to Daddy, and he'd have a huge conniption fit. I don't think I can talk to him about any of this anymore."

We were at the Band Hut, and Rachel had taken her seat as first flute with me right beside her, when she whispered, "Hey! What about Carl? He can drive, can't he? And he's your second assistant. He's supposed to help. Ask Carl."

Mr. Fogel, the orchestra director, started tapping his wand, as we called it, on the music stand, which meant silence and quick, so I just winked at Rachel. A date with Robbie on Friday night and time with Carl on Saturday and the possibility of a long drive in the country with him in the near future. Things were looking up. All I had to do before the weekend was find a time to talk to Trixie.

On Wednesday afternoon, I invited Lucy to go swimming with me one last time before we closed up the pool for the year. Trixie was sitting in a lounge chair reading an issue of *Vanity Fair*, periodically glancing up to comment on a dive Lucy had made. I saw my opportunity and pulled a lounge chair over beside hers, where she was tanning just perfectly.

I tried to look interested in the magazine, but Trixie didn't seem to notice, so finally I just blurted out, "Do you know Mama and Daddy's friends who live at a place called Resthaven?"

She lifted up her bright pink straw hat so I could see her face. "I beg your pardon?"

"Do you know where Resthaven is?"

Adjusting her leopard-spotted sunglasses, Trixie acknowledged, "I've heard of it, but I've never been there. Not sure who owns that place. Did you ask your father?"

"Yeah, but I told you, whenever I start talking about Mama he gets so uncomfortable and elusive. It's just that I found this sketchbook in Mama's studio with all these sketches of this great big brick house. She called it Resthaven. But Daddy won't say a word."

Trixie looked pale all of a sudden, as if someone had come by and wiped off her tan with a washrag. "Then don't bother him with it, Mary Swan. He's grieving in his own way."

"That's what I'm doing. Letting him grieve. And that's why I'm asking you."

Trixie looked miserable. "I really think you should leave it alone, Mary Swan."

"But why? Mama obviously liked the place. Are the people who live there murderers or something?"

"Of course not. It's not what you think, is all."

"Well, then, explain it to me, Trixie. Please."

"It really should be your father. . . ."

"He won't."

She took a deep breath and called out to Lucy, "Great dive, sweetie. Absolutely perrrfect!" Then she turned her attention to me. "Resthaven isn't somebody's private home. It's a place, a place where you go when you're . . . when you're sick."

I sat back, feeling a little quiver in my tummy. Trixie had just confirmed my suspicion. "You mean Mama went there because she was sick?"

Trixie nodded cautiously.

"Sick in the head, is what you mean, isn't it, Trixie? Resthaven is a place for nutty people."

"Stop it, Swan. No. Listen. Resthaven is a private institution where people who are sick—depressed—can go to get better, to be helped, to be away from everything for a while. It's really a wonderful place."

"And Mama went there in 1951 and drew all those pictures of the place." I thought about that. "How long did she stay there?"

"A month. Maybe a little longer."

I ventured on carefully. "So that was where I went to visit when I was a little girl. Daddy took me. I remember."

Trixie nodded.

"And did she get better?"

"For a while."

"You mean she went back?"

"Swan, your dad needs to tell you about all this."

"But he won't!" I said so emphatically that Lucy popped her head over the side of the pool and asked, "What's wrong, Mary Swan?"

"Nothing, Luce. Everything's fine," Trixie sang out.

"Did Mama go to Resthaven more than once?" I decided if I asked the questions in a way that she could answer with a yes or no, maybe Trixie would be more willing to divulge the information.

She nodded.

"More than twice?"

Another nod.

"For a month each time?"

"Yes."

"But that's impossible! I don't remember her being gone!" In my mind I was calculating Trixie's confession and weighing it against the seven sketchbooks. They matched up. But how could they? "The only time she went away for very long was when she was at art exhibitions!"

Now Trixie looked completely disconsolate. But she didn't have to say another word. Suddenly the whole thing got crystal clear, clearer than the turquoise water in the swimming pool.

"Mama never went to art exhibitions, did she?" I accused. And not giving Trixie time to answer, I continued. "Why would he lie? Why did Daddy lie? Why did he say she was going to show her paintings when she was really just going to a place for crazy people?" Hot tears burned my face.

"Swan, whatever your dad did, he thought he was doing the best thing for you and Jimmy. . . ."

"Well, he was wrong! Dead wrong!" I exploded. "He lied so that I'd have to hear the truth from a drunken boy at my first dance! And piece it together from one of Mama's sketchbooks! I hate him! I hate him!"

And to keep Trixie and Lucy from seeing all my tears, I jumped up and dived into the pool and swam under water for as long as I could, until finally I burst to the surface, gasping for air.

Trixie's horrified expression somehow pleased me. I swam fourteen laps without stopping, then threw my arms across the hot pavement. "It's okay, Trixie. Thanks for telling me. I'd have found out soon enough. I'm not a complete idiot, you know."

At last I'd found the thing that would make me paint, make me get beyond the simple sketchpad and to the easel. Anger. Anger, no, fury, made me paint. I locked myself in Mama's studio on Wednesday afternoon after Trixie and Lucy left, dragged an easel across the floor to the windows, grabbed a palette and a handful of brushes, and placed a canvas on the easel. My strokes were so forceful and out of control that I thought I might punch my fist through the canvas. I didn't know what I was painting, but I did know that I had to get this pain, this awful, hideous, all-engulfing pain, out of my soul and onto the canvas.

From time to time little phrases from Mama would come back to me. She'd said things like *"One color at a time, Mary Swan. Use contrasting colors. Opposites. Mix the paints on the palette and dab them on the canvas and have fun. Just have fun. Get the idea and then give the details later. That's what's so great about painting—you can always cover a mistake. Always."*

Poor Mama. If only she had known how *unfun* this was for me at that instant. How painting was my attempt at expressing the insanity I felt, the brokenness of my family, the disappointment with my dad. But somewhere inside, as I experimented with the tiny brushes and the thick wide ones and every color of paint on the palette, the anger dissipated, and I became engrossed in my work.

Two hours must have passed before I put down the paintbrush for the last time. The colors on the canvas resembled absolutely nothing, but it didn't matter. That afternoon I had felt a thrill when I held the paintbrush in my hand. Maybe Rachel felt like this when she held her flute or Carl when he played his saxophone or Miss Abigail when she snuggled a child to her breast. The feeling of "At last! At last! This is what I was meant to do!"

For me, on that horrible afternoon of yet another tragic revelation, I felt a warmth stronger than the momentary tingles, something deep down and satisfying. What I'd always wanted to be true, and what I had always suspected but been much too terrified to admit, had just been confirmed. I was made to paint. When I closed my eyes, I could almost feel Mama there behind me, looking over my shoulder, laughing in the lighthearted way that meant she was happy and saying, "It's good, Swan. Really good."

Chapter 15

E arly the next evening, September twentieth, I was home alone.
Jimmy was still at football practice and Daddy at the office. The
phone rang.

"Swan, quick. Turn on the news. You've gotta see this." It was
Rachel, adamant.

So I ran to the den and flipped on the TV to Channel 5, and all I
could see was what looked like a lot of college students yelling something. The anchorman was concluding his report, saying, "So despite
promises from Governor Ross Barnett and orders from President Kennedy, James Meredith was not permitted to register for classes at the
University of Mississippi today." There on the screen a young black
man was being escorted by a policeman down a short flight of steps
while a crowd of what the commentator said were two thousand white
students chanted, "Glory, glory, segregation."

I imagined Carl with his ear glued to the radio, listening with a
sinking heart to the news. James Meredith wasn't going to be registered tonight, that was for sure. It scared me to see the anger on the
students' faces and hear them chanting in their loud, obnoxious way. I
wondered what Carl was feeling right now, what the rest of the black
community in inner-city Atlanta felt.

Even if I'd had the courage to call him, I would never have been
able to bring up the newest info on the Raven Dare or the possibility
of his driving us to Resthaven. *"Sounds awful silly to me, Mary Swan,"*
he had said the first time I mentioned it. He was right. It was just a
stupid, silly tradition. But it was tearing apart my world with every bit
as much power as the angry students and the stubborn government
were tearing apart the dream of racial equality of James Meredith and

Carl Matthews and every other civil-rights-minded person in the whole country.

Watching the news report made me feel worse than ever. James Meredith hadn't even opened his mouth. Just his simple presence had inspired hatred in two thousand students. Judged and sentenced simply for being black. I understood what it meant to be judged; only it worked out pretty well for me. Where I lived, you only had to say your last name or the name of your street or what school you went to, and everybody thought they knew everything about you. The list was always the same: rich, well-bred, good family, fine education, successful father.

Crazy mother.

"It's not fair!" I said out loud to no one. Nothing was fair.

Trixie rang the doorbell a few minutes later, and when I let her in, she grabbed me up in a hug. "Sweetheart, Mary Swan. I've been worried about you all day. How are you?"

I shrugged.

"I shouldn't have told you. Any of it. It's my fault, sweetheart. I'm sorry." Then she took both of my hands in hers and looked at me as if I were a child and implored, "Please leave it all alone, Mary Swan. It isn't worth it. You can't change anything now. Leave it alone. Forgive your father and get on with life. All that isn't important. What's important is that you were and are loved."

I didn't have the strength to argue with her. Anyway, I'd gotten what I needed from her, even though it had cost me another part of my soul to get it. Scribbled on a piece of paper in my room was the address of Resthaven Sanatorium, located near Dillard, Georgia, five miles south of the North Carolina state line.

I called Rachel back when Trixie left and told her what I thought about life at that moment. "It's not fair. It's awful. Awful for the blacks."

"Of course it's not fair. Not fair for the starving Africans or the persecuted people in Communist China or in Russia or for the folks who woke up one morning last August and found a wall had been built down the middle of their city of Berlin and they were separated from their families. It stinks. I think about it a lot." She paused. "Maybe it's because I'm a Jew. Maybe it's because my mother's family all died in the concentration camps. Murdered, Mary Swan. Good, decent, smart people murdered because they were Jews.

"Think about what happened right here in Atlanta just four years ago. Remember the bomb that blew up the temple on Peachtree Street? Remember how Ralph McGill wrote that great article that blasted the hatemongers?"

I did remember, although I'm sure that Rachel, being Jewish, had that image of the destroyed temple seared into her mind. Ralph McGill was the controversial editor of the *Atlanta Constitution* who had written an editorial after the bombing. The article had later earned him a Pulitzer Prize.

Rachel was saying, "He called all decent citizens to face the facts and said, 'When the wolves of hate are loosed on one people, then no one is safe.' It has happened throughout history. And it's scary and terrible. No, it isn't fair, and James Meredith and all the other blacks in the South are going to keep having to learn it the hard way. The way they have all their lives."

With the pensive, almost bitter mood she was in combined with my despondency, I didn't figure we'd be good for anything that night. But I had to tell her about my conversation with Trixie. "You know what really isn't fair, Rach? You know what stinks to high heaven? Daddy lied to us. All those trips Mama went on weren't to art exhibitions. She went to a sanatorium. That's what I learned from Trixie, and I tell you it stinks."

That took a few seconds to sink in, and then Rachel, for once sounding repentant and almost docile, said, "Gee, I'm sorry I suggested you talk to her."

We never even mentioned the whole Resthaven bit to Carl, because the Meredith issue filled the news right up until the end of September, and when I saw Carl on Saturdays he was different, not his usual happy self. I think he got to watch the news on TV at Miss Abigail's house. Anyway, James Meredith was refused the right to register about three times, and every time the crowds of students and just a lot of other whites would yell awful things.

Finally the army or the National Guard or something had to come in, and there was this horrible riot where two people were killed while Meredith was being hidden and guarded by plain-clothed marshals. And hundreds of white people chanted racial slurs and "Two-four-one-three, we hate Kennedy!" and all the while the president thought things were going well, and he came on TV and said so, and it wasn't until later that we saw the reports of the riot. But Meredith finally did get registered on the first of October.

During that whole time, you could feel that race relations in Atlanta, which historically had been a lot better than other places in the Deep South, were becoming more fragile. In Buckhead, Daddy and Grandmom and Granddad, and probably most everyone else, just could not understand why a black student was so adamant about attending a white college. After all, there were several very well thought of black colleges in Atlanta, like Morehouse and Spelman and Morris Brown and Clark. When I listened to the adults around me talk, I could see their point of view.

But then I'd go with Ella Mae to Grant Park and feel the tension and unrest in the air, like some impending storm. And the blacks in Grant Park sometimes looked at me with suspicion in their eyes. Or at least that's what I thought I saw there, and it hurt. It hurt a lot.

In early October Puddin' broke her arm, and we were pretty sure it was because a white kid yanked her off the swing at the playground at school. But she would never admit it, even though one of her friends saw the whole thing and explained how this big white boy sneaked onto the playground and started roughing up the kids. But the fear in Puddin's eyes replaced her carefree attitude, and she seemed to be forever looking over her shoulder. I think that stabbed me in the heart most of all.

Twice Miss Abigail found the windshield of her car painted with the words "nigger lover," and I could tell that shook up Carl a lot. But she didn't seem one bit worried. I'll always remember what she said to me when I asked her about it.

"Mary Swan, I've got the army of the Lord protecting me, and I'll be just fine."

"You're not afraid?"

She smiled that smile that made her eyes shine. "Sometimes I'm afraid. But haven't you heard the saying, 'Courage is fear that's said its prayers'? I get down on my face before the Lord every morning before I leave my house, and I tell Him that He is in charge and that my day is in His hands."

But Carl was afraid. And mad. Real mad. And I didn't know if his talk about peaceful protests would last. I could read in his eyes that if he ever caught up with the boy who had dared to hurt his little sister, that guy was as good as dead. And that scared me.

We'd barely gotten over the ordeal with James Meredith when the whole country went into hysteria over the Cuban Missile Crisis. If the blacks and whites didn't tear each other apart, then there was the real possibility that the Russians, with missiles in Cuba, would blow us up. And as for logistics, Atlanta was a lot closer to Cuba than, say, California. I think the whole country held its breath for about a week, fearing the worst and praying for a miracle. That miracle came at the end of October when the Russian Prime Minister Khrushchev agreed to dismantle his bases and withdraw all the missiles. So the country let out a collective sigh of relief.

Of course Mr. Jeffries, our history teacher, loved all this "history in the making," as he called it. So not only did I hear about James Meredith and Cuban missiles at home on the TV, but at least an hour a day at Wellington, it was drilled into us about the racial pressures and the changes on the horizon and the menace from Russia.

In early November Rachel and I did get to meet the other members of Carl's band, and, man, could they play jazz! Nickie played the sax, like Carl, Leo played drums, Larry played the trombone, and Big Man played the piano. And we discovered that they could also sing. Nickie was as tall as Carl and skinny as a rail and had a gorgeous tenor voice. Leo, short, stocky, and full of muscles, sang bass. Larry reminded me of Fat Albert, a wonderful character that the comedian Bill Cosby described on one of his records that Daddy and Mama used to listen to. Larry was certainly wide and jolly, and he had the kindest eyes. And he could hit notes so low that Rachel and I could only shake our heads in admiration. Big Man was just the opposite of Larry. He looked like his body had forgotten to grow after the age of twelve, but it didn't seem to bother him one bit. And when he hit his high tenor note or sang falsetto, we knew that in spite of his diminutive size, he had a powerful set of lungs.

"Hey, guys!" I said after they'd delighted us with several renditions of songs from the fifties. "I've got this great idea. Would y'all be interested in playing for the Piedmont Driving Club's Christmas Dance?"

"The *what?*" Larry asked in his deep voice.

"Some fancy club in Buckhead, I suppose," Carl said, nodding to me with a twinkle in his eyes.

"Right. It is this fancy club, and every year there's a dance for juniors and seniors in high school."

"I done finished high school, and I ain't neva' been invited to no dance at no fancy club," Big Man challenged with a smile.

"Oh, hush up, boy, and let the lady speak!" That came from Leo.

"Every year the girls from several of the private schools invite the guys to this dance. Live band. Long dresses and corsages. Gourmet buffet. Stuff like that. Anyway, y'all would be great! And you'd get paid a lot!" I actually had no idea if this was true, but it made my argument sound more convincing.

"Go on and find out about it, Mary Swan," Carl concluded after a brief discussion with his friends. "And keep us posted."

So I called the club and talked to a Mrs. Appleby and found out that she already had reserved the main band, but that she was indeed looking for a start-up band for the evening. And money was involved. When I reported my findings to the jazz band, they all seemed interested in the idea of playing at a fancy white man's club.

So many things I thought were good ideas that year turned out to be not so good and even terrible, but in my heart, I kept thinking I was doing the right thing. Even with Carl, I thought it was right to be his friend, and I felt on fire anytime his hand brushed mine or he rubbed my shoulders or caught my eye. It was always so subtle that, try as I might, I couldn't tell what he meant. I wanted him to mean something deep by those moments of affection. I dreamed of him kissing me in the alley behind the church or when we slipped into Oakland Cemetery and no one else was around. Man, I wanted that! But all he gave me were hints.

Robbie did kiss me, almost every Friday night after the football game. I liked those kisses, and I liked Robbie. A whole lot. I honestly did not think I was two-timing him. Of course, I wasn't, except in my mind. But that kind of kept things exciting. I think the most unbelievable part of that fall was that one boy liked me a whole bunch, and maybe another one liked me too. It had never happened before, and after being jealous of Rachel and all her boyfriends, I finally got a taste of the knock-you-down fun of being with boys.

Rachel told me about all the best spots to go parking, as we called it, but Robbie wasn't like that. He liked to drive me home and kiss me good and hard in the driveway or walk with me out to the back-yard, lean against the hickory tree and talk, with his arms wrapped around me. And since Jimmy's window didn't look out onto the back of the house, that was okay by me. And the thing I liked so much about Robbie was that we talked about all kinds of things. Some dumb gossip from our schools, and of course about his sports and my or-chestra and the horses, but we also talked about church, and why he was an acolyte. I even got up the courage to tell him about going down to Grant Park and what I did there, and about Miss Abigail and Pud-din' and Cassandra and Jessie and a lot of other people I'd met.

I never mentioned Carl, of course, but it felt great that Robbie knew about the things that were mattering to me. I even told him what Miss Abigail said about faith and what Cassandra had said about baptism.

I didn't talk to Daddy much. I still felt furious about his lying for all those years, and I wasn't about to broach the subject with him. And I loved him so much and hated him so fiercely that I found it easiest to blame him for everything that was wrong in my life.

Those women kept coming by to see him, and Jimmy kept being completely obnoxious, which pleased me greatly, and I kept acting polite but distant. Once in a while I'd throw out a comment to shock Daddy and his woman friend at just the right moment. And sometimes Daddy tried to explain to me that he needed a date to escort to such and such a function, but I never acted one bit sympathetic. I'm sure that hurt him.

I avoided Trixie like the plague. I couldn't bear to see her knowing that she knew that I knew all those secrets.

One day I caught Ella Mae bent over the sofa in the dining room, clutching her head and moaning softly. "Ella Mae! What's the matter?"

She jerked up quickly. "Mary Swan! I didn't hear ya come in the room." She tried to smile. "Ain't nothin,' honey, but a bad headache. Been gettin' 'em lotsa times lately. Part o' growing old." She started humming to herself as she dusted a coffee table, but I wasn't fooled.

"Ella Mae, you're sick! You look awful. Go lie down in the guest room for a while. Please."

"Don't ya worry 'bout me, sugar. I'll be fine."

But I was worried. I got her a bottle of aspirin and a glass of water and convinced her to take the pills, but she never lay down. The next day, her husband, Roy, called to say she was "feelin' mighty poorly" and wouldn't be at work. Ella Mae never missed work.

But that fall she ended up being absent two or three times. Whenever I questioned her, she'd just shake her head and say, "Jus' women's problems, Mary Swan. Not much ya kin do but put up with it." I figured she was right, but I certainly hated it for her. I kept my mouth shut, because I knew she felt it wasn't her place to be burdening us with her problems.

But much of my life just went on as normal. Rachel and I rode our mares on Monday, Wednesday, and Thursday afternoons and usually at least once on the weekends, and we went to flute lessons on Friday after school, and I spent Friday nights with Robbie and Saturdays at Grant Park and Sundays at church and the club. And I did my homework, which took at least an hour every night. But whenever I had a spare moment, I sneaked into the studio and painted. I never said one more word to Daddy about the sketchbooks or Resthaven or anything at all about Mama, because I was afraid he would lock up the studio or clean it out. And the studio, the *atelier*, was mine. Mine! It turned out that lots of those books Mama had on painting were pretty helpful, and so sometimes I'd read a few pages and get all inspired and then paint. Mama was right that it was easy to cover over the mistakes.

In English class, we finished *Wuthering Heights* and started reading *Jane Eyre*, so we were talking about the Brontë sisters for half the fall. But we also did poetry by Emily Dickinson, and I liked it so much that I didn't dare transform it.

Once that fall the Wellington orchestra played for the Atlanta Junior League, and we also went down to Savannah to perform for the DAR meeting (the Daughters of the American Revolution) to which Grandmom Middleton belonged. I enjoyed getting dressed in my orchestra attire: putting on my long black satin gown and pulling my stringy hair up into a bun, with Rachel's help of course, and applying Mama's rouge and mascara and lipstick.

But the Raven Dare was as good as dead and buried. I did not want to think about the black bird or Edgar Allen Poe or Resthaven or missing paintings.

It was Rachel who finally brought up the whole thing near the end of October. "I know you don't want to deal with it, and I know you're still mad at your dad and you can't talk to Trixie, but do you think I could just have a look at those sketchbooks with you and go through any other things your mom may have stashed in her studio?"

"I don't know, Rach. It just keeps turning into something bigger than I had planned. Every time I even think about it now, I get this low-level feeling of nausea. What else am I going to find out about my mother? About my whole family? No Raven honor is worth this misery!"

"I think you've learned the worst, Swannee. I really do. And can I just say something, as a not-so-objective observer?"

I shrugged.

"It's true that your dad lied, and that's unfortunate. Well, it stinks. But on the other hand, you had a pretty normal childhood and you loved your parents and they loved you and they loved each other. Lots of kids don't have that. And if your mom was as sick and depressed as it seems, well, I think it's pretty remarkable that your dad and Ella Mae and Trixie could keep things going the way they did. You weren't miserable, after all. Think of Samantha Logan's family. Her mom is an alcoholic, and everyone knows it, and other parents won't ever let their kids go to her house. She hangs out with her older siblings and smokes and cusses and has boyfriends twice her age.

"There are tons of families like that right here in Buckhead, even though they try to hide it. Think of Trixie and the gosh-awful junk she went through. And everybody knew it. I really don't think everyone knew about your mom. I certainly didn't. I never heard a soul whispering that your mom was nuts. Knock-you-down gorgeous, yes. Gifted, yes. But not nutty.

"And as for your dad, don't you think he was coping the best way he knew how? What would it be like to have a wife who was so depressed?"

I scowled at Rachel. "How long have you been planning that little jewel of a speech?"

"Ever since you told me about Resthaven. Ever since you started treating your dad like a scum ball."

"But he is!"

"I've seen worse. So put it aside for a little while, and let's just concentrate on the Dare and the information before us. Okay?"

Dear, practical, pragmatic Rachel.

I gave a long dramatic sigh and acquiesced. "Okay."

Once inside the *atelier*, Rachel knew exactly what to do. She watched me retrieve the Seven Secret Sketchpads and started snooping around for anything else that might be hidden. Over in the corner, Mama had an old desk crammed with papers and bills of sale. I had never even thought to open its three little drawers.

"Excellent! Just what I was hoping we'd find!" Rachel said triumphantly.

It turned out that most of the papers were actually letters of thanks written by admirers of Mama's talent. Many of them were still in their envelopes, so we arranged them by the date on the envelope. Then Rachel started taking them out, one by one, and reading them to me. That was nice, hearing so many people complimenting Mama's work.

And then she came to a letter that turned out to be a nugget of gold, a real treasure—a letter written from Henry Becker to Mama, dated March 1952.

> Dear Mrs. Middleton,
>   *The painting is beautiful. I will treasure it forever. You should have seen my wife's expression when I told her that I knew the artist. I do hope you'll be able to visit sometime and see where we've hung it.*
>   *I am mighty thankful that you seemed so happy and healthy on your last visit to Resthaven. Keep painting.*
> Yours truly,
Henry Becker

We squealed together. Henry Becker! The man in the sketch was Henry Becker!

"We've got to get to Resthaven and talk to that man!" declared Rachel. "He'll know all about the missing paintings."

"Think of it! Mama sold Henry Becker one of her paintings! Or maybe they traded paintings. Maybe somewhere in this house is stashed a painting by Henry."

"I still think he was the yardman."

"The yardman with a talent for painting!" I said melodramatically. "Maybe a secret talent. That's it, Rachel. He's a yardman by day and an artist by night!"

"Impossible. Artists need light to paint by."

"It's not impossible. It's the best explanation. You read it in the papers and in the Raven Dare. One of the artists whose paintings was to be displayed was Henry Becker."

"True." She was chewing on the end of a paintbrush. "But it doesn't really make sense." She shrugged. "Well, the sooner we talk to the man, the quicker this whole mystery will be solved." She got up and went over to the easel. "Hey, are you doing this?"

I lunged at the painting and said, "It's nothing. Don't say a word. It's just my way of getting things out of my system." I couldn't bear to have Rachel make even one tiny, joking comment about my very first painting or about what I had found to be my calling. It was too fragile and new and important to me.

"Cool it, Swan. Anyway, I like it."

"I've barely begun. It's just my first try. It's not—"

"It shows one thing, Swan." I didn't dare ask her what, but she volunteered the information. "It shows you've got a lot of your mom's talent, that's what."

If Rachel hadn't already been my best friend, those last words would have clinched her fate forever. I felt like grabbing her and hugging her till she screamed or giggled. But even Rachel couldn't know how much painting meant to me, so I just said, "Wow. You really think so?" and we headed downstairs to get a bowl of chocolate ice cream.

With the new information about Henry Becker on my mind, I was champing at the bit to talk to Carl on Saturday.

"You got any more information about us playing for that fancy Christmas dance, Mary Swan?" he asked me before I had a chance to speak my mind.

"Well, yeah. Mrs. Appleby said it was possible when I said you played jazz and all the fifties dancing tunes. She'd like to schedule a tryout for your band. Would that be okay?"

"Yep. Okay by me. I'll check it out with the boys." He was heading over toward Cassandra and Jessie, so I planted myself in the way and said quickly, "Carl, could you do me a big favor? It's about the Raven Dare, and it is super important to me and to Rachel, and I don't know anyone else who can help, but we thought you'd be perfect because you can drive, and after all you are my second assistant, so it's okay for you to know everything."

As I expected, he stopped and looked down at me with his forehead in wrinkles. "Slow down, Mary Swan. Way down, girl."

I directed him outside and began to explain. "There's a place in the mountains where my mom spent a lot of time. And a man who works there is one of the other artists whose painting disappeared. So if we could go there and talk to the man, well, I'm sure he'd clear up a lot of questions. But we need you to drive us."

He shrugged. "I can drive, Mary Swan, sure 'nuff. But I don't have a car."

I thought about the big Cadillac that sat in our garage all the time, except when Ella Mae took it out to drive me to Grant Park. "That's no problem. I've got a car. Got the Cadillac over there." I squinted in the bright November sun and pointed to the car, half hidden behind the church in the side alley where Ella Mae always parked it. "Daddy lets Ella Mae use it whenever she needs to."

He moseyed over to the blue Cadillac and leaned on the shiny hood, running his hand over it admiringly. "Nice car you got, Mary Swan. You're sixteen, aren't ya? Can't you drive?"

"Oh no. Not far. Daddy only lets me drive around the neighborhood."

"And your daddy won't mind some colored fella he's never met taking his big fancy Cadillac and driving it way up into the mountains?"

"Well, I didn't think we'd have to tell him."

"You're telling me that your daddy won't notice you and your car being gone for a whole day?"

"Not if he has other stuff planned—like golf. I can figure all that out if you'll just drive."

"Sounds like you're gonna tell him a heap o' lies."

"Oh, come on, Carl. This is important. Please don't start preaching to me about lying."

He didn't outright agree. In fact, he seemed annoyed with me. But he didn't say no. What he said was "When do you plan on taking this trip?"

"As soon as possible. As soon as Rachel and I can work out the details."

"Rachel gonna be comin' too?"

"Of course. She's my first assistant."

He shook his head, really looking annoyed now. "Mary Swan, don't you think this country, this Southern state here, has enough troubles with civil rights without you askin' me, a big black boy, to drive you and Rachel, two fine, young, rich white girls, two hours away from here in a stolen car? Are you out of your mind?"

I shot him a cross look and pouted a little. Rachel said that when I wanted to pout, I had the best bottom lip in Buckhead. And I stuck it out then for Carl to see.

That made him laugh and show his teeth, and then he punched me playfully in the arm. "Don't you go getting saucy on me, girl. I don't need you causing me no trouble." He leaned back so that his elbows were braced on the Cadillac's hood, and then stretched his long torso out in front. I could see his hard muscles under his plaid shirt. "Well, maybe it'll work. Let me think on it a bit."

I grabbed one of his big forearms and said, "Thanks! Thanks so much. I'll work it all out. I promise! If you'll be at the bus stop at the corner of West Paces Ferry and Andrews by nine o'clock next Saturday morning, we'll be there with the car."

"Hold on a minute, girl. I didn't say yes. I said I'd think on it a bit."

I grinned up at him. "By the end of the week I'm sure it'll mean yes, so I might as well tell you the plans now."

"Mary Swan Middleton, you are too much. Go on, girl."

Then my big mouth and insatiable curiosity got the best of me once again, and I found myself asking Carl the same thing I'd asked Cassandra earlier in the fall. With both of us leaning on the Cadillac's hood and the nippy November wind blowing my hair, I asked, "Are you a Christian, Carl? I mean the kind that Miss Abigail would call a real Christian? Did you ask God to live in your heart and then get baptized?"

He scowled at me again. "You sure are one for jumping to different subjects, girl."

I grinned up at him. "Don't stall. Just answer my question."

"Well, then, the answer is, yep, I did. I did become a Christian."

"And so what's different for you? Has God done anything . . ." I waved my arms in the air. "I don't know, anything spectacular in your life since then?" I was fishing for proof that Miss Abigail's thoughts about her almost-adopted son were true.

He looked at me out of the corner of his eye and punched me playfully again. "Why are you askin' those questions, Mary Swan?"

"Why do you think? 'Cause I wanna know."

"Did Miss Abigail ever tell you 'bout me and my family before she found us?"

I swallowed hard. "Yes. Yes, she did."

"Well, then, you know what kinda life I lived growing up. Lived in roach-infested shacks with no running water. Mama had a different man in the place 'bout every month, and sometimes they fought like hell. Never knew if we'd have food or not. And my aunt was jus' as pitiful as my mama. They couldn't help it. Their mama was an alcoholic who left them when they was real little. So they were raised by their grandmama. And then she died when they were about nine and ten. They were completely alone in the world. So they jus' started begging to live, and selling their bodies, and then they got pregnant all those times, Mary Swan, and so none of us children knows who our daddy is. 'Cept for Puddin'. And her daddy was the one who killed Mama."

"Carl, you don't have to talk about it if you don't want. I'm sorry I asked."

"I'm telling you all that so as you can see what is different now. Just hold on and let me finish my story, will ya?" And he gave a soft smile.

"So by the time I was twelve, I was a good pickpocket, and I could take a car apart in less than an hour, and I carried a knife and ran around with guys a lot bigger. Streetwise, I was, Mary Swan. Not scared of a thing 'cause I'd seen it all before. I wanted to grow up better. I wanted to read and learn, but didn't have no place to do those kinds of things.

"And I was filled with hate. I sure as heaven hated God. Mama would drag us to church once in a while to make her feel better, and I hated it. 'Cause those people sang so pretty and talked about a good God, but all I saw was poverty and lots of evil. And we were in a fix. When I saw Mama get killed, well, everything went out of me except the hate. And I told myself I'd save my family somehow.

"So you better believe that I wasn't an easy kid when Miss Abigail found us and took us in. My other sister died two weeks later from TB. We were a sorry lot. Miss Abigail fed us and cleaned us up and gave us clothes and we were a handful. But we felt like we were living in a palace, and we loved her in spite of ourselves. I didn't want to love her. I hated whites, and I didn't want any help. But she won me over. She won me over with her kindness and her firmness. She got me in school, and loads of times the principal called her and said I'd been found fighting with a knife. And she'd come down to school and give me a talking-to. And she dragged us to church and got us singing in the children's choir. When she realized I liked music, she got me in the band at school."

He was getting misty-eyed. "And we heard about Jesus at church. But loads of people who went to church weren't any better than me. You know what got me most, Mary Swan? It was every morning, early, before the little ones were up, I'd come into the den and find Miss Abigail stretched out on the floor just pouring her heart out to someone. I thought she was crazy, talking to herself and crying like that, and at first it scared me real bad. I thought maybe we'd ended up with a crazy lady, crazier than my mom.

"But Miss Abigail started inviting me to come sit with her and read from the Bible, and I found out she was praying, talking out loud to Jesus. So I asked her questions. My brain was just spilling over with questions about everything. She'd listen too. But mostly she told about Jesus being her friend. She said she talked to Him every day, and He was taking care of her and all her problems and now He was taking care of us too. Talked about how I needed this friend who was also almighty God in my life, 'cause He'd show me the way even if it seemed awful hard, and He'd never leave me like all the other folks I'd known had done.

"I was a sponge, Mary Swan. I needed Jesus. And I was a rock. I didn't want to need anyone. But after a while, when you live with a lady who knows Jesus, and you see how He does indeed take care of her, well, it starts to rub off on you.

"But it wasn't just Miss Abigail. 'Cause we were all skinny and sick, and she didn't have enough hands to go around. But she said Jesus did. And all these other white ladies would come down, still do, for that matter, and just hold the little ones and love on 'em and help me with my homework, 'cause I was far behind. Hadn't been to much school. That was hard. Awful hard. 'Cause I loved Miss Abigail, but I didn't want to love any other whites. But after a while, I couldn't help it. They were the hands of Jesus."

The hands of Jesus, I thought to myself. Carl was sounding just like Miss Abigail.

"So when I was thirteen, I gave up and gave in. I'll never forget it. There was this guy at school who was always threatening me. We'd fought a time or two. So I told Jesus one night that I would ask Him to be my Savior if He would just show me what to do with Marvin. I told Jesus that I didn't see no way out, but Miss Abigail said there was always a way out, and if He'd show me a way out, I would believe in Him.

"And the next day at school, Marvin and three of his friends came up to me with their knives. Marvin said he'd meet me over by the cemetery after class, and we'd have this out once and for all. Well, I was so scared I couldn't move, but I said, 'Ain't gonna fight no more, Marvin. I'll be going ta the church after school.' Well, he got a big hoot outta that, if you know what I mean, and you better believe he and his buddies were waiting for me after school.

"They followed me to church, and I was praying all the way like I never prayed before. And about halfway to church they jumped on me, and I thought for sure I was a goner. When outta nowhere two big black men came up and said, 'Leave him alone!' They were big. I mean huge. Twice the size of me. And they had nothing in their hands but a big black book. And they held it up and said, 'In the name of Jesus, if you ever try to touch Carl Matthews again, you'll have us to answer to.' And Marvin and his friends were shook up mighty bad and took off like scared rabbits. It was like those big men were ghosts— they came outta nowhere. Ain't never seen them before or since. And Miss Abigail says they were probably angels."

I narrowed my eyes. "Are you telling me the truth?"

Carl nodded, all serious-like. "Of course I am, Mary Swan. Marvin never bothered me again, and right then and there I gave my heart to Jesus and got baptized the next week. And if you want to hear about the other things He's done in my life, well, I guess we'll have plenty of time on the way to that there Resthaven."

My face broke into a smile almost as wide as Carl's. "I knew you'd take us!"

So, as if I didn't already have enough to think about, with civil rights and Russians and Mama and Resthaven and Daddy and eligible ladies and Robbie and painting, now I had one more thing to keep in my mind: Carl being saved by angels.

Chapter 16

It turned out to be pretty easy to get the Cadillac. Jimmy was invited to spend the night at Andy Bartholomew's on Friday, and I told Ella Mae on Thursday that I couldn't go down to Grant Park, and Rachel invited me to spend the night Friday. I already knew that Daddy was determined to get in eighteen holes of golf at the club on Saturday while the weather was still warm enough. So by the time Saturday morning came, anyone who could possibly be worried about us for the next twelve hours thought that we'd be with someone else.

At eight-thirty, Rachel and I raced from her house to mine, made sure Daddy's Jag was gone, and slipped into the Cadillac. I had rarely driven it, so Rachel volunteered to get behind the wheel.

"Look out!" I shrieked as she backed dangerously close to the BMW that Daddy used for business deals. "And there's the boxwood over there! Turn more to the left, Rach, for heaven's sake."

"Shh. Let me concentrate, will you? Your driveway is a catastrophe to navigate." It was one of the few times I'd seen practical Rachel a bit unnerved.

By the time we made it to the bottom of the hill, I was sure that Trixie and every other neighbor must have heard the screeching on and off of brakes. I expected her to emerge from her front door at any moment, hair in rollers, and question us. But we made it around the corner without being seen.

"You would have to pick the most conspicuous bus stop in Buckhead, you idiot," Rachel said sharply as she puttered toward West Paces Ferry Road. "What time is it anyway?"

"Five 'til nine. Don't worry. He'll be there."

And he was, pulling a jacket around him and stomping his big brown boots on the ground. It took only a matter of seconds for Rachel to put the car into Neutral and hop into the backseat.

Carl was smiling. "Mornin', ladies. Pleased to see you."

"Hi, Carl."

"Now listen, both of you. If anybody questions us about anything, anything, you understand, I'm just your chauffeur."

We giggled at that, but Carl's face was somber. "I can't afford to be getting into any trouble, Mary Swan. I mean it. You get in the backseat with Rachel."

So I obeyed.

Rachel had the map and agreed to play the navigator. I had the letter Henry Becker had written my mother as well as my copy of the Raven Dare and the scrapbook with the sketch of Mr. Becker in it. And Carl had the wheel.

"All right, Carl, you've got to turn here and then go down a ways to get onto I–85." Rachel's head was buried in an Atlanta map.

It took Carl a few minutes of jostling and jerking us around to get used to the Cadillac. He finally made it onto the expressway. "Oh, wee! Mighty fine to be driving out here. Mighty fine," he called back to us, and I could hear the pure pleasure in his voice. It had never occurred to me to ask Carl if he'd ever driven on the freeway before. He pushed his foot down on the accelerator really hard, and we took off fast.

Rachel and I eyed each other, shrugged, and then giggled. "An adventure," she mouthed to me, and I nodded.

The first part of the trip was like a montage from a dozen different Broadway plays. First, Carl's deep bass voice rolled out "Ole Man River, dat ole Man River. He don't say nuttin'. He jus' keep movin' along." He sang it with so much feeling that both Rachel and I got tears in our eyes. Then he sang "Moon River" and moved to "Oklahoma." We both joined in on the chorus: "When I say, yip a yipa yipa yah, I'm only saying you're doing fine, Oklahoma, Oklahoma, O-K-L-A-H-O-M-A," and then we shouted at the top of our lungs, "Oklahoma!"

"Bravo, girls!"

"Sing some more, Carl," I begged him time and time again. Somehow he seemed to know all of the Broadway musicals. I was sitting directly behind him, and since I couldn't see his face, I watched his shoulders. They were enormous. Much wider than Daddy's or Robbie's or anyone else's I knew. But as he sang, they shifted up and down, and the expression I couldn't see on his face translated into his upper body language.

"You have one beautiful voice," Rachel commented when he paused between songs. "Do you sing a lot with your jazz band?"

"Some, but mostly I sing every Sunday in church with the choir. Or sometimes we prepare men's quartet or the like."

"But you don't sing show tunes in church?"

"Oh no. Not in church. That's just when we're messin' around." He turned his head and smiled back at us. "Wanna hear what we sing in church?"

"Sure!" we squealed in unison. And for the next fifteen minutes we listened to a medley of Negro spirituals, songs like "Let My People Go" and "Go Tell It on the Mountain." We hummed right along with him. Finally he belted out in a mournful voice, "Were you there when they crucified my Lord? Were you there when they crucified my Lord? Oh-oh-oh-oh. Sometimes it causes me to tremble, tremble, tremble. Were you there when they crucified my Lord?"

I did start trembling ever so slightly, and goose bumps broke out on my arms. I don't know what it felt like to Rachel, but to me, it felt like someone was putting his finger on my heart and asking me that question, sung out so hauntingly, so mysteriously in Carl's deep voice. I almost expected two big black men holding big black books to appear before us in the middle of the highway and to hold up their books as we zipped by, crying out to me, "Believe, girl. You gotta believe."

When Carl finished that song, he said, "I don't have much voice left."

"Let's stop and get a Coke!" I suggested, relieved to think of something besides black angels.

"Good idea, Mary Swan. We'll be needing some gas anyway."

While we searched for a filling station, Rachel and I started singing a song that Papy had taught me from the war. "It's a long way to Tiperary, it's a long way to go. It's a long way to Tiperary to the sweetest girl I know. Good-bye Piccadilly, farewell Leicester Square. It's a long, long way to Tiperary, but my heart lies there."

About ten o'clock, we pulled into a filling station. I hadn't thought of needing gas, but thankfully, I'd brought a little bit of cash with me. Carl sat straight up and kept his eyes down when the attendant approached the car.

He was skinny and tall with a baseball cap pulled down over his forehead. "What'll it be?" he asked cheerily, and then he noticed the strange combination of teens in the car.

"Five dollars of regular," I said quickly.

The young man peered in the back window, which I had rolled down, and said, "You ladies all right?"

"Perfect," Rachel said, batting her eyes.

"Well, if you're sure," he said, with another wary glance at Carl.

My heart had stopped pumping for a long minute, and when the attendant walked away, it started hammering hard. I hated the way he looked at Carl with a mixture of suspicion and condescension in his eyes. But Carl didn't seem to mind. He took my money and paid for the gas and then bought each of us a bottle of Coke from the machine.

When we left the filling station, I let out a sigh of relief.

Rachel snapped, "That was simply awful, rude, the way he treated you, Carl!"

"You girls did just fine. Keep your calm and smile and don't say a word. And we'll be all right. It's all okay."

We tried to start up the songs again, but the gusto had gone, and instead, we contented ourselves with sipping our Cokes. Every once in a while Carl would exclaim, "Look at that fiery red maple. And that flaming orange oak. Woo-ee, ain't this a splendid view of the Almighty's creation! Have you ever seen hills so full of color? They look like they're on fire!"

Mama had always loved to drive into the North Georgia mountains in late October when the trees' vibrant colors were at their peak. I had grown up admiring that wild beauty. On this day, Mama would have said, "Well, aren't we lucky! First week in November and the trees are still as stunning." But hearing Carl talk, it reminded me of taking him to the High Museum and his looking at an oil painting for the first time. He had an innocent excitement about the things that I knew were supposed to be beautiful.

"Have you ever seen the mountains before, Carl?"

"I haven't ever left good ole 'lanty, Georgia, before, Mary Swan. First time I've been out of the city."

Rachel had traveled extensively in Europe with her parents. I'd been throughout the southeastern United States and even up East. It took us a moment to register what Carl had said.

After a few minutes of silence, Rachel called up to Carl, "Have you ever heard how Coke got invented?"

"Nope, never."

"Well, you know it started right in Atlanta, don't you?" I put in.

"Never thought anything about it, Mary Swan."

"As a citizen of Atlanta, you should know," I said.

So Rachel launched into her story, a story we'd both heard dozens of times. "Doc Pemberton—John S. Pemberton, a cavalry captain during the Civil War—became a pharmacist and lived in Columbus, Georgia. Do you know much about Columbus?"

"Not a thing."

"Well, it's an old aristocratic town right near the Alabama border. But Doc, as everyone called him, believed that Atlanta was an up-and-coming city. So he decided to move his business up here, back when Atlanta was just a railroad town, in 1885. One of his most popular formulas was called French Wine Coca. He advertised it as 'a delightful nerve tonic and stimulant that never intoxicates.' "

Carl looked around and raised an eyebrow. "A nerve tonic, you say? What's that?"

"Something that helped with headaches and other ailments," I answered.

"Exactly," Rachel said. "The only problem was that it had alcohol in it, and Atlanta went bone dry after a November referendum in 1885. But Doc was ready when the saloons closed the next summer. He concocted a new formula to replace the outlawed French Wine Coca. He used two exotic ingredients—coca from South America and kola from Africa and called the new mixture Coca-Cola."

"Ya don't say! This here stuff has ingredients in it from South America and Africa!" Carl held out his half-empty bottle and looked at it admiringly.

"Right! Unfortunately"—I used my dramatic voice—"not much interest came of this formula. But there was a man named Asa Candler who bought it."

"Well, not exactly, Swan," Rachel corrected. "He bought a *fractional* interest in Coca-Cola and then other portions of the formula.

Finally in 1891 Mr. Candler ended up as sole owner of the formula with a total investment in the Pemberton mixture of $2,300. A measly bit when you consider the millions this drink has made."

"And Daddy likes to say," I added proudly, "that if the voters had not briefly outlawed alcohol, there's no reason to believe that Coca-Cola would have been created."

"Ya don't say!" I could see Carl's playful eyes in the rearview window. I could tell he was enjoying our story.

"But this is the best part." I wanted to tell this part of the story. "By accident, one customer who ordered the Coca-Cola—remember, it was still being used to treat headaches—got it mixed with soda water instead of the usual tap water and found it 'refreshing.' " I made a silly face. Then I said in a squeaky little voice, "Yummy, isn't this Coca-Cola stuff great? Made my headache go away!"

Carl let out a belly laugh.

"So a lot of people started buying it to drink for refreshment, not just for headaches. Isn't that a scream?"

"That's a good story, girls!"

"And it's completely true," Rachel said.

"And that's not all. When Mr. Candler started putting Coke in stoppered bottles, like the ones we're drinking it out of now, sales took off like a rocket."

"So Coca-Cola made Candler the first really wealthy man in Atlanta and the first major philanthropist," Rachel stated. "Then later, after the First World War, he sold Coke to a group headed by an investment banker named Ernest Woodruff. And now it's his son Robert who controls all of Coca-Cola. You've heard that ad, haven't you, Carl? 'When you don't see a Coca-Cola sign, you have passed the borders of civilization.' "

"Yeah, I believe I have." He took another long gulp from his Coke bottle and finished with a slurp. Then he raised the empty bottle above his head and said, "Mista Pemberton, Mista Candler, Mista Woodruff, I'd like to thank y'all kindly for this here tonic for headaches. It is mighty fine stuff."

"And you know what else?" I whispered in between giggles.

"What else you got, Mary Swan?"

"The Coca-Cola formula is still one of the world's most coveted and most closely guarded commercial secrets."

His eyes narrowed for a moment in the rearview mirror. "Speaking of secrets, I reckon we'd better figure out just exactly what we'll be saying when we get to Resthaven."

Confident, Rachel smiled. "Don't worry, Carl. We've got that all worked out."

Resthaven Sanatorium, as the brick pediment read, looked exactly as Mama had sketched it. We saw it all at once as we approached it from the tree-lined driveway. Four stories high, stately, red brick, with six white columns across the front. A turnaround led us to the entrance.

Rachel and I hopped out of the Cadillac while Carl waited in the car. At the reception desk, I addressed a plump blond woman in a nurse's uniform.

"What can I do for you, young ladies?" she asked, rather jovially, I thought, for someone who worked with crazy people.

"We are looking for Mr. Henry Becker," I stated, trying to sound professional.

She furrowed her brow and started shuffling her papers. "Is he a patient at Resthaven? I don't recall . . ."

"Oh no! Not a patient. He works here."

She shook her head, "No, I don't believe that we have—" Then her expression changed, and she smiled, "Oh yes. Mr. Becker! Yes, I know who you mean. He did work here before I came. Quite a character, I've heard! But he retired a few years ago. I'm sorry."

My heart fell.

Rachel was quick to the rescue. "Would you possibly have his address? You see, it's rather urgent." She motioned with her head toward the car, where Carl was sitting. "One of his relatives has been searching for him."

I shot Rachel a what-in-the-world look, and she snapped her eyes at me, so I kept quiet.

"Let me see. Just a sec, girls." She came back five minutes later with a piece of paper. "Today you're in luck!"

With the nurse's precise directions, it took us another thirty minutes to find Henry Becker's house. It sat at the end of a dirt road, with pastureland all around. On one side of the house were flower beds, meticulously tended to, with a garden on the other. A rusting metal mailbox and a split-rail fence marked the entrance to the driveway—as did a dog, a spotted hound dog who had been announcing our arrival for the past few minutes. A trickle of smoke came from the chimney.

Henry Becker was old, at least seventy, I'd say, and he had the same tobacco-stained teeth, droopy eyes, and broad smile that I'd seen in Mama's sketchbook. When we drove up to his house, he was hoeing in the garden. I couldn't tell how tall he was, but I could tell he was thin under a pair of baggy pants held up by suspenders. His first look was suspicious.

Carl hopped out of the car and stood off by the fence. "We're looking for a Mr. Henry Becker. A man who used to work at Resthaven Sanatorium."

"I'm Henry Becker."

"Nice to meet you, Mr. Becker. Name's Carl Matthews. These ladies here, well, I've driven them all the way from Atlanta to see you and ask a few questions. I'm afraid it's about one of their mothers, who spent some time at Resthaven."

Henry Becker spit a wad of tobacco in the dirt and called over his shoulder into the house, "Martha, we gots viz'tas." Then he walked over to our car, and leaning on the hoe in much the same way he'd leaned on the rake in the sketch, he peered in at us.

"Well, ya gonna sit there all day or come on in th' house and git ya somethin' ta drink?" He stared at us both for a long moment, and then a trace of a smile formed on his chapped lips.

Rachel and I stepped out of the car.

"Pleased to meet you, Mr. Becker." I stuck out my hand. "Please forgive us for just showing up at your house."

He ignored my gesture and pointed a gnarled hand toward me. "You remind me of someone just a bit, young lady."

"I'm Mary Swan Middleton. Sheila Middleton's daughter."

His face turned into a road map of smiles and wrinkles. "Well, ya don't say! My, my! Imagine that! It's nice ta see ya, Miz Middleton!" He motioned to all of us. "Mary Swan. Yessir, I remember yore mama talking 'bout you. Come on in with yore friends and set with us a spell." He deposited the hoe by the fence. His step was springy. "So yore Sheila Middleton's daughter. How is yore mama, honey?"

His back was to me as Rachel, Carl, and I followed him up the three wooden steps to the front porch. I cleared my throat awkwardly and said, "Um, well, she, she died in the Paris plane crash."

He stopped in midstep and looked back at me with a shocked expression on his face. "Miz Sheila? Lawd, no! Ya don't mean it." He shook his head, obviously greatly disturbed by my pronouncement. "Not Miz Sheila. Such a beautiful young thing. My, my. Yes, I heard 'bout that crash. Mighty tragic." He looked off toward the fields, which stretched on every side far into the distance. Then he continued into the house, saying, "Terrible news. So sorry."

After a moment he regained his composure and asked, "What can I help you with, Miz Middleton and Miz . . ."

"Abrams. Rachel Abrams."

He called to his wife, still lost in some thought. "Martha, I'm bringin' some viz'tas in."

Martha Becker had snow-white hair like Grandmom's and a kindly smile, and she was almost as big as Ella Mae. She walked with a visible limp as she came from the back of the house. "Nice ta meet ya," she replied as Mr. Becker introduced us.

"This here young lady is the daughter of Sheila Middleton." The way he said it, I could tell his wife must have known Mama too. "Poor Miz Middleton died in that plane crash this past summer."

"You don't mean it!" Mrs. Becker's face fell. "Dear Lawd! That dear woman." She seemed every bit as distraught as Mr. Becker to hear the news.

We were in the den with its cozy fire blazing in the fireplace. "Have a seat, chil'un," Martha Becker said, indicating a chair and a sofa, both worn looking. Then she limped out of the room, promising to bring some drinks.

Mr. Becker seated himself in a rocking chair, bent down, picked up a piece of wood and a knife, and began whittling. "I shore am sorry to hear about yore mother. Now, tell me, Miz Middleton . . ."

"Just call me Mary Swan."

Carl and Rachel and I watched his slow meticulous strokes as his knife peeled away a thin layer of wood. "Tell me, Mary Swan, what brings ya ta see me?"

"Well . . ." I glanced at Rachel and Carl, who both urged me on with their eyes. "It's a strange story, and it really has nothing to do with the crash. You see, I was chosen to find the three paintings that were missing from the High Museum last year." I thought he might acknowledge this event, but he kept on whittling, so I continued. "One of the paintings was Mama's and then, as you know, another was yours, and so I thought if I could find you, and talk to you, maybe you'd have an idea of where the paintings are."

He scratched his head a moment and then shook it, saying, "Never painted a picture in my life."

I felt a little confused. "What about the one that was going to be hung in the High Museum in Atlanta last year?"

"Don't know nothin' about that painting, Mary Swan." He chuckled. "I'm no painter. Kin whittle me a fine piece of wood, mind you," and he held up the carving to show the emerging shape of what looked like the ear of some kind of animal. "Yore mama, now she could paint. Yessir. She painted bee-u-ti-ful things."

"But the newspapers, the curator, everybody said that one of the missing paintings was painted by Henry Becker. They'd inspected the paintings. It had to be true."

"Well, there's obviously some mistake. Mus' be talkin' 'bout another Henry Becker. I'm shore there's a whole lotta Henry Beckers in the world, young lady. All's I know is that I ain't never painted nothin' in my whole life."

Devastated—that was the only word to describe how I felt.

He saw it immediately and reached over and patted my hand. "I'm awful sorry, Mary Swan. Sorry that ya came all this way."

"But you knew my mother?"

"Yes, I knew her well."

"For how long did you know her?"

"Well, now, I knew yore mama ever since she first started coming to Resthaven, 'bout ten or twelve years ago, I s'pect."

My throat was tight. I could tell that Rachel and Carl felt miserable for me too, but they didn't say a word. "Can you tell me about Resthaven?" That came out in a hoarse whisper.

"You don't know about Resthaven, young lady?"

"Not much. Hardly anything. I just know that my mama went there when she was . . . tired. And sometimes she stayed a whole month. And I think I visited her there once when I was really little." I swallowed. Then I pleaded, "Tell me about Resthaven, Mr. Becker. Please."

He set down the carving and ran his weathered hands over his face.

Then he let out a sigh. "Resthaven is a home for people who have an illness, I guess you'd say. People who's tired o' dealin' with some of the mean things in this world. It's a good place, Miz Middleton. He'ps folks out. And I worked there taking care of the grounds for over twenty-five years. Just retired in 1960. Yore mama came there proba- bly every six months or so. Sometimes she'd stay a week, sometimes a month or longer."

"Why?"

"To rest."

"Because she was sad, depressed?"

"That's right." I could tell he felt uncomfortable admitting that.

"And did Mama paint at Resthaven?"

"Not at first, I don't b'lieve." He wrinkled his brow as though calculating how much of Mama's story to reveal. "I b'lieve they didn't want her to do nuthin' at first but jus' rest. I noticed her right away, 'cause she'd jus' sit in the gardens and stare at the flowers. And she'd talk to me. Talked ta me lots. Told me I was a mighty fine gard'ner to have such good-looking roses. We talked a bit, yore mama and me."

His face clouded. "And so when your mama came up to me one day not too long after she first arrived at Resthaven, cryin' so hard, well, it nearly broke my heart. She was so young and perty and fragile. And she looked at me with those big green eyes. Jus' like yours, Miz Middleton. Eyes just like yours. And she was crying to beat the band. So I went over to her and asked her what was the matter. Sometimes I'd talk to the patients like that." He wiped his face with a handkerchief while Rachel, Carl, and I sat perched on our seats, totally absorbed.

"She said that she had begged her doctor to take her off the med'cine and let her paint, but he wouldn't listen. She said that if only he would let her paint, she'd git better."

"So what did you do?"

"Well, later I talked to one of the nurses I knew kinda well 'bout what she said. And she musta said somethin' to a doctor, 'cause 'fore you knowed it, Miz Sheila was thankin' me and sayin' I'd saved her life." He shook his head as if he couldn't quite believe his own story. "And eva' after that, whenever she was at Resthaven, she'd be a'sittin' out in the gardens painting. Happiest expression on her perty face, and hummin' jus' like a little girl. Hummin' to herse'f and paintin'. And she swore she'd give me one of her paintings. And she did."

"She gave you a painting?" All three of us sat up straight at that. I could feel Henry Becker's letter burning a hole in my pocket.

"Shore did. Ex-quisite, is what me and Martha says. We calls her paintin' exquisite. Nicest thing we eva' owned." He pulled himself up out of the rocking chair and said, "Come on back to our bedroom, young'uns, and I'll show it to you."

We followed Mr. Becker into his small bedroom. Framed family photos sat on top of two cedar chests of drawers. Several small hand-woven rugs were on the floor, and hanging on the wall above the bed was a real oil painting, looking incongruous in its surroundings. The painting showed Resthaven at dusk, and there was a type of wild energy in the strokes. Flowers bloomed rampantly, and there was a violent wind blowing the trees. But in the distance, beside a tossing magnolia tree, a man was on his knees tending to a flower bed, seemingly oblivious to the imminent storm.

I'd been raised to have an artistic eye, and I could tell it was a fine painting. But I could tell something else right away. "Mama didn't paint this," I said, then added, "But it's a really nice painting. Mama mostly painted portraits."

Henry Becker shook his head and chuckled softly. " 'Scuse me for saying it, Miz Middleton, but I know yore mama painted that paintin' 'cause I watched her do it. She painted it the first time she eva' came to Resthaven. Cain't ya see that's me there beside the tree?" His gnarled hand quivered ever so slightly as he pointed toward the figure in the painting.

"She showed me this here paintin' soon as it was done, and she was mighty proud of it. And so was I. And I convinced her to let the doctor see it. And he said she was mighty talented, and he swore to her she wouldn't eva' have to take another pill while she was there."

"Are you telling me that Mama painted this? While she was at Resthaven?"

"I am."

"But it doesn't look a thing like what she normally painted!"

He cocked his head. "Funny you should say that, 'cause that's what she always told me. She said, 'Henry, I paint so much better and different at Resthaven.' "

I went up to the painting and examined it for a signature. Mama's was easy to recognize, big and flowery. "She didn't sign it," I said, unable to hide my disappointment.

"Shore she did. Right there by the primroses. Don't ya see it? SMM."

I peered at the dark painting and saw the initials, almost planted in the ground beside the purple and yellow flowers. Her initials, all right. But not the signature she usually painted. Nothing in the whole painting seemed one thing like Mama.

My mind felt stuffed and a little panicky. "But you never painted anything? Ever?"

He shook his head.

Suddenly another idea flashed into my mind. "Have you ever heard of Leslie Leschamps?"

"Shore have."

"Well, she was the other painter whose work was lost."

"The Leslie Leschamps I know ain't no painter. She's a nurse."

The pounding in my heart resumed. Stupidly, because I already knew the answer, I asked, "Where is she a nurse?"

"At Resthaven."

We ended up eating lunch with the Beckers and spending a good part of the afternoon with them. When Rachel said, "Mary Swan, we need to be going," Henry Becker smiled politely and put his hand on my arm and asked, "Do ya mind if Mary Swan and I have a little talk 'fore you hit the road?" And Mrs. Becker hurriedly called Carl and Rachel over to look at the garden.

So Mr. Becker and I took a slow stroll around his land. "A fine woman, yore mama. Fragile, she was. But the kind a woman who, as soon as she started feelin' better, well, she wanted to he'p out. Sometimes she let others paint. She'd git them an easel and set them up right next to her, and they'd paint. I tell you what, several of them patients, the ones who didn't hardly eva' smile, several of them started paintin' a little here and there with yore mama lookin' on. And they took to smilin'. Doctor didn't like it much, tho'. Said Miz Sheila needed to concentrate all her energy on gettin' well.

"Like I said, she wasn't supposed to paint at Resthaven. She was supposed to rest. Some of the otha' doctors argued that painting tired her out and made her more depressed. But she said it was the opposite. Paintin' was the way she survived when she got real down. Finally them doctors started talkin' 'bout how paintin' and writin' and other things like that could maybe be used to he'p people git better.'"

We were back at the house. Carl and Rachel stood by the car, and Mrs. Becker joined her husband. Mr. Becker scratched his head before he went on. "Somethin' else I wanted ya ta know, Mary Swan. I ain't never said a word about this to no one, ya understand. So you keep it to yorese'f, please. But mebbe it kin he'p ya. Ya see, Martha and me is mighty thankful for all of Miz Sheila's he'p to our family. She was a very generous woman, yore mama."

I think my mouth must have been hanging open. "What do you mean, Mr. Becker?"

"I jus' wanted you ta know that your mama tried to he'p others even when she wasn't feelin' too good herself. She had a way of talkin' with people and listenin' to ya, listenin' with her eyes, and before ya knew it, she'd heard all about yore problems."

Mrs. Becker suddenly spoke up. "She gave me the two hundred dollars to git my grandbaby to the hospital in 'lanta. Wudda done died if it hadn't been for her." She sniffed a moment, then limped off to the house. She returned a moment later holding the picture of a young girl. "That's her school pitcha' from last year." She gave a big smile. "Fine young girl, she is. Lisa, our Lisa."

"And that's not the only time yore mama he'ped us. Somehow she seemed to know when things was real bad." Henry Becker shook his head. "I thought ya might wanna know, seein' as how you is finding out about Resthaven and all. And she ain't around no more. Jus' wanted you to know."

Then Mrs. Becker caught me in a tight embrace and said, "Means the world to us to meet you, Mary Swan. And we shore is sorry to hear about yore sweet mama. If there is anything we kin do, eva', you don't hesitate to ask, ya hear?"

I nodded in a fog. And found myself wiping away tears.

Chapter 17

We drove the first fifteen minutes in silence, broken only by my unending sniffles. Finally I whispered, "I have to go back by Resthaven. I have to try to see Leslie Leschamps. And the doctor." I'd written his name down. "Alfred Clark."

Carl shook his head. "You can see them some other time, Mary Swan, but not today. I believe you've heard enough for today. We've got a long road ahead, and I won't be gettin' us in trouble." He was insistent.

On the ride home, as I was desperately trying to understand this new revelation, I reasoned out loud with Rachel and Carl listening in. "Mr. Becker says Mama painted lots at Resthaven. But the painting she gave him doesn't look a thing like what she normally painted. And Henry Becker isn't a painter. He was only the yardman, and Leslie Leschamps is only a nurse. Where in the world does that get us except for totally confused?"

"Maybe those names were pseudonyms. You know, to keep the painter anonymous," Rachel volunteered.

"But who would choose those names? Why would anyone choose names of people from Resthaven. Names only my mom knew?"

"Maybe because all the paintings were painted by the same person," Rachel stated matter-of-factly.

"Sounds good to me," Carl piped in.

"But who . . ." And then what Rachel was implying hit me. "Are you saying that my mom painted a lot at Resthaven and that she signed those paintings either Henry Becker or Leslie Leschamps? Why? Why wouldn't she want anyone to know that she painted them?"

"Well, gee, Swan, don't you see? She painted differently at

Resthaven. You yourself didn't recognize the painting in the Beckers' bedroom. It was to protect herself. She already had a reputation in Atlanta. Maybe she thought people wouldn't believe those were her paintings. Or maybe she was afraid they'd find out that she went away to Resthaven, or took medication, or I don't know. Lots of things. Don't you see, Swan? She used his name because she was indebted to him for helping her. And I bet you'll find that Leslie Leschamps helped her too. It was a way of thanking them."

I gave a horrible sigh and said, "I can't talk about it right now. I can't talk about anything!"

And so, of course, we didn't say another word on the way back. Carl hummed to himself, and Rachel stared out the window, and somewhere along the road as the sun went down on the flaming hillsides, I fell asleep.

When I woke up we were entering Atlanta, and Carl and Rachel were whispering about something. "What's up?" I said groggily.

"We're just trying to decide where to let Carl off."

"I wanted to show you the Swan House, Carl."

"It's getting late, Swan, don't you think?" Rachel said cautiously.

I looked at my wristwatch. "It's only five-thirty."

"I need to be getting on home, Mary Swan," Carl said.

I think he was really nervous, but I paid no attention. "It'll only take a sec for you to see it. Just pull over at the filling station on the corner and hide yourself in the back. I'll drive the last few miles."

I knew he didn't like the idea, but he seemed to bend to my desire as if once he'd spoken his mind, saying anything more, rebuking a white girl, well, it just wasn't done. So Carl, all six-feet-two of him, climbed into the backseat and crouched down while Rachel and I got up front.

I dropped Rachel at her house, drove to my house, and maneuvered up our driveway. Daddy's Jaguar was not in the garage. "Wait here a sec," I whispered back to Carl. I ran inside and called around to make sure Jimmy wasn't home. The only sound was my echo. "Coast is clear," I called out.

So he unfolded himself like one of those chairs you take to the beach and followed me in the back door. "One big house you got here, Mary Swan."

I nodded, only half listening, because my ears were pounding with the sound of my heart pumping awful hard. Carl was in my home!

"Come on up to Mama's *atelier*. I'll show you the sketchbooks."

"I don't think I should, Mary Swan. I sure don't want your dad findin' me alone in the house with you. It would get us both in a lot of trouble."

"He's not here. Don't worry." Again, I was oblivious to his discomfort.

He followed me through the back door, his eyes darting all around in every room of the house. He ran his hand along the shining curved hand railing of the marble staircase and gave a low whistle. "You're the one who lives in a mansion, Mary Swan."

"Just wait 'til you see the Swan House."

I opened the door to the *atelier* and gently pushed him inside, closing the door behind us. I quickly took my painting off the easel and placed it against the wall so Carl couldn't see it. He was standing by the window, looking out on the backyard at dusk.

"Here are Mama's unfinished paintings, and over there in her desk is where we found the letter from Henry Becker."

"So this is where she painted," he said softly, almost reverently. "Nice big window she had here, lookin' out on the woods and the garage and the swimming pool. I believe you live at one of those fancy country clubs, Mary Swan."

I felt suddenly embarrassed and tried to change the subject. "And this is where she hid all the sketchbooks." I handed one to him.

"Just exactly what will you get if you find those missing paintings?" he asked, flipping through it.

"Honor. The honor of being a successful Raven. And I get a little silver plaque with my name engraved on it. And money to give away. I'll get to choose a charitable organization that will receive lots of money from different businesses in Atlanta."

"Well, I certainly hope you solve the Dare then, Mary Swan." He sounded distant, unimpressed, maybe even a little bit mocking.

"And, of course, it would help with everything about Mama," I said lamely, almost defensively.

He turned his attention to me immediately. "Oh, don't get me wrong, Mary Swan. It's a fine thing you're doing. I didn't mean it in a bad way. You need to solve it for yourself, more than anything. For you right here." And he touched the middle of my forehead with his index finger. "So you won't keep persecuting yourself about the past. Gotta let it go, Mary Swan."

Hearing the compassion in his voice was all it took. I burst into tears. "I thought it would help to go to Resthaven. Rachel said I'd learned the worst, that it couldn't be harder." I turned my back to him and stood looking out the window, wiping the tears. "But it is. Every time I think I'm closer to understanding, I find out something else, and it just gets more confusing." I was heaving big, break-your-heart sighs now.

"Like why did she sign those paintings with other names? And if they are all by her, well, was she the anonymous donor after all? And if so, why did she decide not to donate the paintings to the museum at the last minute? Why, *why*?" Sniff. "It doesn't make sense. Why did I have to get chosen for this thing? It's a cruel trick, that's what it is. To make me miserable! And why did she have to die right then?"

I was crying so hard that I think Carl didn't know what to do. He kept saying things like "Now, Mary Swan. My, my, girl, calm down."

And then he did what I'd wanted him to do all along. I'm not saying I intentionally planned it, but in my heart, I knew it was what I longed for. He put his big strong arms around me, and he hugged me. Awkwardly at first, like I might break. And then harder, tighter, so that I was crushed into his powerful chest and could hear the beating of his heart. "Shh, Mary Swan. Shh now, girl."

And I kept crying harder and harder, and he stroked my hair and said, "It'll be all right. You'll see."

And I relished every second of his arms around me, so much so that I didn't see his anxiety, didn't feel the terror in his touch, the fear that, at any minute, he might be caught holding a white girl.

I don't know what would have happened next, and I never got the chance to find out. A door slammed, and Jimmy called from downstairs, "Hey, Dad? Swan? Anybody home?"

Carl let go of me in a flash, and I wiped my eyes quickly, and he looked at me with a scared—no, a terrified look. The same expression as when we'd met the rednecks at Oakland Cemetery.

"I gotta get outta here, Mary Swan," he whispered.

I wanted to reassure him that there was no danger, that it was only my pesky little brother, but I could tell that Carl wanted only one thing. To be gone from my house. Far away.

I put my finger to my lips and grabbed his hand and peeked out into the hall. Empty. We tiptoed down the hall at a half run, which felt pretty comical to me, and then down the back steps that led beside the kitchen. I pushed him out the back door, the one with the screen door and the lamppost where Robbie and I liked to stand and kiss. I caught sight of Jimmy's back as he pulled out a bag of chips from the kitchen cabinets, but he didn't see me.

"Wait for me in the woods over there," I whispered to Carl. Then I went into the kitchen, and when Jimmy looked up, I said, "Hi."

"I thought I heard you, Swan. What's up?"

"Nothing," I said in my most nonchalant voice. "I'm just going out for a sec. Dad's not home yet. But when I get back, I'll fix you a grilled cheese sandwich if you want."

"Gee, thanks."

I found Carl crouching behind the Cadillac, which I had not yet parked in the garage. I grabbed his hand again, and we tore off through the woods. We came out at a spot near the bottom of the Swan House property.

"There it is. There's the Swan House," I said proudly, huffing and puffing, as I pointed up to the mansion far away.

He stopped, out of breath himself, and gazed at the fountains and the house and the manicured yard. "Nice, Mary Swan," he said in a polite way. But the excited, innocent expression that he'd had when he'd seen the paintings at the High Museum or the colors of the Northern Georgia leaves wasn't there. "Mary Swan, I don't have time to look at this mansion. I gotta get outta here. Pretty soon there won't be a bus left."

I was hurt, and he could see it on my face. My twisted little game, my adventure, my conquest of Carl was over. I saw in his eyes that he was annoyed, maybe angry, and definitely worried.

"Okay. Follow me. It's just right up the street." I wasn't holding his hand anymore. A huge rock had landed in the bottom of my stomach, and I was thinking to myself, *Stupid girl. Stupid, stupid girl! Now he's gonna hate you.*

I left him at the bus stop. Two maids were waiting there, so I didn't even get to tell him thanks for taking us to Resthaven or any of the other hundred things I wanted to say. I just mumbled, "Bye," and he nodded at me without a word, without a smile.

I don't know why I didn't pick up on it earlier, how uncomfortable he was. I reprimanded myself for being so stupidly insensitive. How could I make flirting with a black man a game? He'd probably seen people get killed over a lot less. He'd been nervous, brooding, like one of Rachel's horses, pacing back and forth in the stall during a thunderstorm. I hadn't seen how preoccupied he was. I should have noticed because Daddy always acted the same way, pretending to listen when his mind was really on something else. All day, Carl had done that. Humoring me, with his mind on something else a million miles away. I'd just been thinking about me and my dare and my life.

What I really wanted was for Carl to be able to hold me and kiss me and care for me. Really care. I wanted it, and so I made it happen in my mind. And while I flipped the grilled cheese sandwiches for Jimmy and me, I let myself relive his hold, his hug, his gentle, kind words.

I went to sleep that night thinking of Carl's strong, powerful grip. And hearing him singing that soulful song. But when I woke up in the middle of the night from a strange dream in which a crowd of people were marching in front of the High Museum and chanting, "Sheila is a fraud," it was Henry Becker's eyes I saw and his voice I heard. "Yore mama did a lot of good things for people, Mary Swan. I jus' thought you might need to know it with all the other things you're finding out."

Thank heaven for chemistry class on that next Tuesday. It was the one time during that week when I laughed, sandwiched in between two very hard Saturdays. Mrs. Tillman, the chemistry teacher, had just reminded us that we had to finish memorizing the periodic table of elements for a test on Thursday. "Now, before we do our experiments, girls, I have a question for you."

We loved Mrs. Tillman's questions. She was a sharp, serious teacher who wore cat-eye glasses and tailored business suits and rarely smiled. But she had a great sense of humor, and she liked to catch us off guard with her "questions."

"Did you hear about the scientist who crossed a sheep with a porcupine?"

Several girls shook their heads as we all waited for the punch line.

"They got an animal that knits its own sweaters."

We giggled lightly among ourselves while Patty Masters rolled her eyes and whispered to me, "I can do better than that. Did you hear about the two TV antennas that got married? The wedding was terrible, but the reception was excellent!"

That definitely made me laugh out loud as we got up from our desks and went to the back of the room to the lab tables. Patty was my lab partner, which was very fortunate because I was hopelessly lost in chemistry and she was a whiz. Not only did she tell great jokes and laugh really loud, she also performed all our experiments single-handedly. All I had to do was give her the beakers and test tubes and matches.

"How's your dad doing anyway? Been out with any eligible ladies lately?" She was reading the directions for the experiment as she talked.

"Too many."

"Well, widowers never stay that way for long." She looked up from the chemistry book and lifted one eyebrow.

"Really?" I was astonished. "Why not?"

"Honestly, Mary Swan. What do you think? A man is a man."

"Oh," I said, pretending to understand. "Well, the worst part is that he's been seeing Amanda Hunnicutt a lot." Patty knew her because Miss Hunnicutt attended St. Philip's. "She has the personality of this cork stopper." I held up a thin test tube and plucked the stopper from it.

"That's not what I've heard," Patty stated matter-of-factly, pouring the clear liquid from the beaker into the test tube.

"What do you mean?"

Eyes gleaming, she said, "I've heard that when she's around a man, she lights up like this Bunsen burner!" And to prove her point, she lit a match and held it to the little rope attached to the burner. It burst into flame.

I blushed, and Patty laughed at me. "You are such a ninny! What about you and Robbie? Are you gonna invite him to the Piedmont Driving Club Christmas Dance?"

"I guess, yeah."

"Well, how are you two doing anyway?" Now she nimbly poured another concoction into the test tube, pushed in the stopper, and swished the test tube carefully to mix the solutions.

"Fine."

"Fine? That's all you can say? Fine? Not terrific or heavenly or at least great?" She attached the test tube to the little metal rack that held it in place over the Bunsen burner. "If all you can say about dating Robbie Bartholomew is 'Fine,' I think you should spend more time worrying about your own love life than your dad's. Robbie's a great guy."

"I know it. He is."

Patty surveyed me carefully, then gathered my hair in one hand and pulled it up above my shoulders. "You should cut your hair, Mary Swan. It's a little bit . . . stringy. No offense, but I bet it would look super in a little bob below the ears, just like Jackie Kennedy's."

"Really? You think so?"

"Sure. Everybody's getting it cut that way. I mean, if you had hair like Rachel's, well, I wouldn't dream of suggesting it. Her hair is absolutely gorgeous. She should be in a Breck commercial or something. But yours would get a little bounce, a little life to it, if you cut it. And wear a little makeup. Mascara. You've got those great eyes. Show them off. I guarantee if you do that, you won't be telling me next time that you and Robbie are just fine. You'll be—"

At that moment, we heard a loud POP and smelled a burning odor.

Julie Jacobs, who was right beside us, yelled, "Look at that!" And we turned around just in time to see a little cork fly through the air and land with a plunk on her partner's head.

"Watch out, flying cork! Danger!" Patty said in a silly voice. By then the whole class was laughing. It was our cork that had taken flight, and our test tube that was black as soot sitting on the Bunsen burner and smelling up the room.

Not missing a beat, Patty picked up the test tube by the top, blew out the fire in the Bunsen burner, and said, as if she'd been instructing me all along, "And that, my dear Swan, is why you must never leave a stopper in the test tube when it's heating!"

"Open the windows, girls! Hurry up!" Mrs. Tillman remonstrated, looking out at us over her glasses with the hint of a grin in her eyes.

Julie was laughing so hard that she was choking, and Patty and I had joined in. "Did you see that?" she squeezed out, with tears in her eyes. "A perfect takeoff from Cape Canaveral!"

"Pitiful landing, though," Patty added, pushing up the window and fanning the air.

"Stop it!" I squealed in between fits of laughter. "Oh, my stomach! You're making my stomach hurt!"

So I never found out what Patty thought Robbie would do when I cut my hair and put on makeup, but that night I stood in front of the mirror in my dressing room and held my hair up the way she had done and put on some of Mama's black mascara.

But I wasn't wondering about what Robbie would think. I was wondering about Carl.

Carl wasn't at the church the next Saturday. I had anticipated the moment when I'd see him and had memorized my speech—my thankfulness, my apologies for being so insensitive, my interest in whatever was on his mind. But none of it mattered at all. He wasn't there. I could hardly keep my disappointment hidden as I brought the pans of spaghetti sauce and noodles from the kitchen and laid them on the tables in the main room.

"Mary Swan, kin we he'p ya in the kitchen?" Carl's little brothers, James and Mike, looked eager to be of use.

"Sure, bring out the bowls of lettuce," I instructed absentmindedly, wondering where Carl could be and if he was purposely avoiding me.

I did open my arms wide to Puddin' when she came running to me. "Look, Mary Swan! I gots my cast off! Arm's good as new!" she bragged.

"That's great, sweetie." I picked her up carefully and held her in my arms. It was then I noticed that the basement was strangely quiet, that many of the regular women weren't around and that several men were talking together in hushed tones. Miss Abigail was nowhere in sight, and Ella Mae was huddled amongst a few other women, whispering excitedly.

With Puddin' hanging on to my arm, I walked up to the group of women and asked, "Where's Miss Abigail?"

"She had an emergency last night," Ella Mae replied, avoiding my eyes.

"Shore did. Had to go to the hospital," another woman added bitterly.

"Is someone hurt?" I asked.

Ella Mae looked over at Puddin' and said to her, "Run along and play with yore brothers, sugah chile."

Obediently Puddin' trotted off toward Mike and James.

"What happened?" I begged. "Ella Mae, you've gotta tell me."

"My, my, chile. A few of our boys from Mt. Carmel decided to attend a youth rally at a church down in Morrow, Georgia. Preacher there was gonna talk to the young folks about civil rights. Whole big group of young'uns from all over was gonna be there. Our boys left on Thursday, they did."

"That's right, Ella Mae, on Thursday, to join their brotha's and sista's in the Lawd. A lotta Christian young people!" Cassandra's mother affirmed.

"There was some kind o' skirmish with some white boys last night as they was leavin' the meetin' place. Them white boys done roughed 'em up real good." Ella Mae's voice was shaky.

"Lawd have mercy!" two women cried. "Our babies! Goin' ta church."

That awful, sick-to-my-stomach feeling swept over me. "Was it Carl? Was he one of them?"

Ella Mae didn't meet my eyes but just nodded.

"Well, is he hurt bad? Tell me, Ella Mae! Is he hurt bad?"

All the women were staring at me with sad, sad eyes.

"Carl's mighty beat up. Whole head full o' stitches. Perty bad. But it's Larry—well, he might not make it." Several women were moaning now. "They liked to near hanged him and beat him somethin' awful." Ella Mae's big brown eyes were misting up. "Imagine someone hurtin' these boys. Weren't doin' nothin' but carryin' their Bibles and singin'."

My head was spinning so that everything was blurry. I sat down in a nearby chair as a wave of nausea made me gag.

"You want me ta take ya on home, sugah?" Ella Mae asked.

I took a deep breath and shook my head. Ella Mae was crouching by my chair, looking caught between her two worlds. Torn. The duty part wanted to scoop me up in her arms and carry me back to Buckhead, away from the reality of the inner city. But the other part wanted to, *needed* to be here, with her people, in a time of tragedy. She was already getting out the car keys from her purse.

"No, Ella Mae. They need you here."

"I shore do hate for you ta havta hear it, Mary Swan. With all you've been through. Shore do hate it."

"I'll be fine, Ella Mae. Just tell me what I can do to help."

"Ain't nothin', darlin', ain't nothin' you can do but pray."

"Does Puddin' know?"

"Naw. We ain't told Puddin' or the boys. Carl's aunt is mighty shaken up. She's at the hospital with Miss Abigail right now."

"Then I'll take care of Puddin' and the boys, Ella Mae. I'll keep them today."

Ella Mae gave a heavy sigh, the kind that made her big bosom rise and fall. "That'd be right fine, Mary Swan. You do that, darlin'. You play with 'em awhile so's they don't worry none."

"Were there any other boys hurt?"

"Two others from the band was there, Leo and Nickie was with Carl and Larry. They's not hurt quite so badly, but ain't nothin' good to see. Some of us women folk, we's gonna see what we kin do ta he'p."

"If you need to take someone to the hospital, Ella Mae, you can use the Cadillac. Daddy would understand."

She patted my head. "Thank ya, Mary Swan." Then she looked at the pans of spaghetti and sauce and said, "Ain't nobody round heah much feels like eatin' nothin' today, I don't reckon."

I don't know what got me through that day or how I smiled while I was jumping rope with Puddin' or throwing the football with James and Mike. Every molecule inside of me wanted to be at the hospital, wanted to know that Carl was going to be okay. Carl and Larry and Leo and Nickie. The boys in the jazz band! I thought of Larry. Big, fat Larry who made us laugh when he puffed out his cheeks as he played the trombone or when he turned his horn upside down and emptied a puddle of spittle on the floor. Ella Mae had said he might not make it. He might not make it!

I took the children to Oakland Cemetery, where we played hide 'n' seek among the tombstones. They assured me that they went there all the time. At least I had a chance to wipe my eyes when they were hiding.

Once I sneaked away for a few minutes to sit beside Mama's grave. "The most awful things are happening in my life, Mama. Some of them have to do with you. So much of it. But a lot is about this part of town too. I'm so tired, Mama. So very tired."

As I headed back to find the kids, I could hear Miss Abigail saying, *"We're the hands and feet of Jesus, Mary Swan."* So while the kids dashed in and out of the tombstones, squealing when I found them, I kept saying in my mind, *God, if you are real, do something. I don't know what to ask you to do. Just please, do something.*

It was almost five o'clock when Ella Mae came to get me at Carl's house. Her beautiful face, her round ebony face, just sagged, and I was petrified to ask her anything. Right off she said, "If it's all right by you, Mary Swan, I think we'll take these chil'un to see their brother at the hospital."

"Sure. Of course."

We herded Mike and James and Puddin' into the backseat of the car. "Yo' brother's gotten roughed up a bit, chil'un," Ella Mae explained. "But he's gonna be fine. Jus' fine. Shore would make him smile to see you'uns, tho'. Sho' would."

On the way to the hospital, Ella Mae said quietly, so that the kids couldn't hear, "Larry's still doin' mighty poorly, honey. Still ain't shore he's gonna make it."

I leaned my head against the window and began to weep.

"We ain't told Carl yet."

When I stepped into the room at Grady Hospital, no bright light shined in my face and nothing said, "Attention! This is foreshadowing," the way it would in a novel. I had no idea I'd find myself there again in a matter of months. All I knew was that a black boy whom I cared about was lying in bed, everything covered in white but a part of his face—a face so swollen that I didn't recognize him. One eye was bandaged shut.

Puddin' ran over to Carl and kissed his cheek, her little face distraught. Then she threw her arms around his neck and started sobbing.

"Don't you be cryin' none, Sissy," Carl mumbled as he rubbed Puddin's braids. "Looks like it's me whose got the bandages now, sweet'un. You jus' got outta that there cast and now I's got me one myse'f. Ain't that somethin'." He tried to smile.

Miss Abigail and Aunt Neta were sitting side by side, grasping each other's hands. Miss Abigail gave me an exhausted smile. "Hello, Mary Swan. Thank you for watching the children." Aunt Neta nodded my way, looking like the life had been beaten out of her, but her eyes were soft toward me for the first time.

Carl looked at me tenderly and said in a raspy voice, which was barely audible, "Thanks for comin', Mary Swan."

There weren't any more chairs left, so I just stood by his bedside, biting my lip and trying desperately to think of something to say. "I let them play hide 'n' seek at Oakland."

"That's fine. Mighty fine. Puddin' and Mike got themselves some tough hidin' spots at Oakland." Carl poked Mike in the ribs with his bandaged hand, and both boys giggled.

Ella Mae motioned to me with her eyes. "Well, we've gotta go now, Mary Swan. Don't want yore daddy to be gettin' worried. Miss Abigail'll git the chil'un home later."

"I'll be thinking about you, Carl," I whispered. "I'm so sorry." And then without knowing why, I added, "And I'll be praying for you."

That's when our eyes locked, for just one second, and he smiled. "You do that, girl. That'll be jus' fine."

Chapter 18

Sunday morning at church, I tried to pray for Carl and for Larry, but I didn't really know how. So I just kept repeating in my mind, *Let them be okay, God. Let them be okay.* I walked to Rachel's after lunch, and we went to the barn. The weather in Atlanta in November can be chilly, even downright cold, or it can be mild. This Sunday afternoon, the air was cool, the sky was perfectly blue, and the woods around the barn were filled with fallen leaves, some of which still retained their orange or yellow or red tint. I picked a few and thought of how much Carl had enjoyed seeing the flaming hills.

"Still thinking about Carl, aren't you, Swan?"

Rachel, of course, knew everything about "the hug," as we'd been calling it all week.

"I've been thinking about him in another way, Rach. He got beat up last Thursday, he and a few of his friends from the band. Coming out from a church meeting in Morrow." I told her about the day I'd spent at Grant Park and seeing Carl at Grady Hospital and the fact that Larry might not make it.

"That's sick," she mumbled. "Absolutely awful. How could anyone do that?"

"Pure hatred."

"Inbred hatred, Swan. People being taught from the time they are little to hate others."

We pulled on our rubber boots and our hard hats and saddled up our mares, leading them by the reins up the hill to the riding ring. Bonnie darted to the side twice at a rustling leaf. The cool weather always left her dancing on pins and needles.

"You'll have your hands full today, Swan," Rachel laughed, putting her foot in the stirrup and swinging effortlessly across the back of her own mare, Brandy, a magnificent bay.

In fact, both our mares were skittish the whole afternoon. We worked them hard at the trot and the canter, practicing dressage, keeping them under control. Then we let them go at a hand gallop, still holding them under a tight rein while we lifted our seats out of the saddle and leaned forward over their necks. I loved the feel of Bonnie's red mane tickling my face as we galloped. I loved to feel her strength beneath me, the way her powerful legs, so fragile and yet so strong, thrust themselves out in front.

The riding ring, which was over half the size of a football field, had ten or twelve different jumps interspersed throughout it. A chicken coop, a fake brick wall (made out of plywood and painted by Mama to look very real), a small brush, and plenty of poles we could set to any height. We started jumping the lowest fences, gradually going to the higher ones, until we felt the mares were warmed up enough to try a series of jumps in a row.

"I'll make up the course!" Rachel volunteered. She hopped off Brandy and began to place the striped poles on their stands. "How high d'ya wanna go today, Swan?"

"Three feet nine."

Rachel lifted her eyebrows. "You sure? That's pretty high when you haven't ridden much this fall."

"Three nine," I insisted.

My mare could practically jump the moon, but Rachel was right. I was out of practice, and I knew it was unwise. Mrs. Abrams would have forbidden it if she'd been there. But I needed to do something daring today. I needed to do something bigger than myself, something to make the adrenaline pump in my ears, something that would require all my concentration so I wouldn't think about Grant Park and black boys lying in hospital beds.

So after Rachel had set the order for the jumps, I cantered Bonnie in a small circle near the gate, then headed her straight for the first fence, a small brush. We took it easily, and I let her gallop forcefully to the next fence, three striped yellow poles, straight up and down. She sailed over it, and I pulled her up a bit to make the turn and came down through the center of the ring, cutting it in half diagonally and taking the wide brick wall and then the chicken coop. All these we jumped with ease.

It was the next line, along the railing of the ring, that would be the hardest. An in-and-out at three six with four strides to the oxer, all three feet nine of it. Three feet nine inches was the height that show jumpers started at. And not only was the oxer three feet nine high, it was also four feet wide with poles mounting gradually in height. I had to get Bonnie to the in-and-out correctly, for as soon as she landed over the first jump, she took only one stride and jumped "out" of the other side. Four more strides then took her to the formidable oxer.

We thundered to this line as I kept the reins taut, Bonnie's head up, me sitting high in the saddle. Bonnie had a thing about in-and-outs. Sometimes she jumped the first one and then took two rough, ugly strides before jumping out. Other times she simply skidded to a stop in front of the "out" part or dodged to the side, missing the jump completely. And once she had crashed through the second, falling to the ground and throwing me hard against a pine tree.

So naturally today, I felt my heart pumping hard as we lifted off the ground. As soon as she landed, I kicked her hard with my heels, driving her to the next fence. She sailed over it without a problem. The oxer ahead looked enormous. For only a second I considered pulling over to the side and galloping around it. Even with that thought I was counting the strides in my head. "One, two, three, four . . ." and again I dug my heels deep into her flanks, moved my hands far up her neck to give her the rein she needed, gripped my thighs tightly into the saddle, and felt her gracefully jump the wide fence.

"Beautiful!" Rachel exclaimed as we hit the ground. "Perfect! You're ready for Madison Square Garden!" As I cantered Bonnie around the ring and then slowed her to a trot, patting her heartily on the shoulder, I smiled to myself. I had conquered my fear.

I showered and finished memorizing the tables for chemistry, then I brushed on some of Mama's mascara. I fiddled with my damp hair, toying with the idea of having it cut in a bob as Patty had suggested. I had an hour before Robbie picked me up for dinner at the Varsity.

Lying on my bed, trying to scratch out a few ideas for an English paper on comparative poetry, I kept hearing all the voices of those I cared about in my head. Daddy saying, *"Mary Swan, the best thing I can give you is a good education."* Rachel saying, *"Oh, Swan, just enjoy it! Enjoy having two boys' attention."* Patty telling me to put on makeup and cut my hair. Trixie pleading with me to leave everything I was finding out about Mama alone. Ella Mae warning me, *"You don't be messin' around none, Mary Swan. Ya heah me?"* And then Cassandra saying, *"I'm gonna try to stop messing around now that I got Jesus."* Robbie saying that he really wanted to get to know me better, and Carl saying that he hoped I would solve the Raven Dare so I could find peace in my head. And then finally there was Miss Abigail telling me that it was the truth that would make me free.

And I think down inside, I wanted to have it all. A good education and a fancy hairdo and nice clothes and the fun of being sixteen in Buckhead. And I wanted to be able to leave all the past alone and just enjoy it. And I didn't want to get anyone in trouble with whatever messing around I might do. But even deeper down, I thought Carl and Miss Abigail were right. I needed to figure this thing out. I needed to know the truth. I wanted to be free.

I didn't much think that going to Wellington or belonging to the club or being invited to the Piedmont Driving Club Christmas Dance or even riding my mare or reciting poetry or visiting the museum were going to help me get free. I wasn't even sure that going to St. Philip's Episcopal Church, or any other church for that matter, would help me. But I was pretty sure that if I would dare reach over and take down the white leather Bible and read some of the stuff Miss Abigail had been harping on me to read, well, then I might find some answers.

Then again, I wasn't sure.

All these thoughts were tumbling around in my head when I went downstairs to the kitchen. Daddy grunted at me from behind the Sunday paper, "Coke stock's up two points, Mary Swan."

"Great, Dad. Now you can afford to send me to an Ivy League school," I said sarcastically.

With an astounded look on his face, he set down his newspaper. "Do you mind telling me what's wrong, dear?"

"Nothing's wrong. Everything's just great. Like always. Why would you think anything is wrong? You've got dates with Amanda Hunnicutt, who's from a fine Atlanta family, and I'm dating a boy from another fine Atlanta family, and Jimmy is best friends with a boy from that same fine Atlanta family, and we are, of course, another very fine Atlanta family. . . ."

"Mary Swan! Stop it!"

My face grew hot. "Sorry, Daddy." I felt like crying, ashamed of my outburst. "It's just that while we're hanging around all these fine Atlanta people, there's this boy, this really great guy who plays the trombone in a jazz band and cracks great jokes and has a heart as big as anyone I've ever known, who is about to die in Grady Hospital. He's not from a fine family. He's black and he's dirt poor, but it's still awful. Absolutely awful."

Daddy looked stunned. "Is this boy someone you know?"

I started to measure my words, but then exploded, "Yes, I know him, Daddy! I know him from Grant Park. You know what happened to him? He and his friends were coming out of a church meeting when a bunch of white guys jumped on them. The white boys had knives and ropes. All the black boys had were their Bibles. They tried to hang him. Beat him to a pulp. Almost killed him, Daddy. And the whole neighborhood of Grant Park is waiting to see if he'll live. But nothing will ever happen to those white kids. Nothing! Who knows, maybe they're from fine Atlanta families too!"

"Sweetheart, I'm sorry about your friend. It's terrible. Barbaric. These are hard times."

I could tell that Daddy was too shocked at my outburst to comment any further, and fortunately, Robbie rang the doorbell at that moment. So I kissed Daddy on the cheek and said, "I'll be back later."

"Be careful, Mary Swan" was all he said.

We were sitting in the part of the Varsity parking lot called Buttermilk Bottom, smiling at each other as we ate. But I felt tired, my whole body worn out from the physical exertion of riding and the mental exertion of everything else in my life, especially leaving my dad with those mean accusations still on my tongue.

Robbie noticed it immediately. "Mary Swan, what's the matter? Is it something I've done?"

"No, not at all, Robbie. Just some bad news. I keep getting bad news." I picked at my onion rings and cheeseburger.

"Is it something you want to talk about?"

"I don't know. Maybe, if you want to hear it."

"Sure, I do." He looked so sincere that I decided I'd just plunge ahead with whatever details I could reveal. "Well, first off, I'm finding out a lot of depressing stuff about my mother."

He didn't question me at all, which I appreciated. He just listened, slurping occasionally on his frosted orange.

"It turns out that what Herbert said about her was kind of true. She did go to a sanatorium. Lots of times. And Daddy didn't tell me."

He put his arm around me. "That can't be fun to find out."

"No, it's rotten. And besides that, some boys I know from the inner city, nice decent Christian boys, got beat up, beaten to a pulp by some white guys when they were coming out of a civil rights meeting at a church in Morrow. It's not like they had knives or something. They had Bibles."

I didn't want him to see that I was on the brink of tears, because it seemed like that's what happened every time I went out with him. "One of them almost died. Can you believe it, Robbie? These white kids almost killed him. Tried to hang him. And last night, they still weren't sure he'd make it."

I leaned forward against the dashboard and watched a black waiter dashing to an old Buick, calling, "Pick up in Decatur." Any appetite I had left immediately.

Robbie reached over and took my hand. "If you want, I'll take you home."

"No, I don't want to go home." I said it rather brusquely. "I'm sorry. I'm really tired, Robbie. But I don't want to go home. You know where I really want to go?"

"No, where?"

"I want to go for a drive. Down to Grant Park. Will you take me?"

"Now?"

"Could you, please?"

"I'm not sure I know how to get there, Mary Swan."

"I'll show you."

"Well, if it means that much to you, I guess we can try." I knew then I didn't deserve a friend like Robbie Bartholomew. He pulled his little red convertible, though the top was up of course, out of the Varsity parking lot and turned away from Buckhead, straight toward the inner city.

"I told you I'd been helping out down here," I said, indicating the road to turn off from Peachtree Street. "Now that this has happened, well, it makes everything in Buckhead seem a bit superficial. Or at Wellington. I mean, who cares where you get your dresses or what club you belong to or who you're dating or how big your car is or how much your dad makes or any of that stuff? Do you think any of that really matters?"

"On a small scale, sure. If you're talking about individuals. But if you're talking civil rights and what's really important, I don't think the superficial stuff is important." He glanced at me. "At least I hope there's something more out there for me."

"You do?"

"Sure. Don't get me wrong. I love Atlanta. I love Buckhead. But I don't know if I'll be able to follow in Dad's shoes. He's a pillar of society. Like your dad."

"What would you like to do, if you could do anything in the world, Robbie Bartholomew?" Then I grabbed his shoulder. "Wait a sec, turn here. Yes, slow down! Right here." And then, "Sorry. Okay, go on."

He gave a mischievous smile, at least it looked mischievous for Robbie Bartholomew. "I think I'd just like to follow you around for a while. You'd find enough to keep us both busy, I'm sure."

I stuck out my tongue. "Now take a left here on Capitol Avenue. We're almost there."

"Where?"

"At the church."

When we pulled up in front of Mt. Carmel, I could tell the Sunday night church service was still going. "Wait here a sec. I just want to peek in."

"Are you nuts, Mary Swan? I'm staying with you. Grant Park isn't the same at night as it is in the day. Just let me park, will you?"

"Maybe you shouldn't leave the car, though. I have friends who tell me they know how to take a car apart in less than an hour."

"Well, then, you better start saving money to get me a new convertible, because I'm parking this car and not letting you out of my sight." We were parked across the street from the church by then, in front of a dark corner with a bent-in-two sign that showed these streets as Capitol Avenue and Georgia Avenue. We both stood by the curve for a moment, grinning at each other.

Then I poked him in the ribs. "You win, Robbie. Come on inside with me."

We crossed the street and went in the front door, the one I never used, the one that led directly into the back of the sanctuary. Music and singing greeted our ears. All we could see were the backs of a lot of black people standing up. Some had their hands raised over their heads, some were swaying to and fro, and some were clapping enthusiastically. We slipped inside, for the moment unnoticed, and huddled together on the empty back pew, almost as if we expected this crowd of black people to turn on us in fury, the way the whites had done to James Meredith.

The singing went on for ten more minutes, and I particularly liked the words in one of the songs. "Jesus on my main line, tell Him what ya want, Jesus on my main line, tell Him what ya want, Jesus on my main line, tell Him what ya want. Ya call Him up, and ya tell Him what ya want."

I could kind of understand how these people might think they saw black angels on the road or some other miracle of God Almighty. There was such a sense of sincerity and expectation and, I don't know, need. Yes, heartfelt need. These people sang like they needed Jesus and, praise God, He was only a phone call away. And in that moment, I wanted it too. I didn't have any idea how to get it—how to get eyes that sparkled like Miss Abigail's and a fresh naïveté that said with Cassandra, "Jesus done goin' ta be lookin' afta' us from now on." More than anything, I wanted God to convince me, as He had done for Carl, that He was real. I didn't know how to get God to do that, so I just belted out, along with all the others, "Ya call Him up, and ya tell Him what ya want!"

Robbie's grin had spread clear across his face, and he looked as if he was enjoying himself every bit as much as the others. "This is great, Mary Swan!" he called over the noise. "Man, can they sing!"

Then, as if on some cue that Robbie and I missed, everyone else sat down, noisily, with a lot of bustling and "Amen!" and "Alleluia!" so that for a split second, we were the only ones standing up.

A few black heads turned to stare at us hard. I heard whispering around us, and then, from over on my left and in front of us, a very loud child's voice trying to whisper, "Hey 'dere, Mary Swan! Look,

Puddin'! It's Mary Swan, and she done brought her a white boy with her." Mike was pointing, and Miss Abigail, sitting beside him, nodded my way with those twinkling eyes. And several of the ladies who came on Saturdays caught my eye, and they gave me the warmest smiles, as though this was where I belonged.

"They all look like they know you," Robbie whispered, while the pastor started praying.

"I *do* know them, Robbie. I see them every Saturday." Then I grabbed his hand and begged, "Can we stay 'til the end?"

He grinned even bigger. "If my dad knew that I was sitting here with you in a black church service . . . see, Mary Swan, I was right. Life with you would always be an adventure. That's for sure." And so we stayed.

I'd heard the ladies talk about Pastor James many times, but I'd never met him, because on Saturdays he worked in a nearby community with a boys' club. Pastor James had a head full of gray hair and bushy gray eyebrows that almost joined in the middle. He was rather short and kind of square looking, and I got the feeling that he had a lot of physical as well as spiritual power behind his words. And I knew from comments made that Pastor James was loved and revered as much as Miss Abigail.

". . . And, dear Lawd," he was saying in his black drawl, "we thank you, we thank you with all our hearts, O Lawd, for sparing the lives of our boys." His voice rose in intensity and emotion as he spoke.

A host of amens followed the pastor's sentence. Relief flooded through me. Larry must be all right!

"We praise you, Lawd Jesus, for overcoming the enemy. We overcome with love, brotha's and sista's, that we do. Where the world says to hate and seek revenge, Jesus, you tell us to forgive and be at peace with all men. Precious Lawd Jesus, do let us overcome with your divine love. Amen."

There was a collective shout of "Amen!" and then the whole congregation burst into a song that would become famous in the following years, but which neither Robbie nor I had ever heard before that night. "We shall overcome," they sang. "We shall overcome, we shall overcome someday-ay-ay-ay-ay. Oh-oh, deep in my heart, I do believe, we shall overcome someday." The way they sang it stirred me way down inside. The piano was silent, no hands clapped, every head was bowed, and eyes were firmly shut, as the haunting, heartfelt spiritual exploded *a cappella*, filling every corner of the sanctuary. And filling every soul.

Robbie had the most solemn expression on his face, and he swallowed hard, and I wondered if he was fighting back tears. Then Pastor James opened his big Bible and began to preach.

"We's talking about freedom, like the Good Book says." He leaned way over the pulpit, peering out at the congregation. " 'What does the Lawd require of you? To act justly, to love mercy, and to walk humbly with your God,' Amen!" Another chorus of amens followed. "And in Galatians it says, 'There is neither Jew nor Greek, slave nor free, male nor female, for you are all one in Jesus Christ.' " He held his Bible up victoriously. "You hear that, brotha's and sista's? We is one in Jesus Christ!"

His message lasted at least forty-five minutes, but neither Robbie nor I noticed the time. We were riveted in place, in part by the message and in part by the brand-new culture of a black worship service. When it was over, Puddin' ran to my side, grabbed my leg, and hugged me tight. I got that pinched feeling in my chest again. She wiggled around my legs, staring up at Robbie.

"Puddin', this is my friend Robbie."

"Pleased ta meetcha," she said, eyes going to the floor and back up to him and back down.

Robbie squatted down to her level. "Puddin'? Good to meet you too." He twirled one of her braids, and she smiled shyly. "Tell me, Puddin', does Mary Swan behave herself when she comes to see you?"

Fortunately, Robbie couldn't see how red my face suddenly got.

Puddin' gave a big grin and said, "Oh, shore, she's jus' fine here. She likes ta serve spaghetti with my brotha', and then sometimes she comes ta my house ta play. Sometimes she and my brotha' and Miss Rachel and the otha' boys in the band, they gets ta makin' an awful racket on their instruments, and then Aunt Neta makes 'em leave the house." She scrunched up her nose. "But that ain't nothin' new 'cause Aunt Neta likes ta run everybody outta the house." She lifted her shoulders shyly and glanced at me. "Mary Swan! I saw Carl today and he's betta'! He's so much betta'! I even got to write on his cast, jus' like he did on mine."

"That's wonderful, sweetie."

"Hello, Mary Swan." Miss Abigail's eyes were sparkling again. "What a surprise to see you here."

"Miss Abigail, this is my friend Robbie Bartholomew. We were—" I blushed. "We were out at the Varsity, and I just had an urge to come down here, and so Robbie brought me, and the service was going on."

"Robbie, so glad to meet you."

Robbie stuck out his hand and shook Miss Abigail's forcefully. "Good to meet you too. Mary Swan has told me so much about you."

Miss Abigail gave one of her dry smiles. "Don't believe everything you hear, Robbie."

"So they're okay," I blurted out. "Carl and Larry are okay?"

"Yes, they are, Mary Swan. Yes, they are." Her lined face softened. "We didn't know for Larry. Touch and go all last night. But they're both gonna be fine. Jesus heard our petitions."

"Miss Abigail done stayed on the flo' in Larry's room all night long talkin' ta Jesus," little James volunteered proudly, the whites of his eyes big. "And Jesus done heard her prayers." He crossed his arms with a satisfied smile.

"Shh now, James. It wasn't my prayers. He heard *our* prayers. Don't you start puffing me up. I won't have it, young man." Miss Abigail playfully swatted at his bottom.

The children darted behind her. Robbie asked, "How long has this building been here, Miss Abigail?"

"Oh, a hundred years, I'd say. Was a white church for decades, a fine white church. But in the early fifties, well, the rich whites started leaving this area. Running away, I like to say." She shook her head as if reprimanding the whole white race. "Running when we needed them to stay. When the Lord *wanted* them to stay. So eventually, well, eventually the Presbyterian Mission gave me the keys to this church. They said for me to take it over." She laughed at an inner joke. "Here I was a missionary with the Southern Baptists, and the Presbyterians were giving me their church. But that's God's heart, anyway, isn't it, children? I work with blacks and whites, rich and poor, Baptists and Presbyterians and Episcopalians and Catholics. And the sweetest group of Jewish ladies you've ever known gets together in their nursing home on Peachtree and knits booties and little sweaters for the newborns."

Robbie was studying Miss Abigail carefully. "You must really love this work to stay here."

"As I've told Mary Swan, it's my calling. This is where God wants me, not because it's easy, but because it's His work for me. Pastor James came about nine years ago, and you can see that the congregation has certainly grown."

"And you're right in the middle of the social reform. Well, it's been great to see firsthand what Mary Swan's been telling me about for all these months. Good night, Miss Abigail." He shook her hand again and rubbed James's and Mike's hair.

"Good night, Robbie and Mary Swan. Take care driving home."

The children followed us out of the church while Miss Abigail turned her attention to another woman. The little red convertible sat untouched where we had left it, but soon Mike and James and Puddin' were crowded around it with several other children.

"See, I tol' ya so. It's Mary Swan's friend's car. Mmm-hmm."

"Mighty nice car, Mista Robbie," little James said with admiration.

"You like it? You want to take a spin with me?"

The boy's eyes grew wide.

"I'd better check with Miss Abigail," I said to Robbie.

I whispered to her inside the church, "Robbie wants to take some of the kids for a ride around the block in his car. Is that okay?"

"Wonderful idea. Aunt Neta's at the hospital tonight, so I'm on duty with the kids. I'll be in here for another thirty minutes. Just let me know when you're leaving and send the kids back in."

So for the next thirty minutes Robbie drove James and then Mike and then Puddin' and then a bunch of other kids around the streets of Grant Park. He even put down the top, which made them squeal with delight. He didn't pay one bit of attention when I said, "It's November, for goodness' sake. They'll catch cold!" I think he enjoyed the rides even more than the kids.

When we left, they stood on the curb and waved while yelling, "Thank you, Mr. Robbie. Y'all come back now!"

Robbie was all adrenaline. "Cute kids. Mary Swan, that woman is extraordinary. Just in those few minutes, I could tell it. Something about her . . ."

"It's her eyes. They sparkle."

"Exactly. Like she has a holy conviction of what she's doing."

"She does. She fully believes God called her."

"Must be nice to be able to do what God says." He laughed wryly.

"My life's already been written in stone by Mr. Robert H. Bartholomew, Sr. Top grades in prep school, Ivy League college, return to Atlanta, and carry on the family business. Marry a nice girl"—he winked at me, and we both said in unison—"from a fine Atlanta family" and burst into laughter.

"But seriously, I wonder what it feels like to do something because it feels right in your . . . in your soul."

"I don't know." I shook my head in wonder. "All I do know is that I think she has had one of the hardest lives I've ever heard of. In many ways, harder than the poor she works with. She's trying to help them come out of their poverty. But she . . . she *chose* to leave wealth and enter into poverty. Can you imagine?"

Robbie was thinking about something far off. He didn't answer right away, but finally he said, "Yeah, I can, Mary Swan. I think I can."

We were driving down Peachtree, the street that cuts through the middle of Atlanta, the street that summed up for me so much of my life. The Capital City Club sat on the corner of Peachtree and Harris Street, my church sat on the corner of Peachtree and Andrews, and the country club was located six miles farther down Peachtree. My dad's office was somewhere in between. Grandmom and Granddad Middleton lived right off of Peachtree, on a wide, calm road not far from Piedmont Hospital.

Robbie slowed down in front of the Fox Theatre. "Wanna go in?" *Gigi* was showing.

"Hasn't it already started?"

"Are you kidding? Not the nine-o'clock show. We've got fifteen minutes."

"Yes, then! Yes, let's watch it, Robbie!" I called the house from a pay phone across the street to tell Daddy that we'd be late, and Jimmy answered.

"Lucky duck. The Fox. All right. Let me tell Dad." He returned a minute later. "Daddy says what he always says."

" 'Be careful and don't stay out too late,' " I repeated from memory.

"Exactly. And I won't tell you who just happened to stop by with a hamperful of Kentucky Fried Chicken right after you left."

"Amanda?"

"Right. I had to sit through dinner alone with them while she cackled and Daddy pretended to think her jokes were funny."

"Sorry, Jimmy. You could always let Muffin out again and get Daddy to help you find him."

"I don't think that will work twice, silly. Anyway, have fun."

"Well, thanks." I smiled to myself. My little brother had actually said something straightforwardly nice to me!

The Fox Theatre was famous for its enormous pipe organ, which played before each film or opera and then disappeared underneath the stage. The theatre's interior walls were made to look like a medieval castle, and when you peered upward, it looked like there was a real sky for a ceiling. As the organ played familiar tunes, we craned our necks to watch the sun rise and shine overhead and then slowly set on the other side of the theater while thousands of tiny stars twinkled above us. Just sitting in the Fox Theatre was magic.

Robbie must have felt the same way, because he put his arm around my shoulder and drew me close to him, and with the other hand he took my left hand and squeezed it gently. I rested my head on his ample shoulder and let myself get lost in a movie about a young girl's discovery of Paris.

It was nearly eleven when the movie ended. When we passed the High Museum on the way home, I had an incredible urge to tell Robbie all about Mama and the paintings and Resthaven. "Can we talk for a little while, Robbie?"

"It's late. You don't think your dad will mind?"

"Not if it doesn't last too long."

"You sure that all you want to do is talk?" he asked with a grin on his face.

I stuck out my tongue, and he shrugged. We pulled into the parking lot of St. Philip's, which was just right up the street from my house. And for the next thirty minutes, I told him about my trip to Resthaven and what we'd found out. I made him promise to tell no one, and I never once mentioned a thing about the Raven Dare or Carl. Maybe he suspected it, but he didn't let on. And when I was done, I let out a huge sigh of relief because it felt like I was being honest with him, almost completely honest with him, for the first time. And I realized anew what I had forgotten over the last ten days. I really liked Robbie Bartholomew a lot.

Before he kissed me good-night, he said, "That was a really interesting evening, Mary Swan. Maybe our best yet."

Chapter 19

On Thanksgiving Day we all went to Grandmom and Granddad Middleton's house for dinner. Their house was on Habersham Road, only a five-minute car ride away. We liked their house because it had a big basement that they'd transformed into a game room. It had a pool table and a ping-pong table, and along one wall there were shelves behind glass that were filled with all of Granddad's trophies from his high school and college days—the days when he'd been a sports hero. Sometimes after a meal, Jimmy and I would escape to the game room and admire the trophies while the adults sipped their after-dinner drinks.

Tradition stood strong on Thanksgiving Day. On Christmas and Easter and the Fourth of July, the Middleton clan sometimes split up to be with their respective spouses' families. But not on Thanksgiving. That was the day when every Middleton was expected to be present, from the oldest to the youngest. This year, with Mama gone and Daddy's youngest sister just having had her third baby, the number went unchanged from last year, and that number was twenty-eight immediate family members. Grandmom didn't mind a bit if other families showed up to join in the fun, as long as she had all her children and grandchildren around. Sometimes, Mama's parents came up from Griffin to join us.

The house was already brimming with children, teens, and adults when Mamie and Papy arrived. I could tell that Mamie had been drinking. She leaned heavily into Papy, and when she kissed me on the cheeks, I could smell the alcohol on her breath. Her bright red lipstick was smeared on, and her eyes looked bright and glassy. Papy supported her under the arm.

"Ma chère Marie Cygne." She always broke into French when she'd been drinking and started calling me the French equivalent of Mary Swan. *"Pourquoi n'es-tu pas venue me voir?"*

Her words stung me. Why *hadn't* I been to Griffin to visit this fall? Mama had been their only child. That big plantation must have seemed terribly lonely since Mama's death.

"We'll be coming for Christmas, Evelyne," Daddy said, rescuing me and giving his mother-in-law the necessary kiss on each cheek. "Ian, so good to see you. Come on in. I believe you remember my sister, Lisa, and her husband, Jeff."

And so I escaped into the kitchen. It wasn't my usual spot on Thanksgiving Day. Normally I played chase with my younger cousins and then went out by the pool and talked with the older ones. We grandchildren ranged in age from Jackie, who at twenty was in her junior year at Hollins, to baby Eddie who was just sitting up at six months. Eddie was actually Franklin Edward Middleton VI, named after Daddy's oldest brother, who was named after Granddad who was named after my great-granddad. Somehow there had been six of them. This new baby had been dubbed Eddie. In that way, when Grandmom spoke of Frank or Frankie or Franklin, only three men would qualify, making things a little less confusing.

I really didn't see my cousins very often, maybe two or three times a year, and I never felt any tight bonds with them. Still we managed to have fun at the family get-togethers. It was Jackie who had given me my first cigarette to smoke, years ago behind the changing rooms at Grandmom's swimming pool. But today I didn't feel like chasing toddlers or chatting with the teenagers.

"Mary Swan, go on out with everyone, honey," Grandmom said as I tried to find something to do in the kitchen.

I pretended I didn't hear her, and she didn't insist. I needed the shelter of the warm kitchen with the delicious aromas of baking turkey and biscuits and apple cake engulfing me and protecting me from the reality around, the reality that everyone was present except Mama. I was thankful for my experience at Grant Park too. Somehow having spent so many hours in the kitchen in the basement of Mt. Carmel made me feel more comfortable in Grandmom's kitchen. That Thanksgiving Day, I found real pleasure in helping Grandmom, the master hostess, arrange the food on her dining room table. The china and silver and white linen napkins were stacked at one end of the table. The crystal glasses and the ice water and tea in their silver pitchers and the wine in its crystal decanter were all set on the long cherry sideboard.

I began to carry out the food. As with every Thanksgiving, each family brought some Southern specialty to add to the feast. Soon the table was laden with the turkey, the stuffing, the mashed potatoes and gravy, the cranberry sauce, the delicious *pâté* that Mamie always brought, fresh from her farm, the artichoke hearts, the blueberry muffins, the sweet potatoes with the marshmallows melted on top, the green bean casserole, the fresh turnip greens, Grandmom's homemade rolls that Jimmy loved, and my personal favorite, her corn soufflé. When it was all in place and piping hot, we stood around the table, all forty-two of us, and held hands while Granddad asked the blessing.

By the time the pies—pumpkin, chess, and apple—were laid out, we were all recovering in various corners of the vast house. Uncle Tim, completely drunk, had launched into the same story he told every Thanksgiving, and the house was filled with merry chatter. The day was bright and chilly, and from the windows of Grandmom's living room, I could see some of the cousins playing in the yard with Muffin, who loved to join us at my grandparents' house. The red mutt, who was mostly hunting dog, ran in wild circles around the children, his rust-colored fur blending nicely with the fallen leaves. Several girls chased him, squealing, while Jimmy tossed a football with two boys around his age.

I made polite conversation until I found my chance to kiss both sets of grandparents good-bye, slip outside, and walk from Habersham Road to Andrews Drive, admiring the stately homes all along the way that I knew so well. Once at my house, I went upstairs to the *atelier* and closed the door firmly behind me. I stood before my easel, looking out the windows, and I painted. My stomach was full and I felt sleepy, so my strokes were not crisp like the autumn air, but lethargic, slow, as if I was clumsily trying to thread a needle with my paintbrush. But I kept painting because over the past weeks, experience had proved that just the discipline of making myself paint was invaluable. And today I was concentrating on a very small part of the canvas, a figure in the background, barely seen, fuzzy like my mood, the figure of a black boy kneeling in a field.

There were few things that brought the city of Atlanta to its feet in those days like the football rivalry between Georgia Tech and the University of Georgia. The Georgia Tech vs. Georgia football game on the Saturday after Thanksgiving was as much of a tradition as Thanksgiving itself. This year it took place in nearby Athens, at the University of Georgia's Sanford Stadium. Granddad had eight tickets, so I'd invited Robbie, and Jimmy had invited Andy, and Daddy had, unfortunately, invited Amanda Hunnicutt.

By the time we got to our seats, the crowd of students for both teams had already had a lot to drink and were bellowing out their rival school songs. Being on Bulldog territory, Tech fans were by far outnumbered. But our minority crowd sang with as much gusto as the Georgia Bulldogs. "I'm a Ramblin' Wreck from Georgia Tech. . . ."

And from the Georgia camp came their song to the tune of "The Battle Hymn of the Republic." "Glory, glory to ole Georgia. . . !"

Of course in our family, with Granddad having played for Tech's illustrious football team, we'd heard a hundred stories of the rivalry and especially the one about when Granddad was the hero of the game. But since Robbie didn't know the story, Granddad launched into it again.

"The game was being played on Georgia Tech's Grant Field. It had snowed at the beginning, and a freezing drizzle settled in for the rest of the game. But the loyal fans stayed. Georgia had a strong team that year, and Tech had a few star rookies but lacked experience."

"Granddad was one of the star rookies," Jimmy added.

"Well, now, Georgia jumped to a fourteen-zero lead. Tech got two field goals, making it fourteen to six."

"It was Granddad who kicked the field goals!" Jimmy persisted.

"Georgia scored again but missed the extra point. At halftime it was twenty to six. We got quite a talking-to by our coach at halftime."

"Tell them who your coach was, Granddad." That was Jimmy again.

"Robbie, our coach was none other than John W. Heisman. You ever heard of him?"

"Sure, Mr. Middleton. He's the man the Heisman Trophy is named after."

"Exactly. Well, he coached at Tech, boy. And he coached hard. Cut our water allowance during the week before the game and had us eating lots of meat, eating it nearly raw. Anyway, in the third quarter, we rallied with a touchdown and made it twenty to thirteen."

"Excuse me, sir? Did you score the touchdown?"

"Well, yes, I did, son. I did score that one. And we managed to hold Georgia on their next two possessions. But with three minutes left, we were still down by seven points."

Jimmy could not contain his enthusiasm. "Then Granddad came in as end, and the quarterback hid the ball on his hip and faked to the tailback. In the meantime, Granddad was streaking down the field, wide open, and the quarterback lofted a pass to him and it sailed into Granddad's hands and he scored!"

Granddad looked more than content. "Of course, with the extra point, that made the score twenty to twenty. Only a minute and a half left. Georgia fumbled the ball and Tech recovered it. Got it down to the thirty-five. It was fourth down . . ."

"And in came Granddad. You guessed it! He kicked the goal and scored. All the Tech fans started flooding onto the field while there was still fifteen seconds on the clock!"

Robbie, always polite, had followed the whole story with seeming interest. "That's really impressive, Mr. Middleton!" he commented enthusiastically. And with the ritual of Granddad's moment of glory behind us, we settled in to watch this game, which in the end proved no less exciting.

All of the fans were already in a frenzy of expectation because the week before, Tech had upset Alabama and Georgia had upset Auburn. They were hoping for something even more explosive in this game. Tech kicked off. Bobby Dodd was the coach, and Billy Lothridge from Gainesville was the quarterback. He scored the first touchdown, and everyone started chanting, "Mr. Cool, Mr. Everything!"

I was huddled as close as possible to Robbie, covered by blankets and protected from the wet seat by a cushion. Our only problem was the drunken man sitting behind me would cuss and stomp when Tech made a bad play, and half of his bottle of bourbon would splash onto me. But Robbie and I just laughed and laughed, and Jimmy and Andy ate hot dogs, and Daddy and Amanda screamed their hearts out. And Granddad let loose a string of curse words when Georgia scored first, and Grandmom just laughed and said, "Frank! Please calm down!" and the men sipped their flasks of whisky and kept warm that way.

Until the second half. By that time, the Tech fan behind us had drunk himself into oblivion. He stopped one of the young black boys who was coming down the concrete stairs with a tray full of peanuts around his neck. "Whatcha selling, black boy?"

I turned around immediately and glared at the man, but he didn't notice.

The boy looked nervous. "Peanuts, sir."

"Well, go on. Give me a bag." He thrust out a fat red hand.

"Yessir. Heah ya go. That'll be fifteen cents, sir."

"Fifteen cents! That's highway robbery. I ain't givin' you no fifteen cents."

Fear sprang into the boy's eyes. "Well, sir, that's the price."

The big drunk man stood up and towered over the boy. "I told ya, boy, I ain't got no fifteen cents for peanuts."

By then everyone around the man had stopped watching the game and was staring at the scene going on around them.

"Robbie, make him quit!" I whispered. "He's awful. He's gonna hurt that kid."

But before Robbie or Daddy or anyone else could do a thing, the drunk man grabbed the boy by his jacket and shook him hard, so hard that bags of peanuts tumbled off his tray.

Granddad stood up then. "That's enough, mister. You'd best be going." I guess the fact that Granddad was every bit as big as the drunken man, combined with the eyes of a dozen people on him, made him reconsider. With a killing look, the man grabbed his flask and his blanket and left the stadium. The boy had laid down his tray on the steps and was frantically trying to salvage a few bags of peanuts off the ground.

Granddad motioned to him. "Come here, boy." He handed him several dollars and said, "Don't you worry about it, ya hear? Everything is going to be okay."

The boy muttered a "Thank ya, sir," and continued down the steps, calling out, a little less enthusiastically, "Peanuts! Get yore peanuts heah. Fifteen cents."

Tech won the game easily, thirty-seven to six, and by the time we left Sanford Stadium all of us were hoarse from screaming, chilled to the bone but good-humored. But, of course, I couldn't wipe out the image of the boy selling peanuts. That scene as well as several others kept playing in my mind on the way home. And I remembered what Carl had told me once: *"You whites think that handing these guys a wad of bills will help. But it's not the money. It's our dignity that matters. It's not pity we want. It's equality. It's not having to cower to another man and keep your mouth shut just because his skin is white and yours is black."*

On the Monday after Thanksgiving, right when I got home from school, Ella Mae handed me a letter that had come in the mail. I tore it open and held up the card triumphantly—my invitation to the Piedmont Driving Club Christmas Dance! I ran upstairs and called Rachel.

"Mine didn't come today," she stated.

"Oh, it'll come tomorrow. You know how the mail is, Rach."

"Sure. I know." We talked for a half hour about what we would wear and going shopping at Lenox Square at Davison's and getting our dresses together.

"And whom are you going to invite?" Rachel asked at last with a hint of teasing in her voice.

"Robbie, of course, you idiot."

"Not Carl? For sure?"

"How can I invite Carl, silly? He'll be playing in the band. You're the one who helped me work that out. Don't forget that we're supposed to take Carl and the rest of the band to meet with Mrs. Appleby next week. I sure hope Larry and Carl will be in shape to play."

"I won't forget. But you're pretty sneaky! You'll have both of your men at the party. You better watch out, Swan."

"I've been thinking about that, Rach. What if they meet? They can't. They just can't."

"Don't worry. I'll be there to help you out."

But she was wrong.

That Thursday night I was stretched across my bed working on a trigonometry problem when Jimmy called up to me, "Robbie's on the phone."

That pleased me because we rarely talked on the phone on school nights. "Hi there!" I answered enthusiastically.

"Hi, Mary Swan. How's everything?"

"Fine, I guess. Except for trigonometry."

He chuckled a little. "Listen. I wanted to talk to you about something—ever since we went to the Mt. Carmel church service, I've had some ideas for helping in the inner city."

"Like what?"

"Well, like why don't you get a group of girls from Welly to volunteer some time at Grant Park? They could go Christmas caroling or raise money and deliver turkeys or repaint Miss Abigail's house. And I could talk it up at Mendon. Wouldn't that be great? I mean, the spaghetti meals are a good start, but there's so much more that could be done. Tons of ways to help out."

I was astounded by his enthusiasm. "Do you really mean it? You think kids from Buckhead would go down to Grant Park?"

"Well, of course! You're doing it. Sure. It'd just take a little organization and a well-defined project."

"Robbie, I'd have no idea how to organize something like that. I mean, it's a great idea, but I don't have a clue how to begin."

"Well, I do. We've done that kind of thing a bunch of times in the Boy Scouts. Community service, you know. If you talked it over with Miss Abigail and the pastor and found out what would be most helpful, well, we could get something going for just before Christmas, maybe right after school gets out, volunteer a day down in Grant Park."

I could feel a smile spreading across my face. "That is one great idea, Robbie. You're brilliant! I've been wondering what else could be done down there. My efforts seem so small and insignificant. But all I came up with was wishing I could write Ella Mae or Miss Abigail a check for a million bucks and tell them to divide it evenly among the poor. Pretty realistic, huh?"

"Not bad. Only problem is that you gotta come up with the money. Other than that it sounds like a piece of cake."

I liked the good humor I heard in his voice.

"But seriously, Robbie. The more we can do to promote civil rights, the better. I never used to even care, but now, well, you've seen it. The poverty, the cruelty, the prejudice. It makes my problems seem so minor."

"True, but then I don't think you can really compare your problems with the inner city. They're both real and hard. Think of Buckhead. It'll take years for everyone to get over Orly. We won't ever really get over it. Bad things happen to rich people too."

"I know it. Of course I know it. The whole reason I started going down there was because Ella Mae was trying to help me out of my problems. But it's become just one more thing that makes me feel awful. These people have become my friends, and it hurts to know what they're going through and not be able to help. I wish I didn't care so much."

"That's insane, Swan. It's great that you care. Someday you may be able to use your experience to influence others, to help them care too."

"Maybe, but sometimes it all just seems too complicated for my pea-sized brain. So many things don't make sense, Robbie. First, my mom had a long, difficult mental illness that never was cured. And my family did the best we could to survive, but Mama never really got better. Then she dies in an airplane crash, and she's gone forever. Forever. And to get my mind off that, I go down to Grant Park, and what do I find? Poverty. And hate. Nice guys getting beat up because of the color of their skin. And what in the world can I do to help any of those things? Nothing. Absolutely nothing. I have no control over anything. I didn't know it before but it's true—no control."

I could hear Robbie's breath in the phone as he contemplated my questions. "True. Not a lot of control on a big scale. You're talking about a lot of different things. A tragic accident, a serious psychological condition, poverty, and prejudice. That's a lot of things to digest. Of course, you can't do much about any of it. Not on a big, national scope. But if you just started on a small level, one project at a time, well, that's helping. Like the spaghetti meals. And taking care of those black children when their brother got hurt. Surely that's important. That matters."

"Maybe. But nothing big is changing."

"Don't think big right now, Mary Swan. Think little. Let's plan something to help Miss Abigail. What d'ya say?"

I hesitated. "Well, I can try to get some girls interested, but according to most of the ones in my class, all I'm supposed to be thinking about is what I'll wear to the dance and how to fix my hair."

"I like it long, just how it is."

"What?"

"Your hair. I like it long."

"You do?"

"Sure. You'll look great."

I had absolutely nothing to say to that. Finally, Robbie spoke again.

"I didn't mean to change the subject, Mary Swan. You've got good questions. I've got a lot of questions of my own. I'm stuck in a mold, with all of these expectations. With all the pressure to succeed. To be at the top of the class. To keep up the good reputation of my brother, the straight-A student who was captain of the state champion track team. Not to mention Daddy's reputation as top financial consultant in Atlanta. It feels sometimes as if I'm carrying a lot more than just a football in my hands. It feels like the Bartholomew good name is going to depend on where I go to school and what I major in and coming back home to help Dad. And everyone thinks that I'm just doing a great job, exactly what I'm supposed to do." There was dead silence for a moment. Then he sighed as if he was getting ready to confess something to a priest. "But these aren't the things that really motivate me, Swan."

"Well, spit it out. What is it you *really* want to do?"

"I want to make things happen in the city. Work with people and projects. A city planner, ya know? Trouble is, it doesn't pay well."

We both groaned at that.

"Well, take your own advice and start small," I suggested. "I'll talk to Miss Abigail and then you can plan the day at the park. Yeah, that's what we'll call it. A Day at the Park. It's a good idea, Robbie." Then I added impulsively, "You know something? You're really great."

I imagined that his cheeks turned bright red with the compliment.

"Thanks, Mary Swan," he mumbled, suddenly sounding flustered. "See you soon. And don't forget, wear your hair long."

I hung up the phone with a smile on my lips. Robbie had the same rumblings in his soul that I was having. Some indefinable feeling, something out of reach, a heart-wrenching longing for something more.

On Friday morning Rachel yanked me into the bathroom after homeroom. Her eyes looked all puffy and red.

"What's up?"

"When did you get your invitation to the PDC Christmas Dance?" It was more of an accusation than a question.

"Duh, it was Monday. Remember? I called you the minute I opened the envelope."

"I still haven't gotten one."

"So, neither have some other girls. It'll come."

"No, it won't." When Rachel was sure about something, she was adamant.

"And why not, Miss Know-It-All?" I wouldn't have teased her if I'd known what was coming. But it was so unusual to see Rachel this upset that I couldn't resist.

"Because I'm Jewish! That's why!" And then she started sobbing. I mean it. Bawling her eyes out.

My eyes got wide and I felt queasy inside and I knew right away that it was true. Just as I'd known about Mama when Herbert had slurred those insults.

"I hate this school! I hate it! Do you understand me, Mary Swan? I hate Wellington!" She spit out that word. "And I hate all these stuck-up hypocrites." She couldn't go on because she was heaving so hard, and her face was contorted with a terrible kind of anguish that made me afraid. I thought she was going to vomit. Instead, she just stood leaning her face over the sink and splashing water on it over and over again.

"Why in the heck does it matter what you believe? I mean, why do people who just happen to be born into a wealthy Protestant family on the right side of town naturally assume that they are better than someone born into a Jewish family?" Her sentences were coming in little gulps, so I had to pay close attention to get every word. "What makes them better? Just the nametag WASP? I think that is the most idiotic notion our society has. You know some of those girls. They're not worth the time it takes to say their names."

I couldn't help smiling at that. Good thing, because it made Rachel smile a little too. "You're right, Rachel. Hypocritical."

"Worse than hypocritical." She sniffed, and an angry hand brushed away the tears staining her face. "Most of these people are too dumb to know how to be hypocritical. Nothing sly or cunning about them. Just stupidly believing and repeating that you're better than someone else simply because of your religion or skin color or job status."

I didn't dare say a thing.

"I hate this. Can you imagine how much it hurts? I was counting on inviting Will. He knows I'm Jewish and doesn't mind dating me."

"You've never had a problem getting dates, Rach," I ventured.

"Oh, who cares! It doesn't matter now. It's not so much the

dance," she reasoned. Then she smiled sadly. "Well, of course it is. It's everything. It's being labeled. It's being different. It's being judged without ever having a fair chance." Her eyes were liquid looking again.

"I won't go to the dance either, Rach, if that'll help."

"Oh, Swan. No. Of course you'll go." She smiled wryly. "You'll go and tell me what everyone wears and how those snooty old ladies take to having Carl and his band playing at the venerable Piedmont Driving Club. What a scream!"

"That will be funny," I said without emotion.

She ignored me completely, in rare form. "And you know what is just great? I mean really idiotic? No Jewish girls will be there, because we didn't get an invitation. But you can bet your little bohunckus that Millie Garrett will invite Harold Wein and Julie Jacobs will invite Mark Goldberg. And no one will be able to say a thing because the girls can choose whomever they want. It's crazy! No Jewish girls at the PDC, but Jewish boys galore. Now does that make one bit of sense to you? Does it?"

I shook my head, not bothering to try to answer.

"And can you please tell me how nametags can really show what a person is like inside? Can you please explain that to me? Because I'll tell you one thing for sure. Those families may go to a Protestant church, those girls may put on their hats and gloves and Florence Eisman dresses, but it doesn't mean one thing in their life. It's just the title. Doesn't anyone care what's inside?

"I mean, for goodness' sake, I don't even go to temple. I'm a lousy Jew! Maybe I should go to Mrs. Appleby and declare I'm an atheist! If it was really religion that mattered, that should work. But it won't. Because it's not really religion. That's the pretext. It's race." She was rubbing her forehead, massaging her temples as if it hurt to reason. She wiped her hand down the right side of her face, her eyes swollen into little red slits.

"Do you understand what I mean, Swan? Can you possibly understand how this feels?" She regarded me with such sincerity that it hurt. "No, of course not. You can't. It's not your fault, though. But I'll tell you someone who could understand. Carl Matthews. Disqualified from society because his skin is black. Not a chance to prove what kind of mind he has." She shut her eyes tight. "But even he gets to go to the dance!"

She started sobbing again, and I had no idea what to do. I thought maybe Rachel was losing her mind. But she just kept talking.

"You know, why does society have to run by this religion thing? I mean, get with it. Sure, some people are great Christians and do lots of nice things. And maybe they put into practice what they believe. Like Miss Abigail. But for the most part, everybody's just the same. Wanting the best for themselves and their families. Making a bundle of money. Impressing the neighbors. Giving the kids a good education. Doesn't matter if you're a Baptist or an Episcopalian or a Methodist or a Catholic or a Jew or a Buddhist, for that matter. I'm just saying they shouldn't make religion the standard to judge by, when it really has nothing to do with it. The bottom line is this place is racist and anti-Semitic, and it's never gonna change.

"I've read the New Testament! Had to for good ole Welly. And it doesn't say, 'Cast people out because they don't have the same blood-lines as others.' It says, 'Love one another.' That's what your Jesus said. Love, forgive, don't judge, go the extra mile, care. Who would ever believe people around here ever even read their Bibles?"

The bell rang for our next class.

Rachel swore. "I can't go to math looking like this." She stuck her face in the sink again and splashed cold water over it, then dabbed it dry with two rough paper towels. She quickly applied a little blush and lipstick, pinched her cheeks, powdered her nose, and took a deep breath. "How do I look?"

"Great, Rach. You always look great. You know it." I hugged her tight and whispered, "I'm sorry."

We walked back out into the hall, and she took off down the long corridor to her math class. I watched her go, thick blond hair flapping gently on the gray jumper. I had never seen Rachel cry like that before. As I gathered my books to my chest and hurried down the hall, I could almost hear Carl saying the exact same words that Rachel had just pronounced.

"It's being labeled. It's being different. It's being judged without ever having a fair chance to prove who you are." I didn't understand it. But I wanted to. Suddenly I wanted very much to understand.

I guess Rachel's outburst became the straw that broke the camel's back. Her words haunted me all day long, so that when I got home from school, I ran up the stairs to my room and took my white leather

Bible off the shelf. I flipped toward the back of the holy book, looking for the gospel of John. The pages were onionskin thin and gold lined, and I liked the feel of them between my fingers. When I got to chapter eight of the gospel of John, I searched for the verse that Miss Abigail had talked about, the verse that had prodded me on in my research of the Raven Dare and of all my other discoveries.

I ended up reading the whole chapter, but I didn't understand much. First there was an incident where the Pharisees tried to stone an adulterous woman, and Jesus caught them in their own game. Then He got into a long argument with these same Jews about who was His father and who was their father. He called the religious leaders all kinds of names like liars and sons of the devil and told them they were going to die in their sins. As I read, I remembered some discussions we'd had in Bible class at Welly about the Pharisees and Jesus' dealings with them.

Sandwiched in between the arguments, Jesus told them that the truth would make them free. I scribbled down the verses in the spiral notebook that Rachel had dubbed "Poems Corrupted by Mary Swan." *As he spake these words, many believed on Him. Then said Jesus to those Jews which believed on Him, "If ye continue in my word, then are ye my disciples indeed, and ye shall know the truth and the truth shall make you free."*

It didn't really sound as though the Jews understood what Jesus was talking about, and I can't say I did either, but I liked the verse, as well as one that followed soon after. *"If the Son therefore shall make you free, ye shall be free indeed."* I wrote it in the spiral notebook too.

I kept repeating the two verses in my mind, over and over, *"Ye shall know the truth and the truth shall make you free. If the Son therefore shall make you free, ye shall be free indeed."* I liked the notion of freedom. I liked it for Carl and all the other blacks in America, and I liked it for Rachel and the other Jews. And I even liked it for dear Robbie, who was trapped in a completely different prison of his father's expectations. But mostly I liked it for me.

I surprised myself by asking out loud, "What do you want to free me from, Jesus?"

Immediately Carl's words flashed into my mind. *"You need to solve it for yourself, more than anything. So you won't keep persecuting yourself about the past. Gotta let it go, Mary Swan."*

Maybe that was it. Maybe God wanted to free me from my past.

For some reason, I started writing a poem, free verse, as ideas tumbled into my mind. It definitely was not my style. I was used to corrupting the poet laureates' works, not inventing one of my own. But it seemed to write itself, and so I let the ink flow.

Everyone wants to know truth,
Everyone wants to be treated fair,
Everyone searches for meaning,
Everyone searches for someone to care.
One brave man, long ago,
Said that truth will make you free,
Then died to prove His point,
But I didn't get it, God, not me,
I didn't understand,
Nor do I now
How
A dead and risen Savior
Who sits somewhere up high beside His dad
Can somehow make me free,
Can somehow make sense of all that's bad,
And so here I am, still searching,
Still holding a paintbrush in my hand,
Still watching the colors blend on my palette
And wondering, if Jesus were here,
What words He would write in the sand.

The poem finished, I closed the spiral notebook and placed the Bible back on the shelf. None of this really helped me solve Rachel's dilemma about the PDC Christmas Dance. I still felt edgy and angry. But somehow I also felt reassured, knowing that the white leather book might someday lead me to a God who made Miss Abigail's eyes sparkle.

I went down to Mama's *atelier*. I thought about painting, but instead all I did was sit cross-legged on the floor and flip through the sketchbooks from Resthaven. Henry Becker's crooked smile greeted me, and for a fleeting instant I wanted to jump into the blue Cadillac and drive into the mountains to Resthaven. Maybe I could meet Leslie Leschamps and ask her the questions I longed to find answers to. But I was pretty sure that wouldn't make the hurt go away.

I suddenly felt exhausted. The things I was dealing with, depression and prejudice and cruelty, were abstract beasts that couldn't be tamed by a visit to Resthaven or the Swan House. They wandered out of control around this city and devoured hope. That's what it felt like as I sat in Mama's *atelier*—some strange beast had gnawed through every cell of hope in my body and was sitting in the pit of my stomach, growling. Could the God Miss Abigail served extract the wild beast and replace it with something that made life matter?

Chapter 20

Fortunately, the next day was Saturday, the first of December, so I figured I'd have a chance to ask Miss Abigail a few questions. That gave me the courage to step inside the basement of Mt. Carmel and face Carl Matthews again. I was embarrassed about the hug in the *atelier* and all my daydreaming. I was afraid he'd just look straight through me and my silly ideas. But of course, he didn't.

"Hi there, Mary Swan. Good to see ya." His arm was in a sling. The stitches had been taken out of the wound above his eye, and all that was left was an ugly scar cutting through his left eyebrow.

I had an incredible urge to grab his hands and say, "I'm so thankful you're okay. I've been trying to pray for you and Larry." Instead, I smiled at him and said, "It's good to see you too, Carl."

"I heard you and a friend of yours came down to church a couple of Sunday nights ago."

"Yeah, yeah, we did."

"Drove the young'uns around in a fancy convertible."

"Well, having the top down wasn't exactly my idea."

"Thanks for doin' that, Mary Swan. They're still talkin' about it with their friends."

"It wasn't much."

"Doesn't take much to make them happy, Mary Swan."

Robbie had said to start small, and Carl had just confirmed the idea.

"How's Larry?"

"Good. Doin' fine, thank the good Lord. He's gonna be just fine." Carl got a big smile on his face. "Even lost about fifteen pounds in the hospital. You'll barely recognize him."

"So do you think y'all can still play for the Christmas dance? I told Mrs. Appleby—she's the lady in charge—that y'all had been in an accident, so she understood why you couldn't audition before now. But she'd still like to hear you play before the dance. She wondered if y'all could come out to the club on Wednesday afternoon."

"I 'spect that there's not much that would keep Larry and the others from goin' to see a fancy white man's club." He smiled. "You tell us where to go, and we'll meet ya there."

I found a pen and piece of paper and scribbled down the address of the Piedmont Driving Club. "Meet you there at five, okay?" Then I added, "You sure you can play, with your arm in a sling like that?"

"Girl, I'm sure." He winked at me.

"And you'll get paid! Two hundred dollars to split among you!"

He whistled low. "Ya don't say. Thanks, Mary Swan. Thanks for working that out for us. You're all right, ya know it?"

I felt the chemistry between us again, but Cassandra and Puddin' came into the kitchen at that moment, so we didn't say anything else.

After the dishes had been washed, I ran upstairs and marched into Miss Abigail's cluttered office on the first floor around the corner from the sanctuary. "I've been reading this book"—I indicated a Bible on her desk—"just like you said, and I have questions. Lots of questions."

Miss Abigail set down a letter she was holding in her hand and leaned back in her chair, an amused expression on her face. "Fire away, Mary Swan."

"Well, first of all, I don't think the truth is going to make me free. The truth is just confusing me."

"What do you mean?"

"All the things I'm finding out about my mother. It's the truth, but it's awful. And ugly things about my school, my side of town, like how much prejudice there is not only toward the blacks, but toward Jews too."

"And what have you read about this in the Bible?"

"Well, I read chapter eight of John's Gospel, like you said."

"And?"

"And I didn't get it."

"No, I see that. Mary Swan, you can make the Bible say what you want. Lots of people twist the meaning to support whatever they believe. So you have to be careful when you read the Scriptures. Ever heard of hermeneutics?"

"Never."

"Well, it's a big word that means there's a way to study Scripture. You can't just grab a verse and use it to defend something without looking at what was going on in the verses preceding and following it, without looking at the kind of literature it is—poetry or proverbs or history or letters."

I wrinkled my brow, confused.

"Here, let me give you an example." She flipped through her Bible until she found what she was looking for. "Look, here it says, 'And Judas went and hanged himself.' " Then she turned to another part of the Bible and read, " 'Go and do likewise.' "

I smiled and raised my eyebrows a little. "Okay, I get it."

"What I'm trying to show you is that you're taking Jesus' words about truth and fitting them into your situation. But you need to understand that Jesus was talking about eternal truth. God's truth. The truth of who He is and who He wants to be in your life—*that* truth will make you free."

"Oh," I said, brightening. "That makes sense. Just the way when you're studying poetry or literature, you have to be careful not to read too much into what the author said. You have to look at the time the author lived and his culture and that culture's traditions and morals to understand the book's message."

"Exactly."

"Hmmm. Okay. But I have another question. You've had so many bad things happen in your life. It doesn't seem fair, when all you want is to do God's work. Why has it turned out that way for you?"

"God's work is never easy. He tells us we'll be hurt when we work for Him, that hardships will come our way."

"Then why do you want to do it?"

"That's part of the supernatural beauty of the gospel. What Jesus gives us is so much better than all the terrible things that can happen here on earth that you almost consider it a privilege to suffer for Him. The Bible is full of stories of men and women of faith and courage. They didn't get some great reward here on earth, but they knew they would get one afterward."

"So what is the reward?"

"Eternal life. Eternity with Jesus. Seated around His throne, singing praises."

"Oh." My face fell. "Sounds a little boring. You're gonna be singing forever and ever? That's all?"

That made Miss Abigail give a full belly laugh, which pleased me. "Mary Swan Middleton, if your middle name isn't honest, I don't know what it is! Heaven is a place of eternal joy. God himself promises no more tears, no more sorrow. Sounds pretty good to me."

"So you're saying that all the awful junk that you have to endure down here will be worth it? Is that what you're saying?"

"Yes. And there's something else very important you need to know, Mary Swan. All the 'awful junk,' as you call it, can either just sit there as awful junk, or it can be used by God to do something good, very good, in our heart."

"Like what?"

"Like making us more like Jesus. The Bible is clear, Mary Swan. It says we all will suffer, and it says if we seek to live for the Lord, we'll be persecuted for our faith. But it's also very clear that God never wastes our pain. And He never leaves us alone."

Then she closed her eyes and smiled, as if she was seeing Jesus on a throne right then, and she started reciting something from memory. " 'For which cause we faint not; but though our outward man perish, yet the inward man is renewed day by day. For our light affliction, which is but for a moment, worketh for us a far more exceeding and eternal weight of glory. While we look not at the things which are seen, but at the things which are not seen: for the things which are seen are temporal; but the things which are not seen are eternal.' Second Corinthians, chapter four, verse sixteen."

"That's beautiful and interesting and hard to understand," I said, momentarily caught up in her reverence. "I like it."

"It's just one of many verses that adorn my bulletin board." She let her hand sweep through the air, indicating the large bulletin board that hung above her desk. It looked a little bit like her refrigerator— filled with old curling pictures on it, snips of paper with addresses, and lots of little white cards with Bible verses written on them.

I inspected the board more closely and read another verse. " 'Blessed be God, even the Father of our Lord Jesus Christ, the Father of mercies, and the God of all comfort; who comforteth us in all our tribulation, that we may be able to comfort them which are in any trouble, by the comfort wherewith we ourselves are comforted of God. For as the sufferings of Christ abound in us, so our consolation also aboundeth by Christ.' Second Corinthians chapter one, verses three through five." I shrugged. "Lots of comfort in that verse, seems like."

"Yes." Miss Abigail beamed. "Our suffering will be used by God to help someone else who is suffering. Never wasted, Mary Swan. Just remember, it's never wasted. And look at that one—James chapter one, verses two through four."

I read the scribbled words, " 'My brethren, count it all joy when ye fall into diverse temptations; knowing this, that the trying of your faith worketh patience. But let patience have her perfect work, that ye may be perfect and entire, wanting nothing.' "

She opened her eyes, those perfectly plain brown eyes, and leaned forward. "God's Word is incredibly rich. His Bible provides us with all we need to know to live in this hard, hard world, Mary Swan. The more you get to know the Bible, the more you'll find what Scripture calls a 'peace which passeth all understanding.' "

My mind was too full of ideas to answer her right then. Something about the way she was explaining things to me made sense. I was thinking that if I could memorize a bunch of poems for school, it probably would be a cinch to memorize some of those Bible verses. I scanned the bulletin board again. One picture, curling at the corners, showed Carl and Mike and James and Puddin'. Carl was about Jimmy's age in the photo and Puddin' only a toddler. My throat went dry, and I felt tears prickling my eyes. There were other photos of this family, school pictures that showed them toothless and grinning. As my eyes traveled across the large bulletin board, I let them suddenly rest on a slip of paper tacked up beside her Bible verses.

I pointed to the paper. "Is this from the Bible?"

She got her sad smile again and said, "No, but it's one of my favorite poems. A blind missionary wrote it, a woman who knew great suffering, a woman who served God by rescuing Indian girls from temple prostitution."

I walked over to it and read the faded writing out loud:

"No wound. No scar?
Yet as the Master shall the servant be,
And pierced are the feet that follow Me,
But thine are whole,
Can he have followed far who has no wound,
No scar?"

Tears suddenly filled my eyes. "That is beautiful," I whispered.
"Yes. Isn't it?"
"Thank you for taking the time to talk to me, Miss Abigail."
"My pleasure, Mary Swan. Any time."

I left her office, deeply moved. This was something so revolutionary to me that my head was reeling. I had tears falling down my cheeks, and instead of hearing "Song of the Chattahoochee" or "Little Orphant Annie" or "The Charge of the Light Brigade" in my mind, all I could hear was one phrase: "Can he have followed far who has no wound, no scar?"

"You look absolutely stunning," Rachel pronounced as she finished rolling my hair on the ends and sprayed it in place. Like the trooper she was, Rachel had gone with me to J. P. Allen's at Lenox Square and helped me pick out my dress. It was pale green with thin straps, what we called spaghetti straps, and there were three layers of thin crepe chiffon material. It fell to my ankles, and Rachel had chosen little gold sandals to go with it.

She had also gone with me to introduce Carl's band to Mrs. Appleby. I could still see her satisfied smile when Mrs. Appleby had exclaimed, "My, you boys can certainly play jazz. I'm thrilled to have you at the dance!"

Later, when we were alone, Rachel had confided to me, "I think just seeing the pride in Carl's eyes, in all of their eyes, when Mrs. Appleby was so enthusiastic was better than even being at the dance."

Now, as I waited for Robbie to pick me up, she inspected me. "Turn around and let me see."

I twirled in a circle, feeling the crepe material swish around my legs.

"Perfect. Very flattering. It shows off your tiny waist and gives the impression that you have a little more up top than you really do." I stuck out my tongue at that. "Well, I gotta get home." She hugged me tightly. "Have a great time. Have a good enough time for both of us, you hear? And don't think about anything else. Just have fun."

"Thanks gobs, Rach. Thanks for everything. I'll call you tomorrow."

"You look beautiful, Mary Swan!" Robbie handed me a corsage, and I awkwardly tried to pin it on.

"You look great too." He wore a black tuxedo, the required attire, which gave him a very sophisticated air, but I noticed that one strand of hair fell over his right eye, just the way I liked.

Daddy beamed from the hallway. "Y'all have a great time, kids." And even Jimmy waved out to us from his window on the first floor.

The Piedmont Driving Club was one of Atlanta's oldest clubs, and in contrast to the Capital City Club, which could be for business or pleasure, the PDC was purely for social events. That night, the club was decorated with red poinsettias and white lace, with red candles burning in silver candelabra in every room. The ballroom was grand, with intricately carved flowers on the tall ceiling from which hung two ornate chandeliers. Twenty or more round tables covered with white linen tablecloths were set for dinner. The centerpieces were mistletoe and holly and thick green candles, and cards with our names written in calligraphy indicated each person's seat. Delicate arches with sculpted laurels lined either side of the room, leaving the center of the room open for dancing on its beautiful hardwood floor. The stage was at the far end of the room.

We had just found our places and were chatting with Patty Masters and her date, Doug, when Carl's band began to play. I immediately broke out in a cold sweat. My palms were sticky, and I let go of Robbie's hand. My eyes were glued to the stage, and I felt terrified and so proud I could burst.

Finally I whispered to Robbie, "Those are my friends from Grant Park. The ones who were in the fight." Carl and Larry and Leo and Nickie and Big Man were all dressed in white tuxedos with black pants, provided by the club. They looked like professionals, but I knew how nervous they really were. I could still hear Mrs. Appleby explaining on Wednesday, "Now, boys, you'll have the introduction, while all the guests are arriving. You'll play for forty-five minutes, maybe an hour. Will that be a problem?"

"Not at all, ma'am," Carl had assured her.

"You see, Mary Swan," Robbie said loudly in my ear, over the buzz in the room. "You can organize things. You did a great job getting them this chance to play."

I simply nodded, not wanting to miss one single note from the band. When Carl played his solo part, I let out a long sigh.

At first the crowd gave polite applause. But the longer and louder and jazzier the band played, the more excited the kids got.

"Do you want to get something to eat?" Robbie fairly shouted.

"Not yet, Robbie," I said. Then I took my eyes off of Carl and the others and faced him. "Do you mind? I really want to hear them play."

"Sure, I'll get some drinks. What'll you have?"

"Coke would be good. Thanks," I called after him.

Gradually, as the band changed from jazz to rock 'n' roll, we all moved out onto the dance floor. Robbie and I jitterbugged gleefully with the rest of the high school kids for at least thirty minutes. As their final number, Carl's band played "Rock Around the Clock." When the song ended, a great "Hurrah!" went up from the crowd for the musicians, and we applauded so loudly that, even though it was supposed to be their last song, they agreed to an encore.

It was a slow dance. Robbie held me tight against his chest. I fixed my eyes on Carl as we slowly turned around and around. Then our eyes met across that wide dance floor, and he nodded in a way that I knew was meant for me while he blew out his heart on that horn.

At the end of the song, Mrs. Appleby came onto the stage and said happily into the microphone, "Well, it's quite obvious that everyone has appreciated Carl Matthews' Jazz Band from Grant Park. Thank you, boys, for coming." There was another round of enthusiastic applause.

As they left the stage, I said to Robbie, "I'll be right back."

He grabbed my hand. "Hold on, Mary Swan. Can't I come with you? I'd like to meet your friends too."

"Sure. Absolutely. Of course." I felt the blood pumping in my temples.

We caught up with them backstage. "Carl! Wait up!" I called, out of breath.

"Oh, Mary Swan! Good to see you, sweetheart," Mrs. Appleby said.

"It was wonderful!" I enthused with my eyes on Carl. Then I smiled at Robbie and said, "Robbie Bartholomew, I'd like you to meet my friends, Larry and Leo and Carl and Big Man and Nickie."

They all shook hands, and my heart fluttered a little when Robbie and Carl's hands touched.

"Nice to meet you," Robbie said smoothly. "I really enjoyed your music. Do you play anywhere regularly?"

"Nope. Occasional high school football game is all."

"Well, you should. You're talented."

"Well, it's thanks to Mary Swan that we've had this opportunity," Carl said politely. I beamed.

"Why don't y'all have a drink with us?" I suggested.

But Mrs. Appleby got a flustered look on her face and said, "Excuse me, Mary Swan, but we've already got a table set up for them in another room." She smiled at me sweetly. "And of course they'll have a choice of all the food from the buffet. And the check. You definitely earned your wages tonight, boys." She nodded at Robbie and me, making it clear we were to stay put, then turned to Carl and his friends. "If you'll just follow me . . ."

"Bye," I whispered to Carl as they left. "You played great. Really great." He just gave me the same wide white smile that had first captured my heart.

The rest of the evening was a blur to me, a blur of dancing and eating and laughing with friends and making polite conversation when the noise of the second band died down or they took a break. Several friends whispered to me that I looked gorgeous, and Patty gave me a wink when we were dancing beside each other. And I thought that I was indeed having the time of my life, fun enough for both Rachel and me, as she'd instructed. It was after midnight when Robbie gave his ticket to the black boy who was working in valet parking.

On the way home, Robbie was strangely quiet behind the wheel, while I babbled on about Carl's band and how they'd been every bit as good as the main band and how glad I was that Robbie had met them and that the band had been appreciated.

Finally, as Robbie was turning into my driveway, he said, "If there's somebody else you like, Mary Swan, just say it. I'd rather know. It's worse to like you and think you feel the same way about me and then find out I'm all wrong. It'll be awful, but it's better for me to know the truth. That's how I am."

I stared at him, dumbfounded. "What are you talking about?"

"I'm talking about your black friend, Carl."

"What?" I said feebly with this terrible sinking feeling inside.

"You're in love with the guy." Robbie's voice had a sharp edge on it now.

"No! I mean, it's not what you think."

"Mary Swan," he said with a sad smile. "You're a lot of things, great things, but you are not discreet."

I shook my head. "You're wrong, Robbie. There isn't anything between us. We're just friends."

"You didn't look at him like you look at a friend." That was an outright accusation. "You've never looked at me that way."

Not one word came out of my mouth. But it was probably hanging wide open.

"I understand, Mary Swan. That's why you go to the inner city, isn't it?"

"That's not fair, Robbie! I don't go there because of Carl! That's not why I go. I swear it isn't. I go to help out. That's plain mean to say, after all you and I have talked about!"

He got out of the car, walked around to my side, and opened the door. When I stepped out, he put his arm around me tender-like and said, "Mary Swan, I'm not accusing you. You've got a great heart. That's what I love about you. Your wild imagination and your sensitive heart. I don't know another girl around like you. I really don't."

I swiped at a few tears. "Do you hate me?"

"How could I ever hate you, Mary Swan?" His topaz eyes looked hurt. "You have a perfect right to like whoever you want. But I can't play that game. I have to know the truth. About us."

"Robbie, you're my friend." I thought of all the kissing we'd done and blushed. "You are so great. You talk to me, and . . . and you're kind."

"Just like every Boy Scout should be. I also help little old ladies across the street." He smiled wryly. "Unfortunately, none of that really counts."

"It does count."

"Yeah, maybe. But not for what I want." He kissed me softly on the cheek and said, "See ya around, Mary Swan. You take care of yourself, you hear?"

And he was gone.

I walked into the house in a daze, tears blurring my view. Woodenly I locked the door and climbed all the way to my room. I flopped across my bed, brokenhearted. Brokenhearted because Robbie had seen through me and I had hurt him deeply. Brokenhearted because in spite of all the hard things I was learning, I could still be so impossibly naïve. Brokenhearted because the stirrings I felt for Carl were only stirrings. With Robbie I could talk. I reassured myself with that one thought. At least we could talk about it. Sometime soon we'd talk.

I had no desire to call Rachel when I awoke the next morning. When I finally did dial her number and she answered, all I said was, "Can't explain it on the phone. You've got to come over."

Which, of course, she did. And she listened carefully to my whole tearful explanation of the previous evening.

"Mary Swan, you're in love with a combination of Carl and Robbie. And it isn't going to work. That guy doesn't exist."

"But what do I do then?"

"Choose."

"But you're the one who told me just to have fun."

"I know. And now you've had fun, and it's time to choose."

"But I like them both a lot."

"Do you really deep down inside think that anything could ever work out between you and Carl? Do you?"

"No. No, I know it's impossible."

"Because if I were you, I'd think about it long and hard, Mary Swan Middleton. Robbie is a great guy. He's like you, from the same place. He understands you."

"But Carl is so different. That's what I want. It's impossible, then, Rachel, for a black and a white to date, isn't it?"

She thought for a moment. "No, not impossible. But hard. Very, very hard. Forever."

"And what if I choose Carl and I make a huge mistake?"

"Well, it's not like you're gonna marry the guy tomorrow, is it?"

"No, of course not. But if I choose Carl, well, I'm obviously not choosing Robbie, and I may never get another chance to go back and fix things up."

"Then you just live with it, Swan. It seems to me like that's the whole point of life. You know? You do your best, flub up, learn something from it, and then you go on. You learn to be strong."

"Have you ever made a really big mistake, Rachel?"

She got up from my bed and walked over to the window and looked out. The day was gray and cold. "I almost did—I almost made the biggest mistake of my life."

I rolled over on my back and stared at her, suddenly very interested. "What was it?"

She didn't look at me. "I almost didn't let you become my friend." She got choked up when she said it. "I hated Wellington when I first got there in sixth grade. I felt like there was this big neon sign around my neck that flashed 'Jewish' all the time. Jewish in the midst of a WASP nest. And so many of the girls were snobby and petty and mean. Really mean. And I hated you from afar, Mary Swan. I hated you. I swear I did."

"You hated me? Why?"

"Because you were funny and creative, and somehow even being different, you fit in. You fit in because you were a WASP like the rest of them. And your dad was really rich and belonged to the Capital City Club and the Piedmont Driving Club."

"But your family's rich too."

"Sure we're well-off. But we'd never be allowed to join those clubs."

"How do you know?"

"Oh, Swan, for heaven's sake. Don't be a total fool. I know. Everyone knows it." She smiled at me. "But gradually I got to know you, and I found out that you were this great, silly, scatterbrained, multitalented Swannee creature with the craziest ideas and the biggest imagination and a good heart. A real good heart."

"Oh, quit it, Rach."

"It's true. Perfectly true. A good heart and a weird name. And you know what I like most is that you don't see color or race—you are so impossibly naïve, you can't tell if I'm Jewish or Carl is black. You don't care about money or jobs or last names or religion. You don't care. That's it—you just don't care. I have always loved that about you, Mary Swan."

I felt a mixture of misery and great respect for Rachel. "I think that's meant as a compliment, so I'll say thanks. But we still haven't figured out what I should do."

We both laughed again, and she gave me an all-engulfing hug, and then she just looked at me, shook her head, and said in her best Ella Mae imitation voice, "All I knows is that yore fixin' to git in a heap o' trouble, girl."

Chapter 21

In spite of the fact that Robbie and I were no longer dating, he held fast to his plans for the Day at the Park. Saturday the twenty-second of December was the first day of Christmas break for most Atlanta students. And almost twenty of them from Buckhead were at Grant Park that bright and chilly morning. Pastor James greeted us warmly. "So good to see you teenagers here. Mighty fine of ya to come out this morning, 'stead of stayin' home in bed." He and Robbie had already bought all the needed supplies and had made a long list of the repairs we were to work on. "Robbie here and I will be helpin' everyone git started. I'd like ta say that Robbie's quite an organizer. So listen to him, and everythin' will run smoothly."

And it did, which made me feel quite proud of Robbie Bartholomew. About ten or fifteen of the older teens from Mt. Carmel were there, Carl and Mike and James and Larry and Leo and Big Man and Cassandra and even Puddin', along with several others I'd never met before.

Robbie walked right up to Carl, stuck out his hand, and shook Carl's forcefully. "Good to see you again," he said, and repeated his greeting to every member of the jazz band. He winked at Mike and James and promised, "If we get all the work done, I'll take you for another spin in the convertible."

A bunch of Robbie's friends had come too. Football players and wrestlers and Boy Scouts and even a few of the fathers were there to lend a hand. Almost every single friend I had invited came, which shocked me. But what really shocked me was the conversation we had that morning while we sanded down the walls in the fellowship hall and prepared them for paint.

"Oh yeah, my mom's Sunday school class has helped out like this in Summerhill," Julie Jacobs said as she filled holes in the wall with putty. Summerhill was another poverty-stricken neighborhood nearby.

"Yeah, Mom takes all our old clothes down there. They have a big clothes closet at the Baptist church," Patty Masters added as she scraped off some loose paint.

Gail Anderson, who went to the big white Baptist church across the street from St. Philip's, even knew some of the young children from Grant Park. "For years, Mom and these other ladies have brought our church bus down here and loaded it up with the kids and taken them roller skating at our church's gymnasium. They come the last Wednesday of every month. And I always help out with the skates."

Millie Garrett burst into laughter as a piece of plaster as big as her hand broke off of the wall. "Oops! Hurry up over here, Julie, with that putty!" Then Millie said to Gail, "My mom's circle from church knits baby blankets and booties for the new babies around here."

I thought of Jessie as a newborn, swaddled in a handmade blanket, and my eyes started to sting.

"It's funny, Swan. I told my grandma that we were going to help down here, and she said that a bunch of the ladies at her nursing home sew and knit for families in the poor part of Atlanta," Rachel added.

Later in the morning, as Cassandra and Rachel and Patty and Julie were working side by side, Cassandra started singing in her beautiful alto voice a chorus I'd never heard before. "Jesus will fix it afta' awhile. Trouble in my way, makes me cry sometimes, I lay awake at night, but that's all right. Jesus will fix it afta' awhile." Just by the way she sang it, you could tell that Cassandra knew what she was talking about. She kept singing that chorus over and over, sometimes with words and sometimes just humming it softly to herself.

When she stopped, Gail said, "You have a great voice, Cassandra. Sing us something else."

Cassandra got an embarrassed smile on her face, but we kept pleading with her. Finally she agreed. "But y'all gotta join in afta' ya learn it. Promise?" So we promised. She broke into a chorus that I had heard the night that Robbie and I had attended Mt. Carmel's service. "Jesus on my main line, tell 'im whatcha want. Jesus on my main line, tell 'im whatcha want. Jesus on my main line, tell 'im whatcha want. Ya call 'im up, and ya tell 'im whatcha want!" It had a strong rhythm, and soon we were belting it out in our untrained voices and clapping our hands together, letting the scalpels and the paintbrushes slap together. That's when I first felt the tingles.

At noon we uncovered the tables in the fellowship hall—they had been draped with white sheets to protect them from paint—and prepared for lunch. It felt funny to be on the receiving end of the spaghetti line, but Miss Abigail and Carl had insisted. Several of the women I usually served were serving me and smiling. Carl brought his plate and sat down beside me, and I got a tummy full of butterflies. "Mighty fine guy, yore boyfriend Robbie. He's done a good job of getting people to work. Hadn't stopped for a second, gettin' supplies, answerin' questions. He's got a head for that, Mary Swan."

I simply nodded, my mouth full of garlic bread. I wanted to look Carl straight in the eyes and say, "He's not my boyfriend! Not at all. *You're* supposed to be my boyfriend! *You're* the one I've chosen." But, of course, I just kept chewing on the bread, even though it suddenly tasted dry and stale.

It was a good thing that Robbie was too busy for us to talk, because I have no idea what I would have said to him. I felt as though I'd betrayed him and stomped on his heart. But he didn't show it that day. That day just brimmed over with a lot of hard work. White hand next to black hand. Side by side. Thirty teenagers, painting and cleaning and scraping and singing our hearts out in our old sweatshirts. And every single one of us was happy to be there.

And my mouth must have been hanging open all day. Once again I had been wrong, thinking in my naïveté that I was the only Buckhead girl who cared about poverty. Seeing these friends around me that day made me feel awful about the way I'd judged so many people from my own neighborhood. Then I remembered that Miss Abigail had told me how she would have never made it in inner-city work without help from the ladies in Buckhead. That day, I finally understood what she meant.

At five o'clock we were filthy and exhausted. Pastor James came by and said, "We's all gonna meet in the sanctuary in about twenty minutes. Y'all start cleanin' things up."

When all the young people got into the sanctuary, Pastor James said, "Let's have a time of singing praises to our Lawd for this glorious day He has given us." So we reached for the hymnals. At first the songs that the pastor chose were unfamiliar to most of us white kids. But we listened, speechless, as the black teens sang and clapped, standing and swaying to the music that was being banged out on the old piano by a beaming Cassandra. Then Pastor James figured out some hymns that we all knew, and we white kids joined in singing for probably another twenty minutes, standing and clapping and even swaying a little right along with the black teenagers. And there was something there. I don't know what. Yes, yes, I do. A presence. Maybe it was God. All I know is that something deep inside made me tingle. When I looked over and saw Robbie with his hair all messy, sharing a hymnal with Carl, I could barely hold back the tears.

Then Pastor James started preaching an extemporaneous sermon. "Young men and women, we surely have witnessed here today a tiny glimpse of what our Lawd wants all across our nation. Jesus is the Great Heart Fixer and Mind Regulator, and when ya let Him in yore heart, well, He starts changin' things. I shore do hope that many of you sittin' here today will be part of fixin' up the problems between whites and blacks in the years ta come. Look at yorese'ves. You's tired and dirty from fixin' up this here church. Ain't gonna be no different if ya try to fix up this country. You is gonna git tired and dirty. But it's worth it, chil'un. It's worth it. I guarantee ya that.

"Some o' you come from white churches that are tryin' to help this situation. But lots of other white churches is tuckin' their tails between their legs and runnin' lickity-split away from the problem. They's afraid. Don't be afraid, boys and girls. If the Lawd is on yore side, ya ain't got nothin' to be afraid of."

While he spoke, Puddin' sat beside me and braided my hair in cornrows, as she'd promised to do for a long time.

"You've come down here to he'p. You've come on a mission. And let me tell ya this. Missions is God's gift to liberate us, to he'p us git outside ourselves. Tonight I know you'll be mighty tired, but I hope you'll feel right good inside, 'cause ya spent a day not thinkin' about yorese'ves.

"An' I ain't jus' talkin' to the white kids here. 'Cause lots o' our problems is our own fault. Gotta quit bickerin' amongst ourse'ves. Gotta quit our fightin' and our stealin' and our cheatin' and our messin' around. Gotta quit our sinnin'. Big sins, little sins, all of 'em make the Lawd mighty sad. Gotta obey what the good Lawd says."

We were all listening intently to Pastor James in spite of the fact that we were tired and sweaty. When he said those words about sin, something stabbed at my heart, and I felt dirty, the kind of dirty, though, that I didn't think ten hot baths could get clean. Dirty inside. But in a fleeting second the feeling was gone, replaced by the feeling that we had done something so very good that day.

It was nearly seven o'clock, and all the Buckhead crew had left the church, except for Rachel and me and Robbie, who was riding Mike and James and a few other boys around the block in his convertible. Rachel and I were talking with Carl, and Puddin' was holding her brother's hand. "She's done a mighty nice job on your hair, Mary Swan. You look right nice," Carl said with laughter behind his eyes.

"Thanks! And thank you, Puddin'. And before you leave, I have something for you." I went to Rachel's car and took out an armful of brightly wrapped presents. "Merry Christmas to all of you." I gave the pile of packages to Carl, saying, "There's one for each of you, and for Miss Abigail and even for Aunt Neta."

Puddin' threw her arms around my neck and hugged me tight. "Thanks, Mary Swan. Thanks!"

"Now, don't you open them 'til Christmas, you understand?"

Her brow creased and she frowned. "I don't have nothin' for you!"

I picked her up and swung her around. "Well, now, young lady, that's where you're wrong. You've already given me a great present. A new hairdo!"

We laughed happily, and as I hugged her to my chest, Carl nodded to me with eyes full of thankfulness, and something else, something strong and sure that would get me through the days before I saw him again. "Thank you, Mary Swan. Mighty thoughtful of ya," he said. "You have a Merry Christmas too."

Then Mike and James came back from their ride and, as they joined their brother and sister, Rachel, Robbie, and I waved and watched them disappear into the dark.

I went over to Robbie with so many strong, good feelings rushing through my heart. "I just want you to know that I was really proud of you today, Robbie. You did a great job organizing everything. Thank you." I kissed him softly on the cheek and whispered, "Merry Christmas," and I handed him a small gift too.

I still had that wonderful, satisfied feeling when I got home and rushed in the back door, the cold air making my cheeks red. Daddy came into the kitchen and started to greet me, but when he saw my hair all braided, his face got a twisted look. "What in the world have you done, Mary Swan?"

"Gotten cornrows, Daddy," I said, ignoring his disapproving look.

"I see that. Where did you get that done?" Now he sounded a bit suspicious.

"Down at Grant Park today while we were helping out. A friend of mine did it for me."

"Well, take it out. You look like a Negro."

"So?"

"So?" Daddy's face got dark, and his voice rose in anger. "Mary Swan, don't you ever say that again, do you hear me? You know why? I'll tell you. Because you aren't black. You're from Buckhead, raised in a decent white family with everything you need. This city is segregated for a reason, you know, Swan. Blacks and whites aren't supposed to mix."

I felt sick to my stomach. "Do you mean to say that blacks and whites can't be friends?"

"Yes."

"And what about Ella Mae?"

"What about her? She's our maid, for goodness' sake."

"She's my friend."

He wiped his brow and sat down, shuffling the newspaper around nervously. "Swan, we all love Ella Mae. But she'll never be like us."

"Well, whoever said all your friends have to be like you?" I asked, incredulous. Then I switched gears. "So you think all blacks are good for around here is to be slaves. Not friends."

"Mary Swan, really . . ."

"I mean it. Think of what would happen to the homes in Buckhead if there weren't blacks to clean the houses and fix the meals and mow the yards and to serve you at the club and park your car and carry your golf clubs. Buckhead would be a mess without blacks!"

"Honestly."

"You don't want to admit it, do you, Daddy?" I couldn't go on. I couldn't let myself keep talking to Daddy like that. I fought back the tears and said almost meekly, "If blacks can help out in Buckhead, isn't it all right for whites to help out in Grant Park?"

"Is that what this is all about?" He shook his head. "Help out, then, if you like, Swannee. But don't go getting your hair braided like a Negro. And don't try to be making friends down there. It'll only get you in trouble. Believe me, I know."

I wanted to beg him to tell me how he knew, but I could tell by the way he said it that the conversation was over. So I ran upstairs and into my dressing room and sat in the chair in front of the vanity and just stared at myself as I took out those braids. Somewhere my heart was breaking. Daddy's philosophy was plain old Southern prejudice. Yet maybe he was right. Even Carl had said it'd be a long time coming before blacks and whites would really, could really be friends. But it was too late to follow Daddy's advice, even if I'd wanted to. I already had friends in Grant Park. A whole lot of them. And so I was stuck with one more big secret.

At least, I thought with a wave of relief, at least Daddy didn't forbid me to go down there anymore.

That special presence, that warm, satisfied feeling of having done something for others had disappeared with Daddy's burst of anger. I had no appetite and declined to come down for dinner when Daddy called to me. I hoped against hope that he might come upstairs and apologize, or at least talk to me. But he didn't. And I realized that seeing him so angry at me had shaken me up a lot.

I'd really only seen Daddy lose his temper twice before. Once when I was about seven or eight, the phone had rung in the evening. I was eager to answer it, grabbing the phone in the kitchen. Daddy must have picked up the phone in his study at the exact same time. I happily listened to the conversation, unbeknownst to Daddy. He was talking to another man, someone named Mitch. Suddenly his voice got gruff, and he exploded, swearing at the man. "No, we are not selling. What do you think you're talking about, Mitch? This is my client and my business, and you can't intimidate us into selling." He had said a lot of bad words in that conversation, but I was petrified to put down the phone, for fear he might notice. So I held the receiver to my ear as if it were glued there until the end of the conversation. And Daddy never found out.

The other time was when I was probably ten. Daddy and Mama had just gotten back from a party. My room at the time was directly above theirs, and I was awakened by Daddy's loud ranting. I'd sneaked into the upstairs hall to listen. He was cursing and saying, "Sheila, why did you have to do that? Half of Atlanta was there, and you choose tonight to have your *crise des nerfs*. You better believe it'll make it into the society page tomorrow!" He swore again.

"JJ, dahling, please." Mama was crying, and I could tell she was drunk. "Please let me explain. It's not at all what you think. Nothing like that."

"Well, it had better not be, Sheila, because I won't have those stories circulating around here. You understand? I won't. If it happens again, I'll send you back, in a second I'll send you back!"

"I want to go back, JJ! I'll run back there myself. At least I'm understood and not treated like a pin-up doll. All you want is for me to dress up and look pretty for your business meetings and clients. Smile and bat my lashes! Well, I won't do it anymore, JJ. It makes me sick to my stomach. Just leave me alone and let me paint. Leave me alone."

I'd heard a door slam shut and Daddy cursing under his breath. And as I tiptoed back to my room, I'd cried all the way.

Those memories were another proof of the way my parents had tried to handle their lives. I went to sleep that night feeling as if a huge wall, built stone by stone over a whole lot of years, stood between Daddy and me. In three days it would be Christmas, but all the hope and love and joy I had felt just a few hours ago had come undone, little by little, like the cornrows in my hair.

It was Sunday night, the night before Christmas Eve, and Daddy had another party to attend. Mama had always decorated the house like a showplace for Christmas, but this year, it was bare. Trixie had finally insisted on taking me to get a tree a few days earlier, but the big blue spruce she'd chosen stood naked in the entranceway by the steps. I gazed at it miserably. Not one present was under the tree. Jimmy and I used to love to wrap presents together and sneak them under the tree during the days before Christmas, but this year no one had thought of presents. At the moment Jimmy was lying in bed with a wet cloth on his forehead, trying to recover from the flu.

Daddy was fiddling with his bow tie, and he could not get it right. Trixie was smoking a cigarette while Lucy and I played a game of checkers. "Thanks for coming over like this, Trixie," Daddy said, flustered with the tie.

"Oh, JJ, you know it's fine."

"I'd leave the kids alone. I've done it dozens of times, but with Jimmy's fever—"

"JJ, it's not a problem. Swannee and Lucy and I are gonna decorate the tree."

But I could tell it really bugged Daddy, as if he were treating Trixie like a maid or something. Or maybe he was just bothered because normally Trixie should be attending this fundraiser. As it was, she and Lucy were spending the evening with Jimmy and me.

He muttered under his breath as he left the room in search of a mirror.

Trixie laughed, put out her cigarette, and got up. "Come he-ah, JJ. I'll fix it for you." And coming up behind him, she laced her tan arms around his neck and fiddled with the tie until it was in a perfect bow. She barely let her hands brush his shoulders, and it was done.

Somehow that felt extremely awkward for all of us, seeing Trixie's arms draped, however innocently, around Daddy's neck.

He cleared his throat. "Thanks, Trixie. You're a doll." He winked at Lucy and gave me a kiss on the cheek and called up to Jimmy, "See you later, son." And he was gone to pick up Amanda Hunnicutt in his sporty Jag.

As soon as he left, Trixie and Lucy and I traipsed up to the attic, which was attached to my room by a door that was cut into the wall. It took us three trips to bring down all the Christmas decorations, but Trixie insisted. "You know that I always used to help you decorate," she laughed. "Some things never change."

We set up the manger scene on the sideboard in the dining room and decorated the tree with dozens of sparkling white, red, and gold balls, the kind you could see your reflection in. Trixie draped real pine boughs that were tied together all along the banister to the second floor. She even put Bing Crosby's Christmas album on the phonograph in the den. It was a good thing that Lucy was there too, because she loved decorating, and her enthusiasm helped me forget all the other things we would have been doing at Christmastime if Mama had been here.

When Trixie had tucked Lucy into bed in the guest room and

checked on Jimmy's fever for the third time, she opened another small cardboard box, and I caught my breath suddenly as she lifted two miniature white swans from the box. Mama's swans. The ones made out of fine bone china that Mamie had bought her in London. They were a pair, small, with hollow backs so that you could put salt and pepper in them and serve it out with two tiny silver spoons. But at Christmas, Mama would always set the swans on a red satin place mat in the center of the dining table and place a tiny gold candle in each one. She had lit the candles every evening in December.

I picked up one of the swans. "Mama said they'd be mine someday. I guess that day has come."

Trixie didn't know what to say. "Would you rather not put them out this year, Swannee?"

"No, it's all right. They need to be here to remind us of Mama." As if everything I was doing didn't already remind me of her.

"How are you doing, Mary Swan?" Trixie asked, when the swans had found their rightful place and Trixie had put the small gold candles inside.

I shrugged.

She lit a cigarette and curled her feet under her on the couch. "Did you have fun at the Christmas dance? Your dad said you went with Robbie Bartholomew."

I felt my face warming. "Yeah, we had fun. It was a good evening."

"That doesn't sound too convincing."

"No, it was really good. But I think my favorite part was seeing my friends from Grant Park there."

Trixie blew a long wisp of smoke off to the side. Her eyes got narrow, and she smiled. "I have no idea what you're talking about, Swan, but it sounds interesting. Explain."

"I have some friends, black friends, guys." I sneaked a look at her, but she didn't flinch. "They're great musicians. They have a jazz band, and I asked Mrs. Appleby if they could play as the warm-up band at the PDC, and she agreed. And they were great. Really great."

"That's remarkable, Swannee! And you say they're friends of yours?"

Suddenly I wished I hadn't told her. "Yeah, but promise you won't say a word to Daddy. He knows I go down to Grant Park, but he doesn't know much else."

"Is there a lot else to know?"

I glanced her way. "Yeah, but I don't wanna talk about it."

She crushed out the cigarette in the silver ashtray. "No more questions, then."

So we listened to the Christmas music and admired the blue spruce. "I have a question for you," I said finally. "You're the only one I can ask."

"Uh-oh, I can hear trouble coming," she teased.

I grimaced. "Do you think—is there any way that maybe you could take me to Resthaven sometime soon?"

"Mary Swan . . ."

"I know you'll say I've got to talk to Daddy, but I swear it's impossible. And I have to go back—I mean, go there."

She didn't miss the slip. "Back?"

I nodded.

"You've been to Resthaven recently?"

Another nod.

Trixie mashed her lips together and reached for another cigarette. "Tell me about it, Swannee."

"I can't now. But I'll explain it all to you if you'll take me. It's important. Very important for Mama. And for me." Now I stared straight into her eyes, pleading.

"My goodness, Swan, you look just like your mother right now. You are a beautiful young lady."

I was so taken aback by her comment that I couldn't think of anything to say. A smile curled on my lips.

"Let me look at my calendar. See if we can work out a time after Christmas." She gave a sigh. "What are you getting me into, Mary Swan?" But when I gave her a quick hug and started up the stairs, she was smiling.

I don't know what time Daddy came in because I was in the *atelier* working on a sketch and getting ideas for my painting when I heard his car drive up. I finished up the sketch, so it must have been five or ten minutes before I left the *atelier*. I was in the hall, about to go downstairs and greet Daddy when I heard Trixie's voice saying, "Don't worry. They're all asleep."

Daddy's answer was muffled. "I don't want to talk about it tonight. Some other time, Trixie."

"JJ." She sounded irritated. "Listen, JJ, she's a girl, a young girl who is trying to figure out a lot of hard things."

"She's got no business figuring them out. If I kept them from her, it was for a good reason! You're the one to blame, Trixie! If you hadn't told her about Sheila's depression, she'd have never known. And why in the world does she want to go snooping around for all this stuff, anyway?"

By now I had seated myself on one of the stairs and was leaning against the banister, straining to hear the conversation taking place in the living room.

"Oh, you're wrong, JJ. She was finding things out on her own. She's trying to figure out who she is and who her mother was." I couldn't see it, but I could imagine Trixie sitting across from Daddy, giving him a stern look, her legs crossed primly. "JJ, you cannot hide things from Swan. Can't you see your daughter needs you? Can't you see she is dying to have you take some time with her? Explain life to her? If you don't do it, who else does she have?"

Daddy cursed, then said, "Trixie, for heaven's sake. It's none of your business."

"Well, then, who will tell you the truth before it's too late? Not your parents! Ella Mae? She'll be loyal to the great JJ Middleton and her memory of Sheila to the grave. But you can't reproach Ella Mae. She did the only thing she thought she could get away with. She took Mary Swan to help out at her church."

That terrible beast in the pit of my stomach had revived and was knocking against my sides.

"I don't know if you've looked at Swan lately, JJ. But she's blossoming in every way. She's a wonderful kid. She thinks about things. About segregation. About poverty. About what part religion plays in her life. And she thinks about her mother. A lot. You're the only one, JJ, the *only* one, who can tell her the truth."

There was a moment of silence, then I heard Trixie's voice again. "Please don't make her hide behind a bunch of lies. Free her! Don't put her through the hell I lived through. The whisperings. The feeling of being completely alone in this world with no one to protect you. I moved here for Tony. Moved from the cotton plantation. And when he left me, I was twenty-five and pregnant. My parents were a long way away, but the scandal nearly destroyed them. They couldn't bear it.

"But you know who I had? I had Sheila! I had your wife! Why are you embarrassed to tell Swan that Sheila was sick? Why do you have to make it seem like everything was always perfect? We're all just miserable fallen creatures. Some of us are hurting in our minds, like Sheila, others somewhere else. But we're all weak. It isn't a sin to admit it, JJ. Swan will understand. Tell how her mama was awfully sick, but tell her about her heart of gold. You fell in love with her not just for her looks, but for her heart. I know it, JJ. You told me. Tell her how Sheila used your money. Tell her how it helped Ella Mae. Tell her about the room at Resthaven."

Throughout the whole monologue, Daddy hadn't breathed a word. Now he sighed, long and hard. I imagined him leaning over, head in his hands, tracing a finger around his eyes and Trixie's small hand, with its perfectly manicured nails, resting lightly on his bent-over back.

"JJ, this plane crash has the potential to destroy the lives of a whole lot of people. People who have lost their civic leaders, workers who have lost their company presidents. And mostly, children who have lost their parents. Their role models. Please talk to Swan. She needs you. Jimmy needs you too. But he needs you to throw a ball with and to take him out to get a milkshake and wrestle with and go to his games. Swan needs her Daddy. She still needs you for a few more years. Either you help her through this terrible time and build something harder, but stronger and more secure, or you let her fend for herself and lose her emotionally forever."

"You're hard on me, Trixie. You've always been hard on me."

Things were quiet for a moment. Then Trixie said so softly that I could barely distinguish her words, "Somebody has to tell you the truth. Sheila was my best friend. She's not here to say it. You loved her, JJ. Do it out of love for Sheila, and for Mary Swan."

"I loved her. God knows I loved her." There was a catch in Daddy's voice. I was terrified for him. Was Daddy going to cry in front of Trixie?

"Tell me what to do with her, Trix. I'm so lost. Do you know what she did the other day? Came in with her hair all braided like a Negro!"

"And that upset you?"

"Of course it upset me, Trixie. She spends half her time in the ghetto with Ella Mae. Before you know it, she'll be talking like them."

"JJ, she's helping down there. You should go and see. Her eyes were dancing when she told me about it! At least she's not getting drunk on the weekends or sleeping around or getting into a hundred other kinds of trouble. There are a lot of different ways to act on your grief, some more constructive than others. Alcohol, or boys, or over-work." I could imagine her looking at Daddy accusingly on that one.

"So tell me what to do."

"Take her out on a date. Girls love that. Take her to the City Club, alone. Just you and Swan. And talk to her. Ask her questions. Answer her questions. Talk. And listen. Try to listen to what is behind her words, JJ."

By now they had stood up and were walking toward the front door. I scurried up the stairs and into the hall.

"This is hard, Trix. Everything is too hard."

"You can do it." Then she gave Daddy a kiss on the cheek and said, "I'll be back in the morning to get Lucy." And she was out the door.

Everything was deathly quiet for five minutes. Finally I tiptoed to the top of the stairs and peered over the railing. Daddy was leaning against the wall in the entranceway, staring up at the painting of me on the tree swing, the one that had hung in the High Museum for several months and now was back home.

Chapter 22

We got through Christmas in a sort of truce, Daddy and I. Neither of us talked much, and fortunately the days were filled with tradition—a Christmas Eve meal at Grandmom and Granddad Middleton's followed by the midnight service at St. Philip's, a day with all the relatives at my aunt's house on Christmas afternoon, and a wonderful French five-course dinner at Mamie and Papy's plantation the next day. And the house looked festive enough, thanks to Trixie's initiative.

I also attended several open house parties at friends' homes, which was another Christmas tradition, and Robbie was at every one. We could make small talk fine, but that wasn't what I wanted to do. I wanted to encourage him to follow his heart and pursue his dreams, and I wanted to tell his father what a great job Robbie had done planning the Day at the Park. I found that I missed Robbie Bartholomew, our dates, our talks, our kisses, just about everything. I missed him, and something inside felt funny just waving good-bye to him at a party instead of driving off with him in that bright red convertible. He didn't bring anyone else to these parties, but it was obvious that we were no longer dating. I noticed several other girls flirting with him, and that hurt like fire. That really stung my heart.

When I was near Robbie, I couldn't imagine how things could possibly work out with Carl. But when I sat alone in my room or in Mama's *atelier*, especially in the *atelier* where I'd gotten "the hug," well, then everything seemed possible.

"How's Robbie Bartholomew?" Daddy asked after I returned from a party two days after Christmas.

"Fine, I think."

"Have you seen him lately?"

"Yeah. I just saw him at the Garretts' house."

"Hmm." Daddy looked a little perplexed. "Everything all right between the two of you?"

"Well, everything's all right, but we aren't dating anymore. We broke up after the Christmas dance."

"I see" was all that Daddy managed to say, but there was a look of disappointment in his eyes.

It was on Friday of that same week, in between Christmas and New Year's, that Daddy and I reached our absolute lowest. Ella Mae was back at our house after her annual four-day Christmas break. I had just slipped into my jeans and pulled on a sweatshirt and was headed to Rachel's to ride when I heard Daddy call out, "Ella Mae. Ella Mae, I need to talk to you." The tone of his voice stopped me cold.

Ella Mae went obediently into the study. Daddy must have thought I'd already left to ride because he did not lower his voice. "Ella Mae, I won't have you carting Mary Swan down to the inner city anymore, you hear? It isn't safe or proper. Not for a girl like her."

I couldn't see Ella Mae, and she wasn't saying a word.

Daddy sighed. "I appreciate your trying to get her to help out down there. Just as you did for Sheila. But not now, Ella Mae. You know I didn't approve of Sheila going down there. I felt it wasn't safe, especially in her condition. But she was an adult. Mary Swan is just a child. A young girl very capable of being influenced in the wrong way. I can't have it. Is that clear?"

"Yessir, Mista Middleton, I understand."

And that was the end of the conversation.

My mouth went dry, and I hesitated at the back door. Did I run to Daddy and tell him I'd heard every word? Beg him to reconsider? Apologize for being insolent with him? In the end, I couldn't say a thing. All I could do was hate whatever it was in Daddy that made him react that way. And I had a clue of what it was. *Mama had helped out in the inner city! This was something to talk to Miss Abigail about!*

When I returned from riding, Ella Mae had finished frying the chicken, and she nodded to me when I grabbed a chicken leg and took a big bite, but she didn't smile. She didn't say a word. She just wiped her hands on a dish towel and gave me a slow nod and walked right straight toward Daddy's study. She knocked on the closed door, something I had never once seen her do before.

"Yes?" came my dad's voice.

"Mista Middleton? I'll be goin' now."

"Fine, Ella Mae. Thank you. Has Mary Swan gotten home yet?" .

"Yessir, she done just arrived."

"Well, could you tell her to come here, please?"

But Ella Mae didn't answer. She disappeared into Daddy's study, and I, of course, listened by the door, which stood slightly ajar. "Mista Middleton, 'scuse me for sayin' so, but I thinks you be makin' one terrible mistake. You be messin' up yore chile, sir, in a bad way. In a real bad way."

"What do you mean, Ella Mae?" Daddy's voice was glacial.

"I ain't neva' seen Mary Swan so happy as when she's he'pin' out with the poor, Mista Middleton. She does a mighty fine job there, an' if'n ya take that away from her, 'scuse me for sayin' it, but I b'lieve you is not the man I worked fo' all these years. I b'lieve ya done lost ya mind and ya heart with yore Sheila. I'm mighty sorry, Mista Middleton, but don't ya treat Mary Swan this way. She's okay. She doin' all right. Don't take this away from her, sir. She done lost enuf as it is."

I think that was the longest conversation Ella Mae had ever had with my dad, and before he had time to answer her, she had turned and left the room. Her face was stern and fearful when she came out, but I just ran up and hugged her before she could amble out the back door. "Thank you, Ella Mae. Thank you."

Right away, things began to change at our house. First of all, on Saturday afternoon, Daddy went out and bought a baseball glove. When he got home, he stood at the bottom of the stairs and called up to Jimmy, "Son, how 'bout throwing a few balls with me?"

Jimmy, who was normally not the king of enthusiasm, came racing down the steps with a wide grin on his freckled face. "Sure, Dad."

While they tossed the baseball back and forth late that first afternoon with dusk settling abruptly around them, I stood in front of the big picture window in the *atelier* and watched. Daddy was throwing the baseball way up high, so that Jimmy had to hold out his glove and run for the ball in the near dark. I heard them laughing together, and that sound, the sound of a father enjoying being with his son, was as beautiful to my ears as Jean-Pierre Rampal playing the "Largo" from Handel.

Muffin seemed to be laughing too, in his canine way, yelping excitedly, and watching for his chance to intercept the baseball. He dashed after every ball that went past Jimmy's reach. He'd grab the ball in his mouth and then, tail wagging, run in circles while Daddy yelled, "Muf-fin!! For heaven's sake, put down that ball! Jimmy, haven't you taught that dog a thing?" Then Jimmy would tackle Muffin and wriggle the ball out of his mouth while Daddy leaned over, hands on his knees, breathing hard and roaring with laughter.

But the most amazing thing happened on Sunday afternoon. I'd just returned from riding at Rachel's, and my face, hands, and feet felt numb with cold. I decided a cup of hot chocolate was imperative. But before I could get to the kitchen, Daddy called to me from his study, "Mary Swan? Could you come here for a sec?" His eyes were down, looking at something on his desk. "Mary Swan, I was wondering if you'd like to go to the City Club for lunch tomorrow. They've got a big New Year's Eve special luncheon. The big tree is still up on the Rich's bridge, and well, I thought maybe you'd enjoy . . ."

"Are you asking me on a date, Daddy?"

He looked up with a hesitant smile on his face. "Yes, sweetheart, I guess I am."

"Then I accept!"

I had butterflies in my stomach as I rode the bus downtown on Monday morning. I had carefully chosen my outfit, with Rachel's help: a light green wool suit, which Rachel claimed showed off my eyes. I wore my hair back in a silky green headband that matched the suit. Daddy's office was in the Candler Building, which sat at a point where Peachtree, Houston, and Pryor streets joined. On the outside of the building, way up high, hung an enormous flashing Coca-Cola sign. Aside from that, the building was very ornate and sophisticated. Two sculpted men sat on either side of the Peachtree Street entrance, and inside in the lobby, the elevator doors were made of brass, and so were the letter boxes, and everything else was made of marble that Daddy said came from a famous quarry in the Georgia hills called Amicalola. The marble winding staircase had all kinds of elaborate objects carved into it. But I didn't take the stairs. Daddy's brokerage firm's offices were way up on the fourteenth floor, so I rode the elevator.

Stepping off the elevator, I pulled open the heavy glass doors leading into the brokerage firm complex. A young woman sitting at the reception desk looked up and asked, "Are you Miss Middleton?"

"Yes."

"Well, come right this way. Your father is expecting you."

Daddy's face lit up when he saw me. "Hello, sweetheart." He gave me a warm hug, which caught me off guard, and I stiffened involuntarily. He didn't seem to notice. "Leslie, could you fix Mary Swan and me a cup of hot apple cider?" He whispered to me, "Those of us fool enough to work on New Year's Eve decided we have a right to a little festivity."

Daddy's office was a square cubicle, three sides of which were glass. Just walking inside brought back memories of other times I'd visited him at his office. I remembered when I was little that I'd pointed to a small plastic tube on his desk and asked, "What's this for?"

And Daddy had replied, "That's a pneumatic tube. It carries customer orders from my desk to the wire room, which in turn sends them to the floor of the New York Stock Exchange to be executed." He had stuck a paper in the tube, opened the hatch, slid in the tube, and it disappeared.

"It's almost like magic, Daddy," I had enthused.

From his desk, I picked up a family photograph of the four of us from a few years earlier. Beside the photo there was a big smooth rock, painted by a childish hand in a variety of colors, that Daddy used as a paperweight. I had painted it for Daddy when I was eight and given it to him as a Christmas gift. I had always felt so proud that my paperweight adorned his desk. On the only real wall hung a painting by Mama, one of her many representations of the Swan House.

"Come around and greet some of the gang," Daddy interrupted my inspection.

I watched the ticker tape move across the wall near the ceiling and remembered how fascinated I'd been by it long ago.

"Keeps us up-to-date on the stocks," Daddy had explained, as though I would understand. "It gives the company's symbol, the number of shares bought and sold, and the price."

He saw me studying the ticker tape. "Today's very slow, since it's New Year's Eve."

It looked to me like most everyone in the office had decided to work on New Year's Eve. Only they weren't really working. They were joking and drinking cider and eating home-baked goodies. Daddy introduced me to a whole bunch of stockbrokers, some of whom I had already met at parties at our house or meals at the club. Most every broker greeted me merrily and said something like "Great to see you, Mary Swan! Merry Christmas and Happy New Year!" Then they'd turn to Daddy and admonish, "JJ, where have you been hiding this beautiful young lady!" which, of course, made Daddy beam. And a few even said, "You look just like your mother, God rest her soul."

Right around noon, we left the Candler Building and walked down to Five Points, so named because of the five roads that came together at that particular intersection: Peachtree, Marietta, Edgewood, Whitehall, and Decatur. Christmas lights were still strung across Peachtree, and lampposts were actually decked in what looked like boughs of holly, just like the song said. The air was biting and fresh and filled with a holiday cheer. We turned onto Alabama Street and walked a few blocks to where it crossed Forsyth Street and stopped across the street from a four-story enclosed-glass bridge that joined the two buildings that made up the Rich's department store. The glass bridge crossed above Forsyth Street and permitted pedestrians easy passage between the buildings without ever stepping outside.

I looked up to see an enormous Christmas tree perched on top of the bridge. Every Thanksgiving night for as long as I could remember, choirs from all over Georgia had performed from metal stands on each floor of the glass bridge. Near the end of the program, all the choirs joined in singing "O Holy Night." When they got to the line "Fall on your knees," a huge Christmas tree, imported each year from the forests of North Carolina, lit up like fire from heaven above the singing choirs, to the delight of the thousands of pedestrians who were standing in the streets, watching. I had wonderful memories of being scrunched in the crowd with Mama and Trixie and Jimmy and Lucy, staring up expectantly, waiting for the lights to flash on.

Seeing the tree, so magnificent in its Christmas garb, brought tears to my eyes. Some things did not change. "Oh, Daddy. Since we're here, can't we please ride the Pink Pig?"

"The Pink Pig? Mary Swan, are you serious? That's for little kids."

"Please. We'll fit." The Pink Pig was as much a part of Christmas in Atlanta as the great tree. It was a children's ride, a monorail with pink cars that curved slowly around the flat rooftop of the Rich's building. Children loved to sit in the front car, which was the head of the pig. And today, rather reluctantly, Daddy joined me in a pink car, his legs pulled up so tight that his knees practically touched his chin. I looped my arm through his as the Pink Pig meandered along. I was recapturing some ecstatically happy moment of my past, when Mama had ridden beside me in the Pink Pig. But today, it was the sweet sound of Daddy's laughter that filled my ears.

"Ready for lunch, sweetheart?" he asked when we were back down on the street. I nodded happily as we took off back up Peachtree, passing the Candler Building and walking several blocks to where the Capital City Club sat at the corner of Peachtree and Harris. The City Club, the downtown subsidiary of the Capital City Country Club and the oldest private club in Atlanta, was housed in a dignified and beautiful beige brick building with a long front porch that looked out onto Peachtree Street. The porch's wrought-iron railings were draped in evergreen boughs, which were tied at the rails with bright red velvet bows. Inside the club, a portrait of Robert E. Lee hung in the elegant hallway, and in the lobby back by the window, another beautiful Christmas tree rose up high, almost brushing the sixteen-foot ceiling.

"Mr. Middleton," said a tall, mustached man with golden skin and a foreign accent. "This must be Mary Swan."

"Yes, Leonard. Yes indeed." Then he turned to me. "Mr. Hourizadeh is the director of the City Club." I had only been there for two fancy meals, and never, ever alone with Daddy.

"Nice to meet you," I answered with a smile.

"I believe you'll be in the Mirador Room." He motioned for us to take the elevator to the second floor.

Philip T. Shutze, the same architect who had designed the Swan House, had designed the Mirador Room. I had heard about this circular room and its famous mirrors. Shutze had lowered the ceilings in a former ballroom to create an intimate supper club feeling. He also wanted to create the illusion of space and openness in a room that had no windows and was small. So he designed mirrors that appeared to be windows through which plants and birds indigenous to Georgia sprang into view from "outside." Shutze had commissioned an artist named Athos Menaboni, a native of Livorno, Italy, who specialized in birds and landscapes, to paint the mirrors.

Daddy and I walked into the Mirador Room, and right away, I began studying the famous mirrors. They were long, in simple gold frames, and did indeed look like windows. One had big dogwood leaves and white blossoms painted all across it along with a crested flycatcher about to snatch a mosquito in its mouth. Another mirror depicted a limb of a magnolia tree with its big, waxy green leaves and white flowers. Still another showed a snowy egret flying out of cattails with their long straplike leaves and dark brown thickly flowered cylindrical spikes. The autumn leaves of a grapevine were entwined beside a big pink water lily with its large bluish green circular leaves, and a hummingbird fluttered above. And I liked the mirror showing Georgia cotton ready for picking, its leaves brown. My favorite mirror was of the Georgia pine tree with its long green needles and the three pinecones, two closed and one fully opened. A blue jay with its crested head and blue plumage sat on the limb, cawing, and morning glory twisted around the lower limbs.

"Swannee?"

Daddy's voice brought an end to my observations, and I sat down beside him at a small table for two. The band was playing "Happy Holidays."

I took the crisp white linen napkin, which had been folded into an accordion, from my water goblet and placed it in my lap. A tuxedoed waiter handed me a leather-bound folder containing the menu. I opened it and began to study the choices. That's when I noticed that Daddy was staring at me.

"You do look beautiful, Mary Swan."

"Thank you, Daddy."

It was after we had ordered and the waiter had brought us our first course, a bowl of vichyssoise, that I asked, "Is it true that I look like Mama?"

"Yes, sweetheart. Yes, it is."

"Does that make you sad, Daddy?"

"Oh no, Swan. No."

"Because I can't change my looks. I could cut my hair, though."

"No, don't change a thing, Swan. You're perfect just as you are."

I set my spoon down beside the bowl of vichyssoise. "Do you really mean that, Daddy? Really?"

"Why, of course."

"Because if you do, it's the first time you've ever told me I was perfect just the way I am."

"I do mean it." His face fell. "And I'm sorry I never said it before. I'm sorry about a lot of things, Swan."

"Like what?" I wasn't about to let Daddy off the hook, now that we at last had this time together.

"Like the way I acted about your going into the slums, to help the Negroes. Things are changing, Mary Swan, and it's not always easy to keep up. You hardly have time to decide whether what is happening is for the good or the bad. It's not how I was raised. Blacks were always our inferiors. Don't get me wrong. You always treated them with respect, fairly, did what you could to help their situation. But there was never any question of friendship. Never ever. It's hard to imagine."

"Do you think, Daddy, that given the right education, a black child could do as well academically as a white?"

"I don't know. Be hard to believe."

"Someday there will be black girls at Welly, I bet you a million bucks."

"It's possible. But it won't come easily."

"It's not Christian to discriminate because of race. It's not what Jesus said. He said there's no difference between slave and free, Jew and Greek." I took another spoonful of the cold potato soup. "But no one seems to pay any attention around here."

"People are afraid, Mary Swan. Many whites don't hate blacks, they're just afraid. Afraid of crime and poverty. And also afraid of change. What will happen to society if blacks start mixing with whites? A lot of things would be compromised."

"Like what?"

"Like safety. You've seen the bad side of whites being mean to blacks. But, Mary Swan, there are so very many cases of blacks being violent against whites, robbing, beating, murdering. And, of course, most of the murders in Atlanta come from the inner city, often black against black."

"But that's because of their desperate situation."

"Maybe. But it's not something that is easily changed. The black and white mentalities are so very different." It was during that discussion that I realized Daddy had thought through a lot of things, and he had good reasons for what he believed, even if I didn't agree with him.

When the filet mignon was served, we started talking about the High Museum as strands of classical music delicately blended with the quiet chatter in the Mirador Room. "Is there much progress being made for the Memorial Arts School, Daddy?"

"Some, slowly. Right now, a lot of families are suing Air France for neglect in the crash. I guess it's to be expected."

"Are you going to sue, Daddy?"

"No, I hope to settle out of court. But it's the kind of thing that will drag on for months, maybe even years."

"Do you think there was neglect, Daddy?"

"I think the plane was too heavy, too much baggage. That should have been more closely controlled."

But I didn't want to talk about the crash, so I dared to broach a different subject. "How did you and Mama meet?"

"You've heard that story, Mary Swan."

"I want to hear it again."

Daddy frowned slightly and then shrugged. "It was in 1941. My sophomore year at Tech. She was about the most beautiful girl I'd ever laid eyes on. Just seventeen. Just about your age, Swan. Wellington had a large percentage of boarders at the time, and your mother was a weekday boarder, going home on the weekends."

"Was it love at first sight, Daddy?"

"For me it was. Absolutely. But your mother needed a little convincing." He stared off into space. "We dated off and on that first year and then the second. But I got drafted in 1943 and headed to England. We were apart for eighteen months, and she wrote me almost every day. Those letters were always filled with whimsical drawings." He wiped his mouth with his napkin, then dabbed his eye. "She'd started college at Agnes Scott and was taking painting classes on the side. She wrote that she'd found her life's calling. She was so excited. Just like a child. I returned from the war in April of 1945, and we were married in July. You came along almost nine months to the day afterward." He winked at me.

"And was Mama fine then?" I asked tentatively.

Daddy seemed ready to talk. "She was always a high-spirited type. I called her a thoroughbred. But we were happy. She loved decorating the house, and we had seats at the Fox Theatre for the opera season.

We used to go across the street during the intermission and have our bourbon at the Georgian Terrace, and just watch the people go by. We supported the symphony. And, of course, anything that had to do with the High Museum, well, she was there. Volunteering her time.

"Ella Mae came to work for us right before you were born. Bless her heart, she knew just how to take care of your mother. I was gone at the office, worked late hours, thought I was doing the right things. I saw that Sheila had odd reactions, moods changing often. I thought it was just the French part of her. Mamie was the same way. And you know, your grandmother had a history of . . . problems. I don't think it was easy to be Evelyne McKenzie's daughter.

"Gradually I saw more and more of Sheila's inability to cope with life. She just, she was just like a child, lost in the world of reality. Fortunately, she had her studio and she could paint. We lined her up with some children's portraits to paint, and she created a fine little business. She wasn't easy to work with, mind you. We had complaints. But during those first years, she was able to get her commissioned work done on time. And she received quite a lot of praise.

"But then Jimmy came. Two little children were more than she could handle. She started going downhill fast. Thank God for Trixie on the weekends. She and Ella Mae half raised you and Jimmy. I think it was a strange, twisted blessing for Trixie when she was going through that awful divorce. She found refuge at our place, and your mother found refuge in Trixie. They'd sit out by the pool and smoke their cigarettes and sip their martinis and laugh. Trixie knew how to make Sheila laugh. To stop her from thinking about the dark side of things so much.

"I'm ashamed to say that I didn't have much patience with your mother. I couldn't understand how raising two children could be so difficult. My mother had raised six of us. I guess I just wanted her to dress up and be my beautiful wife and impress the rest of Buckhead. I'm not proud of it, Mary Swan, but I didn't know. I told her she didn't have to paint if it was too tiring. And she cried for days because painting was what she wanted to do. Don't get me wrong. She loved you and Jimmy more than life itself. But she didn't have the mental reserves to deal with two little ones day in and out.

"One time when Ella Mae was sick, she got real upset with you and Jimmy, and you ran to Trixie's house." He stopped suddenly. "Do you remember that time, Swannee?"

I nodded.

"Trixie insisted I have Sheila tested. We found a doctor who diagnosed her as being depressed and put her on medication. He also highly recommended that she go to a mental hospital for treatment. I refused. I couldn't imagine that would be necessary.

"Then one night I heard smashing sounds coming from her studio. I found Mama cutting through her newest painting with a carving knife. Slashing the thing to pieces." Daddy hung his head for a moment, reliving that nightmare.

"We didn't start with Resthaven, Mary Swan. We started with the dean at St. Philip's. He met with your mother often in the early years. But, bless his soul, he came to see your mother's problems as needing psychiatric care. And then there was a particularly bad incident. . . ." He stopped, took a bite of meat, chewed it carefully, then cleared his throat. "It was the dean who recommended Resthaven. He knew of the private institution. We had to choose between Resthaven and the state institution at Milledgeville."

I had heard of Milledgeville. At school we sometimes whispered stories about kooky people who were locked in the state's mental institution, never to return. Our stories were innocently cruel. We had never really known anyone there. My mouth went dry.

"She was admitted to Resthaven for two months in 1951. And you cried for your mother every single day. More than Jimmy. You were just a little girl of about six, crying your heart out for your mama. So I took you up to see her. You remembered that, didn't you?"

"Yes, when I saw the sketches, I remembered that I'd been there."

"But it was too hard on you and too hard on Sheila. And when it became obvious that Mama wasn't going to necessarily get better, well, I didn't know what to do. The doctor explained that Mama had a problem with cyclic depression. In some seasons it would improve, but the strangest things could trigger it." I watched how a shadow passed over Daddy's clean-shaven face. Noticed again his gaunt cheeks.

"The doctor started her on tranquilizers. Your mother hated it. It took away her creativity, her freedom. Sometimes she was like a zombie. She could hardly paint." From the look on his face, I knew this was hurting Daddy to remember. He brought his fork to his mouth, regarded the bite of filet, and set it back on his plate.

"The medication helped, but she lost the twinkle in her eyes. Thank God her doctor was willing to experiment with lighter doses. He even let her stop altogether when she was at Resthaven and doing well."

He cleared his throat and finally took a bit of meat. I was riveted in my seat.

"What was I supposed to tell you, Swan? That Mama was at a mental institution? How could you understand that your mother was sick in her head? So I said it was art exhibitions. Maybe it was wrong. I didn't mean to hurt you by it. Your mother hated hiding the truth from you. But in the end, we thought it was best. And since the crash, well, I intended to tell you the truth. I would have soon. . . ."

"But everyone else knew she was in a mental hospital!" I accused.

"Oh no. Not many knew. My parents. Hers, of course. Some women suspected something because she broke down twice in a Junior League meeting. But Trixie hushed it up quickly. We all did."

"I'll bet Herbert Thomas's mom knew."

When Daddy looked at me quizzically, I explained the incident at the Back-to-School Ball. "It was so awful, Daddy. So awful to hear him say those things. And worse to somehow know they were true."

"Yes, I'm sure it was." He sighed sadly. "Mary Swan, I really thought what I was doing, keeping Mama's visits to Resthaven a secret, was for Jimmy's and your good. I swear I did. Leila Thomas was a friend of your mother. I'm sure she didn't tell her son about Mama unless she had a reason. Oh, Swan, I'm sorry for all you've been going through these past months. Do you believe me?"

"Yes, Daddy. Now that we can talk, I believe you." I took a deep breath and asked, "Was Mama really considered a fine painter, Daddy, or was that made up too?"

"No, Swan, I swear it, sweetie. Mama was a fine painter. Her work really was loved. And the museum was enthusiastic about her work, excited to have one of her paintings. But she wasn't prolific. I'm afraid she destroyed a number of paintings in times of deep anger and frustration. But, Mary Swan, I didn't make up a thing about her talent. You can see it yourself. She knew how to capture expression. And I was proud of her, Swan. Confused, afraid, at times very angry. But always proud of her."

"And the night of the premier exhibition?"

"She got drunk. Refused to go. Cried about the paintings being missing. She'd worked for weeks on her speech. She knew it by heart. I begged her to give the speech at least, for all the patrons, but she insisted it wouldn't make a bit of sense without the painting to look at. And she was so drunk. Long before it started. Drunk. We made an appearance, but I told the museum she was too ill to speak. They were gracious and, of course, embarrassed by the scandal of the paintings. We stumbled along through that, but I never knew if your mother knew anything more about the paintings. It was all the buzz for a few weeks, and then, thank God, they let it die down."

"I'm sorry I've been so difficult, Daddy. I was just trying to understand."

"No. You deserved to know the truth, Swan. I'm the one who's been difficult." Then, as we ate the strawberry cheesecake, he said, "Swannee, you're so like your mother in many ways. Creative, wild, freethinking. Now you know the other side of her that isn't like you at all. Don't burden yourself with it. Just enjoy life, honey. Don't try to figure out things that are way too hard for any of us to understand."

"I'll try not to, Daddy."

Later, as Daddy walked me to the bus stop, I chirped happily, "It was the absolute most perfect date I've ever had, Daddy." I leaned over and kissed him hard on the cheek and threw my arms around him. "Thank you."

Daddy just stared down at me for a long time. "It's the best date I've had in a long time too, Swan. We need to do this more often."

"I'd like that. I'd like that a lot."

And from then on, it seemed like the wall that had been dividing Daddy and me started crumbling down, one stone at a time.

Chapter 23

Since Daddy and I were talking now, since so much of the past was at least being admitted, I considered asking him to take me to Resthaven. But Trixie had already offered and she had a more flexible schedule, and I didn't want to do anything to upset the fragile balance Daddy and Jimmy and I had found. So near the end of our Christmas break, Trixie and I headed to North Georgia in her blue Chevrolet.

"Daddy took me to the Capital City Club on New Year's Eve," I mentioned casually.

"How wonderful."

"He followed your advice." I looked at her hard. "I heard what you told Daddy, Trixie, that night before Christmas."

"I had no idea." Her slim fingers with their bright pink nails almost imperceptibly gripped the steering wheel a little tighter. She batted her eyes.

I paid no attention. "Then Ella Mae talked to him too. Gave him a piece of her mind."

"Ella Mae? Impossible!"

"No, it's perfectly true." We both chuckled at that. "So between the two of you, Daddy seems to have gotten the message."

"I'm glad. I'm really glad, Swannee." She glanced over at me. "Did you talk about your mother?"

"Yeah. Yeah, we did, amazingly enough. We talked about her and her painting and how you and Ella Mae took care of her and about Resthaven. Daddy admitted it all. And he apologized. He really apologized."

"He's a good man, Mary Swan. He just never knew what to do. It was so hard."

I was nibbling on my fingernail nervously, determined to ask Trixie something that had been on my mind since that night before Christmas when I'd overheard her conversation with Daddy. "Do you like my dad?"

"Well, of course I like him, Swannee. We've been friends for years."

"But do you like him more than just a friend?"

"Swan, I don't know what you mean." She pressed her lips together and fiddled with her pack of cigarettes until she got one out and lit it.

"Of course you do. I think Daddy likes you. I think he likes you a lot."

"Swannee, please."

"I know he loved Mama. But Mama's not here anymore. And I think if you ever gave Daddy a little attention, well, gosh, Trixie, I'd much prefer he dated you than Amanda Hunnicutt."

"Swan, it's impossible. Sheila was my best friend."

"So?"

"So I won't get involved in any other scandals."

"What do you mean by scandals? What's the matter with dating a man whose wife has been dead for seven months?"

"Oh, Mary Swan Middleton. You and your ideas!" There was no lightness in her voice.

"But you told me yourself not to listen to what other people say, especially if it isn't true."

Trixie's eyes were riveted to the highway. "It's more complicated than that, Mary Swan. If your dad and I started dating, well, it'd be the talk of the town. And there would be the possibility of a lot of people getting hurt."

"Why?"

"Rumors. Gossip. I lived through that enough for ten people when Tony divorced me. The rumors flew all around the town, and I went from being a rather helpless victim to a woman of low repute who deserved everything she got. It was horrible, absolutely horrible." She had rolled down the window and was blowing out big puffs of cigarette smoke. "I learned to be strong. I learned to close my ears and eyes and not pay attention to any of the rumors. I knew they weren't true anyway. But it still hurt. Oh, how it hurt to have everyone making snide comments about how much money I was worth and that it wasn't such a bad deal after all since I got to keep the house. Already I'd been through hell with him for all those years, knowing what he was doing. I thought it couldn't be worse, but it was. And I knew he'd never come crawling back and apologize. I think he was happy to have destroyed my life."

"That's why you deserve something better, Trixie."

"Mary Swan." She turned her eyes momentarily from the road. "I would never ever in all my life want to put anyone else through the pain I went through, and certainly not JJ or you or Jimmy. You've been through enough."

"But what would people say? What could they say?"

"Believe me, Swannee, they could make up stories—they could say your dad and I were in love all along, that we'd been seeing each other. Heaven knows what else."

"But that's insane! Completely insane! And who cares?"

"I care. Please don't bring it up again." And that's when I realized how terribly stricken she looked, as if I had guessed her deepest secret, and she was sure it was something that could never happen in a million years.

Trixie left me at the main entrance to Resthaven, and I waved to her from beside one of the white fluted columns. "I'll be back at four o'clock." She glanced at her watch. "That gives me time to shop in Highlands and visit a friend. You gonna be okay, Swan?"

I nodded. I stood on the wide terrace and watched her drive away, down the long, tree-lined road. Then I opened the heavy wooden door and stepped into the entrance hall of Resthaven, its high ceilings and black-and-white tiled floors now seeming a bit more familiar. The same secretary sat behind the reception desk.

"You're Miss Middleton, I believe."

"Yes."

"Please have a seat." She nodded to a cluster of comfortable chairs to her left. "Nurse Leschamps will be right with you."

I had called Resthaven two days earlier and set up an appointment with Leslie Leschamps, so she was expecting me. She arrived almost immediately. She was plump with short, graying hair, and her manner was neat, efficient, and helpful. She led me into a small sitting room that was empty for the moment of other patients or visitors. "Good to meet you, Miss Middleton. How can I help you?"

"Well, I was wondering if you knew my mother. I mean, did you know her well?"

"Yes, I knew her. I'm so sorry about the terrible plane crash." She reached out automatically and took my hand. "I've been here at Resthaven for many years now. Your mother became very dear to me."

I explained to her briefly how my search for three missing paintings had led me to Resthaven. "I met Mr. Henry Becker a month ago. He told me about how Mama loved to paint while she was here. He even had a painting she'd given him hanging in his bedroom. Did Mama give you a painting?"

Nurse Leschamps looked surprised. "As a matter of fact, she did. It's one of my prized possessions."

"And did you help Mama paint?"

She chuckled. "I have never held a paintbrush in my hand except when I repainted the walls in my kitchen. But I loved to watch her paint, and I encouraged her to keep working at it."

"Do you think she signed some of her paintings with your name?"

Leslie Leschamps wrinkled her brow and asked, "Why would she do that?"

"I'm not sure. There are so many questions I still have. But I think it's because of the way her painting changed when she was at Resthaven." Nurse Leschamps pursed her lips and nodded, so I continued, "Could you tell a difference in the way she painted here?"

"Oh yes. Immediately. But of course I don't have a trained eye. I just alerted the doctors and encouraged them to let her stay off medication while at Resthaven." She reached for my hand again. "You know, Miss Middleton, I really think you should talk to Dr. Clark about all this."

"Dr. Alfred Clark?" I asked, remembering his name.

"Yes. He's the main doctor who worked with your mother. A wonderful man."

I grimaced. "But I'm only here for a few hours."

"Well, Dr. Clark is on duty. Sit tight. I'll see what I can do." I understood then why Mama must have liked Leslie Leschamps so much. She knew how to get things done.

In less than ten minutes, I was greeted by Dr. Alfred Clark, who invited me into his office. He was thin, not very tall, and balding. He moved quickly and smiled reassuringly, and his soft blue eyes looked compassionate. "Nice to meet you, Miss Middleton." He stuck out his hand. "So you are Sheila Middleton's daughter. No mistaking that. You look just like her."

"Thank you," I murmured.

"Nurse Leschamps said you have some questions for me?"

"Yes, yes, I do. Thanks so much for seeing me. I know you're busy." Then I launched into my story about my hunt for the three missing paintings by the artists Sheila Middleton, Henry Becker, and Leslie Leschamps. I explained to Dr. Clark about finding Mama's Resthaven sketchpads, of seeing Henry Becker's sketch and knowing he must be the same man who had painted one of the missing paintings. I told him about my last trip to Resthaven and how I had met Mr. Becker and seen Mama's painting in his house, only it didn't look like Mama's painting. And how Henry Becker had never painted anything in his life and neither had Leslie Leschamps.

"I am so very confused, Dr. Clark. I think for some reason Mama painted better at Resthaven, and I think all three of the missing paintings must have been painted by her. Maybe she used different names because she wanted to hide the fact that she painted differently or something. And I know that none of this makes one bit of sense, but you're my last hope, and I really, really need to find those missing paintings."

So intent was I on my speech that I didn't notice at first how Dr. Clark leaned forward with great interest and how gradually a smile spread across his face. "You're a very intelligent young woman, Miss Middleton."

"Oh no. No, I'm not. I'm really confused. But I was hoping . . ."

"That I could answer a few questions?"

I nodded.

"You have come to the right place."

"I have?" I asked incredulously.

"Yes. I can at least answer some of them." He gave the same reassuring smile. "Nurse Leschamps was the first person to talk to me about your mother and her painting. I found her art fascinating. I personally had several art experts come to examine her work—with her full knowledge and agreement, of course. In the past few years, we've started research on art as a therapeutic way to deal with emotional problems, largely based on your mother's experience."

I got the feeling that Dr. Clark really wanted to help me.

"Your mother was diagnosed a long time ago as having something that is called chronic seasonal depression. But what that means is simply that your mother got hurt a lot as a child, and the memories of that pain affected her quite dramatically at different times of the year."

I must have looked uncomfortable, because Dr. Clark paused and his voice grew soft, as if he didn't want to upset me. "Sometimes the bad things that happen to us as children stay with us in a way throughout our lives. Sometimes we can never really understand how the people we love the most could do things that seem to contradict that love. Many adults have never really learned how to accept the traumas of their childhood. It's as though they're dragging their past along behind them into each new circumstance. That makes for very emotionally unstable people. Here at Resthaven, our job is to help the individual admit the pain in his past and move on to a more healthy way of functioning. Does that make sense, Miss Middleton?"

I was concentrating on his every word. "I think so. You're saying that bad things happened to Mama when she was young, and she never really got over it."

"For many years she didn't. But she was making great progress and finding new freedom in her life. I believe her art was a reflection of what she was feeling inside."

"But what happened to Mama that was so terrible?"

Dr. Clark cleared his throat. "Have you ever heard of a term called doctor-patient confidentiality?"

"No."

He chuckled a little. "What it means is that I'm not allowed to talk about my patients to others—what they've confided to me. But the details are not what is important. What you need to know, Miss Middleton, is that your mother wanted very much to function as a normal adult. In her case, particular times of the year were extremely difficult because of the memories they brought along. That is often when she came to Resthaven."

"To be put on medication?"

"Oh no. Not at all. Medication helped her get through the roughest times and reduced the stress that she put on her family, but her best therapy was in doing what she enjoyed—painting. Before she could put into words her hurt, she was able to paint it. And that started her on the path to freedom. She was making progress, and her painting showed this."

"Then are the three paintings all by her?"

"They are."

"And she used pseudonyms."

"Yes."

"But why?"

"She wanted so much to show her work to the public. But like every artist, she was afraid of rejection. With the permission of her two dear friends, Mr. Becker and Miss Leschamps, she borrowed their names. It was also a way to honor those who had helped her. It was through Mr. Becker and Miss Leschamps that I first became aware of your mother's talent."

"But they said they didn't know anything about the paintings!"

"I believe they, too, felt strongly about protecting your mother's confidentiality."

"Yeah. I see what you mean."

"Come with me." He led me down a spacious hall of the high-ceilinged, airy brick building. "Here is our art studio." He opened a door and motioned for me to enter. I couldn't help but smile. All across one wall were big picture windows with light streaming in everywhere.

"This looks just like Mama's studio at home!" I gasped.

"Yes. I imagine it does. She helped design it and paid for it." Easels, paints, canvases, and clay filled different-sized cubbyholes. "This room has become very important in the healing process of some of our patients," Dr. Clark said, almost reverently.

"Mama convinced you to build an art studio?"

Dr. Clark smiled. "Not exactly. It was your mother's paintings that convinced me that art could be therapeutic for certain patients. Mind you, this is all very experimental. Not widely accepted."

"Did Daddy know about how she painted at Resthaven?"

"Actually, he didn't. Not at the time. I don't believe your mother wanted anyone outside of Resthaven to know. There was a lot of shame involved in her being here. She was not easy on herself."

"And she came here often?"

"Fairly often, yes. At least twice a year."

"So she just came to paint!" I accused. "She wasn't ever going to get better, was she?"

"Oh yes, she was improving. She was making great strides." He stared out the big picture window. "Many patients reach a plateau in the healing process. We can keep them fairly stabilized with medication, but they don't make much progress. It all depends on the type of mental illness. But your mother wasn't mentally ill. She was very high-strung and, at times, emotionally unstable. She felt certain . . . certain constraints from the society in which she lived. At Resthaven she left those constraints behind and was gradually able to be herself. A big part of being herself was experimenting with painting. And as she did, her style of painting changed." He turned to me, his eyes intense, concentrated. "I'd like to show you something, Miss Middleton."

He led me down a long hall and out a back door of the main building. All around us were footpaths in the midst of flowering gardens. I had never seen so many colors in the dead of winter!

"The gardens are beautiful!" I exclaimed.

"Yes, we were fortunate to find another gardener who takes as much pride in the gardens as Mr. Becker did."

We wandered in and out of paths, and in the winter chill, I pulled my coat around me. Dr. Clark took out a set of keys and stopped beside a low brick building, half hidden by magnolias and ivy. He pushed open the door, and we stepped inside.

Dr. Clark flipped on a light switch. The room was small, clean, windowless, and definitely not heated. On the floor and in makeshift shelves sat a number of unframed canvases. Some were portraits and still lifes. Others looked more like the raging winds in Henry Becker's painting. Still others had a pastel soft calm to them.

"These are your mother's paintings."

I gasped. "Mama painted all of these?"

"Yes, Miss Middleton. Yes, she did." He was quiet for a moment as I registered my shock. "We all knew your mother had a lot of talent. I suggested to her several times that she let these paintings be seen—even at a small exhibition at Resthaven. She always refused. So we gave her this room. This is where we have stored her paintings for many years now."

I stood in the middle of the refurbished tool shed and just stared. My eyes kept darting from one painting to the next. Never would I have guessed that each of these canvases was painted by Mama's hand. Suddenly I blurted out, "Are the three missing paintings here? Are they in this room?"

But Dr. Clark squelched that intuition with a slow shake of the head. "No. I'm sorry, Miss Middleton. They're not."

"So what happened to them? Do you know anything about the exhibition at the High Museum?"

"Yes. As I said, your mother wanted for her work to be seen in her different styles. I wholeheartedly agreed with her, although I didn't much see the need for the pseudonyms. But she insisted on keeping them."

I walked up close to one painting, practically putting my nose on it as Carl might have done. The signature was splashed across the bottom in a hurry: *Henry Becker.* "Your mother didn't want notoriety. She simply wanted to paint. And when she painted, she felt better. My job was to protect her interests to the extent that it was helpful to her. Your mother came to trust me. She asked me to help her arrange for an exhibition at the High. But she was also terrified of rejection, even after art experts had examined her work and given it praise."

"But why?"

"Miss Middleton, your mother had built a comfortable reputation in Atlanta as a portrait painter, reproducing on canvas the faces of children. But to her, that was not true art. True art was an almost magical experience. It was not calculated—it was free and fast and caught in a moment in the forces of nature outside. Here at Resthaven, she rarely painted inside. She painted nature and whoever or whatever happened to be caught in nature at the time."

I thought about all the different paintings she had done of the Swan House, sitting at the end of the yard with her easel planted in the grass. Dr. Clark was still talking.

"She finally decided on three paintings that she wanted to donate to the High Museum. I helped your mother work things out with the curator of the museum. He agreed to present the paintings as work by three young Southern artists. He met with your mother and understood that she wished to remain protected from the limelight."

"And what went wrong? What really happened to those three

paintings? It's very important for me to know."

"I don't know, Miss Middleton. They disappeared on the eve before the opening of the exhibition. We had kept them here in the
studio, wrapped up and ready to be taken to the museum. I'm terribly
afraid that your mother destroyed them. She had a history of destroy-
ing her work in moments of extreme anguish. A terrible loss."

"This place wasn't locked up?"

"Well, yes, we kept it locked, but your mother had a key. She
liked to bring other patients to this room and show them her paintings.
At times we had different canvases on display in the art studio."

"And no one questioned her? No one from Resthaven?"

"Of course she was questioned—by the police, by the curator, by
me. I met with your mother, and she insisted that she had not destroyed the paintings. That was all she would say."

"Well, you should have told Daddy! These paintings here should
have been given to us! We at least deserved to know about them!"

He flushed and smiled sympathetically. "Of course, of course. But
after I saw the effects of the strain of the exhibition on her, I didn't
want to push her. She was coming along, though. She wanted so much
to tell your father and others she loved. And I believe she would have.
In fact she fully intended to talk to your father on the European tour.
Perhaps she did.

"At any rate, your father knows now, Miss Middleton. I called him
the week after the crash and explained everything to him. I invited him
to come to see the paintings, which he did. Even now he is deciding
what should be done with them. There is no rush. You have all been
through so much."

My head was swimming. "Daddy knows?"

"Yes, he does, Miss Middleton. That is why I felt free to talk to
you today."

I felt tears welling up in my eyes and mumbled, "Would you mind
if I stayed here for a little while?"

"Stay as long as you wish, Miss Middleton. Let me turn on the
heat. Please have the secretary tell me when you are finished." His
voice was soft, and his gaze rested on me for a long moment. "You
know, your mother did a lot of writing while she was here too. And
one of her journals was all about her art. I believe she wanted you to
see it someday."

"For me?"

"Yes, I think she saw an artist in you too."

I swallowed hard. "A journal? For me?"

"Yes, it was part of her therapy. Not simply drawing and painting, but writing about how she felt."

"Could I see it?"

"Of course you may. I'll have the nurse bring it to you. Good day, Miss Middleton."

"Thank you, Dr. Clark. Thank you so much for your time." And then I added, "And for everything you did to help my mother."

I stayed in that shed for the whole afternoon, until the secretary came to tell me that Trixie was waiting for me. I spent my time studying the paintings and then intermittently reading from my mother's journal.

This is true art—this is letting the colors and feelings tell their story without preconceived thought. This is the magic that I have been seeking, the perfection of my skills. I like the way the tree is suggested in different hues of color with the complementary color reflected in the sky. I like the way you can feel the wind because of the way the leaves are moving.

She was talking about a painting of the gardens, and as I studied it, I found myself nodding with her description. It was a stronger painting than the perfectly posed portraits. It made me shiver a little, feeling the chill in the brittle leaves of a thick old oak. The painting was signed *Henry Becker.*

I could not quite figure out the paintings that bore the signature of Leslie Leschamps until I found Mama's own explanation in her journal.

I have experimented with painting inside, away from nature, here at Resthaven. I much prefer the natural light of outdoors, but I have wanted to paint a few subjects from memory. I have found it much more difficult and much more satisfying than a simple portrait. I am reminded of the intense pleasure I felt in painting Mary Swan all those years ago. I knew her soul, and so it was hard and painful and wonderfully liberating to put it onto canvas. So I have experimented with this type of portrait painting again.

And I found to my great delight a portrait of Daddy. He looked like he had been surprised by Mama's entry into his study. He had a brightness in his eyes and an urgent, happy smile as he leaned forward on his desk. In a second he would be out of his chair and coming toward the door, coming toward Mama. She had painted an expression on Daddy's face that I had only seen a very few times. But, I thought to myself with relief, one of those times had just happened during our date at the club.

I would always afterward remember that afternoon in the shed at Resthaven as my private art lesson from Mama, as I read of her struggles to paint truthfully, to paint from her soul. She had even hidden a treasure in her journal, just for me.

I worry for Swannee. She has the same creative bent that I had at her age, but she doesn't know what to do with it. And how do I encourage her when my own path has been so very rocky? What shall I say to her so that she will pursue the passion, the dream? I don't want her to hurt the way I've hurt. May she not walk down the same path, stumbling and fumbling and feeling the searing in her heart! I want her to float gracefully, like the swan in her name, on a serene lake. But no, I will not condemn her to peace if her destiny calls her to something else. She will fly.

Her words were the confirmation I had sought without knowing it. The confirmation that Mama cared and loved and wondered for me, even in the midst of her own struggles.

Months ago Daddy had said to me, *"There seem to be a whole lot more paintings than we knew about."* And then he had changed the subject. He must have been referring to these paintings after receiving the phone call from Dr. Clark. Now at least we could talk about it. Together we could decide what to do with Mama's paintings. At least there was nothing secret between us anymore.

Nothing except the Raven Dare.

The Raven Dare. The reason for the whole investigation. Fate is a funny thing. I am sure if Mama had been alive when I started trying to solve the Raven Dare, I would never have discovered the truth about the paintings or seen the ones she had painted while at Resthaven. *Well,* I thought to myself, sitting in that shed, *I have done my job.* I had found out everything possible about the missing paintings, and the only other person who could clear up the mystery was dead. I had a sinking feeling that the Dare was going to die its own quiet death, far away from the limelight, just as Mama would have wanted.

I would present my case to Mrs. Alexander and the Wellington seniors, and leave it to them to decide. It was the best I could do. And maybe it didn't really matter so much anymore. What were three lost paintings, when I had solved the riddle of my mother?

We were halfway home and Trixie had heard every detail of my afternoon at Resthaven.

"So, Trixie, did Mama ever tell you why she got so depressed at certain times of the year?"

"You don't want to know. Quit asking me such hard questions, Swan, for goodness' sake. Just leave it be."

"Did something happen to Mama to make her depressed all the time?"

"Like I said, you don't want to know."

"You want me to ask Daddy, don't you?"

Strangely enough, she said quickly, "No! No, don't ask JJ." Then with a miserable sigh, "This is the absolutely last thing I'll tell you, Mary Swan. I can't bear to keep remembering. But I know your daddy will never tell you because I don't think he knows."

"He doesn't know?"

"Your mother only mentioned it to me once, and we never ever brought it up again. Her doctor at Resthaven knows, though. I'm pretty sure of that." She took out a cigarette. "Your mother wasn't an only child, Mary Swan. She had a sister, Anne, about four years younger than she." She let that register.

"Evelyne and Ian were insanely happy to have another daughter. And your mother adored her little sister. One beautiful spring day on that big cotton plantation, Sheila was helping her mother push the baby carriage along the road when Anne started choking. Your poor grandmother panicked and started screaming at Sheila to do something, to run get help. Evelyne tried to dislodge whatever was stuck, but to no avail. By the time Sheila came back with help, the baby was dead. Evelyne was cradling her baby and wailing.

"And when she saw Sheila, she started screaming at her. She slapped her and told her it was her fault that Anne died because Sheila hadn't gotten help fast enough. And Evelyne refused to see Sheila for a week." This Trixie confided in a whisper, through blurred eyes. "And then your grandmother started drinking. It was a terrible tragedy. It almost killed your grandparents. And Sheila was such a sensitive child. I think she died inside with her baby sister. And every year in the spring, she would sink into depression. I don't think your grandmother ever forgave Sheila, and I don't think Sheila ever forgave her mother either. She told me that her mother ruined her life by making her live with a guilt that wasn't hers."

I was silent for a long time. *No wonder,* I kept thinking. *No wonder Mama was so very fragile.* I wiped my eyes and whispered, "And now Mama's gone too."

"Yes."

"When did Mama tell you these things?"

"When I'd come over in tears with what Tony was putting me through. Ella Mae would watch Lucy, and your mother and I would drink ourselves silly and smoke a pack of cigarettes at a time. That's how we survived. Talking and crying and then laughing hysterically and drinking and smoking. I don't recommend it, Swan. But that's how we survived. And one day, when she was in that state of mind, she told me her story. And that's why your mother struggled so much with depression. At least, that's what I always thought.

"Now, no more questions! None. It is all terrible and tragic. Nothing more, Swan." And with a last puff of smoke, she crushed out the cigarette in the ashtray and was silent.

As I told Trixie good-bye and walked into the house, I realized why so much of my mother's life had been hidden from me. It was tragic and much too much of a tormented story for a child to handle. Daddy had been right to hide it from me. I slipped into the *atelier.* With one hand I held a paintbrush and dabbed color on my very first and only painting. With the other I wiped my eyes.

We went back to school on January seventh, and as soon as that happened, I felt like I was on a downhill sprint. All the hype about Mardi Gras and the Raven Dare hit me full force, and I knew I couldn't simply give up. The pressure was on. I'd had seven months to solve the Dare, and now I only had seven weeks remaining. Seven short weeks, and I'd exhausted all my possibilities for clues.

The teachers always complained that January and February were lost months, because the only thing we girls thought about was Mardi Gras. But we complained that we worked extra hours every day to keep up with the school's tradition, and the least the teachers could do was to lighten up a little on the homework. But nothing ever changed either way, and that was part of the tradition too.

The senior girls called an assembly that Monday afternoon, and all the girls in the freshmen through senior classes crowded into the auditorium for the announcement of the theme of Mardi Gras. One year it had been "Baskin-Robbins' Thirty-One Flavors of Ice Cream." Another year "The Wonderful World of Disney."

"Is everybody ready for Mardi Gras?" Jane McClatchey, the senior class president, asked enthusiastically.

"Yes!" we yelled back equally enthusiastically.

"This year's theme is 'Shakespeare's Comedies.' The senior class has chosen the play *The Taming of the Shrew*. There are eleven other comedies to choose from. As soon as you have decided, please register your choice with the senior class officers. As you know, you must build a float and write a skit that has something to do with the title that you choose."

In my freshman year, when the theme had been "The Wonderful World of Disney," our class had chosen the film *Fantasia*. We'd decided, for some insane reason, to build a dragon, a great big papier-mâché dragon for our float. We'd gotten so disgusted with the whole thing that by the time of Mardi Gras we didn't care if our dragon breathed fire or soap.

As soon as the theme was announced, we split up into classes and started brainstorming. "All right, everyone. Be quiet, now, y'all. I mean it." Jane Springfield, our class president, was the original organizer if ever there was one. "Listen. We've got to decide quickly, before the freshmen or sophomores can steal our idea."

"The freshmen have already got *A Midsummer Night's Dream*," volunteered Karen Jones.

"And we know the seniors are doing *The Taming of the Shrew*," someone else reminded Jane.

"Great," grumbled Jane. "We've got to get a move on it. Swan, you're our creative dreamer. Any ideas?"

I shrugged, mind spinning. I could hardly wait to get my hands on some of Willie's poetry and make it into mine. Then I'd have the best of the lot turning over in his grave! "Maybe *The Merchant of Venice?* We could have the float be a gondola going under the Bridge of Sighs."

"Good idea," several girls enthused.

"And romantic music."

"And we could have a dance scene in the middle of St. Peter's Square with the pope looking on."

We all giggled, and the ideas started flowing.

"Okay, then is it unanimous for *The Merchant of Venice?*" Jane screamed above our chatter. "Let's vote." We put our heads down and hands up, and *The Merchant of Venice* was chosen. Millie Garrett ran down the long aisle to the front of the auditorium and reported our decision to the senior class officers.

Jane didn't miss a beat. "Now let's form our committees. Let's see. I guess Griffin will head up the float committee again. Is that okay with you, Griff?"

Betty Griffin, stocky with jet-black hair and plenty of muscles, grinned and nodded.

"Good. Well, who wants to work with Griff?" About seven hands shot up, the gals with brains for math who liked to figure out how things worked.

"And what about the skit? Swan, you got a poem dancing around in your head this year?"

I shrugged. Of course I had a poem. I had ten of them bumping back and forth into each other even as she spoke. For the past two years I'd written the skit, almost every word, clever limericks, simple rhyme schemes. It was high time to try iambic pentameter and sonnets.

"And who wants to help Swan?"

Millie Garrett and Julie Jacobs, the essay finalists from last year, both volunteered.

"As soon as you girls have written the skit, then we can set up the different committees for the dances and the costumes and the music," Jane explained. We knew the procedure all too well. The next few days meant lots of pressure for the writers.

"Great. And the last thing we have to do today is choose who will ride on the float and which two girls will pull it."

The girl who would ride the float was supposed to be beautiful. I'd never even gotten nominated.

"Ginny McDougall!" Patty called out. Ginny was petite with straight blond hair that went down below her waist.

"Lauralee Turnbull!" That was an obvious nomination because Lauralee, although not a real beauty, was the cutest, most popular girl in our class.

My hand went up. "Rachel Abrams."

Rachel yanked it down immediately. "What are you doing?" she hissed.

"I'm nominating you, idiot," I hissed back.

"Well, I don't want to be nominated."

"Are you still mad about the Christmas dance?"

She shrugged.

In the end, five girls were nominated. Gail Anderson handed out slips of paper, and we all voted. While the class secretary counted the votes, we started nominating the "pullers." These were two girls who supposedly looked something alike and would pull the float on the night of Mardi Gras. Rachel was pretending not to care one iota about the results of the vote, but she gave herself away by twirling a strand of hair around one finger, something she only did before flute competitions when she didn't know her piece well.

Jane stood up on a wooden pew and clapped her hands together. "Okay, y'all. I've got the name of the girl who will ride the float."

Several girls gave Rachel a squeeze on the shoulder and whispered, "Good luck." Rachel didn't crack a smile.

"This year, the girl who will ride the junior float in the Mardi Gras competition for Wellington School is—" She paused dramatically, which was a bit irritating. "Rachel Abrams!"

"Great! Super!" I yelled so loud that several girls started laughing, and Rachel elbowed me. Everyone clapped happily and started whispering among themselves about what a good choice it was because Rachel was so beautiful. Rachel didn't say a word. I thought I saw a smile on her lips, but then again, you could never tell with Rachel.

Most of the girls hung around in the auditorium. But Millie and Julie and I left to find a quiet room to lock ourselves in for several hours of brainstorming. We had a skit to write.

And I had a dare to solve. What none of them knew except Rachel was that I had a raven flapping its ugly black wings inside my head, reminding me that time was quickly running out.

Chapter 24

"R oy called a little while ago," Daddy announced to me that Friday
when I came in from a late afternoon skit-writing marathon.
"Ella Mae's sick. Very sick. Hasn't eaten in three days. Throwing up
everything she puts in her mouth, even liquids. He thinks he's going
to have to take her to the hospital."

Ella Mae had not been at the house all week. I had never known
her to miss three days of work before. "Are you worried about her,
Daddy? Is there something we can do?"

"I'm concerned, Mary Swan. But she's got a lot of her people
looking after her. I told Roy to let me know if she's hospitalized so we
can visit her."

Feeling sobered and unsettled, I asked, "Could you take me to
Grant Park tomorrow morning, since Ella Mae can't do it? Then
maybe Miss Abigail could take me over to see her after we serve lunch.
I'm sure Miss Abigail knows where she lives."

Daddy's face clouded, so I added quickly, "Besides, it's the worst
time of the year for Miss Abigail. She's said it lots of times. She needs
my help. She's counting on me."

Three long weeks had passed since the Day at the Park, since I had
last seen Miss Abigail and Carl and Cassandra and everyone else at Mt.
Carmel. Even as I considered that, I heard Robbie's accusation in my
mind. *"You just go there to see your friend. That's it, isn't it?"*

"No," I argued back. *"I go there to help out. They need me there."*

Daddy took a deep breath and cocked his head with a funny look
on his face. "You know your mother used to help out among the poor.
Ella Mae got her involved too. I was always a bit wary of her being in
those neighborhoods."

"I'm careful, Daddy. I promise."

"You and Jimmy are all I've got, sweetheart."

"I swear it, Daddy. I'll be careful."

"All right, then." He came over and kissed me on the forehead. "Be sure to bundle up. They're announcing snow for tomorrow."

"Oh, Daddy! Thanks!" I threw my arms around him and kissed him hard on the cheek, and he just shook his head and muttered, "Imagine me taking my daughter down to the inner city on the coldest day of the year."

The next morning I had on my heavy coat, a scarf, and gloves and felt very cozy inside the Jaguar with the heat going. Daddy needed no instructions to get to Mt. Carmel.

"So you've been here before?"

"I've lived in this city for over forty years, Mary Swan. I know just about all the nooks and crannies there are."

"Do you want to come in? You could meet Miss Abigail," I suggested as we pulled up in front of the church.

"Not today. You go on in."

"Just hold on a sec, and I'll see if Miss Abigail can bring me home."

I'd never seen so many people in the fellowship hall. Carl was setting up extra tables, and Miss Abigail was adding noodles to a pot of boiling water. She looked tired. When she saw me, she smiled wearily.

"Mary Swan, thank the Lord you're here. We've got a sell-out crowd today."

"Daddy brought me down because Ella Mae's sick, but I was wondering if you could give me a ride home later on." Seeing her rushing about, I didn't dare mention about her taking me to visit Ella Mae. I'd talk about that later.

"Honey, if you can stay all afternoon, that'd be a big help. I've gotta get a baby to the hospital right after lunch is served, and I'm supposed to be handing out blankets and shoes over at the Baptist church on Moreland Avenue. We've got a nasty night coming. See if you can stay, and I'll get you home later this afternoon."

They need me, Robbie. See! They need me. Miss Abigail just said it. My help is needed! I rushed back out to Daddy's car, which several boys were inspecting from afar. "Miss Abigail will bring me home, Daddy.

It'll be later in the afternoon, so don't worry."

"You sure?"

"Positive."

"Take care now, Swan." He grasped my hand hard, and that made me smile.

As I walked back to the church, I thought about Miss Abigail's question, *"Why do you come down here, Mary Swan?"* and my answer, *"To help out and then I feel better when I go back home."* How that had made Miss Abigail laugh! Was that it, then? Did I help out to feel better about myself and to see Carl Matthews?

"Why do you do what you do, Miss Abigail, and how?"

"It's a calling. God shows me how every day and I leave the why to Him."

I stepped back inside the kitchen, taking off my coat, scarf, and gloves and laying them on a chair in the fellowship hall.

"We need a bread-and-fishes miracle today," Miss Abigail murmured to Carl and me as we strained to set the big pots of sauce on the table. "Too many needy folk. Lord Jesus, you provide today, just as you have always done."

And I guess He did, because over the course of the next hour, every last hungry person in that hall was fed. And in between the "Lord bless you's" served up with ladles of sauce, I told Carl about going back to Resthaven.

"Did you find out anything more about your mama?"

"I found out that she had painted a lot more paintings, beautiful, wild, expressive paintings, and that they are at Resthaven. And you and Rachel were right—she painted all three of the paintings in the Raven Dare. But the bad news is . . ." I paused to take an empty pot back into the kitchen and retrieve the last full one. "The bad news is that her doctor thinks she destroyed those three paintings. So that pretty much means I won't solve the Dare."

"But you did solve it!" He slopped spaghetti sauce on Larry's plate and said, "Whatch you doin' here, brotha'?"

Larry shrugged. "Ain't got much food at home. Mama sent me down here with the young'uns."

"Hi, Larry," I said.

"Hi, Mary Swan. You doin' all right today?"

"Yeah. Kind of cold outside, though. Think it might snow?"

Larry shrugged, smiled, and passed through the line with his younger siblings.

Carl returned to our conversation. "You found out the paintin's were destroyed. That should count for somethin'. And you discovered a lot more important things about your mother and found a bunch of her other paintin's and my, my girl. I think you've done a good job. What's a silly dare compared to knowin' 'bout how fine a painter your mother was?"

"Yeah, I know you're right," I admitted. It was the same conclusion I'd come to myself. I changed the subject. "Rachel's been chosen to ride on the float at Mardi Gras, and I'm writing the skit."

"What kinda skit is it?"

"Oh, it's silly and funny and clever, tells the story of a lost girl in Venice, with modern songs and dances woven in too."

"And you're spending your time on that?"

"It's fun. It's the tradition of the school."

"If that don't beat all, Mary Swan. A float and a skit and a dare. Tradition's okay, I s'pect. And you've got talent. I know it. Isn't everybody who can write somethin' ta make people laugh. I imagine you've got insight when you write your silly poems. That's good. But one day, Mary Swan, you know what?" He pointed a ladle dripping with sauce straight at me. "You're gonna do somethin' from your heart, not jus' somethin' that shows your brains. I'm sure of it. You're gonna do somethin' that makes people cry. Somethin' that touches their soul."

That irritated feeling crept onto my cheeks, making them hot, that feeling that Carl was a combination of a hardworking, down-to-earth boy and someone a little bit other-worldly, like one of the wise prophets from the Old Testament. But deep down inside, I hoped he was right.

"Loaves and fishes, children. Our God always provides." Miss Abigail looked tired, but her eyes were still twinkling as she wrapped a hand-knit shawl around her head and neck so that only the end of her long, gray-streaked hair showed against her coat. "Thank you for all your help.

"I've got to get to the hospital with that baby now. I'll be riding with the mother in her car. Carl, can you please go by the house and load up those bags of canned goods that the ladies' circle brought over yesterday? The coats and blankets and shoes are already in the Ford."

"Yes, ma'am."

"And, Mary Swan, you can help Carl hand them out. They'll be waiting for you over at the Baptist church. I'll be back later, Mary Swan, and I'll take you home."

I could hardly believe that Miss Abigail had just handed me an entire afternoon with Carl. "I'll finish in the kitchen," I told him. "You go on and get the stuff at her house."

"All right. See ya in a minute."

I grinned at him. "I'll be ready."

Thirty minutes later, as I slipped into the passenger seat beside Carl in Miss Abigail's old Ford station wagon, he motioned to the overflowing sacks of food and clothes. "She's got her an office at the church, but the truth is, Miss Abigail works out of her car."

A line of people was already waiting for us when we arrived at the other church. Carl opened the tailgate, and I sat inside and handed him whatever it was these people were looking for. I could hardly bear to look into their cold, hungry eyes. But they smiled at us and murmured, "Thank you" as they left with clothes and cans of food. By four o'clock the car was completely empty. Carl had taken note of several men who still needed shoes. I collapsed in the front seat, anxious to start up the car and get the heat going. A few snowflakes landed daintily on the windshield.

"Carl! It's snowing!" Snow in Atlanta was rare, and the few inches we got each year inevitably caused pandemonium to break out in the city. But that day, snow seemed perfectly fitting and somehow romantic.

He shut the tailgate, climbed in the driver's seat, and started the car. "Well, hallelujah! Welcome, snow!" He tapped his fingers on the steering wheel and started singing, "I'm dreamin' of a white Christmas . . ." and humming the rest of the verse.

"You're a little late," I teased.

He ignored me and kept humming.

Then abruptly, interrupting his song, I asked, "Have you ever seen Willie B?"

"The gorilla? Sure. Lots of times."

"Well, I haven't. Could we go see him?"

Willie B was a silverback gorilla who had been captured in the wild and brought to the Atlanta Zoo in 1961 as a two-year-old. He

was affectionately named after the former mayor, William B. Hartsfield. The big primate fascinated everyone, and rumor had it that the
number of patrons of the zoo was increasing thanks to Willie B.

"Now? In the snow?"

"Sure. We're right around the corner from the zoo, aren't we?" I
was thrilled with my idea. Going to the zoo while it snowed sounded
romantic.

"Yeah. It's not far."

"Oh, shucks," I said. "I left my purse at church. I don't have any
money. Never mind, then."

"That's all right. I've got money."

"No. No, Carl. Some other time."

He smiled. "Are you afraid to let me pay for you, girl? I ain't
broke. I can do it."

He parked the car, and we walked to the zoo's entrance. He
bought two tickets and a bag of peanuts. Invigorated by the snow
whirling in the air, I asked Carl the question that had been on the tip
of my tongue for several months now.

"Would you ever take a white girl on a date?" I didn't dare ask
him if this was a date.

"Naw, Mary Swan. I couldn't do it."

"Why not?"

"Isn't done. No way no black man is going to risk his hide right
now, not with all the civil strife we're dealin' with. No way."

"But what if you really liked her? Liked her a lot."

He gave me a half-irritated sideways look. "You ask the craziest
questions, girl. What good would it do you to know about somethin'
that will never be?"

"I don't know. Just trying to understand. After all, this is kind of
like a date, isn't it?"

He tossed me a peanut and gave me a big smile and shook his
head. "You women are all the same," he said. "Wantin' to understand.
No, this isn't a date. Just two friends out at the zoo." He frowned,
studying my face. "What you thinkin', girl?"

"I'm thinking that you're 'risking your hide' right now, being with
me."

"Maybe, but don't think this is a date. Not in my mind, at least."

He came up close to my face and said, almost accusingly, "You have no idea what it's like to be black."

I swallowed hard. "Then tell me, Carl. I want to know."

"You wanna know, huh?" We were standing in front of Willie B's glass cage by now. The gorilla sat perfectly still, nostrils flared, beady black eyes staring from under his prominent forehead, his mouth turned in a half smile as if he were enjoying our conversation. "There's always an underlying sense of guilt when I'm with you, girl. Like I'm betrayin' my people. I'm not just afraid of what whites are thinkin'. It's more what my people are thinkin'. 'White girl don't need you, but the black girls do.' Liking a white girl is selling out to all the progress we blacks are makin'.

"I tell ya, Mary Swan, sometimes I'm afraid to be seen with you. I know as sure as my skin is black that flirtin' with a white girl will bring trouble. It's just not done. I can pretend in my mind, if I want, but I know it won't go nowhere." He gave me a sideways glance and then said, "Ain't that right, Willie B?"

I just kept my eyes fixed on the gorilla's cage, trying to control the pounding in my heart.

"You know when you come to my house, well, it isn't easy afterward. My aunt and my friends see it as me bringin' trouble in the house. They wonder what you're doin' there."

"So why did you agree to come here with me?"

" 'Cause you're so darned stubborn when ya want somethin', girl. And I figure not many people'll be goin' to the zoo when it's snowing." He laughed a bit wryly. "Don't make much sense, does it?"

"I think I understand what you're saying. But Miss Abigail is accepted, isn't she?" I said, a bit desperately.

"That's a whole different story, Mary Swan, and you know it. But she's paid the price a whole lotta times. You ask Miss Abigail. She knows what it feels like to be hated by whites for helping blacks and to be hated by blacks 'cause her skin is just the wrong color."

"Are you more afraid of blacks than whites as far as I'm concerned?"

"Mary Swan, it's a hopeless situation, I tell you. Blacks feel like I'm betrayin' them, and that's bad. But the whites. Well, I've learned my lesson plenty o' times. I don't fight back 'cause like I told you before, if I do, those white boys'll come back later with more of their friends and with knives and guns. As a black, you know better than to fight back or talk back. That's just the rules of the game. The whites aren't afraid because they've got the weight of society on their side. Black wisdom teaches us to shut our mouths and take a few punches 'cause that's better than being dead."

"So I'm just trouble for you, aren't I, Carl?"

He got a pained look on his face. "Naw, I don't mean to say that."

"But it's true. It's what you are saying. A black boy being with a white girl means trouble."

"Yeah, you're right about that, Mary Swan." Then he grinned. "You liked to get me killed at that cemetery, girl. I'll never forget that. Everywhere we go, we stick out like a sore thumb."

We'd left Willie B's cage and were walking toward the reptile building. Not a soul was in sight. I wrapped my arm around his and said, "But I like you, Carl."

He kept on walking. "No, Mary Swan, you don't really like me. You like the *idea* of liking me. But physically there's no way a white girl like you could really be attracted to some big, ugly guy like me."

"You're wrong! You're not big and ugly! You're handsome! You're really, really handsome. Even Rachel says it."

He laughed and shook his head. "Not handsome to a white way of thinkin'." He saw then how much his talk had disturbed me, because he put both of his hands on my shoulders and looked me straight in the eyes. "You're a great girl, Mary Swan. A bit naïve, but mighty fine. And I do consider you a friend. But don't try to be my girlfriend. You stick with Robbie. He's a good guy. Stick with him."

That was the first time that something clicked in my head. I hated understanding it, because it took away hope, but I realized that Carl's reactions and fears were inbred and automatic. They were a black person's natural response to life and the segregation of our society. Any time a black person stepped out of place, he was uneasy.

We watched a cage full of snakes and stuffed our hands in our pockets and blew out frosty puffs of air until Carl said, "We better get back." We rode home in silence.

Miss Abigail had just gotten home herself and looked exhausted. "Carl, will you make a cup of tea for Mary Swan? I'm just going to lie down for a sec."

"Sure. How's the baby?"

She shook her head. "Not good. Got whooping cough. His mama stayed with him at Grady Hospital. I'll go back later in the evening."

Carl looked lovingly at Miss Abigail. "Go on. Go lie down. I'll take care of everything. You just rest." She gave him a grateful nod and went into her bedroom, shutting the door behind her.

"Her life is one emergency after another, isn't it, Carl?" I whispered.

"Seems that way most of the time. But she does okay." He had set out a teacup and said, "Mary Swan, I got to get home and help Aunt Neta. Let Miss Abigail rest a little and help yourself to the tea. Okay?"

"Sure. Thanks." My throat felt tight. I didn't want him to go.

"Thank you for helpin'." He stopped at the door and added, "I won't be here next Saturday, Mary Swan. A few of us are going down to Albany for a peaceful demonstration."

Shocked, I blurted out, "Carl! Don't go! It's too dangerous."

"I'll be careful. You don't worry about me none."

"I do worry. I worry a lot."

But he was already out the door.

Miss Abigail could not have been resting more than fifteen minutes when the phone rang. I ran to the den to answer it, so as not to disturb her. On the other end of the line was the voice of a hysterical child. "Miss Abigail, this here's George! Come quick—Daddy's got a knife and he's trying to kill us!"

I blinked hard, sure I'd heard wrong. "Trying to kill you?"

"Yeah! Me and my sista's!"

Recovering, I said, "George, uh, honey, this is Miss Abigail's friend. Hold on a minute. I'll get her."

"Hurry! Please! Daddy's drunk, and he's got a knife!"

I threw down the phone and dashed into Miss Abigail's room, where she was stretched out on the bed, breathing peacefully. "I'm sorry to bother you, Miss Abigail," I said, my voice sharp with fear. "But there's a little boy on the phone named George, and he says his daddy has a knife and is trying to kill him!"

She sat up with a start and bolted out of bed, saying, "Dear Lord Jesus!" She hurried down the hall and picked up the receiver, listening intently to the child's stricken voice. She closed her eyes, and a look of great pain crossed her face. "George, there's nothing I can do to calm your daddy down, but Jesus can do something, so let's pray." And she started praying right there on the phone. "Lord Jesus, please hear our prayer. Please calm down Mr. Murphy. Please calm his heart so he won't hurt anyone. And give George courage and peace. In Jesus' strong name, amen. George, you take your sisters and hide under the bed. You hear me? Get all the way under the bed. I'll be right there." She hung up the phone and pulled on a pair of shoes. "Come on, Mary Swan, I need you, honey."

My eyes got wide and I started to protest, but she was already halfway out the door. I followed in a daze. The old Ford wagon took us quickly to George's house, and on the way, I didn't say a word. From the way her lips were moving, I could tell that Miss Abigail was keeping up a continual conversation with the Lord, and I certainly didn't want to bother her. As we parked in front of the house, Miss Abigail barked out instructions. "You go back with the children. Keep them safe, Mary Swan. Whatever you have to do."

"Don't you think we should get Carl or some other man to come with us?"

"Oh no. Mr. Murphy doesn't need to see a strong young man at his door. Better for him to see me. He knows me, Mary Swan." And Miss Abigail walked right inside without knocking.

A burly black man with eyes that looked as if they were on fire met us at the door. He reminded me of a bull facing a matador, as I had once seen on TV. But what I noticed most was the long carving knife in his hand.

"Hello, Mr. Murphy." Miss Abigail's voice was poised, calm. "I heard there was a little trouble here."

"Ain't no trouble I cain't handle myself," he raged.

"I thought I might pray with you, Mr. Murphy. You know how Jesus hears our prayers and takes care of things." She began to hum softly some familiar hymn. Mr. Murphy just kept staring at us with that same fire in his eyes, pacing back and forth in the front room.

"Whatcha done brought that white girl with ya for?"

I closed my eyes momentarily, feeling my legs trembling under me. "Mary Swan came over to take care of the children while you and I talk." Miss Abigail gently placed a hand on my back and urged, "Go on, Mary Swan. Go back and tell George and his sisters a story."

I didn't think I could make my legs move. All I could see was that shiny knife and that big, angry man standing between me and the rest of the house.

"Let's sit down over here, Mr. Murphy. Tell me what's troubling you."

"Ain't nothin' troublin' me that no white folk can he'p."

"Jesus is the one with the answers, Mr. Murphy. Not me. Let's just have a little talk with Him." Then she took hold of his muscular arm, the one holding the knife, and led him toward the sagging love seat. She nodded to me, and I knew that was my cue to go to the back of the house.

I kept thinking to myself, *I'm not like you, Miss Abigail. I can't do this. I might get killed. I don't have your faith and I don't know how to pray and I am scared out of my wits. Please let me leave.*

But her prayers for me must have been stronger, because somehow I did walk through the room and down a tiny hall to a bedroom, where three small children were crowded together on the floor on the far side of the bed.

"Hello," I said softly.

They didn't say a word, just stared at me, their eyes filled with terror. I searched my mind for something to say.

"Miss Abigail's meeting with your daddy. Everything is going to be all right now."

They kept staring at me, eyes wide and suspicious.

"I'm Mary Swan. What are your names?"

The little boy was the first to speak. "I's George and this here is my sista' Angeline and my baby sista' Lissa."

"Well, it's good to meet you. Would you like me to tell you a story?" My voice cracked nervously.

No response.

"What about if we sing a song? A song from church." I frantically tried to think of the songs we had sung with Pastor James after our workday. But the only song that came to mind was the one Ella Mae had sung to me for so many years. "Do you know 'Jesus Loves Me'?"

Just then Mr. Murphy's thunderous voice broke out in a string of curse words, and the children huddled even closer together. I moved quickly to their side of the bed and joined them on the floor, enclosing my arms around them and singing off-key in a quavering voice, "Jesus loves me, this I know, for the Bible tells me so. Little ones to Him belong. They are weak, but He is strong. Yes, Jesus loves me. Yes, Jesus loves me. Yes, Jesus loves me, the Bible tells me so." Slowly the children joined in, singing very softly and very hesitantly. The voices in the den rose again, and I wondered, terrified, what in the world I would do if Mr. Murphy went after Miss Abigail with a knife.

"Maybe we should pray," I whispered. "George, could you pray?"

George could not have been more than seven or eight. He gave me a solemn look and said, "Miss Abigail's always the one who prays first."

"I see." So I was stuck. It had to be me. I decided I'd just try to imitate Miss Abigail. Hugging the children close to me, I closed my eyes and said, "Dear God. I mean, dear Lord. Please help us now. Help Mr. Murphy calm down. Help George and Angeline and Lissa not to be afraid. Amen."

It was not a very convincing prayer, and as soon as I pronounced the amen, George remarked, "You's s'posed ta say 'In Jesus' strong name, amen.' "

"Oh, I'm sorry," I said, flustered. "But I think God understood what I meant."

That seemed to satisfy the children, but I was sweating hard, feeling the pulse in my head, and wishing with all my heart that I had some great idea about what to do next. I started humming any tune that came to mind. Suddenly the children smiled and giggled into their hands while George remonstrated, "You's hummin' 'Rock Around the Clock.' That ain't no song we's ever sung in church, ma'am." A little of the tension dissipated. No sound was coming from the den.

Then we saw through the sheer torn curtains the flash of a red light going round and round. "The poleece!" George whispered excitedly. He ran to the window and pressed his nose on the pane while his two younger sisters cowered in my arms.

Indeed it was the police, and soon I heard Miss Abigail's voice calling to me, "Mary Swan, bring the children out here. Everything is going to be okay." A rather repentant-looking Mr. Murphy gave each of the children a hug and followed a policeman out the door. Immediately Miss Abigail gathered the children around her and announced matter-of-factly, "Your daddy is going to be fine. He's agreed to stay with some nice people for a few days who want to help him. And that means I get the privilege of having you spend a few days with me! How will that be?"

Big smiles erupted on their small faces as we went about gathering pajamas and pillows and three raggedy stuffed animals. George and his sisters filed out to Miss Abigail's station wagon with me, arms piled high with their belongings, following behind. The children climbed into the backseat of the station wagon, chattering excitedly about the snow that was falling in the darkness.

Miss Abigail whispered to me, "Mr. Murphy agreed to get help. They'll be keeping him for some time down at the jail. I'm afraid I won't be able to take you home tonight, Mary Swan. I'll get Carl to drive you."

For some reason that made my heart beat faster than it had when Mr. Murphy was swinging his knife at me. "I can stay and help you if you need."

"I'll be fine, Mary Swan. The question is, are you all right?"

"I think . . . I think I am, but it was awful. I was scared out of my mind. I thought he might kill you or me."

Miss Abigail took a deep breath. "Yes, so did I for a moment." I shot her a surprised glance. She looked more ragged than the children's dolls. "Thank you for your help, Mary Swan. I'm sorry you got caught in the middle of it, but you did a fine job. A fine job."

I wanted to burst into tears and tell her how I hadn't known what to do or how to pray. I wanted to beg her to tell me how she had had the guts to go to that house. But Miss Abigail was worn thin, and she still had a long evening ahead of her, feeding, bathing, and reassuring three fragile kids.

She called Carl right away while I took the children into her kitchen. "Are you hungry, kids?"

"Yes, ma'am. We's starvin'," Lissa volunteered.

I opened several cabinets until I found a box of macaroni and cheese. I didn't know how to cook much, but I figured I could pour a box of noodles into boiling water and stir some milk into the little packet of cheese sauce. The children sat silently at the big rectangular table, and I hoped they couldn't see the tears welling up in my eyes.

Snow glistened on the street as Carl started the car. I groaned, suddenly remembering my purse. "Can we stop by the church for just a sec to get my purse?"

"Sure. Let me get the keys from Miss Abigail." When he got back, he commented, "Miss Abigail told me about the time at the Murphys'. You okay?"

"I guess." I couldn't look at him. "It was awful. Awful. Does Miss Abigail get calls like that all the time?"

"Happens right often. Yep."

"Have you ever gone with her?"

"Oh yeah, Mary Swan. I been in similar situations more often than I'd like ta remember."

"And you aren't scared?"

"Sure I'm scared. But I know the Lord is with us."

"How do you know?"

"I've seen God at work bunches of times. Calmin' folks down, settlin' a brawl, givin' us ideas when we had long since run outta 'em."

"Well, He didn't give me any ideas, Carl. Maybe He doesn't speak to people in Buckhead."

Carl smiled at that. He'd parked the car in front of the church. "I've heard plenty of stories about a whole lotta fine people down where you live. Ladies in that big Baptist church on Peachtree wake up in the night, knowin' they need to pray hard for Miss Abigail. And those fine white ladies get down on their knees by their bed and beg the Lord Jesus to protect Miss Abigail, to protect the children, the families. Happens all the time, Mary Swan. Why, I betcha someday you'll find out that somebody over in Buckhead was prayin' for y'all tonight."

I got a knot in my throat and fought back the tears.

"Miss Abigail calls it warfare—spiritual warfare. She's always quoting that verse in the Bible that says our battle isn't against flesh and blood but against evil forces in the heavenly places. Against Satan."

"I don't know about evil forces and Satan, but I know I was scared. Scared to death. I still am."

"It is scary, Mary Swan, but like I said, I'd be a whole lot more scared if I didn't know that the Lord was watchin' over us and that He was a lot stronger than a drunken papa with a butcher's knife."

"You really believe that, don't you, Carl? I don't. I just cried out some words that sounded like a prayer, but I didn't believe that some God was big enough to calm down that man. I thought he might kill

Miss Abigail. And I'm not convinced it was God who stopped him." It felt good admitting my unbelief.

"That's okay, Mary Swan. If God is God, He'll get you convinced, one way or 'nuther."

"You really believe that?"

"Sure. We all need a Savior, Mary Swan. You know what Miss Abigail says?"

"What?"

"She says the ground is all even at the foot of the cross. Ain't no rich or poor, just a lot of needy folks. Folks needin' the grace of the Lord Jesus. She says that sometimes it's even sadder to see a rich person's pain. Some rich folk got problems more severe than the poor folks down here. You know why? 'Cause the poor folks've got street smarts. They know how to survive. But the rich folks, they ain't never had to fight to live. Miss Abigail and those other white ladies, when they come prayin', they pray for the down-and-out and the up-and-out."

"The up-and-out?"

"People who've got everything on the outside but are hurting mighty bad on the inside."

That's me, I thought flatly as Carl handed me the keys to the church and said, "I'll wait for you here."

My purse was sitting right where I'd left it on a folding chair in the fellowship hall. I picked it up and started toward the door. But something else was tugging at my heart.

Not knowing why, I went upstairs and entered the darkened sanctuary. The stained-glass windows reflected a little of the light from the street so that shadows danced on every wall. I stared up at the plain wooden cross hanging in the alcove behind the pulpit and burst into tears. Something about the way it hung there in the dark, in the silence, sent a chill through me, and I heard Carl's words in my mind. *"The ground is all even at the foot of the cross."* I fell to my knees, right there on the floor, in front of those old wooden pews, beside the pulpit where Pastor James had spoken to us after the Day at the Park.

With tears streaming down my face, I choked out my words. "I don't know what I need, really, God. I guess I need you, but in some way different from just seeing you as high and holy and far off. So I'm doing like Carl said. I'm just asking you to come into my life. I want what he has and what Cassandra has and especially what Miss Abigail has. I want to be able to pray and know that you are hearing me.

"I was so very, very scared this evening. Oh, God, that's when I saw that I have no idea who you are, not really. I had no faith. But I want it. I want you. I want you to take my life, to forgive me for all the times I've messed up, like Cassandra would say. I want you to be in control, God. Whatever that means." I squeezed my eyes shut even tighter, because it hurt somewhere deep down inside to admit these things.

Then I looked up at the cross and whispered, "Thank you for this cross. Thank you for hanging there, Jesus, and for dying and coming back to life. And thank you that you did it for blacks and whites and Jews and Protestants and Catholics and everyone else. It's gonna take me a long time to figure all this out, God, but please, help me."

Something suddenly felt so completely natural about pouring out my heart to this unseen Being. "I want to be free. Like Miss Abigail says. Like you said yourself, Jesus. You said that the truth would make me free. So if you are the Truth, I guess that means I just want you."

I fumbled in my purse for a Kleenex and blew my nose, but I stayed on my knees. "And show me what else to do about Mama's paintings. Poor, poor Mama. And how to love Daddy right. And help Ella Mae get better. And show me what to do about Robbie and Carl and all the other things that are knocking around inside. I am so tired of finding out bad news, God. Will you please just help me?"

I must have stayed there for another ten minutes, on my knees in front of that cross, just weeping, like my heart was completely broken in two. I wondered if that was how God worked. Maybe He let your heart be broken until you thought you couldn't hurt any worse, and then He let you understand a tiny bit of His great love, which was almost as piercing as the pain. When I got stiffly up off of my knees, there was this amazing sense of peace that flooded through my whole body.

"You okay, Mary Swan?" Carl's voice came out of nowhere.

I let out a scream that died down quickly into a whimper when I saw him seated on the second pew. "How long have you been here?" I asked, suddenly ashamed.

"Long enough to know that you've been doing some business with the Lord." A distance of about five feet separated us. He got up, came to me, put his strong arms around me and squeezed me tightly. "That's mighty fine, girl. That's mighty fine." Then he kissed me gently on the forehead and whispered, "I sure do care about you a lot, Mary Swan." He took my hand and led me down the stairs, saying, "Come on, girl. I'm gonna get you home before your daddy starts to worry." And that pure, peaceful feeling flooded through me again.

We drove to Buckhead in silence, watching the snow land on the windshield to be brushed away by the wipers. The streets were shiny, and a little of the snow had stuck to the ground. "You gonna be okay, Mary Swan?" Carl said as he approached my house.

"Yes, I think so."

"I'll be prayin' for you, girl."

"Oh yes, Carl. Please pray for me. I don't know what I've just done."

He stopped at the bottom of my driveway. "You just turned your life over to the God of the universe. Best thing you could ever do, Mary Swan." Then he patted my back and gave me a hug across the seat, the kind of hug a big brother might give his sister. And he left me standing in front of my house with the snow falling gently on my face.

Chapter 25

S omehow it mattered greatly that the snow was still on the ground the next morning when I woke up. It mattered that the sun had barely risen and that I, in my sweatshirt and jeans and wool pea jacket, tiptoed into Mama's *atelier* and retrieved an easel and a palette and an empty canvas and left the house while Daddy and Jimmy were still asleep.

The path to the Swan House was dusted in snow, so that the leaves poked their pointed edges through the white. " 'The woods are lovely, dark and deep,' " I quoted aloud as my boots made soft imprints on the snow-covered leaves. " 'But I have promises to keep. And miles to go before I sleep. And miles to go before I sleep.' "

Promises! *The truth will make you free.* That was God's promise to me. And I had made a promise to Him too. Some sort of surging excitement welled up in me as I remembered my prayer on my knees at Mt. Carmel. "I put my trust in you, God." It came out in a whisper. Then I lifted my face and peered through the bare trees to the white-washed sky and yelled, "I believe!"

When I came out at the bottom of the long yard leading up to the mansion, I took a deep breath and said out loud, "Thank you, God!" The whole long avenue of grass was covered in white, and nothing had spoiled it. Not the imprints of squirrels, or the heat of the sun leaving little pockets of grass where the snow had melted.

I stood the wooden easel out in the middle of the yard near the street, where the wrought-iron fence kept would-be visitors out. I had on my woolen gloves, the ones I'd cut the tips of the fingers out of so that I could play the flute in the raw night air for an outdoor performance the year before. I blew out breaths of frosty air, tightened the scarf around my neck, and began to paint. This is what Mama did at Resthaven, I thought. She painted in what Cezanne called *plein air*, when the light affected everything you saw. I had never painted outside, and certainly not at eight o'clock in the morning, but this day I felt I could have floated to paradise and back. Free! Free and pristine as the untouched snow in front of me.

Mama had written that she tried not to paint subjects, but rather impressions of light. I knew the Swan House by heart and had sketched it dozens of times from this very perspective. But today, I just painted what I felt: the frost in the pure air, the undisturbed beauty of the snow, the majesty of the mansion, which stood unchanged under its new white winter coat. These things I painted without knowing how to make them real on my canvas. I simply knew that I *had* to paint this morning. I had to recall in my own feeble way what rebirth felt like. I wouldn't transform some poet's masterpiece to make it mine. No, this had to be from me, from my heart, as Carl had said.

And so I painted, teeth chattering and goose pimples breaking out on my arms and legs and tingles running down my spine. I painted my representation of what it meant to be free.

Getting home was not easy, holding the easel, palette, and paints in one arm with the wet canvas turned away from me in the other. By now it was almost nine o'clock, and Daddy would be sitting at the kitchen table sipping his coffee and eating a piece of toast with jelly on it while he read the *Atlanta Constitution*. So I avoided the house, traipsing instead through the backyard to where the swimming pool lay empty of water. I quickly stashed my painting and easel and paints in one of the changing rooms in the pool house. Then I walked back to the house and came in the back door.

"Hi, Daddy!"

"Mary Swan! For goodness' sakes! Where have you been? I thought you were still asleep."

"I've been outside walking, Daddy. Isn't it absolutely beautiful?"

"Yes, I suppose it is, Mary Swan. Very rare to have snow stick like this."

"It's like God's giving us a new start, Daddy."

He looked perplexed with that comment, so I just hugged him tight and said, "I'm going to get ready for church." And I raced up the two sets of stairs, still feeling the tingle of cold in my fingers and on my cheeks.

I had never before participated in the church service at St. Philip's as I did that day. When I knelt on the prayer bench in front of the pew, I really prayed, and when we read from the prayer book, the words seemed to speak directly to me. I listened to the sermon and realized, perhaps for the first time, that the dean was preaching about the same Jesus that Pastor James and Miss Abigail talked about. The form was different. No one swayed with the music, and Dean Hardman did not yell out any "amens" from the pulpit. But the service was filled with a radiant and reverent adoration, which laced itself around me so that I felt something holy going on in that cathedral.

Without quite knowing why, I found Robbie out by the gardens after the service. "I have to talk to you sometime," I said, stuffing my hands in the pockets of my coat, barely daring to look at him.

Robbie narrowed his eyes in a suspicious, hurt way. "What about, Mary Swan?"

"About things that are happening to me. Strange, good things."

He looked hesitant, reluctant, so I continued. "I don't feel like I ever really got to explain things to you, Robbie, and I want to. I need to. You deserve that."

He shuffled from one foot to the other. "I guess I owe you that, Mary Swan. We could go to the Varsity tonight, just like good ole times." He grinned sadly. "Guess we'd have to keep the top up on the convertible tonight."

"Yeah, pretty neat, all the snow, huh?"

He nodded, scuffing his tasseled leather loafers through the white powder.

"I'd really like to do that, Robbie."

"Okay. I'll pick you up at seven o'clock, Mary Swan."

When he turned and walked away, I couldn't resist squatting down and making a snowball from the powder. I hurled it at him, but it was already breaking in the air, so that when it hit his back, it simply dusted his coat with snow.

He turned around then, a mischievous grin on his face, scooped up a handful of snow, and said in a playful, menacing way, "You're asking for it now, young lady!" He ran over, grabbed me around the waist with one hand, while stuffing snow down the back of my coat with the other.

I shook all over, squealing as the snow pricked me on my neck. Then we just stood there, breathing hard and laughing at each other and wondering what to do with the way our hearts were melting, as the snow was doing down my back.

"You'll never guess what happened to me yesterday," I told Rachel as we sat curled like contented cats in front of the fireplace in her den, warming ourselves after our ride on our frisky mares.

"Something's always happening to you, Swan." She didn't seem very interested. "Well, spit it out."

"I became a Christian."

"Right. You were already a Christian, you nincompoop."

"No, I mean I've become a real one."

There was this silence as pragmatic Rachel turned that over in her mind. "What in the world do you mean?"

"I don't know, Rachel. But something has happened inside me. Not anything to do with going to church. Something happened in my heart."

"Oh great, Swan," she said sarcastically. "You're not gonna get weird on me, are you? Like one of Mama's friends who keeps telling us that we Jews are going straight to hell."

"Gosh, I hope not." I felt a tinge of regret. "It's just that I've been thinking about what Miss Abigail says about God and freedom and stuff."

"Don't go getting religion on me, Swan. Please."

"It's not religion. It's something else."

"What?"

"I don't know exactly. Faith. I think it's faith."

She rolled her eyes.

I brightened. "No, really. Let me explain. Last night when Carl brought me home, I told him I didn't know what I'd done. And he said this, 'You jus' turned your life over to the God of the universe. Best thing you could ever do, Mary Swan!' "

Rachel wrinkled her brow. "Carl said that? Wait a minute, Swan. What was Carl doing bringing you home last night?"

"It's a long story." I beamed.

"All right, then. I'll put on JP and you can tell me your story." She sounded irritated, but I could tell she was dying to know every last tidbit of my adventure.

So with Jean-Pierre Rampal's flute serenading us and the warm fire blazing in the fireplace, I burst out with my story. "It started with Ella Mae being sick. Real sick. So Daddy took me down to Grant Park. Can you believe it? Daddy? And then it was snowing and Miss Abigail had to get a baby to the hospital and the church was jammed with hungry people, so we finished late and so she asked Carl and me to hand out all the clothes and food over at the Baptist church on Moreland Avenue. So we did, and then afterward Carl and I went to the zoo and he paid for me because I'd forgotten my purse and we had this really neat talk and then I went back to Miss Abigail's and she was lying down because she was tired, and the phone rang and I answered it so she wouldn't be disturbed and it was this kid screaming on the phone that his daddy had a knife and was trying to kill him. So I woke up Miss Abigail and she ran over to the house, and I went with her, and the man was drunk out of his mind, waving a butcher's knife and Miss Abigail told him she was going to pray with him, if you can believe that, and he was mad as all get out and even madder to see me there, but Miss Abigail told me to go take care of the kids. And I was petrified out of my mind. But I went to the bedroom and stayed with the three kids who were hiding by the bed and I tried to pray. But I didn't know how and so we sang and stuff and pretty soon the police arrived and carted off the dad, and Miss Abigail took the kids to her house, so she couldn't bring me home like she had promised, and she asked Carl to do it. But I'd forgotten my purse at church, so Carl took me back there and I got it but, for some strange reason, I couldn't leave the church so I went into the sanctuary and that's when I saw the cross." I paused, out of breath, and not at all sure how to explain the next part to Rachel. She had scooted closer to me and looked more astounded with every detail I gave.

"Well, go on, Swan. What happened?"

"Something big and important. And nothing. Nothing that you could see. But I stared at that cross and I started crying and then talking out loud to God."

"What were you saying?" She was dumbfounded.

"Stuff. I don't know."

"You have to know what you said. You're not making sense."

"Okay, I'll tell you. But it's hard to explain, so please don't laugh."

"No laughing, Swan. I swear."

"Carl had been talking about how he wasn't afraid in scary times because he knew God was with him. And I asked him how he knew. And then he started saying how the ground was even at the foot of the cross, which means, in his words, that everybody needs a Savior. That's exactly how he put it. The rich and the poor. Everybody. Which of course Miss Abigail has always said. And Cassandra had told me that when she cried out to God for forgiveness, well, she'd felt clean and peaceful because she knew that Jesus was in control and He could take care of all her problems and help her choose the right things in life. Something like that." I eyed Rachel. "You following me?"

"Sort of," she said with a strange look on her face.

"So I guess I just combined all that information and told God that I needed Him and that I didn't have faith like Miss Abigail and Carl. When I was in that drunk man's house, I'd seen that I didn't have one bit of faith. But suddenly I wanted to believe so bad. And so I begged God to set me free and forgive me for the way I've been and to please take control of my life." I stopped suddenly. "Do you think I'm crazy, Rach? Was that a big mistake?"

"You are a crazy lunatic, girl, no doubt about it." But she smiled almost sympathetically. "So what's supposed to happen?"

"I think I'm supposed to feel clean and that God is supposed to start showing me what to do."

"Well, do you and has He?"

"I do feel clean, brand-new, like the snow. That's for sure," I said brightly. Then I nibbled my fingernail. "But I don't really know what God wants me to do next."

Rachel didn't say anything for a few minutes. We both just stared at the fire crackling in the fireplace. Finally she sighed. "All I can say is don't drag me into it. Don't go complaining to me if weird things start happening to you."

"But, Rachel, who in the world will I talk to if not you? I have to talk to you. I have to."

"Okay, talk, then, if you want. But don't you dare ever think I'm going to swallow that stuff."

"Of course not," I said meekly.

"Good. 'Cause the way I see it, it's something to make you feel better. But it's not truth; it's just a bunch of sentiments."

"But how do you know?"

"I just know. You're off on cloud nine, Swan. I'm the realistic, practical one. Remember? I'm the one who figures things out. You're the dreamer."

"Then let me dream!"

"Dream then, nincompoop! Dream. But don't call it truth."

"But what if it is truth? Miss Abigail says it's true. She says the truth will make you free. You've got to admit there's something special about her."

Rachel shook her blond mane, and I could tell she was getting mad. "Mary Swan Middleton, if you're so sure this 'faith,' as you call it, is real, if you believe God is real and that He loves the individual, then answer me this question. Where was He when Carl's mama died? Or when your mother died and a hundred other people from Atlanta died, or when all my mother's family, all of them . . ." Here she got choked up. "When they all went to the gas chambers? Where was He? Did He hear their prayers? All the faith in the world won't bring back my family or your mother or anyone else on that awful plane. All the faith in the world can't make sense out of the folly of life. It's much better to believe in nothing. Then you're not disappointed, Swan. You're even occasionally pleasantly surprised."

I had a huge lump in my throat, and my cheeks were burning. "Rachel, you don't have to believe what I do. That's not what I'm asking. I'm just begging you to still be my friend. Even if I do something really stupid, still be my friend, okay?"

She got a great, sly grin on her face, and her blue-gray eyes became slits. "Oh, Swan. Don't worry about that. You've already done so many stupid things, and that didn't bother me a bit."

I stuck out my tongue, and then we both laughed.

"Good. Then that's settled. Now let's get to the important stuff. What in the world is going on with Carl and Robbie?"

"You really want to know?"

"Of course I do."

"I don't have any idea." I glanced at my watch and jumped up. "It's four-fifteen, Rach! I've got to get home. Millie and Julie are coming to my house at four-thirty so we can finish writing the skit. You want to come along? I'll tell you about the guys on the way."

While Julie and Millie and I hammered out the last lines of the skit, Rachel leafed through my anthology of Shakespeare, reading *The Merchant of Venice*. And after the other girls had left she stuck the book in front of my nose and said, "Here, Swan. Read this. A speech by Shylock."

Shylock was the main character in the play. I gave her a questioning look.

"Go on. Read it," she urged. "Read it out loud. It's the part when Shylock is complaining to Salerio about the Christian Antonio." She said it as if I knew exactly what she was talking about. But I'd never read *The Merchant of Venice*. All I had to do was create a skit using some idea sparked by the title. Our Mardi Gras skit had nothing to do with the real Shakespeare play.

I shrugged and began to read the speech out loud.

"If it will feed nothing else, it will feed my revenge. He hath disgraced me and hindr'd me half a million, laughed at my losses, mocked at my gains, scorned my nation, thwarted my bargains, cooled my friends, heated mine enemies and what's his reason? I am a Jew. Hath not a Jew eyes? Hath not a Jew hands, organs, dimensions, senses, affections, passions? Fed with the same food, hurt with the same weapons, subject to the same diseases, healed by the same means, warmed and cooled by the same winter and summer as a Christian? If you prick us, do we not bleed? If you tickle us, do we not laugh? If you poison us, do we not die? And if you wrong us, shall we not revenge? If we are like you in the rest, we will resemble you in that. If a Jew wrong a Christian, what is his humility? Revenge. If a Christian wrong a Jew, what should his sufferance be by Christian example? Why revenge! The villainy you teach me I will execute and it shall go hard but I will better the instruction."

I closed the anthology and stared at Rachel. "Is this some hint to me because I told you I'd become a real Christian? Are you mad at me?"

"No, Swan! Of course not. It's not you. It's me. It's what boils up in me sometimes, only Shakespeare put it a lot better than I ever could. And I'll bet it's what boils up in Carl lots of times too. If you just substituted the word black every time you saw the word Jew in the speech, well, there you'd have it."

"Maybe you're right." I shook my head in wonder. "How in the world did you find this quote anyway? We've never studied this play in class."

"I just read it a little while ago while y'all were working."

"You read the whole *Merchant of Venice* in an hour and a half?"

"It's not that long, Swan. Anyway, enough of all this philosophy. Tell me about Carl and Robbie." And, relieved to leave religion and race alone for a while, we drifted comfortably onto the subject of boys.

It was six-thirty when Rachel left, satisfied that she was filled in on my latest escapades. I felt a quiver of excitement at the prospect of being with Robbie, although I wasn't at all sure what I would say to him. As I started up the stairway, Jimmy called to me from the kitchen, "Swan, Daddy wants to see you." Jimmy's freckled face was drained of color.

"What's the matter?"

"Daddy'll tell you."

I found Daddy sitting at his desk in a daze. "What is it?"

"Roy just called. He took Ella Mae to the hospital yesterday, and they did some tests. They found a brain tumor, Mary Swan. They need to operate immediately. And they aren't sure she's going to make it." His face was ashen, and I was sure that I saw a tear on his cheek.

"When are they operating, Daddy?"

"Tomorrow morning."

"Then we have to go see her now! We have to."

So I never went to the Varsity with Robbie. Instead, after calling him and canceling our date, I found myself once again at Grady Hospital. Roy came out into the hall to greet Daddy and Jimmy and me, his bloodshot eyes filled with worry.

"Mighty fine of y'all ta come down heah. Ya go on in and see her 'fore the nurse says anythin.' And don't ya mind Ella Mae. She don't always make sense o' what she says these days."

We knocked lightly on the door and opened it. Ella Mae gave a weak smile when we came into the room. Her hair had been shaved in preparation for surgery, and she had dark, dark circles under her eyes, as though she hadn't slept in weeks. I barely recognized her.

"Ella Mae, we sure will be thinking of you," Daddy said, patting her hand softly.

"Thank ya, Mista Middleton. Mighty kind of ya ta come."

Jimmy stood at the foot of the bed, looking miserable, his hands thrust into the pockets of his jeans.

I sat beside the bed and asked her, "Are you scared, Ella Mae?"

"Ain't scared a bit, chile. One way or anuther, everythin's gonna be all right. Like the apostle Paul done said, if'n I stay, I'm with the Lawd and if'n I go, I'll be with Him, so much the betta."

"You're gonna be okay, Ella Mae, I'm sure of it."

"Mebbe so, chile." She closed her eyes, and her breathing became heavy. I looked up at Daddy, and he motioned with his eyes to the door. But just as I was about to stand up, she said, "I don't reckon I've ever really helped somebody jus' by the good things that done happened to me, Mary Swan. Seems like it's the hard, sad, break-yore-heart things where I thought I might not git through it, where I had ta grab on ta God, done been the most he'pful ta others, 'cuz I know'd how bad they was a'hurtin' and I also knowed that God was real. Might be one of those times now, if'n the good Lawd wants. We'll jus' have ta wait and see."

Her monologue, so unexpected, stated so calmly, caught me off guard, speechless. It was Jimmy who managed to squeak out, "Do you feel bad, Ella Mae?"

"I'm fine, chile. Don't ya worry none about me."

"But we do worry, Ella Mae," I said insistently. "We don't want you to suffer."

"I ain't afraid of sufferin', Mary Swan. Don't you be afraid either, chil'un. No sir. The Lawd don't neva' waste our pain." I could hear Miss Abigail saying the same thing. "You know what the Good Book says—God uses the foolish things in this world to confound the wise. I ain't afraid ta suffa', Mary Swan. Ain't one bit afraid. You read what the apostle Paul done said. He said he learned to be content, whateva' life handed him. That's what we gotta do, sweetheart. Learn to be content. I'll be okay."

I could tell that all her talking had tired her out. "We'd best be going, Mary Swan," Daddy cautioned.

"I'll be right there."

Jimmy mumbled, "Good night, Ella Mae," and Daddy said, "You get some rest now," and they both left the room. Then I leaned in close and said, "Something happened to me yesterday, Ella Mae," and quickly I told her the whole story.

Her lips turned up in a barely visible smile, and she looked as though she was going to cry. She whispered, "Mighty fine news, Mary Swan. That's the best thing you could tell me right now, chile. Mighty fine."

"God won't let anything happen to you, Ella Mae. Not now. I know it."

"Guess you'll havta talk to Him 'bout that, chile." She closed her eyes, and I bent over and kissed her on the cheek.

"I'll be praying for you, Ella Mae."

"You do that, Mary Swan. That'll be mighty fine."

We didn't say a word on the way home. It was drizzling, the streets gray and slushy. Finally when we turned onto Andrews Drive, Jimmy blurted out, "Do you think she's going to die, Daddy? Is Ella Mae gonna die?"

"It's a serious operation, Jimmy. But she's got a fine surgeon who'll be operating on her. I made sure of that."

"I don't think I could stand it if Ella Mae and Mama both died in the same year," he whimpered.

"Let's not think about that now, children. We've got to hope for the best."

Suddenly I had an idea. "Can you take us by church, Daddy? Just for a sec. They'll be having Evensong. I want to say a prayer for Ella Mae."

"Yeah, that's a good idea. Me too," Jimmy echoed.

We slipped silently into the back pews of the cathedral and waited for the service to end. Then Jimmy and I knelt down on the prayer bench as the others silently filed out the back.

I whispered to Jimmy, "Close your eyes and I'll pray." Then I said, "Please, God, don't let Ella Mae die. Please don't. Please keep her safe. Amen."

Jimmy and I got up off our knees, and the warm glow of the church lit up our faces, and we were both crying. So I put my arm around his shoulders, and we inched out into the aisle slowly toward Daddy, who was standing at the back of the sanctuary with his eyes closed and his head bent down to his chest.

None of us felt like eating dinner, although Daddy did fix several peanut butter and jelly sandwiches. I sat with them at the round oak table and twisted a bright linen napkin in my hands. "What time are they operating?"

"Early in the morning."

"And when will we know if . . . if it was successful?"

"I told Roy I'd meet him at the hospital after work. We'll talk to the surgeon. I'll call you here as soon as I know anything."

I nodded numbly. Jimmy and Daddy went into the den to watch something on TV, and I was thankful for the chance to escape to the *atelier*. As soon as I had closed the door behind me, I started bawling my eyes out. My painting from that morning of the Swan House in snow sat on the easel, right where I'd placed it after having recovered it from the pool house earlier in the afternoon. Only this morning my faith had been so very pure and unspoiled.

Tonight, I wondered if it would slowly melt and disappear without a trace, like the snow from yesterday. Seeing Ella Mae in her fragile condition had scared me. Scared me down to the bone. I wondered if my own fragile faith was enough to believe her through this operation. Now that I was a real Christian, maybe I could bargain better with God. Maybe my prayers had more weight. Surely that was true. But I had a sinking feeling that God was not someone you bargained with. I wished at that moment that I could pick up my phone and call Miss Abigail.

Miss Abigail! Of course! She needed to know about Ella Mae. Had anyone told her? How did the grapevine work in Grant Park, in the whole of the inner city? Was Pastor James even now leading his people in prayer for her? Did Carl know? If only I could call Miss Abigail and ask her my questions. But I didn't even know her last name. She had always been simply Miss Abigail, like an angel who showed up when you needed her. There was no one to call.

"So I guess it's just between you and me, God." This I said out loud, picking up the white Bible from where it sat on top of the scrapbooks from Resthaven. I opened it randomly, glanced at some verses from a book called Jeremiah, and closed it back.

"God, I don't know any better how to talk to you today than yesterday, but I'll just tell you this much. I want to do the right things and help people and love my family, and I want to understand who you are. But more than anything else, more than Robbie or Carl or paintings or Resthaven or Mardi Gras or the Raven Dare or anything else I care about, what I want right now is for you to keep Ella Mae alive. Alive. Please, God! I don't think I could bear it if Ella Mae died too. So take all of these things, please, God, and just do something."

I saw Ella Mae lying in that hospital bed, her black hair gone with her strength. She had looked so vulnerable.

Vulnerable, yes, but also something else. Peaceful. Absolutely calm. More than that. What was it? Ah yes. Ready. Ella Mae was ready, even eager, to see her Savior. She truly believed that dying for her meant eternal life in heaven, a place that was good and safe and without pain.

So was this just one more selfish petition from spoiled Mary Swan? Ella Mae didn't seem one bit afraid of surgery or of dying.

Bible in hand, I left the *atelier*, climbing the steps to my room. I didn't know how to read the Bible, but Miss Abigail had told me to start with the gospels. I changed into my pajamas and got into bed. Then, since I'd already read a little of the gospel of St. John, I decided I'd begin with it. I found the page number listed in the table of contents and turned to it in the New Testament. I read until my eyes grew heavy, read it the way I read poetry for Mrs. Alexander's class, all snuggled under my covers. In fact, the gospel of John reminded me of some of the literature I'd been studying, filled with imagery and metaphors. Beautiful things that Jesus said, and shocking, hard things as well.

What struck me the most as I read through those chapters was all the names Jesus gave to himself. He said He was the Light of the World, the Bread of Life, the Living Water, the True Vine, the Good Shepherd, the Way, the Truth, and the Life. And every time I read one of those names, my heart got this feeling of hope inside. Toasty, cuddle-up-and-let-yourself-be-hugged kind of hope. Better than a kiss from Robbie or a hug from Carl or an afternoon with Daddy. Hope.

I didn't quite get to the end of the gospel because my eyes were too heavy, but I did go back and read one verse right before I fell asleep. It was something Jesus told His disciples, and it reminded me of Ella Mae. *"Let not your heart be troubled: ye believe in God, believe also in me. In my Father's house are many mansions: if it were not so, I would have told you. I go to prepare a place for you. And if I go and prepare a place for you, I will come again, and receive you unto myself; that where*

I am, there may ye be also." And a few lines farther down, He said, *"I am the way, the truth, and the life: no man cometh unto the Father, but by me."*

There was the verse where Jesus said He was the truth. That made sense to me and went hand in hand with the other verse about the truth making me free. But as I fell asleep, it was the verse about the mansions that comforted me most. Jesus was preparing a place for us. At least Ella Mae was right about that. One way or another, she was going to be with Him.

Chapter 26

G od must have heard my prayers and those of a lot of other people, because Ella Mae survived the surgery. The surgeon couldn't
remove the whole twisting mass of the tumor, but he got a large part
of it, and it took him almost seven hours. Ella Mae stayed in intensive
care for a week with no one allowed to visit her but family. I wanted
to tell those doctors and nurses at Grady Hospital that Ella Mae was
part of *my* family, that she was like my second mother and since my
real mother was dead, well, couldn't I please go to visit, but Daddy
said no. I think he did go down there nearly every day and talk to Roy
and the doctors. He never told me how bad it was, but he said things
like, "She's way too weak to see anyone. She's gonna need a lot of
time to recover. Give her time," so that Jimmy and I got the distinct
feeling that she was not out of danger yet.

When I got home from school on Wednesday, I let Muffin into the
house. He jumped up on me ecstatically, licking my hands. "Down,
boy!" I commanded, irritated. I needed another living presence in the
house. Jimmy was at basketball practice and wouldn't be home for
another hour. The house was too big without Ella Mae. I wandered
into the breakfast room, set my books down on the oak table, and
grabbed an apple from off the fruit platter in the center of the table.
But I had no appetite.

I toyed briefly with the idea of starting my French homework, but
memorizing irregular verbs did nothing to lift my mood. I scratched
Muffin behind the ears and thought about the Mardi Gras skit. We had
titled it "The Menace in Venice," and all the parts had been assigned
today. I was to be the narrator. Everyone agreed I had the perfect voice
for it. We had daily rehearsals scheduled all this week and next. Plus,

I knew I needed to talk to Mrs. Alexander. I needed to tell her the whole story of the Dare and what I'd found out. Surely she would be sympathetic.

"But it's such a silly, stupid skit," I said out loud to no one. "Who cares about some love story in Venice when Ella Mae is lying there in the hospital?" Muffin cocked his head the way dogs do and lifted his ears, trying to understand. "Dear God," I mumbled into the empty kitchen. "I feel so confused, so afraid, so disappointed. The snow and my prayer and Carl's words seem so far away. Why does life have to just keep going? Why can't it stop and give a few hints now and then, so that I can be prepared? I'm so afraid for Ella Mae."

The jangling of the phone startled me. When I answered, I was dumbfounded to hear Miss Abigail's voice on the other end of the line. "Mary Swan, dear, how are you?"

"Fine. Fine, I guess." I wasn't about to tell her I'd just been carrying on a monologue with the Almighty. "Did you hear about Ella Mae?"

"Yes, of course. I've been to the hospital. No visitors yet. I know you're worried."

"Scared to death. She can't die, Miss Abigail."

"We're all praying that she'll get well. The surgeon seems to think there's reason to hope." Silence. "I called for another reason too. I wanted to say that I'm sorry I put you in that dangerous position on Saturday at the Murphys' house. It wasn't very wise of me, I'm afraid."

"It's okay. I think I understand more about your life now. How are the kids?"

"They went back home today. Mr. Murphy seems very repentant. Time will tell." Miss Abigail cleared her throat. "Mary Swan, Carl mentioned something about you going into the church after the incident at the Murphys'. . . ."

"Yeah, I figured he'd tell you."

"He didn't go into detail. Would you like to talk about it?"

"It's kind of hard to explain over the phone. I think I did what Cassandra did last summer."

Miss Abigail didn't say a thing.

"You know, talked to God. Told Him, um, told Him I needed Him." I felt awkward saying it, even to Miss Abigail. "But I'm not sure I said the right words."

"The words don't matter as much as the heart. The Lord can read our hearts." Then she added, "Do you want to be sure about what you've done?"

"Can I?"

"Of course. We'll talk about it after lunch on Saturday. Will that be okay?"

"Well, it's just that since Ella Mae can't bring me down there, I don't know if Daddy will want to."

"Can you drive, Mary Swan?"

"Yes."

"Well, just get in that car and come on down! I'm sure your father won't have any problem with that."

I had no idea how she could be so sure, but I wasn't about to argue with Miss Abigail. When she said something, it was almost as if God himself had spoken. "Okay. I'll be there."

"And you'll be fine until Saturday, Mary Swan?"

"Yes. Thanks for calling."

"You're welcome. I'm praying for you. And don't worry about Ella Mae. She's in good hands."

Just hearing Miss Abigail's voice, knowing she cared and knowing that Carl had told her about my experience reassured me a little. Enough for me to pick up the phone and do the next thing I needed to do.

"Robbie?"

"Mary Swan, how are you? How's Ella Mae? I haven't dared call, but we've all been wondering, Dad and Mom and Andy and me."

"Well, she made it through the surgery, but the surgeon couldn't get all the tumor, and I can't visit. But Daddy goes down most every day."

"You must be tired, Swan, with Mardi Gras and this."

"Confused and tired, yeah. But I'm sorry I had to cancel on Sunday night."

"Are you kidding? It's only normal. Do you have any time this week? We could grab a quick bite or just go for a walk or whatever."

"I've got Mardi Gras practice every afternoon after school. Goes till five-thirty."

"Well, I'm done with football practice at five. Tell me where you'll be, and I'll pick you up tomorrow."

"That'd be great," I said.

"You don't sound too convinced."

"Couldn't you come over right now?"

"I thought you'd never ask."

We walked through the woods, stopped and stared at the Swan House, walked up to the mansion and over to the boxwood garden, Robbie listening all the while as I explained Saturday's experience. Back at my house, we perched ourselves on the oak table, feet in the chairs, sipping hot chocolate. "Do you think I'm insane? Rachel does."

"No, of course not, Mary Swan. I believe every word of it. I can see how being in the slums could make you think about life and God. Especially being around people like Miss Abigail and that Pastor James."

"Are you still jealous of Carl?"

"Should I be?"

"No. Like I've already said, we're only friends. Maybe I fantasized that something more could happen, but it can't and it won't and even if Carl wanted it to, which he doesn't, he would never be interested in me. He'd never let his feelings for a white girl get the best of him. He knows better."

"So where do I fit in? First guy didn't work out, so you'll take the reserve?"

I stuck out my tongue. "Do we have to decide that now? Can't we just have fun being together?"

"Maybe."

I wanted to tell him that I liked him, that maybe I loved him, but it was just I was so tired and drained of all energy. I knew I couldn't promise him anything but friendship, and I knew, too, that I certainly didn't want to break his heart again or have mine twisted into a knot. He scooted over near me and put his arm around me, tight, and drew me close to his chest, almost the way Carl had done on Saturday night, in a kind, protective way.

"Don't make any decisions right now, Swan. Not a one." Then he kissed me hard on the mouth, and the color spread up his cheeks. "I've got to get home. I'll talk to you again soon."

I knocked on Mrs. Alexander's office door on Thursday afternoon.

"Come in." Seeing me, she said, "Why, hello, Mary Swan. How's Wellington's Raven?"

"Not so good."

"Aha."

"I'm not going to solve it, Mrs. Alexander. There's nothing else for me to find out. The paintings were destroyed."

"Destroyed! Oh my."

"Destroyed by my mother."

She sat there speechless. "I see. Dear me, Mary Swan. This hasn't been an easy year for you."

"No. So I can't bring the paintings to Mardi Gras, and I can't solve the Dare." My disappointment was scribbled in capital letters across my face.

"Not so fast, dear. Why don't you let me talk to the girls and see what they say? As you know, the Raven traditionally meets with the advisor and the senior class officers one week before Mardi Gras. We'll make a decision then."

"What's there to say? I didn't solve the Dare."

"Well, if you found out the paintings were destroyed, then that's solving it."

"But I have no proof. Just the doctor's word, his speculation."

"Don't you worry, Mary Swan. You've done your job, and now I'll do mine."

"Yours?"

"Yes." She smiled sympathetically, almost with a touch of mischief in her eyes. "I'm the negotiator. You've done all you can. I'll see what I can do. Now's the time for you to concentrate on the skit. I'm sure you've written a delightful poem." She raised her eyebrows with that same look of mischief on her face. "You go on about your business with Mardi Gras, and I'll talk to the seniors, and then we'll all meet on February first. Does that sound okay?"

"Yeah. Thanks, Mrs. Alexander."

"My pleasure, Mary Swan."

"Can I ask you one more question?"

"Of course."

"I was wondering if you might be interested in having a live band play at Mardi Gras. I've got some friends who have a jazz band, and they're really good. They played at the Piedmont Driving Club

Christmas Dance. I know we don't have a band every year, but I remember several years ago that we did and everyone liked it. The audience was even invited to dance after the competition."

"A live band? Well, that is something to think about."

"You can call Mrs. Appleby, and she'll tell you all about them."

"I may just do that." And she winked at me.

For some reason, when it came to driving, I wasn't like a lot of kids my age, eager to hop behind the wheel and speed off into the horizon. So even though Daddy had given me permission to drive the Cadillac to Grant Park, I didn't relish the thought. In fact I hardly slept on Friday night, as I turned over in my mind every road between my house and Mt. Carmel. It took me twenty-five minutes of driving at about twenty miles per hour to get to Mt. Carmel on Saturday morning. I congratulated myself for only having made two wrong turns, neither of which turned out to be very traumatic. When I finally pulled up in front of the church and parked in the open lot, I was sweating hard underneath my pea jacket.

As soon as I walked into the fellowship hall, Puddin' grabbed me around the legs, announcing proudly, "My brotha's done gone on a march with the Reverend Martin Luther King, Jr. Way down in Albany!"

"My goodness! With Reverend King?"

"Yep, and a whole lotta other people. Larry an' Big Man an' Leo and Nickie."

"The whole band?"

"Yep. Ya know how Reverend King got put in jail down there last summer? Well, now he says they's been making lots of progress. Befo' long, Mr. King says they won't be no mo' laws 'bout segregation down there."

"That's really good news, Puddin'," I said, picking her up and swinging her around.

Albany was a flat, sunbaked plain of southwestern Georgia, about five hours due south of Atlanta. Carl had told me about the racial demonstrations that had been going on in Albany for over a year. The town of 60,000 had almost 25,000 blacks, and for some reason, Reverend King had chosen this town to be an example of what peaceful demonstrations could accomplish.

But all I really wanted was to have Carl standing beside me, serving spaghetti.

Instead, Cassandra was taking a turn at it while her mother watched Jessie. A white lady named Mrs. Byers, from a Baptist church in Buckhead, was helping too. Little Jessie was crawling all over the place in the fellowship hall, with Cassandra's mom following close behind. I felt a funny little quiver in my heart just watching her on all fours. She rocked back on her legs and plunked herself on her bottom, looking for her mother. Catching sight of Cassandra behind the long table, she began to wail. In an instant, Cassandra's mom had plucked her off the floor and carried her away, cooing to her as she went.

"I thought you might like to know that I became a Christian last week," I confided to Cassandra a few minutes later.

"Ya don't say. Good for you, Mary Swan! Best thing you'll eva' do. I guarantee it."

"Well, I hope so . . ."

I stopped in midsentence because Mr. Murphy, mean, bull-faced Mr. Murphy, was standing across the table from me. I almost dropped the plate I had just filled with sauce. I expected to see hatred in his eyes, but he didn't even seem to recognize me. He just muttered, "Thank ya."

Lined up behind him were the three children. George's eyes grew wide when he saw me. "Hi there, Mary Swan," he belted out. His sisters were huddled together and giggling into their hands, waiting expectantly for me to say something.

"Hi, George and Lissa and Angeline. Good to see you." It came out in a hoarse whisper.

Mr. Murphy turned around then and looked me over good. "You's the one who came with Miss Abigail last week."

My knees almost buckled under me, and the fear rushed back, as if Mr. Murphy were flashing that carving knife at me again instead of simply holding a plate of steaming spaghetti. I licked my lips and tried to say something.

"Thank ya kindly for he'pin' with the chil'un. We's been havin' a mighty hard time of it eva' since their mama died. But with the good Lawd's he'p, thing's gonna git betta."

My mind went blank, and all I could force out of my mouth was a stuttered "Th-that's great."

When they found a seat at one of the tables, Cassandra whispered, "He done the same thing as you, Mary Swan."

"Huh?" I was still watching the big, burly man with his three kids, surprised that compassion had suddenly replaced my feelings of anger and fear.

"Yeah. Got hisself straightened out with the Lawd too."

This time I heard her, and I was so surprised that I dropped the ladle. "What did you say?"

"I said he done did the same thing as you. He got hisself straightened out with the Lawd."

For an instant I bristled, humiliated to be compared with Mr. Murphy. But in the same second, I could hear Carl saying, *"The ground is all even at the foot of the cross. Ain't no rich or poor, just a lot of needy folks. Folks needin' the grace of the Lord Jesus."*

I fell into a chair in Miss Abigail's office. "You're not going to believe what Cassandra told me." I didn't give her time to answer. "She said Mr. Murphy's become a Christian. Can you believe it?"

"Of course I can believe it. God was working powerfully in his heart during those three nights he spent in jail. By the end of the week, he'd confessed his sins and asked forgiveness. Now he wants to give up drinking and live for the Lord."

"That's really . . . weird. Weird and good. I almost wet my pants when I saw him in line. I was sure he'd reach over and slap me or something worse. But he was . . . he was nice. He didn't recognize me at first, and then when it registered, well, he told me thanks."

"A change of heart, Mary Swan. Which brings us to you. Can you tell me what happened?"

"I told Cassandra I'd become a Christian and she said Mr. Murphy and I were alike. And that bugged me for a second because I didn't want to be compared with him. But then I remembered what you told Carl—that the ground is even at the foot of the cross, that we all need a Savior. So I guess I should be the one thanking Mr. Murphy. If he hadn't scared me clear out of my wits, well, I don't know if I would have ever admitted that I didn't have faith and that I wanted it." Then I recounted once again the story of my conversion in the sanctuary last Saturday.

Miss Abigail was simply smiling. "I think the Lord understood exactly what you did."

"Then I did it right?"

"Yes, Mary Swan. Just right."

"But I haven't told Daddy. He wouldn't understand."

"Why not?"

"He'd say that I was already a Christian."

"God will show you when to talk and when to keep your mouth shut." She smiled. "Sometimes it's hardest to tell our story to the ones we love the most—to our families. We're afraid. Give it time, Mary Swan." Then she sat up straight and announced, "I met your father at the hospital the other day."

"You did?"

"Yes. A fine man. He's making sure that Ella Mae has everything she needs. He's a good man, Mary Swan."

"Did you tell him who you were?"

"He was already aware of that, Mary Swan."

"He was?"

"Your father cares an awful lot about you, Mary Swan. He worries too. He knows the inner city can be hard on sensitive hearts."

"What do you mean?"

"Your mother used to come down here—not to Mt. Carmel, but to another church. I believe she gave art classes. Ella Mae brought her down, just as she did you. Your father felt it was too hard on your mom."

"How do you know all that?"

"Word got around."

"Why didn't you ever say anything to me?"

"What was there to say?"

I took in the new information. "Daddy doesn't want me coming down here because he's prejudiced. He's afraid I'll start talking and acting like a Negro."

"He's concerned for your safety first, Mary Swan. But yes, I'm sure prejudice has something to do with it too. Many otherwise strong, God-serving, Bible-believing Christians are steeped in prejudice. Only they don't see it as prejudice—prejudice that has existed for generations. They simply say 'it's the way I was raised.' Hard, Mary Swan. Very hard to admit that the way one was raised is wrong. Hard to admit that prejudice is a sin that needs to be confessed so that change can begin. So very hard."

"Do you think things will ever change between blacks and whites? The prejudice—will the chain ever be broken?"

"With God, nothing is impossible. Just remember that. He's the one who changes hearts, one at a time. Like for you." She patted my hand. "Then, once His Holy Spirit lives in our hearts, He'll show other things that need to change, little by little. Things like prejudice and pride and selfishness and jealousy. He'll start changing us from the inside out."

"So what do I do?"

She reached up to the shelf above her desk, which was crammed with books, and retrieved a thin paperback titled *Now That You Believe*. "This is a little booklet I often use with new believers. It explains very simply what happens at salvation and how to grow as a Christian— how to read the Bible and pray. Look it over, talk to me and to others about your questions. Most importantly, give God permission to change you. And He will. Live what you believe, care and share what you've learned. And then open those beautiful hands of yours, with those long, slim fingers, and let Jesus do the part that only He can do."

My eyes were stinging with tears, but I couldn't resist asking her a question. "Miss Abigail, why do you put up with me? Why do you take the time to talk to me? Who am I? You've got a lot of other stuff that is so much more important."

She got that twinkle in her eye and said, "Many times after Jesus had been teaching, He said, 'He who has ears to hear, let him hear.' And, Mary Swan, I knew right away that you had ears to hear. I knew right away that God had His hand on you."

"You did?" I was dumbfounded. "How?"

"I saw in you a heart to care and eyes to see and a teachable spirit."

"Wow. You saw all that?"

She nodded. "Let me pray for you, Mary Swan. Remember, God will show you what to do next."

"I've got good news, kids," Daddy said over our dinner of Kentucky Fried Chicken. It was actually quite tasty, but I sure missed Ella

Mae's cooking. "They'll be moving Ella Mae to a private room on Monday. The doctor says that he'll have her home before the end of the month." Daddy's voice belied a tension that made the good news questionable to me.

"Can we go see her?" Jimmy asked, taking a big bite out of the chicken leg and then letting out an obnoxious burp.

"You're gross," I said.

"Give her a little more time."

"That's what you say every day, Daddy," Jimmy complained.

Daddy didn't comment on that. "Stocks up three points today. Market's doing well. Where would you kids like to go on vacation this year?" That was Daddy's way of changing the subject.

But later in the evening, with the news blaring on the TV and Jimmy working on a project with electricity that I was sure would get him electrocuted, I commented, "Miss Abigail said she met you at the hospital."

"Sure did. Nice lady. A little eccentric, maybe. She certainly has a tough job."

"You know she's the one I go to help."

"Yes. I was glad to meet her. She spoke very highly of you. Seems to greatly appreciate your help."

"She liked you too. And she told me that Mama used to help out at a church in the inner city."

"Yes, that's right. She did."

"Daddy, how often did Mama go down to help Ella Mae out?"

"Not too often. She needed all her energy just to get herself well. But occasionally, after she came back from Resthaven and was having a good spell, she'd give art classes to some of the poor kids down there. She loved it. She absolutely loved it."

"And she gave money too?"

"Sometimes."

"But she didn't want anyone to know?"

"Exactly."

"Mama was a good person, wasn't she, Daddy?"

"A wonderful woman. Complicated, fragile, talented as all get out. And she loved you and Jimmy more than the world itself."

Little by little, I was getting a better image of my mother, like paint strokes that gradually reveal a portrait. Yes, these months were giving me a portrait of Mama. Deeply wounded as a child, fragile and prone to despondency, talented and elegant, and generous with what she had. I wondered if I was as complex as Mama had been. Maybe we all were that complicated.

"I had an interesting meeting today, Mary Swan," Daddy was saying. "Met with the mayor and several of the business leaders in Atlanta." He handed me several stapled sheets of paper.

"What's this?"

"The most recent statistics on blacks and whites in Atlanta."

I started to read out loud, " 'Negro families have less than half the income of white families in the city. The average Negro income before taxes in 1961 was $3,307, while the average white family's income before taxes was $6,984. Fifty-seven percent of the white families owned their own homes, but only 19 percent of the Negro families were homeowners. Automobiles were owned by 78 percent of the white families but by only 31 percent of the Negro families. After taxes, the black family used all except one dollar of their income on current consumption.' " I looked up from the paper. "That's awful, Daddy!"

"It is troubling, Swannee, but there are, of course, other reasons besides simple discrimination. Many of the Negroes are coming into Atlanta from rural areas where education was not encouraged. Whereas the whites had an average of eleven years of education in 1960, the blacks had an average of six years.

"On the positive side in this racial issue, in early November of last year, barely two months ago, the H. J. Russell Plastering Company became a member of the 3,000-member organization of the Chamber of Commerce. This made Herman J. Russell the first black man to be admitted to the Chamber of Commerce."

"Well, that is good news, Daddy. That sounds like progress."

Daddy had a wry grin on his face. "Albeit that the invitation to be a member was accidentally sent to Mr. Russell. No one knew he was black."

"By accident?"

"Right. He was invited to join by accident." Daddy chuckled. "Anyway, we all know what Mayor Allen's stand is on these black-white relations. This is his second year in office. During his first year, he got to know many of the black leaders in the city, and as a result he respects their desire for equal treatment under the law for their people. The mayor was most impressed with the black leaders' willingness to let the white community work out the problems slowly, if need be. Mayor Allen insists, and I quote, 'that Atlanta will never become one of the great cities in this nation and of the world so long as black men, women, and their children are held in a state of economic, political, and educational subservience.' "

"And did you agree with the mayor, Daddy? Did you agree with what he said?"

"Let's just say I wasn't quite as adamantly opposed as some of the men. One of my friends, whose name I won't mention, said, 'It'll never happen. You aren't gonna catch my kids going to school with a Negro! Over my dead body! Before ya know it, they'll be wanting membership in the club.' And then another friend turned to me and said, 'I agree totally. JJ, you mean to tell me that you want your daughter sitting by a Negro on the bus or eating in a restaurant with a black, going to the Fox Theatre together?' "

Daddy got this big smile on his face and said, "Swan, I had to bite my tongue not to say, 'Fred, I'm not one bit afraid of that happening. And you know why? Because it already has!' "

"Daddy!" I was delighted. "You would never say that!"

His face grew more serious. "No, sweetie. I wouldn't. I can't honestly say that I'm at ease with it. It goes against all my upbringing. But I'm proud of you, and I know you're the generation who's going to bring change to this city. And so I'm trying to be a little more open-minded."

"Speaking of being open-minded, Daddy, are you still seeing Miss Hunnicutt?"

"Some, yes. Why?"

"Because I know someone who is dying to go out with you, but she would never dare let on."

"Is that so?" He lifted an eyebrow.

I nodded solemnly.

"And who might that be, Swan?" Daddy got this flicker of a grin on his lips.

"Well, you've got to promise not to say a word to her that I told you, and you have to promise to at least consider it."

"Swannee. Remember I asked you to leave the matchmaking alone."

"It's Trixie."

Daddy's face got this creeping red shadow crawling up it, just like the thermometer outside the kitchen window on a hot day.

"Don't object yet, Daddy! Please."

"Trixie is one fine lady," Daddy said softly. "Sure has been an angel to our family. To your mother."

"To me too, Daddy!"

"Yes, of course. A great friend to us all. But just a friend."

"She loves you, Daddy."

"Mary Swan! Has she ever said that?"

"No. No, of course not. But I can tell. I'm not dumb. She loves you."

He sat with his elbows poised on the desk, intertwining his fingers. "No matchmaking, Mary Swan. Please." Then he put his arms around me, and he held me in a bear hug that felt real and true, truer than anything had felt in a long time with my father.

Chapter 27

I t was nearly three weeks after her surgery before I was able to see Ella Mae, and by that time she had just gotten back to her house the day before. I'd never once been there, but I knew that she lived in an area a little south of Grant Park. I decided I could drive the Cadillac to Mt. Carmel, serve lunch, and then find my way to Ella Mae's.

"Do you know where she lives, Carl?"

"Haven't ever been there, but I know round about where it is. I'll draw you a map, Mary Swan. Won't do for you ta get lost in these parts. You sure your daddy doesn't mind?"

"I didn't tell him."

Carl lifted one eyebrow with a disapproving look.

"I can't wait around forever. He's always making excuses why I shouldn't see her. He went to see her all the time at the hospital, and so did Miss Abigail and probably a lot of other folks."

"I 'spect she's still awful weak, Mary Swan."

"I know. But I won't stay long."

He put his big hands on my skinny shoulders. "You're mighty worried, aren't ya?"

"I miss her, Carl. I miss her so much." I could feel the knot growing in my throat, so I said quickly, "You are going to play at Mardi Gras, aren't you?"

"I said I'd play, and the boys agreed, and I've already talked to your Mrs. Alexander."

"You won't be going out of town all of a sudden, will you? I mean, there aren't any more marches planned in Albany, are there?"

"Listen, girl, even if there was, I've already given you my word that we'll be there. Stop your worryin'."

"I met with the seniors yesterday. Mrs. Alexander too."

"And? They gonna give you credit for solving that ole Raven Dare?"

"Kind of."

"Well, good for you, girl. You oughta be right proud, after all you went through to figure it out."

"I guess I should be, but I don't feel too proud. I feel disappointed, like I left something undone. Like something isn't right. You know what I wanted, Carl? I wanted more than anything to present those paintings at Mardi Gras. I wanted Daddy and Ella Mae to be there to see them. It was going to be this great gift to them. But now I don't have the paintings, and Ella Mae won't even be there. Things just aren't working out the way I want."

"Maybe not the way you want, but they are working out. Quit your worryin' and go see Ella Mae, and you be careful."

"I'll see you on Friday night, then. Six-thirty for practice. Don't forget to wear a tie. I have to introduce you as my assistant."

"That'll raise some eyebrows, I 'spect." He laughed, shook his head, and sent me on my way. No matter what I knew in my head, every time his hands touched me, I started to shiver.

Hunched over the steering wheel with Carl's hand-drawn map on the passenger's seat, I putted along the streets of the inner city. Past Oakland Cemetery, past Abe's Fill 'er Up, down one street and up another. I had sketched Ella Mae a picture of our house and written on the back in pencil, "We miss you. Hurry home." I'd even made her a batch of brownies. Ella Mae loved chocolate.

Her house wasn't like the little houses in Cabbagetown or the old Victorian homes around Mt. Carmel. It was red brick, one story, the ranch style of the fifties. Sparse grass grew in the front yard, and there was an old beat-up car that I'd seen Roy driving sometimes parked in the driveway.

Roy was waiting for me at the door. I had called him from the church to tell him I was coming. His eyes looked more bloodshot than ever, but he flashed me a smile. "Mighty fine of you ta come, Mary Swan." He opened the door and motioned me inside. "Little bit dirty since Ella Mae's been sick, but you don't pay no neva' mind ta that."

I took in my surroundings briefly. The first room, a real den, not a front room like the one in Carl's house, contained two easy chairs that were covered in brown corduroy and a big brown couch in imitation leather that was cracking. The carpet was thin and worn. The ashtray sitting on a low coffee table was heaped with cigarette butts, and Roy whisked it away. The ironing board was out with clothes piled in a laundry basket and the TV blaring some talk show.

"Have a seat, Mary Swan. Ella Mae's resting right now, but she'll wake up soon." Roy brought me a glass of Coke and set a thin spiral photo album on the couch. "That there's got some pictures you might want ta see."

"Come show them to me, Roy."

He sat down beside me as I opened the album. "This here's our girls, Gina and Loretta. I don't believe ya eva' got to meet Gina," he said in a whisper. "Lawd done took Gina good while back."

His pronouncement shocked me profoundly, but I had no idea what to say. Roy flipped through several pages of pictures of his two daughters, blinking his eyes really hard.

"You eva' meet Loretta, Mary Swan?"

"No," I said, feeling suddenly ashamed.

He furrowed his brow. "I's perty shore you's seen her when you was a little girl."

But I had no recollection of it. I had never once heard Ella Mae talk about Loretta.

The album was old, turning yellow around the edges of the pages. And the sticky surface had worn off, so that some of the pictures fell out when I turned a page. There were pictures of Loretta as a baby with Ella Mae cuddling her or Roy holding her on his lap. Such pride in their eyes! Then a whole series of pictures from grade school.

"What a beautiful little girl," I commented, my mind still racing with questions I didn't dare ask about Gina.

"Shore is right about that. Our Loretta's mighty perty." He flipped to the back of the album. "This heah's when she done gradgeated from high school." A striking young black woman in a blue robe with a mortarboard on her head smiled out at me.

"She's beautiful," I mumbled again.

"Done had her a gran'baby for us now. Lemme see if I kin find one of those pictures." His pride was evident as he got up and went in search of the photo, talking as he went. But all of a sudden I couldn't hear him anymore. I had turned back to the pictures of Loretta as a child, and on the next page, I saw pictures of little white faces interspersed with the pictures of Ella Mae, Roy, Loretta, and what must have been other cousins and friends. Little white faces in an album filled with black faces, most of whom I didn't recognize. *Our* little white faces. Picture after picture of Jimmy and me.

Roy caught me staring at one page and said, "Oh, Ella Mae was awful proud of you and your brotha'. Miz Sheila done give her lotsa photos, and Ella Mae kept them in this here album jus' like you was a part of our family. She always called ya her chil'un, ever since you and yore brotha' was babies."

He said it like it was the most natural thing in the world, and for some reason it hurt to think about how much Ella Mae loved us.

"It's a privilege to be in your photo album," I said softly, my face suddenly wet with tears.

Roy saw it and was embarrassed, so he said, "Lemme go see if she's awake yet."

I was glad he left me to cry. I cried for my ignorance and lack of interest in Ella Mae's life, and I cried for her obvious interest in mine. Mostly I cried for this poor, kind, godly woman whose love and sacrifice came through the pages of a worn photo album.

"She ain't really awake yet," Roy apologized, coming back into the den, "but you kin stick yore head in if ya want."

When I walked into her bedroom, I almost gasped. Where was my Ella Mae? Her dark brown skin was splotched. Her head was wrapped in a large white bandage that covered her shaven head and her forehead. A cheap gray wig sat awkwardly on her head. Black circles hung below her eyes. Her ample bosom sagged pitifully under the white cotton hospital gown. Ella Mae had shriveled up and died, it seemed to me. Shriveled up and died. She did not even manage a smile when she saw me, but whispered "Chile" and it came out as a low cough.

I was too horrified to speak. This was why Daddy hadn't wanted me to visit her. The shock of seeing Ella Mae, well-padded Ella Mae, looking like a skeleton of her former self was almost more than I could bear. I forced my legs forward, praying the disgust and fear did not show on my face. I went to her side and clasped my hands around hers and whispered, "I'm so sorry, Ella Mae. I'm so sorry."

I'm not sure she even heard me. She closed her eyes, and I tiptoed out of the room.

Roy, seeing my obvious distress, assured me, "She'll wake up in a little while. Then there won't be no stopping her talkin'." His lips parted, and he attempted to give a toothless grin. "Doctor says they got out most of that tumor. Couldn't git it all, though. And it's funny I guess how things work in yore brain. Somethin' done happened ta Ella Mae 'cause she cain't quit talkin' now. Whereas before she didn't hardly say two words tagether, now she jus' talk own and own ta beat th' band."

"But she ain't herse'f, that's for shore." The smile faded. "Come on and see what she calls her art gallery. You'll like seein' this." He closed her bedroom door behind him and led me down a narrow hall. Halfway down he stopped and pointed to each wall. "Have yorese'f a look at this, Mary Swan. A regular art gallery, yessiree!"

On either side, the walls were lined with sketches, some in cheap frames and others merely taped to the wall. I glanced in both directions, and my heart jumped. These were Mama's sketches! All of them. Many, many of Mama's sketches! I began examining them closely. I'd never seen any of them.

"Mighty talented yore mama was, Mary Swan," Roy was standing beside me.

I could not take my eyes from the two long walls. "How did she get all these sketches of Mama's?" I asked.

Roy chuckled, "I reckon I'd better let her explain that to ya."

"Can I just stay here and look at them?"

"Shore, honey. Do as ya like. Like I said, Ella Mae'll wake up in a little while." He left me there alone.

My mind was racing. A month ago, I'd discovered a room full of Mama's paintings at Resthaven, and now, in the place I'd least expected it, were walls papered with her work.

Most of the sketches had either been wadded up or torn in two, but it looked as though Ella Mae had lovingly smoothed them out and taped them back together. I could almost feel the tension in Mama as she drew and grew more frustrated with each stroke of the charcoal, could almost hear the paper ripping and being wadded and thrown into the trash can.

I stood in front of each sketch and memorized it. There were several of the boxwood garden at the Swan House. There were sketches of Ella Mae, one of her ironing, another as she fried chicken. She was bent over the stove, but had turned around, I guess to look at Mama, and seemed to be protesting, with her brow all puckered out and a half frown on her face. But her eyes were laughing.

There were two unframed canvases. One had a hole slashed right through the middle. Mama must have stood her easel by the big window in her *atelier* and looked out on the backyard in spring. The main thing in the painting was the big hickory tree with the swing. She'd placed it on the right side of the canvas. The slash was to the left of the tree. Ella Mae had punched the canvas back into place. I reached out to touch it, squinting to decipher what exactly had been slashed. And then I made it out. It was the tiny figure of Mama, standing there by her easel, painting. A strange, far-off self-portrait that had obviously displeased her.

"Roy! Roy Maddux!" Ella Mae's voice came out loud and shrill.

Roy called to me from the den, "She done woke up, Mary Swan. Like I tol' ya. Lemme go see what she needs."

A moment later, I heard, "Come on in, chile." That was Ella Mae, calling to me in a weak but certain voice.

I went to her bed and once again clasped her hands. "Ella Mae, you're gonna get better. I've been praying for you every day."

"Have a seat now, chile." She motioned to a chair in the corner. "Drag it on ova' here, honey. That'll be fine."

I obeyed.

"So how'd ya like my art gallery, chile?"

"I like it a lot. All Mama's stuff."

" 'Course right here with me is what I call the finest gallery. Better'n any one in that High Museum." I furrowed my brow and then looked around at the walls. A chill shot up my spine and went back down in a mere second. Three beautifully framed oil paintings hung on the walls of this tiny, dingy bedroom. I let out a tiny, stifled cry.

The three missing paintings! *Mama's* three missing paintings! It had to be them, hanging right here in Ella Mae's bedroom. I covered my mouth with my hand, stood up, and walked over to the painting that hung on the wall to the right of Ella Mae's bed. It was a portrait of Ella Mae in her gray maid's uniform, cuddling a white baby in her arms. Mama's painting entitled *Child at Rest*.

"Dat's me an' you, honey, when you weren't more 'n' a coupla months old. That there always was my favorite."

I couldn't say a word.

"Thought you might be surprised," Ella Mae said, pleased. "Ya wonderin' how I ended up with three such nice paintings, aren't ya, chile?"

I nodded, speechless.

"Yore mama gave 'em to me. Gave 'em to me and made me swear I wouldn't neva' tell no one 'bout 'em. And I ain't neva' breathed a word, not even ta Mista Middleton. But afta' yore mama died, well, I jus' kept wonderin' what I should do. 'Cause there's a mighty fine story behind those paintings, and I reckoned yore daddy needed ta be told 'bout it. So I jus' kept askin' the Lawd what ta do, and I guess He done answered by sendin' you heah."

I heard Ella Mae talking beside me, as if in a dream, but it didn't really register. These were Mama's paintings! The second painting hung beside the first and was of Resthaven's gardens, no doubt about it. I was certain that this was the painting named *Spring Bouquet*. Henry Becker was raking in the background, and the azaleas and dogwoods were in full bloom around him. Part of the building itself was painted on the right. Some of the detail that characterized her portraits was absent in this painting. Henry Becker's name appeared in the lower right-hand corner.

"The Swan House," I whispered when I turned to the opposite wall and saw the painting that hung there. But it didn't look like the other paintings Mama had painted of the famous mansion. This painting had more energy and life, as if the trees and wildlife and the house itself might just burst off the canvas and into the room. *Joie de Vivre,* I thought to myself, the name of the third painting I was supposed to find. Of course. This was Mama's third style of painting. As a confirmation, Leslie Leschamps' name was painted across the bottom of the canvas.

I was not sure of what it all meant, but I was sure of one thing. I had given it all up to God just a couple of weeks ago, the Dare, the paintings, the mystery of Mama. And now it looked like He was giving it back to me, to do with as I willed.

My mouth was surely hanging open. A terrible tumor had almost destroyed Ella Mae's life, and simply through love for her, I'd dared to come to visit. Or maybe it was God who had brought me here where Ella Mae was sitting in bed, looking pitiful and weak, surrounded by those paintings. Those works of art in gilded frames. I wondered briefly how the plastered and cracking walls could hold their weight.

I finally recovered from my shock and choked out, "You don't have to tell me anything, Ella Mae. I just want to be with you."

"Well, then, come sitcha a spell. I do believe I got some 'splaining to do."

"I don't want you getting tired."

"Ain't gonna be tirin' to me. I jus' woke up, and for some reason, when I'm awake, I cain't stop talkin'. I think it's the tumor. Me who never liked the sound of my own voice, well, imagine that."

She looked off at one of the paintings, cleared her throat, and said, "The first time I's seen yore mama, I knowed she was different, special, Swannee. She was a beautiful little thing, full of spunk and ideas enough to change the world. Proud and fragile and tough somehow all at once. Oh, I didn't like her at first. The way she talked and her fancy house and money. I didn't think no white folks who lived in Buckhead knew nothin' about the hard things in life. They jus' lived in a shallow dream, they did.

"But I started lovin' her right away, Swannee. 'Cause she didn't have no problems with money, but I saw the problems she did have. Heap o' problems. Every day she had to decide to fight somethin' strong and terrible in her brain. She knew sufferin' all right."

A sharp pain shot straight through me, and I bit my lip. The image of Mamie cuddling her dead baby to her breast and then slapping Mama in the face flashed before me.

"That firs' time I found her in tears in front of her paintin', I was mighty frightened for her. It was that paintin' in the hall of the hickory tree. And she'd taken a knife and cut through the canvas, tried to cut herse'f right out of the picture she was paintin', and then she held her head in her hands and cried like a baby. You could see the sufferin' and the anguish all bottled up inside and spillin' over.

"Yore daddy done told me about his Sheila then. He told me she was different. Told me she needed he'p sometimes. And he begged me to stay and help. And so I did." She let the phrase trail and stared at the painting of herself holding me as a baby. "That's me 'n you, honey chile, in that paintin'. We done had us a whole lotta fun together, Mary Swan. You was the sweetest baby. Yore mama loved ta sketch me holding on to you. Didn't neva' paint us 'til she got to Resthaven. Took her sketches there and painted.

"Then after Miz Sheila had Jimmy, it was jus' too much for her sensitive mind to handle. She could paint or she could cuddle her babies or she could go to a party, but she couldn't do it all or she'd start havin' those fits real often.

"They put her on some of those drugs, you know, the tranquilizers, to he'p her calm down. But she couldn't bear it. They made her dry up, she used to say. Took away all her creativity so as she didn't know who she was no more. And, Mary Swan, I do believe that was a million times worse for her than the battle in her mind. To have no battle, to be calm and without no feelin's or thoughts. Scary kinda calm.

"One time she jus' up 'n stop takin' her medicine. You was jus' a little thing and Jimmy a baby. And she was a mess." I could see the tears in the rims of Ella Mae's eyes, could hear the quiver in her voice. "I came into her studio ta ask a question, and there she was on the floor, blood everywhere. She'd done cut those tiny wrists of hers with a carvin' knife. So I ripped up some ole T-shirts of yore daddy's and wrapped 'em around her wrists ta stop the bleedin'.

"And I picked up that little wisp of a woman, and I cried to her, 'Sheila, now you ain't gonna die on me here! You ain't!' And I carried her down the hall and those windin' stairs and into yore daddy's study and put her on the couch, and I called the ambulance for her like I's done for a lot of my people. And while they was comin', I jus' took her little hand in mine and I prayed and prayed that the Lawd Jesus would spare her life. I sang her favorite songs, and then they came and took her away."

While she talked, another scene flashed in my mind, the one that had come to me at the Back-to-School Ball, after Herbert's drunken announcement. Ella Mae carrying Mama, the blood on the carpet, the siren, the confusion, and Mama leaving.

"And that was the first time she went to that there place up in the mountains. That's when yore daddy and me and Trixie done realized that we couldn't take care of her alone. So for all those years we's done our best and them folks at the Resthaven done he'ped out a whole lot. And she was doin' okay, ya know it. And you and Jimmy growing up so fine and strong. An' her paintings bein' in some of those museums. Ain't neva' gonna figure out why the Lawd done took her now. No, sir. I got me a list a mile long with some questions I'm gonna ask my Jesus when I see Him. And that's one of 'em." Her eyes were closed, and there were tears on her lashes.

I wiped my own eyes.

"When she was really sad, I'd rock her like I did with you, and I'd hum those songs and pray. She loved for me to pray. It calmed her down, and she'd fall asleep, she would. And then she would wake and say to me, 'Ella Mae, if God has given me this talent, I am going to use it for good, no matter what.'

"I made it my habit ta clean up in her studio last every day. And when she threw away those sketches and paintin's, I pulled 'em outta the trash and brought 'em home with me. And one time when Roy was real bad off and she came ova' to he'p out, well, she discovered my gallery. She was mighty mad at me at first. Then she jus' laughed and said, 'As long as you don't show 'em to another soul, Ella Mae, you can keep 'em. Keep 'em and enjoy.' They said she wadn' very pro-lific, but it wadn' that, it was jus' that she threw away so many things. The things at my house. And I done seen otha' things at that place in the mountains. Loads of paintin's."

I couldn't breathe a word, couldn't bear to ask her to tell me more, but she wasn't done talking.

"These three paintings here, you know about them, Mary Swan?"

I nodded slowly. "They're the ones that were going on exhibition at the High last year, weren't they?"

"Yep, you done got that right, Mary Swan. Don't know how you know it, but you is right. Yore mama was gonna give them paintin's to the museum. That nice doctor worked it all out with yore mama. But she was afraid, Miz Sheila was. Terrified to reveal the other side of herse'f. Part o' her wanted to real bad and the otha' part was scared stiff. And so I tells you what we did. I tell you that story, Mary Swan, becuz you done figured out the rest.

"I swore to Miz Sheila I wouldn't neva' tell nobody, not yore daddy or Miz Trixie or no one, but you is here now and you see these paintin's. It was the day before them paintin's were gonna be delivered to that museum. And yore mama started getting all panicky, and I could tell she was jus' terrified. So she comes to me while I was ironin' and she begs me to go with her to Resthaven and git them paintin's. And I said, 'Aw, Miz Sheila, don't ya be doin' that now.'

"But she wouldn't have none of it. And so we drove all the way up ta Resthaven, and they jus' thought she was comin' as usual to check in, and I didn't peep a word. She went right to that studio of hers where all her paintin's was kept and where those three paintin's was all wrapped up and ready to be delivered to the museum and she took 'em out ta her car, and I he'ped her. And we put 'em in her car and drove off jus' like that, with nobody askin' no questions. An' I don't think yore mama had any idea what to do next, but I was mighty afraid she was jus' gonna cut 'em up like I'd seen her do before. She was so upset. So I says ta her, 'Miz Sheila, lemme take 'em. I'll be real careful with 'em. And nobody'll find 'em. I promise you that. Won't tell a soul.' I figured that afta' she calmed down a bit, she might change her mind and give 'em to the museum.

"So Miz Sheila done agreed, and she drove me home, and I took those paintings inside and put 'em right where they is now.

"And I neva' did say a word. Wadn't easy, but then again, they was yore mama's and I figured it was up ta her ta decide. Once when I told yore mama she should give 'em back, well, she flew into a rage. She said they were for me and no one else and that she didn't want me eva' ta say anuther word about it. So I didn't. And so you see, they's right here in my room, and I have my own private art show every day. I enjoy them so much. Every day I'm at the museum. Every day I kin almost hear yore mama hummin' away as she paints.

"I think the Lawd done prepared it 'fore I got sick, 'cause He knew I'd need some cheerin' up. So I sits here and smiles seein' you on my lap." She nodded toward her portrait. "Or I stares at that one there, with all those dogwood trees and azaleas and the roses and ev-erythin' testifyin' to spring. She was a mighty fine painter, yore mama."

Her head fell back on the pillow, and she closed her eyes again with a peaceful look on her face.

It took me a minute to quit sniffling. Then I said, "Thank you for telling me, Ella Mae. You'll never know how much it means to me. I think you saved her life a hundred times. I think you saved her life, and then you saved Jimmy and me too. I'm glad you have these paint-ings. You deserve them."

I knew in that moment that I'd never breathe a word to her about the Raven Dare. And I'd never tell Rachel or Carl that I'd found the missing paintings. The Dare was finally solved, but it didn't matter at all. What mattered was Ella Mae. She was going to need all the help she could to recover. Maybe God really had planned it this way so that Ella Mae would be surrounded by beauty, surrounded by the memory of a woman she loved like her own child when she needed it most. This was a much better place for them, right here at her house.

"But you mustn't think it was jus' me he'pin' her, Swannee," she said all of a sudden, obviously not finished with her story. " 'Cause she came down here lots a times ta he'p us out too. Every time Roy and me was in a scrape, she somehow knew it without me sayin' a thing. Maybe the Lawd done revealed it to her. I dunno. But she'd give me the money and stuff. Sometimes wadn't for us. Was for somebody else she'd heard was havin' a rough time. So she'd slip me the money and make me swear I wouldn't tell who it was from. She had a tender heart for those who was hurtin', yore mama did. She loved us blacks. And she'd say, 'I can't do much, but I can write a check and I can buy a bag of groceries.'

"She told me once that what she liked about Resthaven was that everybody there was jus' the same. Didn't matter none if'n you was black or white or young or old or had lots a money or nothin'. Everybody there needed he'p. She said she didn't have ta pretend at Resthaven. She could laugh and cry and hug the black janitor and he'p the little teenager with her problems. An' nobody saw her as some rich and uppity woman from Atlanta. She was jus' Sheila with a heap o' problems. An' she said that she learned there how to tell the truth and how to depend on others and on God. 'Cause there it was okay to admit that her life was in a mess. There it was okay. An' she never put on no fancy gown or suit, and on Sundays she jus' took off her paintin' smock and went to the chapel like she was, a mess, and she'd jus' git on her knees and cry her heart out and ask forgiveness." A tear was trickling down Ella Mae's cheek.

"An' then she'd be all better, she would. An' she told me how she thought every church should be like that. A place where you could go without no makeup or fancy dress to hide behind and you could jus' hug yore friends and cry and tell the Lawd how bad you'd messed up and ask Him to forgive ya and let ya git up and keep goin'.

"And I do believe that's the kind o' church Jesus had in mind when

He spoke ta us, Mary Swan. I do. Place where ya feels comfortable jus' like you is. Place where we gives each other a lotta grace, jus' like our Savior done give us."

Then Ella Mae got this serious look on her face and said, "She knew you had some of that wonder in you. She cried and laughed about it. And worried. You be shore ta remember, Swannee, that no matter what, life is a gift, a wonderful gift from the Lawd. Everything about it. The good and the bad and the borin' and sad. All of it is a gift, and don't you waste it now, Swannee. Please don't waste it, chile."

"I won't, Ella Mae. I promise you," I murmured. I thought surely Ella Mae would fall asleep, but she still had things to say.

"Lawd, He done knowed I'd need Miz Sheila and Mista Middleton and you and Jimmy in my life. He done brought yore mama in my life right before I done lost my baby, chile."

I jerked my head up. "Gina? I saw her pictures."

"That's right. Still got me my Loretta, thank the Lawd. But I done lost my Gina. She was jus' a young girl, 'bout yore age, smart and beautiful and with a voice like an angel. Got hit by a car right ova' by the church. Comin' home from school late one afta'noon in winta'. Kinda dark outside. Man was already drunk outta his mind. He neva' even saw my Gina. . . ."

I fell onto the bed, clasping her hand again. "Ella Mae, why didn't I ever know it? Why didn't I ever know any of it? I'm so sorry. I'm so sorry I never asked, I never cared. I was so selfish." I was sobbing into her sheets. "Ella Mae, please forgive me for being so selfish."

"Hush now, chile. Ain't tryin' ta make ya cry. Wadn't no reason ta tell you. Yore mama knew, though. She come ova' and cry with me. Bought a mighty fine casket for Gina, she did. That was the first thing she done for me, afta' I'd only bin workin' for her for a few months. Bought a casket and paid for a nice funeral and had her buried at a cemetery not too far from here. And then the Lawd done give me you and yore brotha' ta take up my time. And you done brought me a heap o' happiness, that's for shore."

"Oh, Ella Mae. I wish I could change it all. I want to make your life easier."

"Ain't askin' for an easy life, Mary Swan. Don't guess there's any time much that I r'memba' where me havin' an easy time of it has he'ped anyone, chile. I cain't 'member a one, honey. Like I'd done already told ya when I was in the hospital, it's been through the hard times that I been able to he'p someone else. It's been through believin' that the Lawd somehow gonna git me through that the others done wanted to hear about my Jesus. He ain't never used no polished perty words to draw them ta Him. Ain't neva' been nothin' I kin brag about myse'f, honey. I guess the only times I could really he'p was 'cause I knowed what God had done for me when I couldn't do nothing myse'f."

You're right, Ella Mae. Even now, in your suffering, you're helping me, reminding me of what is important, showing me what Mama was like, telling me loud and clear that three paintings are needed a lot more in a poor maid's house on the south side of town than at a fancy exhibition in a museum. I don't need the recognition at Wellington for being a successful Raven.

"You's had some hard things happen in yore life, Mary Swan. And you's learnin' some hard lessons. But don't you stew over those things. Give 'em back to Him and let Him make somethin' beautiful out of them. I guarantee He will. But it won't be nothin' to make you proud of yourself. It'll be some way where you'll jus' praise Him for what He's done. Now that you done asked Him ta take ova' in yore life, and you got the Holy Ghost in ya, well, ya be listenin' ta Him, honey."

I nodded, feeling all of the pain and the hurt of the past months and wondering about the way God's timing worked. And I felt something else, something like what I'd felt on my knees in the sanctuary of Mt. Carmel. Something pure and simple. I think it was what Miss Abigail called "the peace that passes understanding." Could it be that the terrible tragedy of Mama's death and the emptiness it left—that wrenching pain—and my desire to paint, and my challenge as the Raven and my friendship with Carl and every other circumstance in the past year were like pieces in a puzzle that God was putting together, slowly and patiently? Maybe life really did matter, and maybe, just maybe, God wasn't going to waste all of the pain.

"I don't know why you don't hate me, Ella Mae," I said softly, resting my head in her lap as she slowly stroked my hair. "Seeing how selfish I've always been. Selfish and rich and spoiled. I don't know why you don't just hate me. Aren't you ever jealous?"

"Been jealous before of what folks have. Shore. Ain't been jealous of them, tho'. I gots my own people to love, my family, and yore family and my problems and yours, and that's enough. Guess I ain't got no business tellin' the good Lawd that He put me in the wrong place. He done shown me 'nuff times that He knows exactly what He is doing, and I better jus' agree. 'Cause one way or anuther, He'll show He's right and git me there anyway."

All of a sudden, I knew I needed to say something to Ella Mae that I'd never said before. "Thank you for bringing me down to Mt. Carmel, Ella Mae. It's changed me. Changed my life."

"Glad it's he'ped ya. Mighty glad."

"I love you, Ella Mae."

"Aw, go on, Mary Swan. I knows it. I love you too."

And we just sat there together, my arms entwined around shriveled-up Ella Mae with her golden heart, and I don't know if she was crying, but I was sobbing like a baby.

Chapter 28

O n the night of Mardi Gras, Rachel came to my house early to help me with my makeup. She insisted that I wear mascara, eyeliner, rouge, and lipstick. "You'll be in the spotlight, Swan. You need it. I promise you won't look overdone."

So I let her fix me up. My braces had come off two weeks earlier, and last week I'd gone with Rachel to her fancy hairdresser and gotten my hair cut just above the shoulder, even though both Robbie and Daddy had told me they liked it long.

"They'll like it short when they see it," Rachel had insisted, and as usual, she was right.

She fiddled with it now, curling it on the ends. "Gosh, Swan. Your hair is a great length. Getting it cut gave it just the right amount of body. And it's got the greatest shine." She peered closer. "Even some red highlights there. Natural highlights, like your mom's. No matter if they hose you down up there, your hair won't wilt," she added, satisfied, after emptying half a can of hairspray onto my head. "Now you're ready for the dress! Hurry up! Put it on."

Rachel had helped me pick it out. It was a simple, strapless white dress. It had a built-in bra so that I didn't look flat-chested at all, and I almost had to hold my breath to get it zipped, so there was no chance of it falling off. It was perfectly plain, a winter white, shimmering satin. The top had a wide pleat across the bust. The dress fell to my ankles, and I had on gold sandals. And around my shoulders I wore a short black velvet cape, tied at the neck.

When Rachel had seen the dress and cape at Rich's ten days ago, she'd exclaimed delightedly, "This is it, Swan. This is it *exactly*. It's the perfect combination of the graceful swan and the black raven."

"Wellington's unsuccessful Raven," I had added.

"No. Not at all, Swan. You did your absolute best and found out everything you possibly could. The judges have the last word. They may decide that you did indeed solve the Dare."

I nibbled on a fingernail. "Yeah, who knows?"

Remembering that conversation now, I shivered slightly. If only Rachel knew what I'd discovered at Ella Mae's since then. . . . But I wouldn't tell. Not even Rachel.

She twirled me around and proclaimed, "You'll charm your escort. That's for sure."

That was another tradition of the Raven Dare. At Mardi Gras, the Raven was presented with her "secret" escort, chosen from one of the boys' private schools. Rumors had slipped out that I'd be escorted by Christopher Allen, who was knock-you-down handsome, six foot two, captain of the All-Star basketball team, and every girl's heartthrob. That didn't do anything to calm my nerves either.

"You look absolutely gorgeous," Rachel prattled on. "That dress shows off your terrific figure."

I blushed a little, shrugged, and corrected her. *"You're* the one who's gorgeous."

Rachel did look stunning in her red taffeta dress that was fitted around the bodice and then poofed out at the waist with a skirt full of crinolines that fairly danced to her shins. She wore a small tiara on her head. Her blond hair fell thick and shining down her back.

"But I'm all right, I guess. Yeah. I look okay." The truth was that I liked what I saw staring back at me from the full-length mirror in my dressing room. I liked it a lot.

Rachel drove us to the Wellington gymnasium, which sat on spacious acreage far behind the other buildings. For this one night the basketball court was transformed into a stage, and the bleachers would soon be filled with Wellington students, their parents, and friends. I glanced at my watch. One hour until the festivities began. One hour, and where were Carl and the rest of the band? They were to play for fifteen minutes before the official ceremony began and then again at the end of the evening, with several songs interspersed while the audience and the girls awaited the judges' decision on the float and skits.

The four different floats were hidden under sheets in the corners of the gym. Rachel and I lifted the sheet off the junior float and inspected it—a gondola, sitting on a piece of plywood that had been painted blue and made to look like a river. A bridge rose in a wide semicircle above the gondola. "Wow. It looks great," I whispered to Rachel. "They've done a lot of work since Wednesday when I saw it last."

"Are you kidding? Griff and Patty and Jane were up practically all night getting it into shape."

"Have you sat in the gondola yet?"

"Yeah, I came by this morning and tried out my perch. I think it will hold me." She flashed her eyes. "Wouldn't it be hysterical if the whole thing fell apart right in front of the audience?"

"Don't be stupid. It looks solid enough." But I knew Rachel was thinking of the disaster three years ago when a huge crepe paper chicken had toppled over onto the girl who was riding the freshman float. "You'll be fine."

My own heart was bouncing in several different directions. First, the skit still had a few rough spots we were desperately trying to iron out, and there was a general feeling of happy panic in the air. As writer and narrator, I was more or less in charge, so I found myself dashing here and there to reassure the star-struck cast. And then the little speech I had prepared, as every Raven must, was growing soggy in my hands, just like that piece of paper had done nine months ago in Latin class. That soggy wad of paper had changed my life. And finally, where in the world were Carl and Leo and Big Man and Larry and Nickie?

I unfolded the paper where I'd scribbled my Raven speech. I wondered, with butterflies flitting inside my stomach, if what I was going to say was appropriate. I felt terrified and excited, as if there was something new about me, something good and right. Mary Swan after the crash, Mary Swan the believer, Mary Swan thinking of someone else. And Mary Swan willing to let go. Still I doubted my decision tonight when I thought about Daddy and Jimmy sitting in the bleachers, hearing that I had been the Raven. I had so wanted to have those three paintings here to show. For Daddy. For Mama.

But Ella Mae, weak, struggling Ella Mae, was lying in her bedroom, able to open her eyes at any time and see Mama's work. Her Sheila's work. That was exactly as it should be. Ella Mae and Sheila. They had lived a tight relationship of trust and love. They had pulled each other through attempted suicide and the death of a child. They had been survivors. And they had been conspirators—together keeping Mama's paintings a secret. Who was I to destroy that?

I checked my watch again. The competition started in thirty minutes. First the skits, beginning with the freshmen, then the sophomores, then us, followed by the seniors. Afterward the floats would be pulled in one at a time in the same order. And while the judges were making their decisions and tallying the points, the Raven Dare would be revealed and the Raven presented. It was going to be a long night.

The band arrived, and Carl looked more harried and out of breath than I'd ever seen him before.

"What's the matter? Are you okay?" I asked, relieved by their presence and trying not to sound irritated at their tardy arrival.

"Everythin's fine, Swannee. Don't you worry." He flashed me a smile, but it wasn't very convincing.

"I've got to go out there later and talk about the Dare, Carl."

"You'll do fine. You jus' go out there and tell the truth. The truth is all. Remember."

I nodded, my head spinning. *But you don't understand, Carl. You don't know that I really did find those paintings. And I am not going to peep a word.*

"Pray that I say the right things, Carl. I'm scared stiff. I'm terrified."

He looked at me slowly as he pulled his saxophone from its case, gave me a wide smile, and said, "You know, girl, I b'lieve you are." He put one hand on my shoulder and looked me straight in the eye. I'm sure Patty and Jane saw him do it, because they'd just run over to ask me a question. Carl didn't flinch. "You'll be just fine. Do it for your mama's memory. You'll be fine."

He walked over to where his band was set up under one of the basketball hoops. Larry and Big Man and Nickie waved to me. Leo winked at me and gave a drum roll.

"Shh!" I reprimanded, my face growing hotter by the second.

Then Carl glanced back over his shoulder at me and said, loud enough for those around me to hear, "You look really beautiful tonight, Mary Swan. A perfect reminder of the white swan and the black raven."

That made my face turn beet red, which was probably good,

because I'd been pale as a ghost up until then. In fact, I suddenly felt so light-headed and hot that I untied the black cape, took it off my shoulders, and draped it around one arm, thinking to myself, *A swan and a raven. Good grief, Rachel and Carl, cut the symbolism and just help me get through this night.*

The lights were down in the big gymnasium, and Larry was playing a solo on his trombone. I was seated in the bleachers with my class, and I kept looking up behind me. Where were Daddy and Jimmy? Then I caught sight of Amanda Hunnicutt, and my heart stopped. Did Daddy have to bring *her* to Mardi Gras? For heaven's sake, now everyone in town would know that my dad and Amanda were dating.

But as I squinted in the dark, it looked like Amanda Hunnicutt was sitting between two other women. I breathed a sigh of relief. But where was Daddy?

The freshman skit was announced and performed—the sophomore skit too. Carl's band played a brief interlude. I was working like mad to get one of the junior girl's costumes right. Another glance into the bleachers. Still no sign of Daddy and Jimmy. Or Robbie for that matter. He had promised to be there too. No more time to worry about that.

"Put your cape on!" Patty whispered, and I quickly threw the black velvet around my shoulders, tied it in place, stepped up to the microphone, and was blinded by the spotlight. I couldn't see a thing. My hands, which held my copy of the skit, were trembling, and I cleared my throat, turning from the mike. This was supposed to be the easy part, but I didn't know if I could get a sound out of my mouth.

I leaned toward the microphone and began,

" 'Twas a warm day in Venice, the streets filled with crowds
The canals all a-shimmer, the sky filled with clouds
The pigeons were pecking at bread in the square
And everyone seemed to be going somewhere.
But alas, a fair maiden, with hair down to her waist,
Was alone, searching listlessly for something to taste
Her visage was thin, hunger hung in her eyes
When suddenly she fainted on the Bridge of Sighs."

As I read the skit, my classmates enacted it before the audience.

Julie Jacobs was playing the fair maiden, and she was a born actress.
The spotlight left me and panned the floor, focusing on each player.
Millie Garrett held a flashlight on my script so that I could still read.

"Below on the water a gondola passed under
The bridge just as the maiden slipped into her slumber
And Antonio, the gentle, brave gondola driver,
Happened to look up and on the bridge spied her.
He parked his long boat by the side of the river
And ran onto the bridge, where, with a gasp and a shiver,
The maiden had awakened. He took her by hand.
'Can I help you, Fair Miss?' She whispered, 'Sand.'
'There's no sand on these banks,' he replied with a frown.
'A sandwich is all I need.' She hung her head down."

The audience chuckled, just as they were supposed to, and Antonio, played by Jane with a long, thin curving mustache drawn above
her top lip, picked up the maiden, Julie—not without difficulty—and
carried her to the gondola. I was into the skit now, my voice rising
and falling with the rhythm, smiling with the corny jokes and feeling
an occasional swell of pride at a particularly clever line. We'd peppered
our medieval love story with plenty of 1960s humor and puns, and it
seemed to be pleasing everyone.

After fifteen minutes of entertainment, I came to the end of the
skit and pronounced these words,

"Ladies and gentlemen, that alas is our story
Of how a simple gondola man found his princess and glory.
'Tis a tale for romantics, but never forget
A kind deed done from the heart's a sure bet
To receive abundantly more than the clouds in the skies.
So ends our story of Venice and the Bridge of Sighs."

The applause was enthusiastic as the spotlight was turned off and
the lights came up. All of us who had taken part in the skit, which
was almost everyone in the class, joined hands and took several bows.
At least that part was over. As I glanced up into the bleachers, I finally
saw Daddy clapping and laughing with Jimmy. Then he turned and put
his arm around the woman beside him and gave her a warm, affectionate hug. My mouth fell open. It was Trixie! Daddy was sitting by Trixie

and laughing with her and punching Jimmy, and suddenly they were all waving down at me, Daddy and Jimmy and Trixie and Lucy. And Mamie and Papy and Grandmom and Granddad were sitting there too, looking as though they might burst with pride.

My eyes lit up, and I waved back with what was probably a foolish-looking grin on my face.

I got a stinging in my eyes when Jamie and Jessica, the two junior "pullers," slowly, matching step for step, pulled our gondola float out into the middle of the floor, and the spotlight focused on Rachel. She was a princess, a movie star, a Persian cat, eyes sparkling, a soft curl of a smile on her lips. Light bulbs flashed all over the room, and everyone was whistling and yelling, "Great job, juniors!" while Carl and the band played a hyped-up version of "The Carnival of Venice." All the girls in the junior class were hugging each another and squealing with relief and delight. And I think that Rachel, beautiful, Jewish Rachel was happy, maybe even delighted, to be the fair maiden of the junior class at Wellington Prep School.

"We've got it hands down," Patty stated, when we finally hushed up and the lights dimmed again. "The skit was perfect, and our float is tons better than the others."

But all I could think about was that there was just the senior float left, and then it would be my turn again as the Raven was revealed.

Mrs. Alexander came to the microphone. "As most of you know, it has been a tradition at Wellington since its inception in 1929 to pick a rising junior girl at the end of the school year to be Wellington's Raven. She has nine months to solve a riddle or dare, if you will, that has been thought up by the incoming senior class officers. As you well remember, it has been very rare that the Raven has solved her riddle. Traditionally, the Raven, the Dare, and the results are presented at the end of Mardi Gras.

"I would like to clarify that this year's dare was thought up in late May, cleared with me by the rising seniors, and given secretly to the would-be Raven on June first. I say this due to the odd nature of the Dare and in view of the circumstances that followed on the heels of the naming of the Raven. I will read the Dare and ask that our Raven join me now. The Raven for 1962–63 is . . . Mary Swan Middleton."

There was polite applause as I wiggled my way out of the bleachers. I could hear comments all around by classmates, saying, "Wow.

She never breathed a word. We wouldn't have guessed." Out of the corner of my eye, I saw Daddy and Trixie whispering to each other.

When I was standing by Mrs. Alexander, again blinded by the spotlight, she said, "Let me read to you the dare that Mary Swan received on June first of last year. 'You, Mary Swan Middleton, Raven of Wellington for the school year of 1962 and 63, have been chosen to locate three missing works of art before the end of the annual Mardi Gras Festival on Friday, February 8, 1963. These paintings were given to the Atlanta High Museum of Art by an anonymous donor and were due to be delivered on April 29 of the past year, 1961. But the paintings never arrived. There was rumor of theft, but the donor never complained to the authorities. In fact, there was never another word received from the donor, and no one knows who this mysterious person is. Locate the paintings and become one of the few successful Ravens in Wellington's history.'

" 'And here are the titles of the paintings and the artists: *Spring Bouquet*—Henry Becker, 1958. *Child at Rest*—Sheila Middleton, 1952. *Joie de Vivre*—Leslie Leschamps, 1956.' "

I heard murmurs from the audience when she pronounced Mama's name. I glanced up at Daddy, who had just flashed a picture and now leaned intently forward, elbows on his knees.

Mrs. Alexander placed her arm around my shoulder. "Mary Swan has always been one of my most"—she looked at me slyly—"shall we say, *creative* students. I love her enthusiasm for literature and her talent for poetry. She wrote the junior skit. But Mary Swan received a task much harder than simply being chosen as the Raven this year. She was asked to solve a mystery in which her mother was implicated, and then, as a tragic twist of fate, her mother was taken from her in the Orly crash.

"I spoke with Mary Swan during the summer, offering that she back out if she wanted. But Mary Swan is not a girl who gives up easily. As I have watched her conduct herself this year in spite of the terrible personal tragedy that came upon her and her family, I have been most impressed. And now I will let Mary Swan tell you what she discovered.

"But first, I'd like to present Mary Swan with her escort, who happens to be a close personal friend. Robbie Bartholomew asked to be beside you as you speak." From behind the bleachers, Robbie appeared. My knees grew weak as he lifted his eyebrows, gave a quick wink, and showed his dimples. Then he took me in his arms and whispered in my ear, "Surprise, silly girl," while the audience clapped and whistled.

I was eternally grateful for his presence there. I held on to his arm for dear life as my other hand clutched the speech I'd prepared. "Um, thank you, Mrs. Alexander. You've been a great help in spite of all the times I corrupted poems in your class." Several of the junior girls were giggling and nodding. I took a big gulp of air. "Well, as Mrs. Alexander said, it was a strange twist of fate that made the Raven Dare end up being very personal for me. I was determined to find Mama's missing painting and the other two so that they could hang in the High Museum where they were supposed to be. I felt it was the least I could do for my mother . . . and my dad." I glanced up at Daddy.

"But it turned out to be a whole lot harder than anything I've ever, ever done before. I'd like to thank my two assistants, Carl Matthews and Rachel Abrams, for all their help. I wanted to give up many times, and they were always there to encourage me. Rachel's the one on the float. Wave, Rach!" She glared down at me from her perch on the gondola, and then broke into a smile and waved.

"And Carl's the one on the sax." Carl stood briefly, and people murmured amongst themselves. "They've been wonderful friends to me, better than I could possibly say. And Robbie . . . Robbie came along after I'd chosen my two assistants, but he helped me, more than he knows, to walk through a whole lot of pain."

I licked my lips and realized I was taking too long. I unfolded the paper in my hands and looked down at the words. "What I want to say, what I need to say, is that my mother was a very talented woman. But she struggled as we all do at times with hard things." Herbert Thomas's eyes were locked on me. "Mama struggled with seasonal depression, and my dad and some other great people helped her. And a really good doctor was willing to work with her. And what I found out, what I found out is that Mama had three distinct styles of painting, and that actually, the missing paintings were not by three artists, but by one and one only, my mother, Sheila McKenzie Middleton."

There was another murmur in the crowd. Robbie felt me trembling and placed his hand over mine.

"What I discovered was that my mother loved life and painted passionately and differently according to her moods. Many people in Atlanta know her for the portraits she painted, but she also did many paintings of the outdoors, following a technique that was used by some of the great Impressionist painters. Mama actually used pseudonyms for many of her paintings, in homage to two dear people who had helped her through her illness. I had the privilege of meeting these two people, Henry Becker and Leslie Leschamps."

Again people whispered among themselves as they recognized the names of the other two artists.

"I also met Mama's physician, Dr. Clark. And he showed me many other paintings painted by my mother while she was in therapy." I paused. "Although she longed to show her different styles of painting, I think she was also terribly afraid to reveal them to the public. Dr. Clark believes that she destroyed the three missing paintings. In any case, I cannot present them to you tonight.

"But even though I'm not a successful Raven, the things I learned about Mama and the people I love are far, far more important. It's been the hardest year of my life, but I'm glad for the Dare, because I found out the truth about Mama. She was a fine, complicated, extremely talented woman.

"I just want to say thank you to everyone who helped me this year. And I'll end with a quote from a very famous man. It's been my favorite lesson from this year. 'You shall know the truth, and the truth will make you free.' Jesus said it, and I've found that it's true."

Tears were blurring the words on the page. Robbie put his arm around my waist and whispered, "Great job," and we turned to leave.

But Mrs. Alexander stopped us. "I believe someone has one more announcement." She caught my eye, and I'll swear hers were filled with mischief, as if she'd just corrupted one of *my* poems.

Suddenly Carl was beside us, and Leo and Big Man were busy setting up three big easels right there on the basketball court. Then Nickie appeared carrying a painting and Larry came in with two others, one under each arm. I watched in shock as they carefully placed those beautifully framed paintings, Mama's paintings, on the easels!

Carl stood in front of the microphone and squinted into the spotlight. "Hello there," he said, his voice shaky. Then he whispered to me, "Man, Mary Swan, how'd you git the nerve to do this?" My eyes were wide, and I just mouthed to him, "What in the world are you doing?" But he paid no attention and turned back to the mike.

"Hello. Like Mary Swan's already said, I'm Carl Matthews. I know you might be surprised to see me here, but the fact is, Mary Swan is one of my very dear friends. She taught me a lot when I helped with her dare. I must admit, I thought it was a silly waste of time 'til I started understanding the significance and 'til I started understanding Mary Swan. 'Cause she didn't look at me like I was a Negro. She just looked at me like I was a person, and she saw the good things in me.

"But that's not what I wanted to say. I wanted to tell you the end of the story. 'Cause here before you are the three missing paintings."

Hushed conversation rippled through the audience. "Her mama's paintings. Mary Swan did find them. She found them hanging on the wall in her maid's bedroom. Her maid, Ella Mae Maddux. Mary Swan went to visit Ella Mae the other day and found them there. But she didn't say a word to Ella Mae about the Raven Dare, 'cause she knew it was a whole lot more important for Ella Mae to enjoy these paint-ings than for Mary Swan to solve a dare. Ya see, Ella Mae's been sick. Had a brain tumor removed.

"And that's how the story would have ended if I hadn't just hap-pened to go see Ella Mae this afternoon. I wanted to bring her to Mardi Gras if I could, 'cause Mary Swan is just like family to Ella Mae, and I knew Ella Mae would want to be here to see her Mary Swan. And that's when I saw these here paintings. I guessed where they came from, and after a little prodding, Ella Mae told me the story of how they got there. I don't have time ta tell ya the story, but it's a good one. When I explained to Ella Mae about the Raven Dare . . ." He paused and looked at me. "Sorry, Mary Swan, but I had to tell her. When I told her about the Dare, well, she insisted I bring the paintings and that she come along with me. There she is, up there in the wheel-chair."

I saw her as in a mirage, way up on the section of the gym without bleachers, with Miss Abigail and Roy on either side, that white band-age all around her head. She lifted a weak arm and waved to me.

"She wanted more than anything for these paintin's to be presented tonight. Mary Swan found them. She solved the Dare." He backed off from the microphone.

For a moment no one said a thing. I even think a lot of people were wiping their eyes. Then someone yelled out, "Congratulations,

Mary Swan!" and the whole junior class erupted into hysterical cries of joy. I was soon engulfed by what felt like hundreds of arms and hands, all congratulating me and saying, "Great job, Mary Swan" and "You are one brave lady" and stuff like that.

By now Mrs. Alexander was back at the mike, trying to calm the girls down. "Mary Swan Middleton, Raven of Wellington for 1963, successful in your mission, I present to you a sizeable check and gifts in stocks to be given to the charity or nonprofit organization of your choice." Then she handed me a shiny silver plaque with my name and the year engraved on it.

I don't remember what she said next, but it didn't matter, because all of a sudden I could feel Daddy's arms around me, squeezing me tight. "I'm so proud of you, my Swannee, so very, very proud. Bless your heart." His voice was cracking. We walked together over to the three paintings and just stared at them in silence. Daddy was all choked up.

"So it was Ella Mae who had them. Well, that doesn't surprise me one bit." He was looking straight at the painting of Ella Mae holding me in her arms, and there were tears streaming down his face, and no one else in the whole gymnasium dared come near. They all with one accord just seemed to know we needed this private moment together. Finally Daddy whispered, "Your mother would be very proud of you too. You did the right thing."

Those words from Daddy were the sweetest possible. That was the highlight of the evening, that and seeing Ella Mae in the balcony. So it hardly mattered at all that the junior class won the skit competition and came in second in the float competition, which gave us the overall victory, winning over the seniors by a mere three points. That announcement was followed by an invitation for everyone present to join the Wellington girls on the basketball court to end the night with dancing.

The three paintings were carefully moved into the foyer of the gym and guarded by two policemen, and all throughout the rest of the night, I could see people standing there, observing Mama's work. The expressions on their faces were sad and sweet and, I don't know, like something had touched them deep down inside. Just like Mama had said that art could do.

Mamie stood there for a long time with Papy, reaching out as though she wanted to feel the texture in the paintings, as if in so doing, she could feel Mama again. And she cried a lot. When I saw her standing there crying, hard yet frail Mamie, the anger I'd felt toward her kind of melted. Mamie was someone who had been hurt by life. I was sure there were many other secrets about Mama and her parents that I did not want to unveil.

Before they left the gymnasium, Mamie found me on the dance floor and kissed me hard on both cheeks, leaving bright red lipstick smeared there. *"Magnifique, Marie des Cygnes. Absolument magnifique. Ta maman serait fière de toi."*

Very proud, my mother would be.

"I did it for her. For her memory." Something like compassion welled up inside me and I said, "I'll come see you soon, Mamie and Papy. I promise."

"You do that, Lassie," Papy said in his Scottish brogue.

I was never sure afterward if I had really seen Ella Mae or if it had been, after all, a mirage, because when I looked for her and Roy and Miss Abigail later, they were nowhere to be found. Neither did I have the chance to ask Carl to explain the events of the afternoon in detail. He and his band were busy playing. Robbie and I danced together, and it reminded me of the first time we'd danced at the Back-to-School Ball. And there, jitterbugging right beside us, was Daddy with Trixie. And the look on their faces was like that of two love-struck teenagers.

Chapter 29

I t was somewhere around 11:00 P.M. and the last people were leaving the gymnasium. "See ya at the house in a minute!" I called out to Daddy and Trixie and Jimmy as they headed to the parking lot. Carl and the band waved back to me as they stepped outside, lugging their instruments. Robbie and I stayed in the foyer, carefully rewrapping the paintings, which we'd decided to take back to my house until we learned what Ella Mae wanted to do with them. Rachel, tiara in place, had her arms wrapped around Will.

"I'll get the car," Robbie said.

"Yeah, me too," Will echoed.

"What gentlemen!" Rachel giggled.

"We wouldn't want the two stars of the evening to catch cold in the night air," Robbie quipped. "Anyway, those paintings are heavy." And they took off.

"There's the real reason! They don't want to have to carry the paintings too far."

"Oh, who cares! It's been the most magnificent night, hasn't it, Swan?"

I nodded. "I think when I get home, I'll stay awake all night thinking about everything. How it all worked out."

"Were you surprised about Robbie and Carl and the paintings?"

"Everything. Did you know about it?"

"Only about Robbie being your escort. Nothing else. Why didn't you tell me about finding the paintings at Ella Mae's?"

"I couldn't, Rach. Couldn't tell a soul. I was afraid I'd change my mind and convince myself that I should have the paintings at Mardi Gras. And somehow I knew that wasn't right."

"But they got here anyway."

"Yeah. But not by my scheming." I picked up the biggest canvas with a grunt, then set it back down. "You know what I think?"

"No idea."

"I think God himself sent Carl to Ella Mae's this afternoon, and then brought her here tonight."

"Silly, scatterbrained girl. I told you not to get religious on me!" But she was laughing.

Glancing outside, I said, "What is taking them so long? Let's go tell them to hurry up!"

I walked out into the brisk night air, drawing my coat over the dress and cape, Rachel's arm draped through mine, both of us leaning back and laughing, our eyes bright and our cheeks red from cold and excitement. When we got to the parking lot, I was surprised and pleased to see all of them talking together in a tight little knot—Daddy and Trixie and Jimmy and Robbie and Will and Mrs. Alexander and Carl and the rest of the band.

"Can you believe it?" I commented to Rachel. "Black and white together!"

It was only as we drew closer that I saw that none of them were smiling, that Jimmy was in fact crying as Trixie held him and that Daddy and Robbie and Carl were gesturing and nodding, looking much too serious for the end of such a spectacular occasion.

Jimmy saw me first and came running over. "It's Ella Mae! She's dying! She's dying right now in the hospital. Miss Abigail called the gym and told Mrs. Alexander."

Daddy came over to me and said, "I wish you didn't have to hear it tonight, Swan."

I swallowed hard, feeling my knees give way beneath me and clinging to Rachel, who was supporting my weight. "Is she still alive?"

"I think so. We just got the call about fifteen minutes ago." This was from Mrs. Alexander.

"Then we've got to get there fast!" I cried.

The news, so sudden, so unexpected, left me numb, just like the aftermath of the Paris plane crash. I was still holding the plaque with the inscription for the successful Raven of 1963 in my hands and still seeing in my mind the blurred faces of Ella Mae, Roy, and Miss Abigail smiling down at me from the balcony.

"Why did she come out when she was so sick? She didn't have the strength! She shouldn't have come! That's what did it!" I wailed.

Then Carl, oblivious, I guess, to the fact that everyone else was right there, took me tenderly by the shoulders and said, "I'm so sorry, Mary Swan. So very sorry." He hugged me tight, all the while explaining, "I don't know what made me go ta see her. Something did. Went with Miss Abigail. When I went in her bedroom and saw those paintings, well, right away I knew whose they were. And I don't know why I told her all about that dare, but I thought it was the right thing ta do, and I still do. 'Cause when she heard it, her face got all radiant and she said, 'Praise the Lawd! If there's somethin' I can do to help my Swannee, I'm gonna do it. That sweet chile neva' breathed a word ta me when she was here last week.' And she was bound an' determined to come. That's why I was late tonight, Mary Swan. Like ta neva' git those paintings and Ella Mae in th' car. Roy and Miss Abigail and me, we told her she was too sick to go, but she started hollerin' and sayin' she was going to see her Mary Swan if it was the last thing she did. She knew, Mary Swan. I think she knew she wasn't gonna be here much longer. She wanted to see you tonight."

"They couldn't get the whole tumor," Daddy added softly. And at the sound of his voice, Carl let go of me quick, staring awkwardly at his shoes. "It was intertwined around the brain stem. The doctor said it was a matter of months, maybe just weeks."

"Why didn't you tell me? Why didn't you tell me! I thought you were done with hiding the truth."

"Sweetheart, we didn't know how long she had. She was so weak. She needed every ounce of strength to pull through. That's why she couldn't have visitors for so long. Ella Mae's smart. The doctor told her he couldn't get the whole tumor. She knew she didn't have long. But she didn't want to die at the hospital. She wanted to go home. She said she had everything she needed right there at home. More than any doctor could give her. I didn't see how it could help to tell you there was no hope. You've seemed . . . you've seemed so full of hope these last few weeks."

Hope. The word suddenly sounded flat.

Daddy's hand was on my shoulder. "She knew. She was ready. She told me so."

Me too, I thought. She told me too, only I didn't want to hear it.

She told me she was going somewhere better and that one way or another it was all going to be okay.

Robbie hugged me hard and said, "Mary Swan, you go on with your dad to the hospital. The rest of us will deal with the paintings."

So I climbed into the backseat of Daddy's Jaguar and buried my face in my hands. Jimmy was up front with Daddy, and Trixie sat beside me, arms wrapped around me, not saying a word.

We met a nurse in the hall outside Ella Mae's room. "I'll tell Mr. Maddux you're here," she said.

A moment later Roy came from her room, followed by a young black couple. Roy looked skinnier than I'd ever seen him, vulnerable, like a lost child. "She'll be right happy ta see ya, Mista Middleton. Mary Swan and Jimmy too," he mumbled.

Daddy's face was set, and he just nodded.

We entered the hospital room and saw Ella Mae lying there, her black skin swaddled in white sheets, her eyes glazed, her breathing heavy. Miss Abigail sat very still by the window, looking as though she'd wept every tear that she'd ever had. That set me to crying, seeing Miss Abigail so torn up.

Daddy spent a moment whispering something to Ella Mae, and then Jimmy went over to her, sobbing. "Ella Mae, I'm sorry. I'm sorry for you, and I'm sorry that I've been such a pest! So bad."

"Loved every minute of bein' with you, boy." That came out in a raspy whisper.

Then I bent down beside Ella Mae. At first all I could do was moan, a pitiful, gut-wrenching painful sound from inside. Then a sob. "I'm so sorry." I grasped her hand and felt the effort of her fingers closing over mine.

"Mighty proud o' ya, Mary Swan. Mighty glad I got ta see ya there tonight." Her breathing was labored. "It's gonna be all right now, Mary Swan," she whispered. "Don't ya worry none, my girl. It's gonna be all right now." Her eyes fluttered and closed.

"No!" I spat out through the searing in my chest. "No, Ella Mae!" Again her fingers pressed against mine, the warmth of her life still there. "You can't die, Ella Mae! God wouldn't take both you and Mama in one year."

"I'm ready, and so are you. Go on, honey."

I let out another soft wail and bent down and kissed her softly on the cheek.

Miss Abigail took me gently by the shoulders and said, "It's time to let her family say their good-byes." And as I left the room, Roy and a beautiful young woman whom I recognized as Loretta and the young man who must have been her husband came back into the room. Pastor James must have just arrived, because he came into the room with them.

I squeezed Roy's hand and then caught him in a hug, and he patted me on the back and said, "Now, now."

Loretta went straight into the arms of Miss Abigail, and I figured she must have been there many times before, and then they all gathered around Ella Mae's bed and Pastor James started praying. I wanted to stay there with them. I hesitated, knew it wasn't my place, and left the room. About ten minutes later Miss Abigail came out into the hall and nodded slightly in the way that let us know it was all over.

When the rest of them came back into the hall, no one said a word. It struck me as bittersweet and ironic that Ella Mae's two families had been brought together for the first time simply by her death. Daddy put his arm around poor Roy, who was crying his heart out. Loretta's husband was holding her around the waist, and her head was buried in her hands. Pastor James came up to Jimmy and me. "Mighty sorry, chil'un, about this."

We must have stayed there like that, Daddy, Trixie, Jimmy, Roy, Loretta and her husband, Miss Abigail and Pastor James for an hour. At one point, Loretta came over to me and said, "Hello, Mary Swan. I don't think you remember me, but I'm Loretta."

I looked deep into her eyes, remembering only the face I'd seen ten days ago in Ella Mae's photo album. She spoke in a soft, melodic way. "When you were tiny, just a baby, I used ta come over to your house with Mama. I watched you sometimes while Mama was cooking and such. I was about ten at the time. Mama thought it'd help me, seein' as how I'd lost my big sister."

"Gina, right?"

"Yeah. Gina died right around the time Mama started working at your house."

"I'm so sorry, Loretta. Sorry I don't even remember you."

"Not your fault. I stopped going over there soon after Jimmy was born. I was old enough ta stay home by myself." She took the young man by the hand and said, "This here's my husband, Reggie."

"Nice to meet you, Reggie."

He nodded somberly and said, "Sorry to meet under these circumstances."

I just nodded. "Do you live around here?"

"Reggie's training to be a doctor. He's in his last year of residency. We live in Monroe."

"Loretta's a nurse," Reggie added proudly.

"And you've got a baby. Roy showed me a picture of her. An adorable little girl."

Loretta smiled for the first time. "Mattie Mae. She's nineteen months old. Named her after both of our mothers."

"Your mother was a wonderful woman," I sniffed. "We're all gonna miss her so much." I teared up again.

"I know it's been hard on you, since the plane crash. I'm awfully sorry."

It was time to go, so we just awkwardly said good-bye.

"I'll talk to you tomorrow, Roy, about the funeral," Daddy said.

When I hugged Miss Abigail good-bye, I whispered, "I can't bear to think she's gone. Not with Mama gone too."

She held on to me tightly for a moment and then took me by the shoulders, looking me straight in the eyes. "Let Jesus carry you now, honey. As only He can. Just be sad, and let Him carry you and your father and your brother. He'll do it. He's promised that He will."

So I did stay awake all night, but not for the reasons I'd expected. When we got home, I laid my satin gown and cape on my bed and pulled on old jeans and a sweatshirt and tiptoed down one flight of stairs. I listened for a sound from Jimmy's room, but there was none. I let myself into the *atelier*. The canvas I had started a month ago, the one I called *The Swan House in Snow*, sat on an easel, bright and hopeful. But I couldn't bear to touch it with a paintbrush while the sorrow was so very heavy in my heart.

Instead, I took the first canvas I'd ever painted, the one I'd started in anger after Trixie had confirmed to me that Mama had spent a lot of time at Resthaven. It was the one that Rachel had glimpsed and had then commented that I had talent like Mama's. It was the painting I had hidden from Carl the day that he'd ventured into the *atelier* with me.

I plopped it on the easel in front of those wide windows and stared out into the dark. For a while I didn't turn on a light, but just watched the background of the star-flecked sky that rose from above the tree line of our yard. Finally flipping on the light switch, I took a paintbrush and palette and began the only exercise I had found to calm the running emotions of my heart. I painted.

It was a painting of a cemetery, and I had almost finished it. The old tombstones in Oakland had inspired me, tombstones from the nineteenth century, everything from simple stone markers to ornate mausoleums and tall obelisks with intricately carved sculptures.

In the foreground of my canvas I had painted a large stone angel, almost life-size, reminiscent of a marker I'd seen in Oakland. God's emissary was holding a book in one hand and pointing heavenward with the other as a confirmation of life after death. Beside this dramatic tombstone a young woman knelt, her head bowed in prayer, a bouquet of flowers draped across her lap. Her face was hidden by her long hair.

Far to the right were white dots representing the plain stone markers for the Confederate soldiers, and even farther in the distance spread a green field, Potter's Field, with the tiny figure of a black man kneeling, hat off, head bent, a lone rose lying on the ground beside him. I had taken artistic liberty and painted Mt. Carmel Church behind Potter's Field, its red-brick exterior reaching, like the angel in the foreground, to the sky. The rest of the canvas was dotted with mausoleums and obelisks and other tombstones that I had found particularly poignant.

Now I knew that one more thing needed to be added, and I worked almost feverishly to get it right. It must have taken me almost half the night. When I set down my palette and brush and studied my work, I shuddered. Behind the angel tombstone as the cemetery gradually descended in slope, between the white girl kneeling in the foreground and the black man in the background, I'd painted a young black woman, also kneeling beside a much smaller tombstone. Her head was also bent, and she too held a bouquet of flowers in her hand.

My eyes were almost as heavy as my heart by the time I put the paintbrush in a jar of turpentine and turned off the light. The climb up the stairs to my room seemed to take an eternity. I flopped onto my bed, beyond exhaustion.

Miss Abigail had said, "Let Jesus carry you now." And somehow, as I lay on my bed, drifting off to sleep, the heaviness lifted and something else replaced it. A lightness. Yes, a sensation of being surrounded by a presence or by an abstract quality. Freedom.

Saturday dawned gray and drizzly, and the three of us hovered in our fresh grief around the breakfast room table. Daddy was trying to read the *Atlanta Constitution,* and Jimmy was making paper airplanes out of the want-ad section, and I just leaned onto the table, closing my eyes and resting my head on my arms. Around ten, Trixie brought over freshly baked cinnamon rolls, but none of us felt like eating. I wondered to myself how in the world this big old house, which had seemed so empty after Mama's death, could seem like anything but a downright hollow shell with Ella Mae gone too. The only sound in the house was the clinking of our knives and forks as we cut the piping hot cinnamon rolls and brought the bites slowly to our mouths.

Later we moved into the living room, where Daddy lit a fire in the fireplace.

"Can I let Muffin inside, Daddy?" Jimmy asked.

"Yes, of course," Daddy answered, sounding almost relieved.

Muffin bounded in the back door, dashing through the kitchen, into the entrance hall, and around through the living room, with Jimmy in hot pursuit. Muffin's tail was wagging so hard that it almost knocked over a small porcelain object on the coffee table, but Daddy didn't even seem to notice. Normally not allowed inside, Muffin brought life and energy to us that morning. He effortlessly entertained us, and I even saw Daddy smile in approval when Jimmy got on the floor and began wrestling with his mutt.

"Mary Swan, would you like me to take you to Mt. Carmel?" Daddy volunteered a little later in the morning.

"I don't know. I don't know if I could bear it today." Then I cuddled up beside him on the sofa, stretching my feet onto the ottoman and resting my head on his shoulder. "But thanks for offering. Thanks a lot."

Then Daddy and I had the exact same thought. We'd bring the three paintings into the living room, set them on easels, and just watch them by firelight.

"Do you mind if I go outside to play with Muffin?" It was Jimmy's way of dealing with grief. We both knew that by now.

"By all means, go ahead, son. I'll be out in a little while to throw the baseball."

"So you were chosen to be the Raven and received the Raven Dare right before the crash." Daddy was standing in front of the paintings, his back to me. "And you never breathed a word. And that's why you asked all those questions about the exhibition and the disappearance of the paintings and Resthaven."

"I kept finding out more and more things about Mama. Bad things. And since you wouldn't say a word, well, I asked Trixie. She hated telling me anything, but she saw how torn up I was. And I couldn't tell you that all my questions were for a good cause. I'd be disqualified!"

"I'm sure, under the circumstances, Mrs. Alexander would have understood. She called me last week, wanting to be sure I was planning on attending Mardi Gras. She suggested I bring your grandparents too."

"She told you I was the Raven?" I asked incredulously.

"No, no. She was very discreet. I really didn't have any idea. She just strongly suggested that I would want to be there since you were the author and narrator of the junior skit. Of course, I was already planning to come."

Mrs. Alexander. She certainly was emerging from this whole affair as a friend. Then I announced bluntly, "I've seen the paintings at Resthaven, Daddy."

"Yes, Dr. Clark mentioned your visit."

"He did?"

"We've been talking quite a bit off and on since the crash. I, too, have been to Resthaven and seen the paintings."

"Yes, he told me. But why didn't you say anything to me?"

"Sweetheart, I don't think you can understand. It is still very hard to talk about Mama, to think about the past. It was very painful—very painful. Every time she left for Resthaven, it was like a death. The death of our family."

The same grayish expression that he'd had when he returned from Paris outlined his face. I felt, maybe for the first time, some of Daddy's misery across the years. I wanted to console him, but there was nothing to say.

Daddy cleared his throat. "I've decided what to do with the money for your mother's memorial fund. Your mother had already created a room at Resthaven for art therapy—an *atelier*."

"Yes, I saw it!"

"And so, what would you think about transforming the room where her paintings were stored into a small gallery for different artists' works from Resthaven to be hung? And then maybe offer a scholarship there for aspiring painters."

"Oh, Daddy, that's a great idea!"

"I hope Dr. Clark will be pleased with it. I also plan to talk to the High Museum about an eventual exhibition—with the three paintings you found at Ella Mae's and then a loan from Resthaven for the others."

"Would that work, Daddy? Would people want to come to an exhibition of just Mama's paintings?"

"That is for the museum to decide." He nodded to the paintings before us. "What should we do with these three?"

"Don't they belong to the museum?"

"Technically, but no one will claim them now that the truth is out. They'll respect the wishes of the family."

"Don't you think Roy should be able to choose, Daddy? After all, Mama gave them to Ella Mae."

"Roy?" He shrugged, then caught himself and said, "Yes. Yes, that's a good idea. I'll talk to him." He got that preoccupied look on his face and said, "Better get outside with Jimmy."

But as he was walking out the back door, he turned and said, "There's been a lot going on for you, Swan, so you may not remember, but last week two paintings arrived from Paris, on loan to Atlanta from the Louvre. A gesture from France in commemoration of the crash. A way to show their sorrow over our tragedy."

"Which paintings?"

"*Whistler's Mother* and *Penitent St. Mary Magdalene*. The Art Association organized a big welcome party for the ambassador from France and his wife. I've heard they made a representation of the Eiffel Tower out of flowers and put it in their suite! Anyway, I thought maybe you and I could go down to the High sometime next week, if you'd like."

"That's a good idea, Daddy. Something to look forward to after . . ." My voice cracked.

"Something to look forward to, sweetheart." And he went outside.

Ella Mae's funeral was on Monday afternoon at Mt. Carmel. The sanctuary, which had been empty when I bowed before the altar a month ago, was now crammed with people. Loretta found me as we were walking down the aisle looking for a place to sit and said, "If you and your family would like to sit up front with us, we thought that would be just how Mama would have liked it."

So the five of us, Daddy, Jimmy, Trixie, Robbie, and I sat next to Roy and Loretta and Reggie on the front pew. The pianist was softly playing the hymn, "What a Friend We Have in Jesus," and I could hear sniffling all around me. Ella Mae's casket, a beautiful shiny mahogany one, sat right in front of us with a bouquet of flowers on it. Dozens of other flower arrangements were spread out across the front of the sanctuary.

Pastor James stepped to the pulpit and started to speak. "Dearly beloved in Christ, we are gathered here today to honor the memory of one of our most precious sista's in the Lawd, Ella Mae Maddux. Ella Mae was a member of Mt. Carmel for almost forty years, ever since she and her husband, Roy, moved to Atlanta from Monroe, Georgia, back in the 1920s. For most of those years she he'ped in various ways here at Mt. Carmel, ways ya didn't often notice. With the chil'un, in the kitchen, cleanin' up afta' a meal, he'pin' Miss Abigail with the lunches on Saturdays. We sure do remember her fried chicken and her fine pies and that delicious strawberry shortcake she was famous for."

There were murmurs of "Sho' do," from behind me, and I glanced over my shoulder to see many men and women nodding their heads.

" 'Cause Ella Mae was a servant of Jesus. That's what she was. Not one to eva' go on about herself, she was known for her kindness to her family and neighbors when they were in difficulty, and for her joyful disposition.

"Not that she wasn't acquainted with grief. Ella Mae and Roy raised two fine young women, Gina and Loretta. Gina was killed in an automobile accident right near the church ova' fifteen years ago. Yes,

Ella Mae has known sufferin', and she shared in others' pain with her tender heart.

"As many of you know, Ella Mae also worked on the otha' side of town, ova' in Buckhead for a white family who are with us today. John Jason Middleton and his children, Mary Swan and Jimmy. One of the hardest things Ella Mae had to face was the death of Miz Middleton in that plane crash in Paris last June." He got a little choked up and paused for a moment. "She worked for this family for more than sixteen years, and Roy wanted me ta make sure and say how much she loved them, and how much she appreciated all they did ta help her and Roy out." He glanced our way and nodded solemnly.

"We sure are gonna miss Ella Mae, 'cause we weren't ready for her ta leave us. No, we weren't." He leaned against the pulpit and stared intently into the congregation. "But ya know what, my brotha's and sista's? She was ready. Ella Mae was ready to meet her Savior. She loved her Jesus with her whole heart, and it was that faith in Him that allowed her to live through a heap o' trouble with a song in her heart and a smile on her lips. And so I know she would want me ta ask ya this question today, the question that was the most important for her. Are you ready? Are you ready ta meet yore Savior? It's the most important decision you'll eva' make in yore whole life. He's waiting fo' you, arms outstretched, yore Savior and friend."

Pastor James talked on about Jesus for another ten minutes, and then the whole congregation sang three hymns. Then Pastor James spoke again.

"Before we leave here today, I want to tell you that the church has received two beautiful paintin's in memory of Ella Mae. The first one was painted by Miz Sheila Middleton. This here paintin' was given to Ella Mae by Sheila, and the Middleton family has kindly given it to our church." Pastor James brought out the painting of Ella Mae holding me. The congregation seemed to strain together as one, trying to get a better view of the painting. Many of the women dabbed their eyes. "I think this painting is a poignant reminder of the times we are living in, times of unrest and change. Times of hope. Hope."

He motioned to me, and I stood up. "The second paintin' has been given to us by Miss Mary Swan Middleton. I believe she would like to say a word to us today. Mary Swan?"

I made my way beside Pastor James and looked out onto the congregation of black faces. And what I had to do then seemed a hundred times harder suddenly than the speech I'd made on Friday night. The knot in my throat wouldn't go away, and fresh tears threatened to spill from my eyes at any second. My legs trembled slightly.

"I just wanted to say how much I loved Ella Mae. How much she was like a second mother to me. Like Pastor James said, my own mother died in the Orly crash, and well, with Ella Mae gone, I sure am going to miss them both. But I also wanted to give something to your church. I kind of feel like it's my church too, because I come down here on Saturdays to help with the lunches. Ella Mae brought me down when I was grieving for my mother, and she was right—it helped me a lot. She was like that. She knew how to help people get beyond themselves.

"So I wanted to give you the first painting I've ever painted." I turned around and retrieved my painting of Oakland Cemetery from the alcove. "I'm not a famous painter or gifted like Mama, but all through the fall I've been working on this painting. Painting this has helped me grieve, and well, I think we're all gonna be grieving some more. But this painting is about hope. I found hope in this sanctuary about a month ago. And I'm not sure why, but I think this painting should be for you all."

Pastor James held up my unframed canvas of Oakland Cemetery— my representation of the year of death. This was Carl and Loretta and me, brought together in one place by the graves of those we had loved. Faced with death, we were, in fact, exactly the same, bent forward in prayer and grief. You could not tell what color the person's skin was under those heavy tombstones.

"Thank ya, Mary Swan. Thank ya kindly. It's a lovely gift," Pastor James was saying. Then to the congregation he encouraged, "Please feel free ta come by and admire these paintin's afta' the service."

I caught sight of Carl beaming back at me from the congregation, nodding his head in approval. And as I sat back down, I thought of what he had said to me. *"One day, Mary Swan, you're gonna do somethin' from your heart, not just somethin' that shows your brains. You're gonna do somethin' that makes people cry. Somethin' that touches their soul."* So now as I looked out at the congregation, I saw that nearly every face was glistening and wet. The black faces and the white ones. Even Daddy's.

Carl had been right. Painting revealed my heart. If I really felt something strong enough and dared to put it onto canvas, maybe the real Mary Swan would come out after all.

Chapter 30

T hank goodness spring came early to Atlanta that year. As soon as
February neared the end of its twenty-eight-day countdown, the
weather warmed, and nature began proclaiming a rebirth. The pansies
and primroses were still tossing their winter heads when the tulips
bloomed, and then the first shoots appeared on the dogwood trees and
the azaleas came out and covered the lawns of all the houses in Buckhead. Just driving from my house to school was a feast for my eyes.
The trees and shrubs boasted every possible shade of pink, and there
was plenty of red and white and purple and yellow splashed across the
yards too. For me it was a sign that the terrible year of death was
maybe behind us, and that life would indeed continue.

On a breezy Saturday in early March, I drove to Mt. Carmel for
the first time since Ella Mae's funeral two and a half weeks earlier. I
felt a pinching in my chest without Ella Mae at the wheel, and I
blinked back tears during the whole drive.

As soon as I stepped into the fellowship hall, people called out,
"Mighty fine ta see ya, Mary Swan." Then Carl and I began our weekly
routine of serving spaghetti and garlic bread.

As we were finishing up the dishes, Carl said, "Puddin' and the
boys and I were wonderin' if you'd come with us to the cemetery."

"I don't know, Carl. I've been to too many cemeteries this year."

"It's beautiful right now," Carl commented wistfully. "I think you'd
like to see it."

So once again we all walked from Mt. Carmel to Oakland Cemetery. We passed under those brick arches and along the uneven road,
and I found myself smiling. Life was blooming all around us at

Oakland. We stopped beside a dogwood tree and examined its pink blooms.

"Do you know that there's a story in the dogwood blossom?" I asked the children, and they shook their heads.

"Look at the flower. It's in the shape of a cross, and at the end of each petal it looks like there are nail prints. There's even what looks like a tiny crown of thorns in the center. It's like God is reminding us through His creation of Christ's death and resurrection." The children peered intently at the dogwood blossom while I thought to myself that none of these things had ever seemed remotely important to me before. But now they did. My, how it mattered that there was hope.

Carl helped each sibling pick a blossom from the tree, and then we walked to my mother's tombstone. I knelt by the simple marker. Puddin' got down beside me, squinted at the writing on the marker, and read, "Sheila McKenzie Middleton, 1924–1962. Beloved wife, mother, artist, friend." Then she looked up at me, perplexed, and said, "I cain't make one bit o' sense outta the otha' words written there."

I laughed. "Of course you can't! That's because they're written in French. My mama was half French. And one of her favorite painters was a Frenchman named Claude Monet." I slowly pronounced the words, *"Je sais seulement que je fais ce que je peux pour exprimer ce que j'éprouve devant la nature."*

"That sounds perty, Mary Swan! What does it mean?"

"It's a quote from Mr. Monet, and it says, 'I only know that I do what I can to express what I feel from nature.' Something like that. Anyway, we chose the quote because it was one of Mama's favorite's and because it's what she tried to do, too, as an artist."

"I wish we had a place to visit my mama's grave," Mike said solemnly.

I stood up. "You don't know where she's buried?"

"Nope," he said sadly.

"Didn't have any money for a burial," Carl explained. "Miss Abigail tried to find out. She thinks Mama's buried at a cemetery a far piece from here. So me and the kids come here to Oakland and go down to Potter's Field and lay our flowers down in the field full of unmarked graves. The children take whatever nature offers." He nodded to them. "Y'all kin go on." And they took off down the gently sloping hill to the back of the large cemetery.

"I was pretty sure you were praying in Potter's Field every time you came here with me," I said.

"Yeah. You got that right in your painting, Mary Swan. Every time you visit your mother's grave, I jus' go down there and kneel in the grass and thank the good Lord for my mother. 'Cause no matter how messed up she was, she still gave life to me and my siblings, and I'm thankful for that."

We were slowly walking toward Potter's Field when Carl stopped and sat down beside the bronze statue of a wounded lion that was set in the part of the cemetery where all the Confederate soldiers were buried. I took a seat beside him.

"I wanted to tell you, Mary Swan, that I won't be coming down to Mt. Carmel on Saturdays much anymore."

I couldn't hide the surprise on my face.

"I've been accepted at Morehouse College for next year." He smiled with satisfaction.

"That's really great, Carl. Right here in Atlanta. So you can still live at home?"

"Yeah. But I've got to take a couple of classes starting soon to catch up. They meet on Friday nights and Saturday mornin's. And then I'll be workin' on Saturday afternoons at the gas station. Gotta git in extra hours to help pay for tuition."

I felt my chest constrict.

"So I won't have much time. But I sure hope you'll keep coming down to help Miss Abigail. She really appreciates it." He looked slightly embarrassed. "I mean, I hope that now that Ella Mae isn't here, and well, I won't be around as much, well, I hope you won't think you're not needed."

"No, Carl. I'll keep coming," I said too quickly. Then after some thought, I added, "I don't know if they need me, but I need these people. They're my friends."

He looked me in the eyes and said, "Well, then, that's mighty fine."

I felt a sweet closeness and an unexplainable distance from him at the same time.

"I wish you wouldn't keep staring at me with those green eyes of yours, girl."

"I'm sorry. It just seems like this is good-bye."

"Ain't good-bye, Mary Swan. That's one good thing about the Lord. In the Lord, we just gotta say, 'I'll be seein' you around sometime.'"

I threw my arms around him, and he held me tight against him in that quiet, empty section of the cemetery, me crying into his chest. Then he let go of me and stood up and sauntered off down the hill to where Mike and James and Puddin' were playing in the field.

Jean-Pierre Rampal was playing on the stereo in my room, and Rachel was lying on her back next to me on my bed. "Do you think Carl was trying to say good-bye permanently?" Rachel asked.

"I don't know. But I think he wanted to make sure I'd still help out down at Grant Park. And I want to. Only, it makes me wonder if I've changed at all. Or if I only went down there because of Carl."

"You've changed all right," Rachel assured me, but she had a funny little smile on her face. Suddenly I realized she was staring at my chest.

"Oh, Rachel! For heaven's sake. I'm not talking about my body. I'm talking about what's inside. About my soul!" I said it in my best melodramatic voice.

"Well, of course you are, Swan! And that's precisely why I know you've changed. Last year all you could think about was your body. Now you're thinking about real, important matters. You've changed."

"You really think so?"

"Absolutely. You've got a purpose or something. You believe in something bigger than yourself or your upbringing. You're religious, open-minded, less sheltered, artistic. . . ."

I sighed.

Rachel affirmed, "You've done well, Swannee. I didn't know if you'd make it, but you have. You're just great, you know it?"

"Thanks, Rach. Thanks. That means a lot."

We listened to Jean-Pierre until the record ended, and as I lifted up the needle and turned off the record player, I said, "Speaking of changes, Rach, are you ready to tackle the *atelier*?"

"You bet!"

So we ran down the steps and into Mama's studio. I'd decided to clean it up and make it mine, and Rachel had offered to help me get everything organized.

Right away she wanted to start throwing things out. "I'm not sentimentally attached like you."

"But I can't just toss out Mama's things."

"You can't, but I can."

"You have to check it out with me first," I insisted.

"Fine. Take this, for example. It's a half-empty tube of paint that's all dried up. Please don't tell me you feel a sentimental attachment to it." And to prove her point she pushed hard on the middle of the small tube with red paint caked on the top. Suddenly a long flow of oil paint squirted out at me, and the look on Rachel's face was priceless.

I started giggling, and then she joined in, and before long we were in hysterics. That lasted a few minutes, but Rachel quickly regained her composure and went about her task in complete seriousness.

As I carefully stacked up different sketchbooks, I came across the one that Mama had used on the European trip, the one that Daddy had brought home in his suitcase. Slowly, reverently, I leafed through the pages. She'd sketched in Paris, London, Edinburgh, Amsterdam, Vienna, Madrid, Florence, and Rome.

"I'm going to Europe," I announced.

Rachel didn't even look up. "Good—you'll enjoy it." She'd been to Europe three times.

"No, what I mean is that I'm going to Europe, and I'm going back to visit each of the museums Mama visited, and I'll sketch and paint to my heart's content."

That got her attention. "Wow, Swan."

"I have to do it, for her memory. You can come, too, if you want."

"When will you go?"

"I don't know. I guess I'll have to wait and see. I'm sure someone will make it clear to me."

"Someone?"

"Yeah." I nodded heavenward. "Someone."

Rachel just rolled her eyes at me and said, "No doubt about it. You've changed."

Near the beginning of May, Daddy and Jimmy and I drove up to Resthaven on a Sunday afternoon. By now the long treelined drive and the stately brick mansion with its white columns looked familiar to me. Dr. Clark greeted us at the entrance.

"I hope we haven't inconvenienced you, Dr. Clark, coming on Sunday."

"Not at all. My pleasure. Please come have a seat."

After a few minutes of polite conversation in his office, Dr. Clark led us outside and through the gardens, which were so very similar to what Mama had painted in her *Spring Bouquet*. The colors!

I recognized the path to the old tool shed immediately. But I certainly didn't recognize the shed when Dr. Clark threw open the door and we stepped inside. The ceiling had been lifted, the walls repainted, and comfortable leather furniture offered plenty of room to sit and browse. Two rooms had been added to the shed, so that the building had the appearance of a small, intimate art gallery.

And all of Mama's paintings were framed and hanging on the walls.

Daddy was nodding his head in approval. "It's amazing that you've been able to complete it so quickly. It looks beautiful. Just what I had in mind."

"Yeah! What a change from the way it looked in January!" I added.

"You'll want to read the plaque by the door," Dr. Clark said, and Jimmy and I joined him at the entrance where a bronze plaque was engraved with these words: *The Sheila McKenzie Middleton Room. This gallery has been donated in loving memory of Sheila Middleton (1924–1962), an artist who found great inspiration for her work at Resthaven. It is the wish of her family that many others who come to Resthaven will find refuge and hope through art.*

"And her paintings will always stay here?" I asked.

"Actually, Swan," Daddy said, "the High Museum is very interested in having an exhibition of your mother's work. They've already scheduled it for next fall. Many of these paintings will be featured there, as well as the original three that were lost. The Metropolitan Museum in New York has also agreed to loan the High three Impressionist paintings—one by Monet and two by Cezanne. After the exhibition is over, we'll decide what to do with all of Mama's paintings. The one of you and Ella Mae will return to Mt. Carmel. Some will come back here, of course, but the purpose of this gallery is to display many artists' works. The money from the memorial fund helped create this gallery and also will provide supplies for the studio and art classes for patients."

"It's just what Mama would have wanted."

"Yes, I think so. And Mrs. MacIlvain at the museum told me that you decided to donate the money from the Raven Dare to the memorial arts school. That's a good idea, Swan."

"It wasn't just me, Daddy. The whole junior class voted to do that."

Jimmy was inspecting the paintings. "Hey, Swan. Look at this one of you and me and Muffin!" In the painting, Jimmy, around ten, was trying desperately to yank a football out of Muffin's mouth, and I was doubled over laughing. "That's a really neat painting," he added. It was the first time I'd ever seen Jimmy interested in Mama's art. "And look at that one of you, Dad! It's *exactly* how you used to look when we'd interrupt you in your study." Jimmy was pointing to the painting of Daddy rising from his desk with the smile on his face.

"I hope I'll look that way again, son," Daddy said, coming over to Jimmy and putting his arm around his shoulder.

"Oh, sure, Dad. I'm sure you will."

For the rest of the afternoon, Daddy and Jimmy and I walked round and round in the little gallery and relived the life that Mama had captured for us on canvas.

"Your dad said *that*?" Robbie asked as we sat in his red convertible, staring at the stars.

"Those were his words. If you'll set up another Day at the Park, he'll be glad to come down and lend a hand. So I think you should— maybe another workday with a cookout in Grant Park afterward. He said he'd pay for the supplies and the burgers for the kids."

"What made him all of the sudden want to do that?"

"He said Mama always wanted him to go down with her and just get to know some of the people, but he never thought it was a good idea. But now he realizes how important it was for Mama to help out among the poor—how helpful it was for her as well as for the ones she taught, and he told me that he's really glad I've been helping out too. 'That Ella Mae was one wonderful lady,' he said the other night. 'She had the biggest soul of anyone I ever knew.' I think he wants to do it in memory of Mama and Ella Mae."

"Well, there certainly is plenty to do. And what did Miss Abigail say?"

"She said, 'Fine. Plan it.'" I smiled at him. "Just like Daddy, she thought *you* might like to figure out all the details."

"Aha! Well, sure. As long as it happens before mid-June. Dad's taking me on a trip to visit colleges."

"And?"

"And what?"

"Are you going to tell him that you don't want to go up north to school?"

Robbie got an uncomfortable look on his face. "Not yet. I figure I can at least check them out first."

"I hope you can choose what you want to do with your life."

He grinned suddenly. "Me too. I already know what it would be anyway."

"What?"

"I've told you. Long time ago."

"A city planner?"

"Well, yeah. Maybe. But that's not what I mean."

"Well, spit it out, Robbie!"

"I'd just like to follow you around for a while and see what happens next."

"It's a deal." And the way I felt right then, I hoped Robbie Bartholomew would follow me around for a very long time indeed.

Late one night, right before the first anniversary of the Orly crash, I went into Daddy's study and got out the folder where he'd stashed all the newspapers that told about the crash. For some reason, I knew I had to read them again. Hugging the thick folder to my chest, I crept up the steps to the *atelier*, went inside, and shut the door. For at least two hours I cried through every article in every paper. The first one I read was a column that Doris Lockerman, assistant editor for the *Atlanta Constitution*, had written two days after the crash, on Tuesday, June 5. "The Sunday of disbelief is past. The wounding, restless, agonizing night is over. A weakened Atlanta moves into the long misery of realization."

Long. All the adults had known it would take time. A very long time. The deep, painful eyes of my orphaned classmate, Lanie Bradshaw, haunted me. *I'll call her,* I told myself. I couldn't let her disappear into bitterness. Maybe she just needed a friend, someone to understand. Maybe she needed something to do, the way I had.

Then I reread Ralph McGill's editorial from the *Constitution*, written on the Monday after the crash. Ralph McGill was the editor, a controversial man who certainly supported civil rights. *"You know what they say about Ralph McGill,"* Daddy liked to remind us. *"Half the people of Atlanta can't eat breakfast until they've read Ralph's editorial, and half the people can't eat breakfast after they've read it."* I smiled to think of Daddy's words.

But no one could disagree with what he had written the day after the crash:

> *It is an awesome thing to be confronted with the ancient truth that in the midst of life we are in death. It is a difficult enough fact to accept when it is an isolated, personal one. When it occurs in the mass, as in a battle, the loss of a Titanic at sea, the wrenching crash of steel trains, or the explosive, flame-wrapped smash of aircraft, the shock of it is one which makes a community grow silent and put its mind to the business of trying to understand the swift transition of more than 100 men, women, and children from life to death. A rector put his arms about a sobbing woman, "In the inscrutable mystery of life and death," he said gently, "there is no glib answer. There is faith or there isn't. Faith is an assuagement of grief, though not of your sorrow. With faith one can accept the painful reality of loss. With faith one can accept the finality of death. We are created, we live, we die, we live again. 'In my Father's house are many mansions. If it were not so I would have told you.'"*

There is faith or there isn't. Yes, that was what I had gained from this tragedy. Faith. Faith that let me accept it all. It didn't hurt any less; in fact, I think it may have hurt more. But I had faith. And I had something else. A scar. A scar that I would carry with me forever on my heart as a reminder of how I found my Savior.

On a sweltering Saturday morning in June, Robbie stood in the fellowship hall of Mt. Carmel with an assortment of men, women, and teens seated around him at those long tables. Many of the same teens from Mendon and Wellington joined us again. Rachel and Julie and Millie and Patty were all present, oohing and ahhing over baby Jessie's fledgling steps. Cassandra beamed at her daughter. Larry and Big Man were telling Robbie about an invitation the jazz band had received to play at another "white man's club," as they put it.

"Carl shore wishes he could be here," Leo said. "Poor guy. 'Bout ta go crazy with those classes he's takin'."

There were several new faces among us. Lanie Bradshaw, orphaned Lanie, had agreed to join us when I'd called. Several of the fathers who had volunteered at the first Day at the Park had returned. And Daddy was there, sitting next to them and talking about the stock market. Trixie and Lucy were talking to Cassandra's mom. And Jimmy was, of all things, admiring Mr. Murphy's pocketknife. That made me almost give a belly laugh. Mean old Mr. Murphy had become meek as a lamb and volunteered for every project or activity offered at Mt. Carmel. *Rachel says I've changed, but he has really changed. That's for sure,* I thought to myself.

"As far as the work goes," Robbie was saying, "Miss Abigail has given me a list of homes that need emergency repairs. I've divided you up into five different teams. Each team has a leader who, I hope, knows what to do." Robbie nodded to the men, and they chuckled among themselves.

"Plus another team of teens is going to do some painting around the church. Later this afternoon, we'll all walk down to the park with the kids and have some games and a cookout."

And so the second Day at the Park began. Miss Abigail got in her Ford, and the rest of us followed in an assortment of cars. At she stopped at each house, Robbie got out and unloaded the supplies and handed the team leader a long list of instructions.

Unbeknownst to Miss Abigail, Robbie had put her house on the list too. Mr. Murphy was the leader of that team. When I drove by after lunch, heading back to church with supplies, I saw Jimmy and Mr. Murphy repairing the screen door on her porch. Jimmy waved at me, grinning broadly, and Mr. Murphy nodded my way.

"A regular engineer, this brotha' of yours is, Mary Swan," he called out.

Around four o'clock we met back at the church. At least thirty children were waiting for us. We all walked down to the big open park for which this part of Atlanta was named. Rachel and Cassandra played freeze tag and Red Rover with the youngest kids. The men and teens got some of the older kids involved in a softball game, and Trixie and Lucy brought out coolers of lemonade from Daddy's car and began pouring it into paper cups.

Robbie made sure everyone was involved in some activity. He attracted the kids to him like a magnet and was never too busy to stop and answer a question or cheer a child on in a three-legged race or a game of Red Rover.

Just before dinner he found Mike and James admiring his convertible and told them, "We'll go for a spin around the block in a little while, guys, if you'd like."

"We shore would!" James exclaimed. "And kin we bring some friends along? They's been hearing 'bout yore fancy red car for a long time now."

"You bet!" Robbie chuckled.

As soon as dinnertime rolled around, Daddy was kept busy flipping hamburgers and hot dogs on an old grill with some of the other fathers. The adults sat at a few picnic tables, and the kids sat on blankets that we had spread on the ground. We passed around bags of potato chips and served coleslaw and brownies. While we munched on the food, Miss Abigail told the children a Bible story.

Later Robbie suggested, "Anyone for a game of touch football?"

Soon he was explaining the rules to a dozen eager boys. Daddy and Jimmy even joined in the fun. I think my favorite moment of the whole day was when little James tackled Robbie too hard and they both went sprawling on the lawn. They started laughing really loudly, and then Robbie pulled himself off the ground and, huffing and puffing with his hair falling in his face, he helped James up and gave him a big hug.

"It's been a lovely day," Miss Abigail said as we walked back to the church. "Thanks to everyone's hard work, several families have more comfortable homes." And turning to Robbie she added, "Including myself. Thank you, Robbie. I really appreciate it."

Robbie grinned. "Don't thank me. It was Mr. Murphy and his team who worked on your house."

Mr. Murphy's dark face turned a shade darker, and he said, "Aw, shucks. Wadn't nothin'."

Daddy kept stride with Miss Abigail, and I think they were discussing the different projects she hoped to start up in the future. "We'll talk again soon," Daddy told her enthusiastically before he and Jimmy and Trixie got into his car. "We've all had a wonderful day."

Then he added with emotion, "And thank you—thank you for all you've done for Mary Swan."

"It's been my pleasure, Mr. Middleton."

I followed Miss Abigail into the fellowship hall and said, "I think I understand now."

"Understand?"

"I think I see what you've been trying to tell me. This is what I'm supposed to do—share what I've got with others. Be thankful for all I've been given and trust God to show me what's next. Something like that."

Miss Abigail's eyes were definitely sparkling as she said, "Exactly. And don't worry about what others are or aren't doing. That's really none of your business. Remember, God has a special plan for each of us. The Bible says, 'Whatsoever thy hand findeth to do, do it with thy might.' "

"My hand has found painting."

"Yes, a wonderful gift to have."

"And serving spaghetti!"

"That too."

"And you know what else, Miss Abigail?"

"What?"

"I love Buckhead!"

That made her laugh out loud. "Good-bye, Mary Swan. See you soon. The Lord bless you. "

We walked to the convertible, Robbie's arm draped around my left shoulder and Rachel's arm linked through my right arm. Then we climbed into the convertible. As we drove away, I glanced back and saw Puddin' standing in the middle of the road, waving at us and grinning from ear to ear.

When we arrived back at my house, we all congregated in the carport.

"I'm exhausted," said Trixie, and she did look tired. But even with ketchup on her shirt and her hair a little wilted, she still looked fantastic.

"Well, that was a fine day!" Daddy sounded tired but happy. Really happy. "Robbie, thanks for all your hard work." He shook Robbie's hand forcefully.

"I'm beat!" Rachel said. "I haven't played that many rounds of freeze tag before in my life! I'm going straight home to take a bath!"

"You could use one," I teased, scrunching up my nose.

"Well, look who's talking, you silly, scatterbrained girl!" And she started chasing me around the yard.

"Who needs a bath when you've got a pool?" Robbie said, and before I knew it, he'd picked me up and tossed me over his shoulder. With everyone else following behind, he marched me through the backyard past the big hickory tree and threw me, clothes and all, into the pool.

It was almost dusk when I, still damp, walked Robbie over to his car. "Thanks for making this day happen, Robbie. It was great! It was . . . it was, I don't know . . ."

"It was just what I get for following you around!" And he kissed me on the mouth right in front of Daddy and Trixie and Jimmy and Lucy and Rachel. Then he hopped into his car and took off down the driveway.

"Fine boy, that Robbie Bartholomew," Daddy commented, his arm around Trixie's shoulder. Jimmy made a grimace, definitely disapproving of the kiss. Lucy hugged her mother around the waist and seemed perfectly content to be sharing Trixie with Daddy.

"Smitten," Rachel whispered as I walked her down the driveway. "You'd better keep him, Swan."

"I'm planning on it, Rach. Now go take your bath!"

She rolled her eyes at me and said, "You go change into some dry clothes! See ya tomorrow."

Every muscle in my body was aching, but instead of going inside and flopping on my bed, I walked through the familiar woods to the Swan House and sat at the bottom of the hill just staring up at the mansion. A dozen different memories flashed before me: running through the house, counting swans; clinging to Mama's skirt while she painted, swatting at the gnats when I was a little older; holding my new sketchpad at twelve, trying to draw the mansion; bawling my eyes out on the day after the crash; finding that I still could sketch even with a black eye; and finally setting my easel in the snow in this very spot and painting.

Mrs. Inman had said I was trying to find myself in this house. And I had. I had found my inspiration in the Swan House. But my real

Swan's House was something a whole lot bigger. *In my Father's house are many mansions.* That was what I had found this year—an answer to the longing in my soul. A swan and a raven, a little of each. In this year of contrast, stark, heartbreaking contrast—life and death—God had brought color too. He had brought me a palette full of color to last my whole life long.

# Epilogue

We're standing in the sanctuary of Mt. Carmel, Abbie and I, where we've been bawling like babies. And we're looking at the painting of Oakland Cemetery. I smile to myself. Oakland Cemetery now has a board of directors and is a very popular historical site in Atlanta.

"I really love that painting, Mom. Almost as much as the one of the Swan House in snow."

"I was so very young and inexperienced back then. I'm amazed they still have it here."

"I imagine they consider it a privilege, considering that it's the first painting you ever painted and who you've become."

"Now, don't start going on about that."

"Well, even if I've never painted anything but the walls in my house, I'm very proud to have a famous mother and grandmother."

"All right. Enough. Come on downstairs where the other painting is." I want to hurry her along so I won't start crying again.

We are walking down the stairs to the fellowship hall now. Abbie has her four-month-old son, Bobby, on her hip.

"Thanks for telling me the whole story, Mom. It is absolutely the saddest thing I've ever heard. I can't believe it's all true and that it happened to you."

"Every bit of it, baby." I can't bear for her to see how much the telling of it cost me, how vivid it seems even now. I can still see the sparkle in Miss Abigail's eyes and hear Rachel calling me a "silly, scatterbrained girl." I can almost feel Puddin' pulling on my hair, forcing it into braids. And I can picture myself bending over Ella Mae's hospital bed again, kissing her cheek

"I feel like I really know my namesake now. Miss Abigail was certainly a remarkable woman."

"Miss Abigail brought faith into my life . . ."

". . . And you wanted it to be a family legacy forever," Abbie chimes in with the familiar words I have often repeated to her. "I've gotten to know and love all the people in your story. Keep telling me about them, Mom—until I can remember for myself."

"Some other time, Abbie. Maybe when the next baby is due." We both smile at that.

I close my eyes and think of Robbie and Jimmy and Carl and Daddy and Trixie and the paintings. Because more than anything else, that has been my life. The paintings. And it seems perfectly fitting that I put my arm around Abbie's waist and we stand silently in front of Mama's portrait of beautiful Ella Mae cradling a little white baby girl in her arms.

"I'll tell you the story soon," I promise. "But for now let's just look at the painting."

And so, with Abbie's infant son asleep on her shoulder, that is what we do.

Author's Note

The Orly plane crash in June 1962 was a true and terribly tragic event that affected the lives of many, many Atlantans.

The High Museum of Art is part of what was long called the Atlanta Memorial Arts Building (in commemoration of the Orly tragedy) and is now known as the Woodruff Center—home to not only the High Museum but also to the Atlanta Symphony Orchestra, the Alliance Theatre, and the Atlanta College of Art.

The Swan House is indeed a well-known historic site in Buckhead and is now owned by the Atlanta Historical Society. It is open to tourists throughout the year.

Oakland Cemetery is likewise open to the public, and the Historic Oakland Foundation is dedicated to the restoration and preservation of this historic cemetery.

The immensely popular Varsity still sits across the expressway from the Georgia Institute of Technology, its menu virtually unchanged.

In the Grant Park section of Atlanta, a small church provides spaghetti meals for the needy each week, as it has done for several decades. Many homes in this area have been remodeled in the past years and the residents reflect great racial and social diversity.

The Middleton family and all other characters, except those of known historical importance, are fictitious, and any resemblance to real persons alive or dead is purely coincidental.

Acknowledgments

As a young girl, I remember standing in the lobby of the Atlanta Memorial Arts building and staring up at a stone-engraved list of names of Atlantans who perished in a plane crash. That stone marker with its long list broke my heart, for it represented great human suffering. Over the years, the tragedy continued to haunt and inspire me. This story begins with that tragic event, but it is also about where I grew up and about so many things that have made me who I am— things I have loved and things I have learned. I am deeply grateful to my heavenly Father who has used all of my life's experiences to shape and change me and has allowed me to write stories from the heart. *"Delight yourself in the Lord and He will give you the desires of your heart."*

I also wish to express my sincerest thanks to:

Atlantans:

My grandmother, Allene Massey Goldsmith, one of Atlanta's *premières dames*, in my humble opinion, still inspiring and encouraging me along the way. Thanks for lending me the newspapers from those fateful days in June 1962.

My parents, Jere and Barbara Goldsmith, who raised me to share the same love for Atlanta that they have, and who have modeled to me generosity and love among Atlanta's richest and poorest. Thanks for all your help with research and publicity.

My brothers and sisters-in-law, Jere and Mary Goldsmith and Glenn and Kim Goldsmith, who encourage me from across the ocean. Many thanks, Jere and Glenn, for all the help with computer complexities.

Louise Adamson, whose real life stories and sacrificial love in the inner city inspired parts of this novel. You are an amazing woman of God.

Laura McDaniel, Kim Huhman, Margaret DeBorde, Valerie Andrews and Heather Myers, for helping me remember the past. We grew up together, we laughed and cried and prayed and dreamed together, and we still do. Lifelong friends—I am richly blessed!

Jill Steenhuis, fellow Atlantan living in southern France and gifted artist. Thanks for your thoughtful insights and advice about art.

The Girls' Class of '78 from The Westminster Schools, for so many crazy, wonderful memories that live on . . .

Other Atlantans who helped me with research: my aunt, Jay Goldsmith; Coobie DeBorde; Bill Crawford; Doris Lockerman; Thom Shelton; Pam Meister; Rebecca Moore; Molly Lawson; Frances Francis; Mary Rose Taylor; Ivan Allen Jr.; Michael Rose; Camille McDuffie; Julia Shivers; plus many others who whispered words of encouragement along the way.

The High Museum of Art; the Atlanta History Center; the Swan House; the Martin Luther King, Jr. Center, the Historic Oakland Foundation.

Others around the world:

Dr. Michel Cannat and Dr. Daniel Shoultz for helpful advice in psychiatry.

Marcia Smartt, precious friend, mentor, artist, counselor. God has used your wise words to speak to my heart hundreds of times throughout the years. Thanks for your insights on art and mental illness.

Todd Burkes, fellow missionary and friend who helped me get into Carl's skin. *Merci beaucoup.*

Trudy Owens, soul mate, teammate, encourager, editor, fellow mom, and missionary, with whom I've shared these past twelve years. My love and prayers go with you as your family steps out into a new adventure.

Odette Beauregard, teammate and precious friend for almost twenty years, you are truly part of our family. *Merci pour tout!*

Cathy Carmeni, prayer partner, gifted editor, and invaluable friend, who is not afraid to speak the truth about my writing and about life.

All my friends in Montpellier who encourage me along as I write *en anglais* and wait patiently for the translation.

Dave Horton, who started me on the road to writing novels and who is still encouraging, editing, and generally being a wonderful friend! *Merci!*

All my new friends at Bethany House Publishers. Thanks so much for your hard work.

Lora Beth Norton, expert editor, who reads my mind and finds the right word and whose late-night emails across cyberspace could somehow make me giggle instead of groan! What a treat to be working together again!

My husband, Paul, my best friend and critic and the one who knows how to make me smile. Nothing I do would be worth it without you.

My sons, Andrew and Christopher. No mother has ever been prouder of her boys. What a delight to watch you grow up. Thank you for truly encouraging me in my writing.

And finally:

All those who lost loved ones almost 40 years ago in the Orly crash and in memory of those who perished in the crash.

And in memory of Mary Maddux, the woman who worked for my family for over twenty-five years. I sat on her lap while she sang me lullabies, and that changed the way I look at the world.

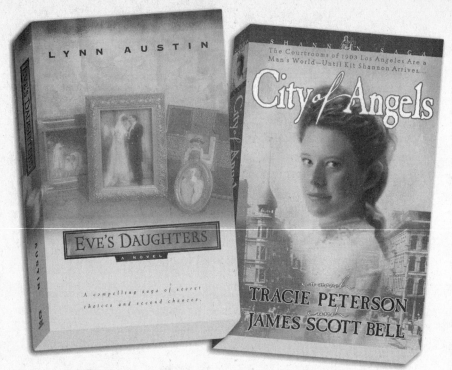

THE COMPELLING STORIES
OF UNFORGETTABLE HEROINES

A Compelling Saga of Secrets, Choices, and Second Chances

Yearning for love and dignity, four generations of women must come to grips with the choices they've made and those their mothers made before them. At the heart of their struggle rests a dark secret that, if told, may have the power to heal old wounds—or may tear the family apart forever. *Eve's Daughters* by Lynn Austin

Will the Light of Truth Direct Her Fight for Justice?

Kit Shannon arrived in Los Angeles feeling a special call to practice law despite the fact that few in her family understood her burning desire to seek justice for the poor and oppressed. Soon Kit finds herself working with the city's most prominent criminal trial lawyer and is drawn into a high-profile case. She longs to discover the truth but struggles with her personal doubts about the suspect she must defend.

City of Angels by Tracie Peterson and James Scott Bell